THE SHADOW OVER LONE WOLF LAKE

D.W. HITZ

ISBN-13 (Digital): 978-1-956492-77-4
ISBN-13 (Paperback): 978-1-956492-78-1
ISBN-13 (Hardback): 978-1-956492-79-8

Edited by Heather Ann Larson
Cover Art by Matt Seff Barnes & Don Noble at Rooster Republic Press
Interior Design by D.W. Hitz

Also by D.W. Hitz

Judith's Prophecy (Big Sky Terror Book 1)
Judith's Blood (Big Sky Terror Book 2)
Judith's Fall (Big Sky Terror Book 3)
Gods are Born
Brady: A Novella
Bloodtooth
Our Trip Through Hell
Garrets Lodge
Food Court of the Damned
Black Creek Mystic
The Shadow Over Lone Wolf Lake

Stay up to date with D.W. by becoming a member at
patreon.com/dwhitz

THE SHADOW OVER LONE WOLF LAKE

D.W. HITZ

For Dad,
Order a rum and Coke and a plate of wings on the Underhill's
account, watch out for Cato's old hiding-in-the-closet ploy, and I'll
meet you in the clubhouse. We'll say we picked the wrong week to
quit smoking, and I'll know you'll have the cigars.

Part One

The Move

Chapter One

DREW KLINE STOOD ON THE PATIO, entranced by the violet shimmer sparkling across the lake's surface. It was a curious sight for the twelve-year-old. His previous visits to his now-deceased grandmother's house had been during the morning or midday, and the sun had shone brightly. The water's depths had struck him on those days as being an endless abyss. Lone Wolf Lake was the deepest lake in Montana, after all. The shimmer today made it feel different than those other days—light, even magical, like he was on the cusp of something that would carry him away. It was a welcome greeting after what had been a tedious late-August afternoon of packing, loading, and carrying.

He wondered if it shimmered every dusk, if it was something he could look forward to. He had a lot of questions about the house and about his grandmother, though he didn't expect Dad to start answering those. Drew's previous half-dozen visits only lasted for a few hours at most, and they felt awkward and rushed. Dad's relationship with Grandmother always reminded him of those jail visitations in the movies where enemies sat on opposite sides of the glass, stressed out and forced. But he had all the time in the world to get answers about Dad, the house, and the lake now that this was his home.

Dad had driven off in the moving truck, Mom following him so they could drop it off before their forty-eight-hour rental expired. The boxes were scattered throughout the house in their approximate destinations, though the placements of the ones without labels were just guesses.

Dean, Drew's fifteen-year-old brother, was setting up his room—what had been Dad's room when he was a kid. Maggie, the seventeen-year-old and incoming Lone Wolf High School senior—she wouldn't let anyone forget that—was in Aunt Joan's old room. Mom's and Dad's things were waiting for them in Grandma's old room, which Drew was sure was a bad idea. She had died in that room just a few weeks ago, and he was sure her ghost was hovering some-where nearby.

Drew was lucky enough to get Bobby's old room. It was a little smaller than his siblings' rooms, but he had been told there was a crawlspace you could almost walk into, and Bobby had been missing for like thirty years. No ghosts—Drew was assured of that much. The room had been locked up since his young uncle went missing and had all this cool stuff waiting for Drew to explore.

But he wasn't ready for that just yet. After spending the whole day loading the truck at home—what used to be home, he had to stop doing that in his head—and then unloading and moving boxes around, he was ready to just sit and do nothing. The lake looked like the perfect place to do that.

He walked down the hill along the overgrown path from the back patio. Grass that was too tall and in need of a mow reached from both sides, caressing his legs and shoes. It somewhat tickled and then immediately itched, and he moved faster toward the dock.

"There's a whole lake to explore," Dad had said two days ago, when the idea of the move was thrust upon the kids. "A dock and all kinds of trails. There's woods—my brother used to have a fort out there. You guys'll love it."

Drew wasn't convinced. He didn't understand why the move was even necessary, but at the same time, he wasn't opposed to it. He wouldn't have to change schools; the town only had one. The idea of the lake and actually having his own room for once appealed to him. He'd had enough of dealing with Dean's weirdo ideas of when he needed the room to himself and his nightly flatulence. Having a room to himself and the lure of the lake were winning Drew over.

He didn't know why he was drawn to the water. Maybe it was some attraction hard-wired into humans to keep us hydrated, or maybe a primordial thing since life came from the sea. What he knew as he looked down the hill was that the thing Dad had called a dock was more like an ancient latticework of splinters waiting for an unlucky soul to step on and crash through, but not without a thousand shards of wood stabbing them. Besides, only a few feet of it were actually over the water. Dad said the water was low because of the drought.

He passed a hump in the path where the hill descended at a steeper incline. It felt like he could see the whole lake from there. At the bottom was the shore and Dad's *dock*. In the distance were acres and acres of water, lined by woods. Closer, along the right shoreline, were patches of lawns that must have belonged to neighbors with their own lake houses. All of it was set within the valley and surrounded by deep-green mountains.

At the bottom of the hill, Drew stood at the edge of the twenty-foot dock, a rickety construction from the mid-nineteenth century that probably hadn't been maintained in thirty years. He shook his head. He was not stepping on that thing, and if Dad thought he should, he would have to wonder if the man was trying to kill him.

Rocks of a thousand colors covered the shore, washed smooth by eons of ebbing and flowing tides. The water's shimmer colored the beach in a purple hue as the sun kissed the emerald mountain wall. Boulders littered the shore to the left, growing in size as they formed lines toward the woods.

Drew followed the line of stones with his eyes. There were no woods, no nature hardly at all, at the old house. It was a tract home in the middle of town with only enough grass around it to make it a pain to mow. Unlike here. These woods, the lake, the boulders, they were somehow magical. He looked into the shadowy path between the boulders and the tall trees in the distance, and what he saw was Middle Earth or the forest moon of Endor. He saw a vast world of the unknown waiting for him to conquer and make his own. He breathed in the piney scent and felt surrounded, hugged by the eager green wild.

His heart pounded at the sensation.

A feeling of expectation filled him from his toes to his chest as he stared into what felt like uncharted wilderness. There was an adventure in there. There were things to discover, races to win, hunts to be had, and maybe, like Dad mentioned, a fort to build.

His adrenaline spiked, the exhaustion of the move relenting, and he took a step toward the woods. He wished he had a cell phone like all the other kids in school so he could call Lance and tell him to get over here. He hadn't seen his best friend since he left for camp two weeks ago, but Drew was pretty sure he was supposed to be back now. He could see them both heading down that path between the boulders and spending what was left of the summer making this place into a real gem. That was if Lance's mom let him come. She was always iffy about when he could visit the old house, but this—this place was like a resort compared to the old house.

There was a splash, and Drew spun back toward the water. He saw a large fish's tail flutter below the surface, and before he could blink, a hawk appeared. Its talons dipped into the water, snagged the fish, and it flapped up into the sky once again. The green fish flailed in its grip as the bird soared across the lake.

"Wow." Drew's jaw hung open. He glanced back at the shore, looking for any other fish waiting to get plucked by passing avian predators. He didn't see any. What he did notice were large footprints on the rocky shore. "What the?"

There were no footprints on the shore a few minutes ago; he was sure. He had taken it all in, studied each aspect of his new beach, and the pebbly ground had been smooth.

He stepped beside one of the prints, placing his own shoe next to it for comparison. It was definitely larger than his size nine, and considerably so. It was not a kid's mark. He traced the path the footprints were taking, and strangely enough, they were headed between the boulders into the same woods he had been about to walk into. But when he was planning his and Lance's future adventures, there had been no footprints. There had been no one to make them, either. He was sure of it.

The thought of someone sneaking right past him and leaving those marks gave him a shiver.

"Weird." He needed to see what this was about. Grandma's land was supposed to be big, something like fifty acres. That was a lot of land to explore and a lot of woods for a hiking stranger to hide in.

He started down the path between the boulders. "Hello?" he shouted into the gloomy forest ahead.

"Drew!" Maggie stood at the hump, the midsection of the overgrown path toward the house. She gripped her phone in her hand by her hip and snarled at him. Her sharply trimmed red hair was nearly as pointed as her tone. "Mom and Dad are on the way back. You need to set out plates for dinner."

Drew hadn't felt super hungry, but as he envisioned Mom arriving with a pizza or a bucket of chicken, he remembered how long ago lunch had been and how hard he had worked today. But still, his gaze returned to the woods. He felt something calling him there. He looked toward the footprints—he needed to know where they went. Who had left them?

"Now, shrimp! They're on the way!" Maggie shouted.

Drew sighed and gave in. He walked toward his sister. She was probably right. He needed to go set the table if that was what Mom wanted. She wouldn't be in a good mood if she came home and it wasn't done, and Drew really wanted to explore those woods. He didn't want to get in trouble, maybe even get grounded, if she and Dad were fighting again and she was in a bad mood when she got there.

He climbed the path up, and Maggie spun, headed back toward the house. She raised her phone as she walked and tapped at the screen. She was the only one of the kids to have a phone, and she saved for like six months to afford it. Even so, she still had to work a weekend job at the frozen yogurt shop in town to pay the bill.

Drew wished he was old enough for a job.

He stopped at the hump in the hill. It was as if something was tugging on his shoulder, pulling at him to come back. He couldn't help himself from turning and taking one last look before going inside.

The sun was barely set behind the western mountains, and the lake was bathed in an orange glow, not indigo as before. It was still pretty, but somehow, it was like something was missing. He glanced at the dock, the shoreline where he had found those prints. They were gone.

Drew was tempted to run down there and verify it wasn't a trick of the light. He wanted to. They had vanished all the way from the dock to the bouldered path, and he needed to go down there and find out what happened. How was he going to follow the trail and learn what the mysterious stranger was doing with no footprints?

"Doofus, come on!" Maggie shouted. She was halfway across the large yard that spanned between the hump and the house.

"Shit," Drew muttered. The enchanted piney smell seemed to wane the farther he got from the woods. The soft lap of the shoreline's tiny waves was an imperceivable hush from there. He hoped there would be enough of a trail when he went back tomorrow.

Randy Kline held three large pepperoni pizzas in his lap. The smell was making him drool. After spending the entire day lifting, carrying, heaving, and rushing, his stomach demanded to be refilled, and though his skin felt grimy with the day's sweat, he was ready to get back to his childhood house and eat.

He glanced at Emma. Her teeth were clenched, hands tight on the steering wheel. He knew this move was tough, but she would see; the whole family would see how good this move was for them... in time.

He remembered loving the house when he was young. He

remembered the joy it had brought the family, living on the lake. There were constant boat trips, games in the woods, and picnics on the lawn. The house was a gathering spot for his and his siblings' friends. It was host to a hundred dinner parties—Mom used to love throwing those.

And, yes, everything changed when Bobby went missing. Yes, it was like a bomb dropped that Mom could never get over, but nothing like that had happened in his marriage. For them, this move could be like it was in his youth, before they lost Bobby.

Besides, it wasn't like they had a choice.

It had been nine months since Randy was laid off from his job at the mill. The first few weeks weren't bad, but as time went on and the only work he could find was a part-time job at the grocery store, the regular pile of bills went from late to disconnect notices to plain envelopes from debt collectors. They had less than a month before their old house would have been in foreclosure.

Then Mom died.

Randy thought it was odd but understandable how Mom had left the house to him and not split it between him and Joan. Of course, Joan never spoke to Mom anymore. When she was done with high school and old enough to leave, there was no looking back. As uncomfortable as it felt, Randy stayed in touch with Mom. He called her every few weeks, even brought the kids by for short visits a few times a year.

As much as he couldn't stand the constant cloud of blackness that surrounded his mother and the vile assaults she delivered because Randy was still around and Bobby was not, he couldn't stomach the idea of permanently abandoning her the way his sister had.

He hated to admit it, but when he heard he had inherited the house, a wave of relief washed over him. He saw a beacon of hope somewhere in the distance. The will declared he couldn't sell it, though, which was what Emma wanted and something she still sneered at when the topic came up. Not for five years. It was a weird thing, but Randy thought he could make it work. With Emma's income, his measly check, and hopefully a little bit of equity from the old house, they might be able to get back on their feet. He hoped.

They pulled up the driveway, and Drew and Maggie disappeared into the front door.

Emma shook her head. "They haven't done a thing since we left. I guarantee it."

"They've been working hard all day. A break is good."

"The house looks like a tornado went through it, and I'm just supposed to—" She stopped the car and closed her eyes. "Yeah." She smiled at him. It was shallow and restrained. "You're right. It's been a long day for all of us."

Her phone lit up in the cup holder, and she snatched it up and made it dark again.

"Let's eat." Randy raised the boxes. "We'll all feel better once we've eaten."

Chapter Two

LANCE BROWN HUNG UP WITH DREW, the screen briefly flashing "Drew's Mom" before it faded to black. His smile was wide and his brain flush with ideas. He lived on a decent half-acre lot, and there was ample room around his house, but he had never wanted to build a tree house or a clubhouse there. It didn't seem to fit the property. Everything was too new, and frankly, as much as Dad used to complain about them, he was pretty sure the HOA wouldn't allow it. But at Lone Wolf Lake? In the real woods with Drew? The idea got his heart pumping.

He saw a palace made of plywood and two-by-fours suspended in the arms of a giant spruce. There were stacks of comics and a shelf with various guns, all of them shooting foam darts of various colors and capacities. He saw ropes and pulleys for bringing stuff up into their clubhouse and setting traps for intruders and wild animals alike. There were heads on the walls, deer and elk and rabbits—they were old and bare, the kind he had seen for cheap at the flea market, but they would be perfect. He pictured a pair of sleeping bags and a lantern for sleepovers and a hidden stash under a loose floorboard where they would keep dirty magazines—he knew there was better stuff online, but Mom kept his phone locked from that stuff and there was a box of magazines he'd found while exploring the attic that would have been perfect.

All he had to do was convince Mom.

He slipped out of his room and listened over the railing for clues to what Mom was doing downstairs. He heard the television blaring, a woman was complaining about a man, and Lance was pretty sure she was either one of the ladies on the yacht show Mom liked or the dating show where twenty-somethings made out with one another on some island. Usually Mom was in a good mood while watching the island one, but if it was the yacht show, it would depend on how much wine she drank. He would need her in a good mood if he was going to ask to go to Drew's house.

He slipped around the railing and stepped down the first few stairs slowly and quietly. He was a ninja when he wanted to be. His socks helped as he stepped with toes first and gently lowered himself bit by bit, stair by stair.

He imagined how he was going to phrase the question. Mom hated when he went to Drew's old house, but she might be better about the new one. She always said the old house was in the ghetto, and she didn't want Lance hanging out there. Lance had to look up *ghetto* online, and what he read was nothing like the place where Drew lived. Yeah, the houses in Drew's old neighborhood were older and smaller than his, but there was only one black family there, and he never saw hustlers on the corner selling crack cocaine.

Sometimes he just knew Mom didn't make any sense, and he decided not to push it. She had always been more protective of him than he saw his friends' parents acting, but when Dad was killed by that drunk three years ago, she seemed to go into overdrive. She went on rants weekly about how all of Lone Wolf were hillbillies on meth, and she wouldn't dare drive anywhere at night, not with all of Montanans being alcoholics and speeders. She talked about people going missing around the state as if Montana had its very own serial killer just waiting to be named. She packed his lunch every school day just in case a lunchroom worker went psycho and decided to poison the lunches. She told Lance constantly that one day they were going to move, she just needed to decide where. She had been researching and looking for that perfect, safe place for two-and-a-half years.

Lance reached the bottom of the steps and tiptoed behind the wall separating the foyer from the den. He held his breath as he peeked around the edge.

Mom sat on the couch, a half-glass of red wine in her hand and her back to Lance. She sucked in a gasp as a shirtless man walked on screen, a sly grin on his face and a rose in his hand. A woman in a short, silky dress (one Lance thought he had seen in one of his Dad's boxes of old nudie mags) stood and sauntered over, and she and the shirtless man began tongue wrestling.

That was good. Mom was always happy watching this show, especially when her wine glass was full.

"Eh-hm." Lance cleared his throat as he walked into the room.

Mom jumped from her seat, grabbed the remote, and paused her show. "Lance!"

Her eyes were wide, and he wasn't sure why she seemed so surprised. It wasn't like he had never seen that show or known the depravity that the island-goers practiced on each other.

Then he saw the haze in the room and smelled the skunky smoke.

Back in the early days of elementary school, Lance went to assemblies and had teachers preach about drugs. They always mentioned pot as if it was a killer. When it became legal and Mom started bringing it home (though hiding it until he was asleep), Lance was stunned.

She cried every night back then. He was supposed to be sleeping, but he could hear her through his bedroom wall the first time he smelled that skunky scent. He had poked his head out from his room into the dark hallway, hoping she was okay, and then he smelled it. He wondered if something had died in the house at first, and the image of death, of his father in that coffin two weeks prior, made his stomach sink. They had tried to fix his face, but it wasn't right. Billy Hornwall at school told him it was never right. But it was that skunky smell in the hallway that sent him to Mom's room to make sure she was okay.

He reached the door, and it was stronger. He could see smoke rise from the crack below the door, and his heart skipped a beat. Was there a fire in there? A death and a fire?

Lance couldn't hold himself back. He turned the knob, but it only rotated a quarter inch before clicking. Locked.

"Mom?" He knocked on the door. "Mom? It's smoky. Are you okay in there?" His heart was pounding. He had lost Dad; he couldn't lose her too. He knocked harder. "Mom!"

There was a shuffling on her carpet, feet moving toward the door. A cough—God, could she breathe in there?

"Are you okay, Mom?" He knocked again.

"Fine," she said through the door. Her voice was harsh, and she was out of breath. "I'm fine, sweetie. Go back to bed."

"But the smoke, Mom—are you sure?" His fingers traced the wooden grooves on the door. He wanted to hug her and feel that she was alive in the flesh and not some disembodied voice.

"Yes, Lance, I'm fine. I just let my incense get away from me. It's okay. Go back to bed." It was a command, and he had better listen.

His hands dropped to his sides. Why was she being so distant? Didn't she know he was worried? That he wanted to hug her? That tone in her voice, he hadn't heard it since they found out about Dad.

"Oh. Okay." It was all he could say. It was a weird smell for incense, and Billy Hornwall and Drew would both agree that the smell was more than likely pot when he went to school the next day. But that night, it was the smell of rejection.

Lance turned back toward his room. The hallway seemed darker than before, and a chill brushed over his shoulders. He eyed his bedroom door a dozen paces away, and there was a certainty creeping through him that he needed to run there. He didn't know why just then, but he didn't want to be in this hallway anymore. The chill was like looking into Dad's casket, into that dead-man's face. There had been a feeling that Dad was and wasn't there at the same time. He had felt the best and the worst in Dad. The anger when Lance stumbled in the garage, knocking five wrenches and the new carburetor Dad had bought for his '69 Camaro project car to the hard floor. The sounds of metal objects crashing, rattling, and clanking into one another, scraping on his nerves. Then there was the sensation of loving embraces, the hugs that, no matter how long, were never enough. The warmth as Dad pulled him near and tussled his hair after every baseball practice.

Both of those feelings were in that funeral home as if death wasn't sure which was the real Dad and which was the false one. They hung over his body, teasing Lance one after the other, and both clamped onto him in the hallway between his mother's room and his own.

He wanted to make the run, but there was a feeling that whatever he was sensing was between himself and his room, that if he ran, he would go straight through it.

He could see the warm yellow light through the crack in his door. His bed was in there, waiting. His TV, where he could throw on his favorite episodes of *One Piece* and drift to sleep, forgetting everything wrong that had destroyed his life in the past four weeks.

That sense of love caressed his right arm, and the feeling of anger, disappointment, and rage gripped his left. In the long, shadowy hallway before his door appeared a shape that started his teeth chattering. Ten feet into the gloom was the dark outline of his father's face.

It wasn't him, yet it was, the face floating in shadow. It shifted from a sneer to a smirk as the sensations on his arms fought. Teeth showed through the darkness, and tears ran down Lance's cheeks.

"Dad?" It was a mumble, barely more than a breath.

The face twitched, and the grip on his arm burned. Overwhelmingly, Lance knew that if he didn't run he may not make it to his room tonight.

It was like when he rounded third base and headed toward home after Jason Cranson hit a ground ball that the Custer Falls Sluggers just couldn't get their grips on. His heart slammed, and he filled his lungs and pushed off from the carpet by Mom's room. He didn't allow another thought into his brain until he was in his room and the door was shut.

He had made it with heaving breaths and couldn't sleep for half the night. But that wasn't the last time he saw Dad. And every time he smelled that smoke, he was reminded of that day.

This time, with Mom shocked in front of her show and smoke lingering, he fought to push those feelings down. The fear, the sorrow, the anger and rejection, they all needed to wait right now because he wanted—no, he needed—to go to Drew's house. He had to get away from here, from Mom's smoking and Dad's ghost and the bullshit of it all.

She probably would have given him a thousand dollars if he had asked for it. He didn't. But she said yes to him going to Drew's for the weekend.

Chapter Three

EMMA KLINE TOOK HER PHONE back from her son and felt the familiar wave of relief that James hadn't called or texted while it was in her son's hands. Sure, she could have explained that James was calling about a work thing, that he needed her advice about an open house or something, but the more often that happened, the more likely it was to raise suspicions.

"He's gonna ask," Drew said. His eyes were hopeful, but Emma knew it was fifty-fifty at best that his friend would be allowed over. The mother didn't seem to like them for some reason; why, she wasn't sure. But the woman was odd, had been since she became a widow a few years back. Either way, she hoped the kid would come. If Drew was busy, it was easier for her to sneak off and see James.

"I hope she says yes." She sat at the end of her bed and offered Drew a smile. He went off to his room to unpack and sift through thirty-year-old junk, and her eyes went back to her phone.

She glanced at James's text from earlier that evening: "I need to see you. Come over!"

She hadn't responded. She wasn't sure yet what to say. Maybe she could invent some excuse to go to the store and stop by his place for a quickie. Her pulse sped up at the thought. But if she was being honest with herself, she was tired. She didn't want to touch the pile of boxes against the wall, the one leaning into her mother-in-law's ancient dresser—the dresser Randy had insisted on keeping despite how ugly it was. At least he had cleaned the thing out, though he probably just moved all his mother's junk into the attic.

Emma leaned back into the bed and typed a single word into her phone: "Tomorrow"

Her eyes closed, and she repeated the word in her mind. Tomorrow, for the boxes and rearranging the living room and—God, everything in this house needed it. It was basically a time capsule from the 1990s, and since they didn't own enough furniture or have the money to buy more to fill the place out, they would have to keep some of Randy's mom's. She had already started a mental list of what would stay and what would go, but it would have to wait until tomorrow.

Randy sat in the living room. He hadn't meant to take a break; it just kind of happened as he sipped a can of generic strawberry-flavored water, smelled the room's dust and his mother's still-lingering scent, and the images from years past caught up with him.

He was six years old, racing toward the Christmas tree with Bobby by his side, and Mom and Dad were cuddled on the couch with coffee and cinnamon rolls. He was nine and playing Artie Crenshaw's copy of *Mortal Kombat 3* with Joan on his Sega Genesis while Bobby watched from the doorway, a lookout so Mom and Dad wouldn't catch them playing the bloody, forbidden title. He was twelve, and his father sat where he was now, drenching the couch in whiskey stench after Bobby hadn't come home in three weeks.

Mom would have been in the kitchen, her head in her hands at the table. Joan up in her room. If she didn't, Mom's crying would set off hers. The house was a cold, quiet place then.

Randy watched the years pass in front of his eyes. The room didn't change, but the people did. Dad left, unable to cope with Mom's unending sadness. Joan left once she was accepted at the college in Bozeman, the meager grants and a campus bookstore part-time job waiting for her.

Randy had been the last to leave.

He tried to empathize. He got a job at the mill to help with the bills. He never left for college, not that he wanted to, really, but he knew with a degree he could get a better job in a bigger town. He lived in the same room. He cooked and cleaned and tried to buy Mom things, thinking that one of these days she would wake up from her gloom, that she would snap out of it.

The food he made was never good enough—she could have made it better. The cleaning was never good enough—he was just like his father and couldn't clean for shit. A figurine to match her angels or a new CD by the BGs, her favorite band back when she liked music, was never right. Bobby would have chosen better. Her baby boy knew her best and wouldn't have made such stupid mistakes.

The sourness was turning to hate when he left, and he couldn't live hating his mother. He would hate himself for that. He had to go.

Randy shook his head and stood. He walked into the kitchen. He had to get back to work or the tears would come. Moving into this house was going to be hard in some ways; he had known that. After her death, though, the memories were somehow amplified. Every visit over the last few years had been short, only long enough to let her see the kids, whom she barely showed any interest in, and his thoughts during those times were mostly on deflection. He made sure her comments on how Maggie dressed like a slut (which she didn't) didn't register with the kids. None of her remarks that Dean should have had a job and was lazy or that Drew was too small and probably stunted ever found them. He sent them outside to play after ten minutes in the house with his mother, and they left five minutes after that.

But in this house, in the silence, alone, the past screamed at him. The fights. The tears. The slamming doors and fleeing.

Randy opened a box of dishes and lifted them, setting them on the counter below where Mom kept hers. He opened the cupboard, took out the stack of chipped 1989 Sears everyday china, and set it beside his own. The ring of curling vines and roses over cream-colored porcelain on the edge of her plates brought tears to his eyes.

He looked outside and saw the lake. The moon was shattered into a thousand pieces across demure waves. He saw Bobby on the dock twenty-five years ago, fishing with his half-size pole. He only caught something with it once, and that had been enough to fuel him for the next two months of summer. Bobby turned and waved at the house.

Randy waved into the empty night.

Bobby left the pole on the dock and walked to the left. He headed into the woods, bobbing as he moved, hiking into the shadowed path with a plan that only he knew.

The counter creaked under Randy's grip. He didn't realize he was holding it so tightly.

He shoved Mom's dishes to the side, refusing to look at them, and lifted the ones from the old house. He slid them in place and bit his lip.

This was going to be much harder than he thought.

There was a shelf of Denver Broncos bobbleheads, tiny footballs, and cups all mixed with plastic cowboys, a six-shooter, and a brown hat. Drew studied each item, putting together an image of who his room's last resident was.

He saw a kid wearing a cowboy hat tossing a small Nerf football high across the room, catching it himself, and collapsing into a bed covered in Mighty Morphin Power Rangers logos. He looked at the models of fighter jets hanging from fishing lines around the room and imagined Bobby sitting at the table under the far window, meticulously cutting out the pieces and gluing them together. He saw his dad as a kid coming in every once in a while and helping his little brother with the tougher parts, the same way he helped Drew when he went through a rocket-building phase a few years back.

He felt life in this room, even knowing that it hadn't been occupied in twenty-five years. There was an energy there that gripped him and made him wish he had gotten to know his long-lost uncle—*dead uncle*, the realist side of his brain chimed in. *If he was alive, he would have come back at some point.*

Drew wouldn't let realism hold him back. He went to the door on the right side of the room. It was three feet tall, made of vertical clapboard, and painted white to match the trim. There was a small brass knob on the left, and Drew's heart pounded as he took it in hand.

A feeling of discovery rushed through him. He wasn't opening a door; he was entering an undiscovered tomb, a hidden treasure chamber that had gone undisturbed for a lifetime. He was venturing into the secret realm of the Lost Bobby, and it was only more special because it was his family's treasure that he was about to discover. It was rightfully his now.

The door was stiff, shuddering inside its frame at first, then it squealed as it relented, belching forth a wave of dusty wind and revealing a dark cavern inside the wall.

Drew coughed, and his breath hitched as he tasted the dirty air and smelled dry wood and insulation. It itched his eyes, and he had to blink several times before focusing on the only object he could make out in the gloom: a skeleton the size of a cat.

Drew shivered and stepped back. That was not what he was expecting. His hand fell from the doorknob to his side, and he squinted, wondering if he still wanted to see inside the tiny room or if he would have been better off slamming the door and never opening it again. He spotted a hanging string and leaned forward. His eyes shifted from the heap of bones to the string, back and forth.

There was a mountain of dust on the skeleton. It curved up from the coarse floorboards to the sides of the bones and made little curly Qs over the skull. There were cracks and dotted lines in each piece. The head was under an arm, and the tail was a stiff line around the outer edge.

Drew's hand touched the string as his gaze remained glued

downward, and he jumped, startled at the feeling of the old strand on his skin. It was light and made him imagine his fingers wrapped in spider silk. He yanked the cord, and the crawlspace flooded with a yellow wave of brightness.

He gasped.

The thing on the floor became clear, and he crouched to look closer. Under the light of a hanging bulb, he saw what was not the remains of a cat or dog or any earthly animal; it was a plastic replica of what had to be a dragon skeleton. Its long, bony tail, its claws, and its fangs were all distinguishable. It was buried under two and a half decades of dust, but that was what it was.

Drew reached, then stopped. His gaze was distracted by something else in the small space. A shiny model was on a far shelf, another dragon, but this one was glossy green and a foot long. It sat beside an army of smaller creatures. There was a shelf of books, a shelf of modeling tools and paints and yet-to-be-completed projects. There were little orcs and elves and trolls in a battle that had been frozen in time on the top shelf, and Drew felt himself pulled in that direction.

Before he could go, though, he remembered the skeleton. Drew gripped it by its spine and raised it up to chest level. Dust that smelled of a thousand minutes fluttered into the air and made him sneeze. He pictured the years passing and this little closet sealed in darkness. He pictured his dad growing up in the halls and rooms beyond, and his grandmother after that, roaming the house alone.

He felt bad for them, for their loneliness without Bobby. He felt loneliness for the books and toys and the soldiers in the endless battle of mythical creatures.

His fingers ran across the skeleton, brushing away ages of fine dust. It rained over the floor and coated his digits.

He uncurled the arms and legs of the great beast, expanding its tail to a full foot long. He raised it up to the bulb to get a better look and spotted something inside the monster's jaws.

At first, he thought it was a stone, but as he unlocked the lower jaw and the object tumbled into his hand, he saw exactly what it was: a tiny human skull. A *real* tiny skull.

Chapter Four

J AMES VAUGHN DROVE A RED 1999 Ford F250 with a red cap over the bed. Every time he started a hunt and climbed inside it, he wished the windowless van idea wasn't a stereotype. He blamed *Silence of the Lamb*s most of all. A windowless van probably would have been easier, but he didn't want to scream *Serial killer!* when he went out.

The engine rumbled, and he turned on the lights. The three-bedroom cabin he called home for most of his life lit up in the chilly night. He backed up and turned the truck around, grumbling to himself as his headlights skidded from tree to tree across the wooded lot.

He didn't want to go out tonight. He had wanted Emma to come by and relieve the pressure. She had been doing a good job of it for the past few months, and he hadn't needed to go out. But it had been a week now. A week of her spending all her time with that pathetic excuse for a husband. A week without release.

James would just have to go back to what worked before this relationship started, what had always worked since he found the pit.

It was funny the way the pit crossed his mind as he traveled his eighth-mile driveway and found the road. He had been with his sister when he found what it could do—he hadn't thought of her in years.

He remembered the crispness of the leaves on the ground near the house as he chased her into the woods. Melody squealed the way Hanson, the old hound, would before James made him disappear.

She was eleven then. Her red hair bounced over her shoulders as she ran and looked back at him, smiling. He followed, wearing his new Michael Myers Halloween mask they had just come home with. She was going to be Fiona from *Shrek* but was in no hurry to put on her costume, unlike her brother. He had been wearing it since they left the store, and when the car door opened and he raised his rubber knife, what else was she going to do but run?

Twigs snapped as she passed under the breadth of never-ending conifers. She grinned as she darted left toward the rising slope that ended at a rocky cliff face. It was where the creek ran south and they used to catch frogs when they played together. They never played these days, and the rush of having James play with her now made her giggle.

She looked back, expecting to see him running, to see his knife raised in faux aggression so she could scream again and prolong the game.

He wasn't there.

Melody slowed. She felt the October wind pass over her cheeks. It was getting cold now that the day was almost done, but she wasn't going to let her smile fade.

But where was he?

"James?" she called, and her voice reverberated with a flatness that felt odd in this forest. It was as if something was eating her tone as it traveled through the trees. "James!"

There was a crunch to her right, and she spun. She saw the white mask, and that time, when she screamed, it was real.

Fear wrapped her skull, and she felt the coldness run down her spine. Somewhere inside, she knew it was just James, but there was something about the blank look of the mask, the emotionless facade, the way he held that fake knife and took a step toward her, that told her the truth. The person in that mask was not her brother.

She forced herself to smile and scream again. She forced herself to believe that they were just playing in the dusky woods and he was doing his job to make the game fun. She forced a laugh and turned, running along the bottom of the cliff.

He walked steadily behind her.

She glanced back, and he was right there, right behind her, his rubber blade high. Only the blade didn't look rubber. It held a mirrored image of the forest on the side, complete with an orange and red sky above. How could a rubber knife reflect like that?

The blade came down and scraped across her back. There was a ripping sound.

She screamed for real as she felt the cool autumn air rush inside her outfit. The knife had cut her clothes. It *was* real.

She ran faster. With the hard rock wall at her side, she could only move ahead or right. She could feel the cold radiating from the stone at her left. She could hear the breeze flutter through boughs on her right.

"Stop it!" she howled but kept moving. "I don't like this game anymore, James!"

The wind whipped behind her, and her back stung. It was a slice. It was her skin, and she didn't dare think of what else had been cut as hot liquid ran down her.

"Stop!" It was a loud, squealing cry. She looked ahead and right, praying to see a break in the woods where she could turn and loop back toward home. She didn't look down.

Something hooked Melody's foot, and she was immediately ripped from her path into an arching drop. Her hands flew in front of her, but there was no ground to brace herself.

James watched his sister disappear into a gaping hole they had tossed rocks and sticks into a dozen times in the past. It was somewhat humorous that she didn't see it coming and was diving into it.

He stopped at the edge in time to see her head crack against the pit's uneven stone wall while she continued to rotate and fall. Ever lower.

They had speculated at one point that this hole had been an attempt at a well by some long-forgotten settler. Before Lone Wolf was there and the town expanded the way towns do. It was never covered or filled in, though. It just sat and waited for them to come play and giggle as they watched their offerings tumble inside. The way Melody was now.

Under the mask, the sides of James's lips curled as she thumped against the bottom of the pit. She groaned and shifted. Her face was in the dirt, and he could see the slice on her back and the stream of blood.

That was when he saw the pit perform its magic.

The sunlight shifted, making the dusky rays look more indigo than before. At the bottom of the pit, the floor below Melody changed. It turned somewhat foggy and vanished.

James's mouth dropped as he saw his sister plummet into an even deeper space drenched in the bluish-purple shimmer of a tunnel he had never seen. It was like she was dropped down a chute and rushed off to some other place.

He watched the pit for the next forty minutes. His mind reeled, trying to understand where she had gone.

He wanted to climb down there and follow the chute, take it like a playground slide to its eventual destination. But how would he get back up? He had no rope or flashlights—it was bound to be dark down there.

Just as James decided he would run back to the house for rope and flashlights and a snack—he had grown an appetite over the last little while—another oddity occurred.

The sun passed from view, and the shimmer within the pit faded. The bottom of the hole fogged and returned to the dirty floor he remembered. The chute was gone. Wherever it led was blocked by a floor of stone and debris.

"Vanished," James mumbled as he drove the truck onto Highway 14, headed south. He'd follow that for a while, take a few turns, and eventually find himself in Bozeman. He liked hunting in

Bozeman. It had the same stupid college kids to choose from as Missoula, but the town was more deserted at night, easier to slip through without catching anyone's eye.

He cruised past the college, tucking his hat tightly over his face just in case he passed any cameras he didn't know about.

The sidewalks and cross streets were bare. No coeds, no one walking their drunk friends home from parties. It was like every kid in Boseman was being an honor student tonight and home studying.

His fingers couldn't help but strangle the steering wheel. His legs flexed over the pedals, wanting to stomp down the accelerator and run the few cars he saw off the road.

He needed to find someone. He needed release.

James was about to scream as he passed the gas station at the corner of campus. It was a shithole Wesker Pump from the '80s that must have raked in the dollars by being the first set of pumps outside the college, yet it looked like the owners had no interest in modernizing it despite the flood of cash. The awning over the front was a dingy red, and the roof over the pumps looked ready to collapse with only the slightest push. But at pump 3 stood something that calmed his tension while putting his heart into overdrive.

Standing between the pump and a blue Subaru was what he assumed was a ninety-pound female freshman with bobbed, black hair and a frustrated look on her face. She plugged her credit card into the machine and sneered, then did it again. Finally, she banged on the side of the pump before dropping into her driver's seat and shaking her head.

James's mind reeled with the possibilities. What could he do with her back in his shack? What was he going to do to get her there? Both questions fought for dominance. He settled himself down and decided on a plan.

She was about to shut her door when he pulled up to the pump on the opposite side.

"That one giving you trouble?" He pulled out his wallet and then his bank card.

She just shook her head. He could see the embarrassment radiating from her.

"I've had that reader give me crap before. If you pay inside, it works better." He looked around as if embarrassed as well. "And when I've had less than a hundred bucks in my account... that machine always tries to authorize a hundred. If I pay for twenty or thirty inside, it usually works."

Her face lit up.

He pretended to slide his card into the reader. There was no way he would do it for real—leaving that kind of trail was for amateurs. Just like making sure there were no cameras on these pumps—he always rechecked for that.

"Thanks." Her voice was a mumble. She clutched her card tightly and scurried toward the store.

He nodded, and once she had a hand on the door, he stepped in front of her car, placing a pair of nails face-up against her front and rear tires. Before she returned outside, he was parked in the shadows on the side street, watching.

James grinned and waited.

Chapter Five

DEAN KLINE LINED UP HIS TROPHIES on his dresser. They barely fit. He knew he should ditch the lamer ones from Little League, but he liked how it looked with them all crowded together, like he was some big sports' star. Bowling, track, baseball, even his pinewood derby prizes from Cub Scouts, they all shined. They all made him feel accomplished, like he was going somewhere. He had to, after all. If he was forced to stay in this hayseed town for the rest of his life like his parents, he would kill himself.

Well, maybe not that, but it would suck.

It seemed like no one in town ever amounted to anything. He would always hear stories about athletes, musicians, and actors who were from small towns in the middle of nowhere, but no one had heard about someone from Lone Wolf, Montana, doing anything other than growing grains or raising cattle.

Dean had asked his dad once, "Has anyone famous ever come from Lone Wolf?" and Dad pondered over his morning oatmeal for a long time before saying, "Ruth Darby was from here."

No one knew who Ruth Darby was, no one younger than fifty, for the most part, and no one outside the border of the great state of Montana. Dean didn't know until his father informed him that Ruth was the president of the Montana chapter of the Grain Farmers Association in the 1970s. "She even got to fly to Washington and meet President Carter," Dad had said. He grinned and nodded at Dean as if Dean should share his excitement.

No. No one interesting had ever come from Lone Wolf. Maybe Dean would be the first, and maybe not, but he was definitely getting out. He had to.

Dean looked around his room at the old furniture, out the window at the dozen dim streetlights he could see in the distance where downtown was, and he sighed. He wasn't going to lose fingers at the mill. He wasn't going to work with cows as a ranch hand. He wasn't going to work one of the minimum wage jobs at the Dairy Queen or John-Hoss Marketplace, where the only people who shopped were the ones who didn't want to drive a county over to the Super Wal-Mart.

This shitty town was dead. It just didn't know it.

He wasn't going to die here with it.

Maggie's laugh came through the wall. She was on her phone again—she was always on the phone. Dean wasn't sure how Mom and Dad paid the power bill with as much charging as she had to do to support her talking.

He would have a phone next year. He'd be old enough to get a job, and he would have a phone and a bank account where he'd save for his move, save for a car, and, of course, he would spend just a little so he could ask out Nancy Hanning, who he had crushed on for nearly four years.

Each year, something different stood in his way. She had a boyfriend, then she didn't but he had to focus on track and then watching his brother. Then she moved to the far side of town, into a bigger, nicer house, and he just knew he couldn't ask her out until he could at least pay for dates.

In the back of his head, he knew he was just too scared. But he wouldn't be once he had a job.

Maggie laughed again, and Dean wondered if she was talking to Janet Green. He loved it when Janet drove her dad's old Nissan Z to pick up Maggie. Not that he gave a shit about the car, but sometimes she would come inside and wait for Maggie, and her smell would fill the hallways. That smell and the shape of her hips were enough to make him forget about Nancy for a solid few hours.

He flopped onto his bed and stared at cream-colored swirls of textured plaster on the ceiling. He couldn't wait for time to move faster, to have some control over his life.

Dean closed his eyes, and in the darkness behind his lids, he found himself down at the lake. He sat on the rocky shore and watched the water. It shined with a bluish shimmer, and he watched a bulge emerge from the water, a head tilting back as water rushed down the sides of her face. It was Janet Green.

He wondered if his sister had invited her over to swim, and another bulge lifted from the water, another head. It was Nancy Hanning.

His heart thudded against his ribs.

They moved through the glittering water toward the shore, and he watched their shoulders emerge, then their arms and their bikini-covered breasts. Their eyes were on him, and they smiled slyly as water caressed their hips and thighs, and they came onto shore.

Dean sat up on his towel and found he was in his swimsuit, a tattered black thing with a faded white print of a shark on the side.

The girls winked at him, looked at each other, and nodded. It made his hair stand upright and his blood run hot.

"Holy shit," he whispered to himself. He had no idea what was happening, but he wasn't about to question it.

Janet and Nancy took each other in their arms, and their lips met. They kissed and giggled, and they looked back at Dean. They kissed again, and each found the catch on the other's top and undid them.

Dean stood. He looked around the beach. Obviously, someone

was playing a trick on him, but there was no one else there.

Gray fog blocked his view of the new house, and the shimmer from the lake highlighted the boulders and the edge of the woods. A feeling of calm overwhelmed him—until he saw the girls again.

Janet and Nancy were on the shore. Bathing suit tops hung from their fingertips, and they were walking away. They turned and flung their tops at him. He watched their garments sail through the air, and he just missed a full glimpse of what he knew were their perfect breasts. Perfect.

He stared at their dripping wet asses, their suit bottoms barely covering their skin, as they followed a path between the boulders into the woods.

"Come on, Dean," they called together. They laughed, and his heart ached.

Dean leaped across the stony beach after them. He still didn't understand, but nothing in the world was going to keep him from this opportunity.

"I'm coming!" He followed into the path between boulders. He saw them pass into the woods, swallowed by the fog as blue light glistened on their skin.

He thought about touching them, running his fingers over their soft shoulders and across their bellies. He wanted to caress their legs and gently wrap his hands around their chins as he leaned in to kiss each of them.

As Dean reached the edge of the woods, though, something inside him forced his legs to halt. He felt the cool moisture of the fog as it passed before him. He saw a flicker of something behind the obscurity, and though he wasn't sure what it was, it sent shivers across his skin. He smelled a sour, rotting odor, like when he had to clean out the mousetraps in the old house and the creatures had been dead for a few days. It was a scent of wet decay, and it made his stomach stand up inside his midsection.

"Dean!" Janet called. Her voice was sultry. It was longing.

"Dean! Where are you?" It was Nancy. It was nearly a whine. "Come play with us, Dean."

He could envision them both, pouty-faced and staring, holding each other close, one of each of their hands moving over one another and the others waiting for him, curling mid-air, calling him over.

A breeze blew from inside the woods. The smell was stronger. It curled inside his gut and made his bile rise.

They laughed.

He wanted to step inside the fog. His insides burned hot for him to move ahead and find them. Surely, the sensation holding him back was just fear. It was the same fear that had stopped him from asking Nancy to the eighth-grade dance. It was the fear that told him once he had a car it still wouldn't be enough to get her. It was a fear born of poverty and watching Dad take orders from Mom as if no man in their family was good enough for her.

As much as he hated it, he succumbed. He stepped back from the fog.

"No," they called together. "Dean?" they cried.

The ground around his feet softened. He felt his toes sink into the mud, and the stench grew stronger. The dirt folded over his toes, and as he backpedaled again, he was forced to look down.

It wasn't mud he was walking in—or, not a mix of dirt and water like he would have expected. Liquid flowed over his toes, deep red. The dirt was more than dirt. He could see it in his mind, and though he had no reason to believe his thoughts, he knew they were true. What he was standing in was only partially earth. The rest was once living. It was the crumbled dust of muscle. It was the dark-red desiccation of skin and hair and bone. The land below his feet was, in fact, the source of the smell. It was layer over layer of decomposing flesh soaked in the rotting blood that was once contained within it.

The fog moved toward him. It swirled around his back and hid the rest of the world. The lake, the shore, the path back to the house were all hidden. Everything ahead and behind Dean was a gray blob coated in a glimmering shine of blueish light.

"Dean, come on," Janet whined.

But he couldn't tell where she was calling from. Was it in front or behind? If he knew, he could run—but it was all around him.

"Dean?" Nancy called.

Dean opened his mouth to scream, and fog climbed inside him. He howled into the clouds and only heard a wet whimper. The muddy ground softened further, and his feet sank, then his ankles, then his knees.

His heart pounded as the idea screamed within his head that he had to get out of there. He was surrounded by Death. It was swallowing him from below. It was pulling him like the current of a hungry ocean, drawing him deeper into those woods, into the arms of something he knew was not the girls he dreamed of but the luring end of a dirty trick.

"No!" his muffled voice fought from his throat. He tried lifting his legs from the muck, and they only sank deeper. "No!" He was quieter still. "*No!*"

Dean's eyes shot open, and he saw his ceiling once more. He spun and rolled from his bed, thumping onto the floor. The hardwood smacked the back of his head, and pinpricks of white floated into his vision.

He raced across the floor on hands and knees until he thudded against the wall, turned, and pressed his back hard into the plaster.

Dean's lungs pumped air heavily in and out. He smelled the dusty old room, the stench from his track sneakers he kept forgetting to deodorize, and his open stick of Old Spice antiperspirant by his gym bag.

There was no stench of death.

Maggie laughed through the wall.

He wanted to laugh too; he was being so dumb. He had drifted away thinking about girls and somehow ended up in a nightmare. He smirked until his eyes fell on his feet, on the dark red dirt that clung to the bottoms of his soles.

"No." He panicked and shook his head and rubbed his toes. He brushed the bottoms of his feet.

It was gone. Not red, just the remnants of a nightmare.

Chapter Six

RANDY KLINE GLANCED AT HIS sleeping wife as he entered the bedroom. The lights were on, but her sleep mask was tight on her face. That meant she was officially in *Do Not Disturb* mode until morning. He supposed she had earned it. Emma hadn't been the easiest to deal with today, but she had gotten them through it. Moving into his childhood home wasn't high on her list of must-dos for the year, but once the arguments were over, they were both on the same page—they had to vacate the old house if they were going to get a dime out of it while avoiding foreclosure. He knew it wasn't ideal for her. She hated the water and his mother, but he had to hope it would grow on her after a while.

He walked to the old brass-framed bed that Mom had inherited from her grandparents and watched Emma sleep. Her mouth twitched, and her dimple showed itself for a split second. The sight punched Randy in the gut. He didn't know why until the memory landed of them in Mrs. Harmon's math class in tenth grade. He watched her from the back row, smiling when she answered Mrs. Harmon's question. Harmon had praised her, and the little divot in her cheek showed itself. It planted itself in his mind that day and that night. It gnawed at his thoughts, how perfectly it fit the side of her face when she laughed with Haily Jones and Stephanie Osborn as they smoked outside the cafeteria. It drove him nuts until he asked her out three days later.

But like that dimple faded into her cheek when she stopped smiling, it seemed their connection faded over the years. It wasn't just their money problems, which definitely didn't help; it was everything. It was a gap between them that started as a stream when Maggie was born and he couldn't console Emma enough about her inability to breastfeed. Her postpartum depression stressed them further, and he was clueless how to help. After Dean came along, he found himself actually resenting her. He didn't want to be home, so too often, he wasn't. She was a ball of raging sadness, and it felt like it was always aimed at either him or the children.

She had found medication that helped by the time Drew came along, but they both knew the damage was done to their relationship. Though he tried, he found himself unable to completely forgive the screams she had aimed at him and the kids—the people he loved more than anything and whom he found himself defending daily.

Of course, the grudges went both ways. She never seemed to forgive him for his absence. They had fueled each other, her sadness and anger, his desire to be away, her rage at his lack of duty to her and the kids, his hurt and fear that the kids were growing up to think screaming and crying and fighting were normal.

Those days had mostly faded into the background of their lives, but the scars were still there, raw ridges over their emotional reactions and wounds left gaping to color any minor disagreement with pain. There was a chasm between them. They made their marriage function on a daily basis almost out of routine; they tried to have date nights to rekindle what they could when money was available, but those nights were rare. The constant sense of trying and failing was exhausting. And the chasm never seemed to shrink.

Randy sat on the edge of the bed and shed his shoes and pants. The stubs of his fingers ached as he worked the button on his jeans. He laid his head on his pillow and closed his eyes.

Maybe this would be the step they needed to pull themselves back together. After the old house sold and they had a little cash flow, after a few years they could sell this one, and maybe then they could afford a house Emma liked. He could make a better effort to do things for her. He could try some online courses and maybe find a better job—show her he was trying hard to help this family and take some of the strain off her shoulders.

God, he hoped it went that way.

The wind blew outside, and the sky rumbled somewhere over the lake. He hadn't heard that a storm was coming, but if it was, he was happy they finished getting everything inside this afternoon—or had they?

There were a handful of boxes on the porch when they left to drop the truck off, and he had asked Dean to bring them inside. He fought to remember if he had seen them while carrying in the pizzas, but he just could not remember. He wouldn't stress it normally—the house was set back from the road, and it wasn't like anyone would come along and steal them—but a storm.

Another rolling wave of thunder lightly shook the house, and it was louder than the last. Wind whistled beyond the bedroom window, and Randy imagined cardboard boxes on the porch getting soaked through with rain. He saw their meager possessions toppling out as they lifted each box and the seams split. He didn't remember what was in those boxes, but whatever it was, it probably wasn't good to leave it soaking overnight.

He groaned as he sat up and reached for his pants. His nubs ached as he buckled his belt and pulled on his shoes.

The house was dark as Randy moved down the steps, but the ambient light from a neglected living room lamp showed the way. He was halfway down when blinding white light flashed in every window and the house shook from a belt of bone-rattling thunder.

Randy blinked at the brightness and froze. When he opened his eyes again, the house was drenched in gloom. The living room light was out. Everything was out. Hissing, then ringing, then the heavy sound of rain pounding on the roof came through the walls and ceiling.

"Shit."

Whatever was on that porch was likely getting drenched. He gripped the railing tightly and felt the edge of the step with his toes. One step at a time, he lowered himself down through the darkened stairway.

He was ten years old all of a sudden, and Bobby was crying in the darkened living room. He was rushing to get to his brother on that stormy night when Mom and Dad were across town at some dinner party and Joan was supposed to be in charge—but Joan had gone off with Buddy Miller on his dirt bike five minutes after their parents were gone.

Boom. Crack. The house shook, and something crashed in the woods.

In the lightning's flash, Randy saw the front door and buckets of rain flowing from the roof. He was steps away from the door, from saving whatever belongings waited out there, and the light was out again.

"Randy!" Bobby's shaky voice called from the living room. The seven-year-old was crying. Randy knew he'd slipped from the couch when the lights went off. He had been walking on its back, pretending to be Spider-Man, and lost it. He slammed against the wall and tumbled to the floor, bruising three ribs and spraining his ankle. "Help, Randy."

It was just a memory, but it sounded like it was happening right then. He could swear if he walked into that living room he would see his brother in pain on the floor. He wanted to go and check, even knowing it was just in his mind.

Randy stopped with his hand on the front doorknob.

"Randy!"

The voice was so clear. It was so loud. It was just a memory, but in the midnight black, he wondered. It felt like more than just something in his mind, and with that thought, others bloomed.

What if Bobby returned? What if it was Bobby's ghost? Had

Mom gotten so mean because she was being haunted? Was Bobby going to haunt his family now?

"My chest." Another sad tone from the living room, one on the edge of weeping. There was fear there, and a hint of betrayal.

Was that what Bobby felt in those woods? Did he think no one cared? That he had been betrayed and left for dead by his family?

"I tried," Randy muttered. "I looked for you so many times."

"Randy, help!"

It couldn't be. Really. It was the stormy night and the stress of moving. It was his mental state, worrying about money, and—he hadn't processed losing Mom; that was it. But what if it wasn't those things? What if Bobby was in the living room?

He had to see.

His hands out and walking slowly, he turned left until he had done a U-turn. He passed the stairs, and under the racket of crashing rain, he heard sobbing.

It was that night again. The pitch black house and Randy looking for his brother. The sounds of his kid brother whimpering and breathing shallowly with injured ribs. The fear was fresh in his mind that something had happened, and because Joan wasn't there, it was his fault. He had been left in charge, and he was to blame for what-ever happened, even if Joan had snuck out.

His heart raced. His fingers trembled.

He expected that at any second he would feel the back of Dad's recliner against his fingers, the start of the room. Bobby would be curled up on the floor, one hand on his chest and one on his ankle.

But Mom had taken that chair to the dump years ago. Instead, what he touched was a tower of moving boxes he had piled there thirty minutes ago. With one hand on them, he continued blindly into the room.

He smelled the rain. The deep humidity brushed his skin as if he was out in the downpour, not under his roof. He took another step into the room, his hand threatening to leave the box tower, and he paused.

What was he doing? What did he think he was going to find? Did he really think he was going to relive a memory from almost thirty years ago?

The wetness on his cheeks told him he had to know. The tears he hadn't shed for far too long were coming out and streaming through his beard, and when he sniffed, he smelled something foul.

"Bobby?" His voice was low and sheepish, barely more than a whisper. "You're not here, are you?"

He prayed there would be no answer.

He breathed hard, his chest pounding, his nose taking in more and more of that disgusting smell that he refused to identify.

Lightning crashed over the lake, and the room flashed bright, white horror.

Bobby was on the floor, but not the Bobby from that night. What he saw was a moldering thing, a wet, dead thing the size of his missing nine-year-old brother when he went into those woods and never returned. Green, slimy meat showed through broken skin. Lines of bone protruded through cracks in the skull. Yellow drips leaked from broken, blackened skin, and the head slowly turned toward Randy.

Randy couldn't comprehend what he knew to be true. It didn't click, no matter how hard the gears tried to turn.

That thing was where his brother should have been. It was the size and shape of his missing sibling, but it was not him—he couldn't accept that. This decaying corpse was something else. It had been snuck into his home to scare him or ridicule him or something. This thing...

Randy sank to his knees as the face found him. It was the face of his brother, but it wasn't. One eye leaked green pus, its entire surface overtaken with rot, but the other—the other was the emerald-green shine of Bobby's ever-bright gaze. His hair, though drenched in oozing rot, was light brown, medium-length, and split on the back quarter of his head with a cowlick that Mom had fought with every morning.

"Help!" Only a rasp of air made it through Bobby's lips, but Randy heard it loud and clear in his head. His brother was calling him. His brother—no matter how he looked—needed his help.

The lightning faded, and darkness consumed the room.

"Bobby!" Randy cried, and slowly moved forward.

The living room filled with amber hues as the power surged back on, and the end table lamp illuminated all.

Bobby was gone.

Randy reached into the empty space his brother had occupied as if his hand might find something his eyes failed to discern. Where Bobby had lain was empty, other than the old rug his mother had worn to bare threads. The rancid smell was gone, but the humidity remained.

As thunder boomed from somewhere down the lake, Randy remembered the boxes he was trying to rescue. To fulfill every last doubt, he ran his hand across the empty patch of floor, then stood. He wiped the tears from his cheeks and headed to the front door.

Was he going crazy? How could he have imagined that? It was stress. It had to be.

He sniffed and wiped his face one last time and opened the door. Stress, that was it.

On the front porch was a single box labeled: *Dad.*

Randy kneeled, taking a moment to observe the downpour and the steamy August night. Other than the newer vehicles in the drive-way, he could have been ten, staring out there and crying for Mom and Dad to get home so they could take Bobby to the hospital.

"No." He huffed and shook his head. He scooped the box up, carefully supporting the bottom in case it ripped from wetness. He carried the thing into the kitchen and placed it on the counter. The last thing he wanted to do was unpack a box that late, but the contents could have been ruined if he didn't dry off whatever it was.

Randy flipped open the box's top, and staring back at him was the severed head of Bobby Kline. The emerald-green eye bore into Randy's mind as he heard the scream, "Help me, Randy!"

Chapter Seven

THE ROAD WAS SERENE. THE wildlife stayed clear of the two-lane stretch, and there were almost as few travelers from either direction. It let James drive and relax and bask in the knowledge of what was to come—the games he could play with his new toy when they got back to his shed.

It had been too long since he had a toy; he realized that now. He had let himself be tamed by the mundane, by something as simple as regular sex. It was great sex, that was true, but he had let it drain him of his urges, urges that brought the greatness out of him and led him to explore. He had failed by letting himself get sidetracked, because what greater calling did man have beyond exploring? Even if what he explored was through steel and flesh, he pushed the boundaries of himself and his toys. He was an explorer at heart.

The sky ahead was darker than he had left it. Black clouds covered the mountains and the town of Lone Wolf within. Lightning flashed across the mountainside, and as its white flare fell on his toy, she whimpered.

She had heard his directions when he placed the tape on her mouth and limbs. She could ride on the back floor of the cab as long as she was quiet. Otherwise, it would be the truck bed, and he would have to take other steps to ensure she was silent. She had nodded her head, and they formed an understanding.

He let most of the whimpering slide. It was normal for them to cry at that point. They couldn't control it. The shuddering of their chests, the rapid breathing, the shaky limbs and soft whines, it was expected. They learned control over the following weeks. They learned that this ride was nothing and that his patience would not last.

James chuckled to himself, thinking about Emma. She had been so convincing in the way she treated him. She had made him feel like she was the key to his needs and all he would ever want. As much as he allowed the sheet to be pulled over his eyes, deep inside, he had known it was all temporary. It couldn't have lasted. And as he thought about it, he was sure he would have to end it the way he ended all of his relationships. He hated to take a toy so close to home—it was a bad practice—but she had to be removed from the board. And she had to experience what his toys got to enjoy. So did her family.

The more he thought about it, the more sure he was. Once he took her, the family would be an issue. They had to disappear too. All of them. It was the only way to wipe the board clear of any links to him.

He could wait a few weeks and play it out slowly and thoughtfully. Long enough to finish with this one.

James glanced at her between the seats. Her head was against the rear passenger door, and her eyes were on him—wide and studying his every move. She was a sharp one; he could tell. She was going to be fun.

And then he would take care of Emma and her kin.

Donna Latham watched the psycho drive with tears in her eyes. Her heart had stopped pounding, but the shivers still ran over her flesh. They knew what she didn't.

She had repeated the thought over and over in her mind. *Why didn't I know better?*

She didn't need the gas that badly. She walked everywhere on campus, and she could have easily gotten a ride with Meredith to the girls' night tomorrow. But no, she had to push it. She had to listen to a stranger and leave her car with him, she had to talk to him again when he showed up beside her car while she had two flats—two!

I should have run. The moment I saw him pull up, I should have run. Campus was only a block away, with lights and cameras and security.

But she hadn't. She had frozen in a moment of indecision like too many other times in her life. Should she say yes and go out with Mike Halstead before she packed and went away to Bozeman? Should she sign up for political science or sociology this semester, or risk losing out on both? Should she scream and run from the psycho or stand there slack-jawed and hope he wasn't as bad as she feared?

She feared the worst now. He was taking her somewhere she would never come back from. He was going to rape her and cut her into tiny little pieces. He hadn't said those things, but she knew it, and in some ways, she guessed she deserved it for being so stupid.

How did she let this happen?

It wasn't even the first day of school yet, in her first year of what was supposed to lead to her engineering degree, supposed to start her life off with a leg up on a good job and possibly her dream of working in aerospace design.

She remembered drawing rockets and shuttles with her father on the kitchen counter when she was six. Watching dumb, old science fiction movies with him on the couch, like *Flying Disc Man from Mars* and *The Man from Planet X*—she had wanted so badly to see space. Later, she settled on designing for space; it was a lot more likely to get a job doing that, and she would still be in the ballpark.

What was her dad going to do when he found out about this? He had warned her about being alone in a city. Granted, it was Bozeman, not New York, but he had warned her. And she failed.

Rain patted on the windshield, then it came down like a sheet. The psycho looked annoyed as he flicked on the wipers and slowed, turning onto what felt like a dirt road under the tires. He glanced back at Donna, and a smile returned to his face.

She didn't like that smile. It wasn't a normal smile. Normal smiles were from joy and laughter. A smile was supposed to bring people together. This one was one of deep mischief. It was one of internal fire being stoked by something unmentionable to others. It made her shiver more, her skin rising into goosebumps and a cold wave washing over her insides.

The psycho turned the truck again, and the road became bumpier. They were going slower now, under trees that stifled the rainfall. He wrenched the steering wheel, and she felt them ascend and then lower over a small hill.

They were near the end of this trip, and all of a sudden, the fear of their destination rose like a kaiju from the sea. It was no longer going to be a thing to come. It was a thing of here and now. Whatever he had planned was about to happen, and the fear within that question made her heart pound and her chest heave with quickening breaths.

She was going to die with her hands and feet taped. She was never going to say goodbye to anyone. She was a statistic now: Number of Missing College Women, Number of Students to Enroll and Not Graduate, Number of Cars Abandoned Yearly.

She was nothing. Unless she made up her mind to do something.

The truck stopped, and the psycho turned off the engine. He looked back at her, this time without a smile, this time with a leer that left one side of his mouth sagging more than the other.

"We're here," he said in a low sing-song tone. He looked her over, his eyes lingering on her taped hands and feet. He stared into her eyes, and she saw an eagerness there, a kid ready to unwrap a present.

She had to do something. She had to control herself. She had to watch and wait—he was bound to take this tape off. When she had her chance, she would take it.

The psycho opened his door, and lightning cracked nearby.

Flashes of white flooded the cab as the door slammed shut. He walked around the front of the truck, around to her side, and she squealed under the tape. She flexed and stretched and demanded the tape break.

It didn't.

The door opened behind her, and rain slapped her forehead as her top half fell backward and hung from the door frame. He was above her, looking down. Rain traced the lines of his skull as shadows covered his features but let his eyes shine.

She was frozen. All of her raging desire to flee short-circuited the wires inside her brain. Fear and indecision held her once again.

He tucked his hands under her shoulders and pulled her from the truck, lifting and twisting until she hung from his shoulder like some clubbed woman in a caveman cartoon.

Rain soaked her head and clothes.

The world spun as he turned and shut the vehicle door. He carried her under some trees, opened a door to a structure, and flipped on a light.

Her heart thrummed, and she tasted acid in her mouth.

The door closed, sealing them inside a small wooden building. There was a wooden floor covered in painter's plastic sheeting. As he dropped her on her ass, she saw chains on one side and a pit on the other.

Something told her to fear the pit.

Rain tapped on the metal roof. It sang in a sympathetic tone, trying to calm Donna as the psycho slid a knife from his belt and held it in front of her face.

"We're going to move you from here—" he pointed with the knife at her belly, "—to there." He swung the blade until it pointed at the chains hanging from the wall behind her. "This can be painless, or it can be bloody. It's entirely up to you."

A flash of cold raced down her spine as she took his words to heart. He was being honest now. He was ready to cut her or chain her. Her pick.

She nodded slowly. Her hair felt greasy from sweat. Her body was stiff and tired from trembling in the car. Her joints ached. She wished she could go to sleep and wake up at home with her dad in the kitchen making breakfast like her high school days.

"Good." He brought the knife down to her ankles. "I'm going to cut you free, and you're going to behave." He waited, watching her eyes. Only after she nodded again did he proceed to slice through the gray tape that bound her ankles together.

He peeled the tape outward and around her leg. It stung her skin, and she flinched, but she did not move.

With one hand, he peeled it free of her first ankle and started on the second. With his other hand, he caressed the freed skin as a parent might check on a child's wound. Once it was halfway off, he jerked the tape sideways, ripping it from her leg.

Donna gritted her teeth and whimpered under the burn. She didn't move.

"Good." He ran his fingers over her ankles and up her calves.

She felt slimy things running down her spine. She tried to remind herself to look for her chance, but all she saw was that knife. All she saw were those chains. She tried to decide what was better, the chains or the blade, and she wasn't sure. The blade would hurt now, but with those chains, her chances were gone and she was sure to meet that knife again eventually.

"Very good." He untied her right shoe and lifted it from her foot. The plastic below her crinkled.

He unrolled the sock from the ankle down, and she could feel his giddiness. She could feel the excitement in his fingers as he stroked her flesh, teasing the cloth from her toes. The look in his eyes was cold. It was hungry.

She didn't want to know for what.

The psycho dropped the sock by her shoe and took her other ankle in hand. He untied the second shoe, and the thought occurred to Donna that this may be the last time she would ever wear shoes. If he got her in those chains, she might never walk out of that shitty little shack. She might never touch the outside world again.

She had to do something.

He slid the sneaker off and tossed it. It tumbled beside the other, making a crackling sound on the plastic floor.

The plastic floor...

Why was the floor covered in plastic? Why—a vision took her mind: other girls in this same position, others bleeding on the plastic sheeting, and the psycho just balling it up and tossing it out. That was going to happen to her.

He slid the second sock free just as he had the first, stroking her skin in quiet eagerness, and she panicked inside her mind. She screamed for a clue of what to do. She looked around the room for anything that she could use to—

Donna's eyes fell on the pit as he tossed her second sock to the side. She imagined him tossing the shoes and socks of a dozen girls as he prepped them for whatever his sick fetish was.

He grabbed her waistband, and their eyes met. He raised the knife and opened his gaze wide as if to say, *I know you see this.*

She took a deep breath and held still.

"Wise," he said, and gripped his knife in his teeth as he unbuttoned her shorts.

She had to act now. She couldn't; he would kill her. He was going to kill her anyway. Would she rather get raped or eaten or whatever the fuck his twist was first?

She was a statue as he unzipped and spread her shorts.

Should she fight or deal with it? Was this her chance, or was it later?

He raised her ass and pulled the shorts down, careful not to take the panties with them.

Part of her was thankful for her underwear—the other part knew why he was doing it. This sick fuck wanted to enjoy each step.

He slid the shorts down, caressing her rump, her thighs, her calves, her feet. He lifted them from her feet and raised them, his eyes locked onto hers, and he breathed the crotch in deeply.

From her neck to her toes, chills ran their tingly legs over her skin.

The psycho tossed the shorts over the pile of shoes and socks and walked his fingers slowly up her legs.

She sucked in air through her teeth. Her body tensed as he hooked one hand around each side of her panties.

Donna's vision was a shower of spots and redness as her heart pumped and adrenaline ran wild. Her skin felt slimy and gritty at once. Her arms and pits were hot, and her legs were freezing. He pulled on her underwear, and she felt it stick and then give as a waterfall of dread ran through her system. It unpeeled from her bottom. She felt the sticky plastic on her skin. She felt his fingers on her, probing as he moved the cotton cloth down her thighs, his eyes fixed on the inches he had uncovered.

It was now or never. She knew it in her heart. She could stay a frozen little coward and die here with him, or she could take this one and only moment before she was forever locked in those chains and—

He reached her feet, and his eyes were glued between her legs. His lips quivered.

She breathed deep, and as fast as she could, Donna curled her legs up to her chest and fired both feet forward.

Her heels slammed into the psycho's chest, and she felt a crack as he reeled backward. He was tumbling, losing his balance, and rolling toward the pit. A glimmer of hope rose in her gut until he grabbed her legs and pulled her along.

She slid and kicked. He slammed onto the ground a foot from the hole, and one of her heels found his face. His jaw clacked and jerked back, and the knife between his teeth sliced the meat of her sole wide open.

She screamed under her tape.

He rocked toward the pit, and his eyes shot wide. He reached with one hand at the side of the hole while he rolled uncontrollably into it, and his other hand clamped tightly on Donna's leg.

"Fall!" she screamed, but the tape made her words a muffled howl.

The knife glimmered as it fell into the chasm.

She kicked again, a bloody footprint on his face as he teetered.

His hand slid from the wall, and his head went down. His shoulders and upper arms went next. And he refused to let her go.

Donna skidded across the plastic. Her arms flailed, taped and unable to grasp anything but painter's sheeting. She held it in her fingers as her waist crossed the edge and her legs went over.

He screamed, and it echoed, burning her ears. He released her as both of her legs dangled, and she balanced with her belly on the ridge of the giant pit.

There was a thump as he hit the bottom. She would have thought that would have relieved some stress, but it didn't. She knew she was next if she didn't figure this out and pull herself up. She was slipping farther, with only her elbows gripping and the plastic slipping away from the world above.

Her breath was hot through her nose. Sweat ran down her face, splatting on the plastic. Every part of her seemed to be on fire, stressing to hold her in place as millimeter by millimeter was stolen from her.

Her eyes searched the room for anything that could help. The plastic between her and the ledge whined as it slipped free.

She plummeted down, trailed by a flapping, failing parachute of translucent sheeting.

Part Two

Friends

Chapter Eight

THE MORNING SUNLIGHT IGNITED DUST motes in the air. Inside his room, the day was cooler than the one before, and though Drew couldn't see the lake from his window, it was like he could feel it out there, calling to him.

He wanted to go, but not just yet.

He sat at the inherited desk that was part of his new room, with the tiny skull to his right. He studied the back of a box, a still-sealed model he had found in the crawlspace. It read *Dragons of Middle Earth* in large letters, and below that, it read *Glaurung the Golden*. Drew thought it was kind of squat and stumpy for a dragon, and it had no wings, but as he looked at the detailed drawing where the giant beast waged battle, he couldn't help but want to play with it.

His fingers ran down the cellophane's sealed edge, and his lip curled in. He wondered if he had what he needed to put it together. He had seen cutting tools, paints, and glue in the closet, but he highly doubted twenty-five-year-old glue still worked. Same for the paint. The bottles probably held nothing but hardened globs inside.

He would need to go by The Gilded Lady, the only hobby store in town. It was mostly geared toward quilting, crocheting, and fake flowers, but it had a small section for model building and rockets. They would have some paint and glue.

His fingernails scraped and curled the plastic seams.

He could still open it and look, even if he didn't have the stuff to put it together. He'd be super careful not to drop any pieces or lose anything.

Drew scratched across the box, taking a line of clear plastic with him. His eyes opened wider as he ripped into it.

"What's that?" Dean's voice invaded his moment.

Drew sighed and raised the box, but he didn't turn to his brother. "It's a model I found. I'm going to build it."

"No, dumbass, that."

Drew turned and saw Dean pointing at the small jawless skull on the side of the desk. In the morning light, it seemed even smaller, a little larger than a golf ball. "Oh. It's cool, right?" He set the box on the desk and picked up the tiny head. "I don't know if it's a baby head or what."

Dean stepped closer and plucked it from Drew's hand. "I'm sure it's a fake. A Halloween prop or something. Babies' heads aren't fully sealed when they come out, anyway. They're all soft and shit until their skulls harden. And this—it's the size of an *unborn* baby, like someone took home their abortion."

He held the miniature skull up to his face and examined it. He probed it as Drew had the night before, running his fingers over the rough patches and joints. He tapped it, trying to decipher if it was really bone. He peered into the eye sockets as if expecting to see a tiny inscription reading *Made in China*.

"Definitely fake," Dean finally surmised.

"What d'ya mean?" Drew's head cocked to one side. "It's made out of bone."

"Yeah, maybe. But I saw this one YouTube where a guy was sculpting all kinds of stuff out of bone. They do it in third-world countries to sell to tourists. I bet that's what this is. It was probably part of a hippo bone or something. It's cool, though."

"Maybe not." Drew fought against conceding, but his voice was already shallow. "It could be a monkey head... those are small like that." He figured Dean just didn't want to claim it was real because he didn't want to get tricked. If he agreed with Drew and his buddies came over and saw it, he didn't want to get roasted. Drew had to find some string to cling to; he really wanted it to be real.

"Maybe." Dean sat on Drew's bed and lay back. He set the skull aside on the bed. "So, how do you like your new room?"

Drew picked up the skull and scanned it once more. Had Dean actually seen something? *No.* After a second, Dean's words finally registered.

"I like it. Uncle Bobby left some cool stuff here." He pointed at the hanging models and then the crawlspace. He didn't really want Dean in there, but he was conflicted. He wanted to keep it all to himself, for it to be his special place, but at the same time, he wanted Dean to be jealous. His brother couldn't be jealous if he never saw it. "There's so much cool stuff in there."

Dean turned. "In there? Isn't it just like the attic?"

"Kinda. But it's special, like a secret room."

Dean rolled his eyes and sat up. He went to the door and kneeled, placing his hand on the tiny door's knob. His mouth parted slightly, and he took a breath. Drew had to squint as he watched because Dean didn't take anything slowly. He was the type to jump headfirst into everything—and that sparked another question in Drew's mind: Why was Dean even in his room?

Yeah, they used to share a room. Yeah, they were almost always around each other. But that was out of necessity. They *had* to be in the same room. Now they didn't. They were free to spread out and do their own things, and in the old house, it seemed like that was all Dean wanted. As much as Dean used to bitch, it seemed odd for him to even be in Drew's presence right now. It was as if he didn't want to be alone.

Dean opened the door. He looked puzzled for a moment, and then he reached in and pulled the light cord.

"Huh." He crawled inside on his hands and knees.

Drew shoved the skull in his pocket and followed his brother in.

"All this stuff was here when we moved in?" Dean picked up dragons and set them down. He fingered books and scanned over the modeling supplies.

"Yeah. Can you believe that?"

Dean raised a small elf to eye level and then blew, sending a cloud of dust toward Drew. "Yeah. I guess I can believe it."

"Wow, look at that." Dean pointed and then shuffled a few model boxes around from the bottom right shelf. He emerged holding a cardboard box illustrated with a black 1969 Chevy Chevelle. "Is this…" He shook the box. It was empty.

"That's Dad's!" Drew couldn't help but envision the model car that had been on the top shelf of the family bookcase ever since he could remember. It was a car he wanted to pull down and play with a thousand times but was never allowed to. He had nearly scaled the shelves in secret several times, he wanted it so badly.

"All it needs is to be painted navy blue with an orange roof."

"That's it." Drew was sure. "That's Dad's car."

"You think…" Dean paused as it sank in, "…that car was Bobby's?"

"Sure looks like it."

They both stared at the image on the box.

"I want to see it now," Drew said. He was itching to run out of the crawlspace and find it, but he just couldn't leave Dean in his secret spot alone.

Dean shook his head. "Dad hasn't unpacked it yet. It's in one of those thousand boxes in the living room, I'm sure."

Drew sank. "Oh."

"But still. I want to see it again too."

"You think they made it together? Dad and Uncle Bobby?"

Dean didn't answer right away. He slid open the box and looked inside. There was an instruction sheet and a few frames that must have held the car's parts before they were sliced free, and that was it. He closed the box and set it back on the shelf.

"Maybe." That was all Dean said. He had this look on his face, a sad look. Drew tried to understand what it was, but it didn't seem to compute.

Dean turned and crawled past Drew. His interest in Drew's new, special place had fled.

"I'm going to ask Dad about it." Drew reached over and picked up the box. "Let's see what he says."

"You go ahead. I'm going to go watch some YouTube or something."

That was more like it. Drew wasn't sure what was bothering Dean, but going off to be alone was much more what Drew expected.

Box in hand, Drew yanked on the light cord, closed the crawlspace door, and went searching for Dad.

Emma sat on her bed and hit send, then stared at her phone's screen. It was the third text she had sent today, and none of them had been answered.

First, there was: "I can sneak out now. Are you at home?"

Then: "I hope you aren't mad at me. I really want to see you"

Finally: "I need to feel you. Please let me come please you"

She sounded desperate, she knew that, but if that was what it took to get his attention, it was okay. She didn't want it to be okay, but it was. She had never let herself get to a place like this, so powerless, not even with Randy, but part of her thought she deserved the desperation.

She had been cruel to Randy. She knew that, and she didn't care. Her postpartum depression had been a medical condition, and he should have just gotten the fuck over it. He should have been a man and served her how she needed it instead of letting things get strained the way they did. It was his job to make her happy—wasn't that what their vows were all about?

But even still, not that she would ever admit it, but she was sorry. She knew she shouldn't have been seeing James, she knew she should have been working harder to mend the gap between herself and

Randy, yet those minutes with James made all of that melt away. Those minutes of being his slave and letting him punish her for all the wrongs she did made her feel like she had paid for her crimes—until she returned to the bright light of day and her children's faces reminded her that all of that was just a fantasy.

She was wrong. She was treating her husband wrong and her kids wrong, and she needed to be punished—and though she fought it, her mind went to James doing the punishing, even if that would just start the cycle all over again.

"Text back," she whispered.

"Mom?" Drew called from the doorway.

Emma shot upright, slamming her phone face down into the comforter. She spun to face him. "Drew, sweetie," she tried to calm her breath and talk slowly, "what is it?"

He stepped in sheepishly, scanning the room with his eyes. "Is Dad in here?"

"Dad?" A brief moment of terror passed through her mind as she considered Randy being in the same room while she texted James and her not knowing it. *Jesus, thank god he wasn't.* "No, sweetie. I think he's downstairs."

"Okay." He left, and she exhaled relief.

Emma dared another look at her phone. *Maybe he sent a message while I was talking to Drew.* Nothing.

She shook her head and walked to the sealed stack of boxes by the dresser. "I guess I better work on you."

She put her phone on the dresser where she would see the screen light up from notifications, and she opened the first box.

Drew passed Maggie's room and glanced inside. He knew she wasn't there—she had gone to her friend Janet's or something—but he was curious what her new room looked like after she had unpacked her stuff. It turned out she hadn't really unpacked anything, and the space resembled a cardboard city more than a teenager's room.

He descended the stairs and heard noises in the living room, paper rustling and things scraping against the cardboard surfaces of a box. He reached the bottom and turned into the living room.

There he was. Dad had opened a new box, this one labeled *Living Room*, and he took a breath as he opened the flaps—as if he was scared of what might be inside it. Drew stopped where he stood. He couldn't really comprehend that.

Dad surely wasn't a brute or anything—he was a manly guy and a mill worker, after all—but he didn't think he had ever seen the man look genuinely scared. Frightened, maybe, like the time a squirrel got into the ducts of the old house, and while they were trying to get it out, it leaped past Dad's face. He yelled and jumped, and then he was tearing right after that thing, but he didn't seem *scared*.

It was only a brief expression, but it was there. And as the look faded from Dad's face, it left a trace of fear inside Drew. What could be in one of those boxes that could scare him that badly? Should Drew be worried? Could he open the wrong box and find a rabid wolverine or something?

Before he could shed the idea from his mind, Dad must have noticed him because he said, "Drew? You okay, pal?"

Drew saw his dad had stopped unloading what turned out to be the books and knickknacks Mom kept on the end tables and was staring at him.

"Sorry, Dad." He smiled. Then he remembered why he was looking for his father in the first place. He raised the box. "Look what I found."

Drew sensed Dean coming into the room behind him—he must not have found anything on YouTube—and Dad's face went white.

Chapter Nine

RANDY DIDN'T SEE HIS SON holding the model's box. It wasn't August 2025, it was June 1999, and it was Bobby who stood before him with scruffy brown hair and a dopey look in his eyes.

"Come on, Randy," Bobby whined. "You can do that later."

Randy looked at the controller in his hands and the digital Denver Broncos on the television screen. The score was Denver 21, Miami 28, a near mirror of his team's depressing late-season loss seven months ago. He wanted to keep playing and return the honor to the Broncos' franchise. He wanted to teach those Floridians a lesson. But that look on Bobby's face was hard to say no to.

"Yeah. Okay." Randy set the controller down gently beside the TV, praying no one would touch it while he was gone and he could whip up on those Dolphins after this model. He wouldn't get the pleasure, unfortunately—Joan would find the console on and hit the off button just to be a pain in the ass while they were upstairs.

"But," Randy insisted as he turned, "we have to paint it Broncos' colors."

Bobby squinted. Randy knew that would be a tough thing for his brother to agree to. Bobby was usually true to the packaging. If the car on the box was some hideous green or lame, boring gray, Bobby wanted to use the same colors so they would match. Asking him to use a different color was like asking him to disobey Mom and Dad.

"Well?" Randy reached for the game controller. "Should I just keep playing?"

"Fine," Bobby surrendered. "We can use the stupid football colors."

Randy smirked. "You won't say that when you're older. Trust me." He followed Bobby out of the living room and up the stairs. "You'll learn to appreciate football. Why do you think I give you all my old stuff? You'll thank me when you're in sixth grade and all your friends are asking where you got that sweet Broncos' gear."

He hoped Bobby would come around, but he had his doubts. He had to try, though. If a boy didn't like football by sixth grade, the other guys would start to wonder about him. It usually meant he was a geek or some kind of a weirdo. He didn't want that kind of reputation for Bobby, even if he was way too deep in the fantasy-creatures' zone right now. He still had time to grow out of it before it counted.

They went into Bobby's room, past the piles of sports merchandise Randy had handed down and Bobby had accepted for no other reason than it used to be his big brother's stuff. Football or not, he always loved anything Randy gave him.

Bobby had set the model-building stuff up on his table by the window. The paints and glues were on the right. The car parts were on the left, organized by section of the model and ready to be dissected from their plastic frames. The instructions were in the middle, propped up against an older box from an F-14 jet they had built months ago.

Randy walked over to the table, where Bobby had already set up two seats, as well.

"Hold on," Bobby said. He picked up the jar of black paint and took it into the crawlspace. He returned a minute later with the correct Denver colors and set them on the desk.

"You still have those, huh?" Randy remembered using them to paint a lamp he had found at a garage sale last year. It had been perfect for his nightstand, the only problem being it was blue, green, and gray, a combination that would not stand in this house.

"Yeah. Why wouldn't I?" Bobby prided himself on his collection of tools and supplies. He wanted to be ready to build anything at a moment's notice. If he had to go downtown and pick something up at The Gilded Lady, it was guaranteed to slow him down half a day, what with the chatting Mom would do with the Lewis sisters or half the town, if they happened by. It didn't seem like they could ever get in and out of downtown without a dozen people wanting to talk to Mom and ask her opinion on something or tell her some piece of gossip—relationships that would all end in just a few months.

They sat in their places and got started. Randy used his steady grip and blade control to cut out the pieces. Bobby gently sanded the extraction points where the parts had been connected to the frame and placed them methodically on the table, where they could be drawn from to assemble. Every now and then, he held two pieces together, matching their future connection and testing both the fit and his expectations of how it would all go.

They talked about their upcoming summer. They talked about Bobby's weird friend Jeffrey Wingard, who was going to some kind of math camp. They talked about Randy's plan to try out for the JV football team at the end of summer—with the search for Bobby, the toll on Mom and Dad, and the general stress in the house, he would not try out. He would never play football on a real team.

A breeze came in the window on one side of the desk and went out through the other. It crossed Randy's arms, marking a chill that he didn't realize warned of an oncoming darkness.

One piece at a time, the model came together. It was the best job they had ever done on one of Bobby's models. It was the last thing they would ever build together.

As the reality of 2025 returned, Randy blinked and took a seat on the couch. That box in his son's hands was not something he expected to see again, and after last night—Bobby's dead body on the living room floor, Bobby's severed head in that moving box—it was the last thing he thought he would have to remember.

But now it was like that build had happened yesterday. He could still smell the pungent scent of model glue in his brother's room.

He remembered Mom's tone a few months later on that fateful night when she asked him to go down to the woods and call Bobby in for dinner. She wasn't worried or angry, just a bit tired, but she didn't want Bobby to lose track of time like he sometimes did, and they were just about ready to sit down for dinner. They didn't want to make Dad wait.

A tear ran down his cheek.

"Dad?" Drew asked. "Are you okay?"

"Yeah." Randy spoke softly. His insides burned. It was like he had been hollowed out and was collapsing in on himself. He had not thought of that day in so long, maybe not in twenty-six years. He hadn't missed his brother so much since—he didn't know why, but he hadn't. It was like those memories had been buried and just now dug up.

Randy pictured Bobby in the fort he had made in that rock formation, the one he had checked over and over, day after day after Bobby went missing. He pictured a man grabbing him and pulling him away, never to be seen again. He pictured a bear seizing Bobby by the foot and dragging him off to a distant cave. He pictured a mountain lion taking Bobby by the neck and hauling him up into a tree.

The blood would have come down like rain.

And somewhere under those thoughts, he knew what had happened, even if he still couldn't (or wasn't allowed to) remember.

Randy hadn't had those thoughts in so long—had he blocked them out of his mind? Had he forced himself to just think of Bobby as missing, like his kid brother had gone off on a hike and just decided to live happily in some other town like Judith or Custer Falls, and they just never saw him again?

He knew those things weren't true. Wherever Bobby was, he wasn't happy. He likely wasn't anything.

Thinking of his brother as dead filled his stomach with a rock that pushed him back into the couch and drained every ounce of energy. It made him want to close his eyes and sleep. Just sleep for a long, long time.

Randy looked up and saw his boys standing in front of him. He took a deep breath and invited them to sit with him. He explained just how his model Chevelle came to be. He looked over his boys from head to toe as he talked, marveling at how much they reminded him of himself and Bobby while hoping with all his soul that they would never have to go through the pain he had—or what Bobby had.

"So, yeah," he told them, nodding, "that's my car. Bobby's car."

"He really liked models, right?" Drew asked.

"Models, books, adventure. He was a hell of a kid brother. I wish you guys could have met him."

"I wish so too, Dad," Dean said.

Randy took a deep breath and stood. He couldn't keep thinking about this. "Anyway, I need to get back to work. Mom will be a lot happier once all this mess is put away and this place starts feeling like a home instead of a house-shaped storage unit."

"Okay." Drew stood. He leaned in and hugged Randy.

Randy let himself release what tension he could. He let the pain slip away for just a moment to feel this. He draped an arm over Drew's shoulder and held him tight. After a moment, he patted his youngest on the back.

"Why don't you guys go check out the property. You've only seen bits and pieces. I know our visits to see Grandma were always pretty short, but Bobby and me really had a blast out there when we were kids."

"Yeah." Drew smiled.

"I don't know," Dean said. He glanced out at the dock with a distrusting stare.

"You'll be fine," Randy said. "Just stick together. Two are less appetizing to a bear than one."

Drew's eyes widened. "A bear?"

Randy patted his back again. "You'll be fine." He thought of Bobby out there, disappearing, all alone. "Just stay together."

Drew and Dean went outside, but not until after they ate lunch and Drew checked in with Lance. Amazingly, Lance's mom had agreed to let him come for the weekend. Drew wondered if she was on some new medication to put her in such a mood, but he wasn't going to ask and jinx it. Since the fair was in town this week, they made a plan to meet at the fairgrounds at eight, ride a few rides, and then come back to Drew's. But first, Drew was itching to take his first real steps into the woods as their proper owner. Well, son of the landowner.

Dean wasn't himself. He came outside and, just like earlier, hung out as if he didn't want to be alone. Drew tried asking him if everything was okay, but Dean just blew him off. Now, they stood at the precipice of the forest between the rows of massive boulders, and Dean's eyes kept darting between the dock, the house, and the path into the woods. There was definitely something going on, but Drew knew his brother would get pissed if he asked again.

He looked at Dean. "Dad said Bobby had a fort or something in there. Think we can find it?" He imagined ten-foot walls made of tree trunks, their tops sharpened to points, and a huge wooden door with a bar that could be lowered to lock out bad guys and bears.

"After twenty-five years? That thing's probably rotted into sawdust."

The fort grew moldy and covered in moss in Drew's mind. Logs from the wall had fallen in or were decayed into something more resembling a tall picket fence than the medieval wall he had been imagining.

"We can still find it."

"Maybe."

Drew took a step inside the woods and instantly felt cooler. The shadowy underbelly of the tall pine canopy was like another world, and it took a moment for his eyes to adjust. There were hollows under bushes where he imagined pixies or brownies running through the greenery. There were long-dead branches, abandoned by growth, where the larger trees had decided to focus on their higher boughs.

Drew saw elves and magical furry things bounding along them, running and leaping, headed out for magical adventures.

After seeing Bobby's collections in his room, Drew felt like he understood why his uncle would have loved these woods. He felt like he understood who his uncle was more clearly.

Drew was about to take another step when he realized he was alone. Dad had said to stay together, and though he wasn't necessarily scared of the woods, the idea of hanging out in the same place someone had vanished from was a little creepy. He figured that feeling would go away once he was used to it and the place felt more like his, but right now was another story.

"Dean?" Drew glanced back into the sunlight.

Dean was staring at the water. He ran his hands over his pockets, then rubbed his neck. He breathed slowly and scanned the shore back and forth as if he expected something to come crawling out of the water and come after him.

"Dean!" Drew called louder.

Dean spun, meeting Drew's eyes.

"What's going on, man?"

"Nothing." Dean shook his head and walked into the woods. He paused next to Drew. "Which way?"

Drew gazed into the long, green paths ahead. They went forward. They followed the lake's edge. They went inland and curved around boulders and up the hill. He imagined Dad and Bobby walking through here and thought, *Which way would Bobby go?* He had to find the fort, after all, even if all he found was a rotten pile of branches.

There was a feeling of nostalgia going left up the rocky hill that seemed to belong to someone else. It was like the path held memories he was yet to have, and only the warm, tingling afterglow was present right now.

He pointed. "That way. I think the fort's somewhere over there."

"Lead the way, short stuff." Dean gestured toward the path.

Drew felt a note of hesitation in every word his brother spoke. There was something he was hiding, but the world ahead was too vast and exciting to let wait. He just had to hope Dean would tell him what was going on when he was ready.

Drew led the way, and there was a sense that Dad and Bobby were right there with them and a sense that they might be a little early to find what they were really looking for.

Chapter Ten

DEAN WATCHED THE TREES AS he followed his brother. He was being stupid, and he knew it. The forest was not filled with dead things. The zombified corpses of Nancy Hanning and Janet Green were not waiting to jump out. No fog was waiting to creep on him and fill him with evil. It was just a dense stretch of woods like so much of Montana, and he had nothing supernatural to fear.

But he couldn't shake it.

That dream was so real. It wanted him to come into these woods so badly, and here he was, offering himself up with no defense whatsoever. He couldn't have brought his .22 rifle, Dad kept that locked away with his own rifles, but he could have brought his BB gun. He could have said they were going to target shoot at pinecones or something. Why didn't he do that?

He hoped he wouldn't come to regret the decision later.

"This way." Drew climbed up the hill on the left, around a boulder, and between a pair of massive, dead spruces. Their rotted limbs hung over the world thirty feet up, swaying gently in the breeze, and Dean felt he would be lucky if he was able to pass underneath them without getting crushed.

"Yeah, bro." Dean followed, his heart pounding as he climbed and matched his brother's steps. He glanced up and told himself those branches had been hanging like that for years; why would they choose today to fall?

He cursed himself as he watched his brother smile. Drew was having a blast. It was a new world to explore back here, a world they couldn't have dreamed of at the old house, and it was all theirs. This was their backyard.

He made himself smile. He needed to get over that stupid dream and enjoy himself. He had been sidled up to his brother all morning as if something was going to jump out and grab him if he was left alone. He wasn't going to do that anymore. Regardless of the feeling in his gut that this was not a good place, he was going to find something good about it. He was going to ignore the feeling that he was on the edge of danger and ignore the feeling that Death was watching. This was a chance to have some fun and enjoy himself.

"Look at that!" Drew called from thirty feet ahead.

"What do you see?" There were a half-dozen ponderosa saplings between them.

"It's like a cave, but it's not!" The joy in Drew's voice climbed even higher. It was palpable. It was like the first time they went to the water park in Billings, and they slid down the giant tube together because once they got to the top of the stairs, Drew was too scared to go alone. They climbed into the innertube and shot down the tunnel together, and the joy in his brother's voice was like magic. Like this.

Dean rounded the copse of small pines and found his brother ducking into what looked like a tepee made of enormous, flat, black boulders. They had to stand thirty feet in the air, and they rested on each other in a seamless joint as if the three things had been masoned to fit perfectly.

"Wow." It was awe-inspiring, even if the sight made his stomach rise into his chest, like when a roller coaster drops and your stomach doesn't know it until it's crammed into your lungs.

"Come on!" Drew leaned forward to fit through the only discernible hole, and he slipped inside. "Awesome!" his voice reverberated like he really was inside a cave.

Dean approached the structure and got on his knees at the entrance. His heart pounded. A cool draft hit him, smelling of damp earth. He climbed through the opening on all fours with a feeling of otherworldliness clawing at his limbs. "What do you see?"

"Oh, man! It's awesome!" Drew was on the other side of the structure.

Though gloomier than the forest outside, there was a faint ambiance of gray light over the dirt floor and the deep-black walls. The stone sides held scratches, and shallow lines ran in hundreds of different directions. Those were what Drew was inspecting.

"Look at this." Drew pointed.

There was a carving in the far side of the rock. It was actually legible. *BOBBY KLINE WAS HERE*

Another was to the right: *RANDY KLINE WAS HERE*

"Dad was here!" Drew ran his fingers over the etched-in name. "We should write our names too. You think this was the fort Dad was talking about?"

"I don't know." Dean looked at his hands. "I didn't bring any carving tools. Did you?"

"Shut up. You know I didn't."

"Then we aren't writing our names there."

"Still, it would make a good fort. You could make a fire in the middle, easy, and it would be awesome to defend—no one could break through the walls." Drew's fingers felt along the letters of Bobby's name. "Dean?" he stopped cold, the excitement stalled in his tone.

"Yeah?" Dean lay on his back, looking up at the peaked roof. On the inner right, at the very top, there was a small crack where he could see sky, then dark, then sky as the highest of the forest's boughs passed over them in the breeze.

"What do you think happened to Bobby?" Drew followed along the wall, searching the darker crevices along the base. "I mean—do you think he was taken, or ran away, or what?"

"Don't know, man. That was so long ago. If they don't know by now, I don't think they ever will."

"I wonder if he was exploring the woods and just got lost. They're pretty big." He paused and picked something up.

Dean heard the movement but closed his eyes—his energy was draining the longer he lay still. Between the sleepless night and the dark, cool space, he was realizing how tired he was.

"I don't know, man." Dean yawned. "They seem big because you're used to living in a tract home. I bet you'd run into a neighbor if you walked for more than an hour in any one direction."

Dean couldn't help but think of their old house. He remembered the toys he would have to step over to get to his bed when Drew was smaller. He remembered lying in bed and rolling over on some stiff plastic thing, and the sharp pain when his brother had been playing in his bed and left his toys behind. He would scream at the top of his lungs, "Don't play in my bed!" and Mom would rush in to settle them. But he also remembered saying yes to Drew when he was bored. They'd play King of the Monsters and sometimes sneak a few of Maggie's dolls into the game—they could either become the monster or the victim, depending on the day.

Maggie had such a fit when she found out. She would scream to Mom, and Drew and Dean would laugh.

Their last day in that house was only yesterday, but it already felt like another chapter in their lives. Something had ended, and this was their new reality.

Dean wished it hadn't. He liked having his own room, but those dreams... They made him want to go back. He couldn't admit that, not to Dad or Mom, and definitely not to Drew. But he couldn't get those images of Nancy and Janet out of his head. It was like they were still out there, wandering the woods, waiting for the fog to come back. Then they would come back too. And maybe they wouldn't stop at the forest that time. Maybe they would find their way up to the house.

He saw them limping up the path and trying to turn the knob. The stiff metal slipped through their slimy grips, and they banged on the doors. They smashed the windows and crawled up the stairs. They stumbled into his bedroom, where he was sleeping, and they grabbed him and ripped into him with green, bony fingers.

"Look at this!" Drew called from the far side of the room.

Dean shivered and sat up. He felt a cold tickle moving up his legs as if frozen ants had crawled under his pants and were marching up his legs. He pulled his knees to his chest and rubbed his fingers over his legs, dispelling the feeling and hoping to squish any imaginary pests that may be not so imaginary.

"Look." Drew was beside him now. In his hand was another miniature skull. "There's more over there. Come look."

Dean had to shake loose the thoughts of zombie Nancy and Janet, but not before checking that the entrance to the stone tepee was clear.

Drew was back in the far corner, brushing away dirt with little strokes of his fingers like some archaeologist in training. And he was right. Against the wall was a stack of the tiny heads, each a little different than the others. Each had a different tooth or teeth missing. Each had a slightly different shape—some more egg-like, some more rounded. Some of them had gashes in them, cracks in the bone like they had died in battle.

"Look at that." Dean lifted one with a hole in its right side. "It's almost like he was stabbed with a tiny spear or something."

"Whoa." Drew stopped in the middle of what he was doing.

"Imagine that." Dean held the tiny skull toward his brother. "I know these aren't real—I figure Uncle Bobby was making them out of clay or something—but what if you had a little army of these guys with little spears? You think that's the game he was—" Dean caught sight of what was below Drew's fingers. It wasn't just another skull. It was an entire tiny skeleton. "Is that what I think it is?"

"I—I think I dug up a tiny grave." Drew's voice was softer, somewhat solemn.

"No. They're not real." Dean had to get closer to see.

The body was about a foot long. It was wrapped in ragged cloth littered with holes. There was a gash from its eye socket to where its ear must have been, and its jaw was shattered inward. Under the burial cloth, it wore a shirt sewn together from hides of some sort. The legs were still covered, but Dean could clearly tell it must have been the most intricate sculpting project he had ever seen.

But why?

"Why would Bobby make a fake grave out of little skeleton toys?" It was morbid, and Dean was stumped.

"I—I think it's real."

"Real what?"

"Like, they were real creatures."

"You mean you think tiny little people lived in this cave?"

Drew's head sank, and he looked away. "Well... it looks pretty real to me."

"Bobby made these. He probably used clay and sculpted them. We'll ask Dad, and he'll tell you." Dean reached down to pick up the figure. He took it by the shoulder and lifted.

The skeleton fell to pieces as it moved, the bones of the arms first, then the clavicle and ribs. The head toppled back, and the skull rolled free of its broken jaw. Only the shirt dangled from Dean's fingers.

"Uh." He didn't know what else to say. He expected the whole thing to come up like a Halloween decoration, the bones tied together at their ends with little wires. "Did he piece together the skeleton here as he buried it?" He looked at Drew, whose mouth hung open.

"That's real." Drew backed away. "That was a real tiny person, and you just messed up his death bed. If he was a mummy, you'd be cursed right now."

"It's not real. We'll ask Dad about it."

"Yeah. We'll ask Dad."

They both said nothing. They both stared at the tiny graveyard as Dean placed the shirt back into its hole and pushed the bones into a pile as close as he could to where they were.

"I think we should go," Drew said.

Dean wasn't going to argue. He had had enough of this place—

enough of these woods. He was ready to leave, maybe all the way back to the old house, and he hoped really Dad had some answers that would make sense.

Chapter Eleven

THE MCGREGOR COUNTY FAIRGROUND WAS packed to the brim, or as busy as Drew had ever seen it, at least. Kids he hadn't seen in months, high schoolers, and those folks from the county's outskirts all mingled between rides, food trucks, tents filled with hand-crafted oddities, and the big tent where the 4-H show was wrapping up. Lights from every ride lit the dimming sky, and though the start of school was still two weeks away, the summer's end weighed on the incoming night. It whispered that time was almost up, and they better get their fun in before the rigidity and pressure of the new school year descended.

Drew hopped out of the car, followed by Dean. Dad said something, but it faded into the background rumble of amusement screams and teenage chatter. Dean headed toward the 4-H animal pens to meet his friends, and Drew marched to the ticket kiosk for a wristband. Lance should be there at any moment if they synchronized correctly. Dad drove off, and Drew caught something about picking them up later, but he couldn't make it out completely with the call of electronic amusements beckoning him so fiercely.

At the kiosk, five people stood in line for tickets and bracelets ahead of Drew, and by the time he got to the counter with the thirty dollars he had been saving for the past four weeks, Lance had joined him. They each bought a bracelet—the carnies called it that, though it wasn't much more than a thin strip of yellow paper with a dab of glue—and they stepped into the horseshoe-shaped ring of rides, feeling like they owned the night.

The bracelet meant they could ride anything they wanted as many times as they wanted until close, and with no parents there to tell them otherwise, they were free to eat junk and spin and rattle until they puked.

The Gravitron hummed on the far right, and Odin's Beard, the Viking ship-inspired torture device, was on the far left. There was a Tilt-a-Whirl close on the left, a Flying Swings in the middle, a Ferris Wheel, a smaller wheel where the seats flipped you upside down as you turned, and a half-dozen other rides Drew didn't recognize.

His heart pumped, and the smells of popcorn, cotton candy, and funnel cakes begged him to get going. It was an imperative. The twinkling lights shone, and the screams called, and a drive told him it was his mission to fit in every minute of fun that he could. There was a timer ticking down for the end of summer, for the seconds he had tonight, and, in the back of his mind, for something more serious than a boy of twelve should be able to contemplate until much later, a subconscious knowledge that none of this could last forever.

"What do we do first?"

Lance's eyes rested on the Flying Swings, his smile growing. "That one first!" He pointed. "But we have to go to the Fun House sometime tonight."

Drew always felt the Fun House was for the smaller kids. It was even set up in the next field of the fairgrounds, to the right of the good rides, where all the little kid amusements were. But he agreed to go for Lance, and he would hope no one saw them over there.

Lance held out his hand for their private handshake, his index and middle finger together, his pinky and ring finger together, and a gap in the middle. It looked like he was offering a Vulcan sign from *Star Trek* to the uninformed, but it wasn't. It was a dumb sign they invented for their team during a game of Sharks and Minnows too long ago to remember. It had evolved between Lance, Drew, and the other member of their team, Eric, and it had grown to mean so much more as time followed. Since Lance's dad's death. Since Eric's folk's divorce. Since Drew's family seemed to get poorer and poorer and Lance and Eric stepped up to help him where they could.

Drew made the sign, and they slapped palms so loudly the sound traveled over the nearby screams, and they both winced in pain before laughing.

The line for the swings was shorter than a lot of the others, which Drew didn't quite get. It raised you like fifty feet and spun you in circles, making you feel like your organs were going to sink into your legs and squeeze out your toes. He was happy to take advantage of it, though.

Lance counted the people in line. "We should get on in the second group. Not too long to wait." Lance had a gift for math, and logic in general. He was always counting and trying to figure out the way things were going to work out.

"Sweet." Drew sniffed, and the smell of cotton candy gripped his stomach hard. He had made sure to eat before he came, that was a must to make sure he didn't spend every cent he had on food, but at this point, his stomach was demanding it. "Next stop is a snack, okay?"

"Sure. Whatcha thinkin'? I want a caramel apple. They have the best ones here." (And his mother wouldn't allow him to eat them.)

"Cotton candy."

Lance nodded. The ride stopped, and the attendant directed the swings' riders to the exit and let in the next group.

Lance counted again. "Ten people ahead of us. We're definitely getting on the next round."

People strapped into the double-occupancy seats two by two, and the operator walked to his controls, trusting all the patrons to secure themselves correctly. The hydraulics whined as the frame holding all eight dangling chairs lifted them from the ground and started to spin with sixteen pairs of feet rising ever higher.

"Here they go," Lance said.

Screams and laughter drifted down as the seats rose and tilted outward. Legs swung, and Lance bobbed up and down.

Drew could feel the night's electricity in his veins. The sun was gone, and the stars twinkled above the neon lights. He took in a crisp breath and held tight to the railing that surrounded the ride.

After a few dozen rotations, sixteen riders descended and exited the area, and it was Drew's and Lance's turn. They rushed past the attendant, who nodded as he spotted their bracelets. They chose the farthest seat, a green chair, suspended by the slightly rusted steel wires. They climbed into their seats and strapped themselves in with the scratchy leather strip.

Drew's limbs tingled with excitement. Soon, they'd be cradled fifty feet above the crowd. He saw the same glimmer in Lance's eyes.

The motor on the center pole whined, and they were off. Drew's feet rose from the fairgrounds' dirt floor. The wind rushed harder and harder into his face as they were slung around the central pole.

"Oh my god!" Lance screamed.

"Wooo!" Drew called. He hadn't felt this free since he rode the swing a year ago, and he had forgotten just how exhilarating it was.

Their chair swung outward as centrifugal force pulled them farther out from the central pillar. Drew wondered for a moment if his shoes would stay on. He felt the pressure pulling him down in the seat, and he breathed deeply. He wondered if life could possibly get any better than this.

His smile lasted through two dozen rotations and held strong even once they were back on the ground. It was the perfect start to the night.

They unbelted and walked toward the ride's exit, where Drew noticed a hand waving in the air.

"Drew! Lance!" it was Eric Steward, probably the happiest kid Drew had ever met and the third member of Drew and Lance's posse when they roamed the halls of Lone Wolf School.

"He's back," Lance yelled as they neared the ride's barrier. Eric had to go to his dad's house in South Dakota every time there was a break from school. He usually wasn't back from his summer visit until a few days before school started up again.

"Eric!" Drew held his hand up and waved. The night was only getting better. "You're back!"

Eric's hand formed the secret shape, and he slapped it against Lance's and then Drew's. "Yeah, Dad and his new girlfriend had this cruise planned, so I got to come home early."

"I thought you liked going to your dad's?" Lance asked as they gathered between the traffic of fairgoers and the line to ride the swings.

"I do, but his girlfriend is, like, jealous of me or something. She kept trying to go everywhere we went and then kept saying I was being rude to *her*."

"You?" Drew scowled.

"I mean, I'm sarcastic. It's just this thing me and Dad do. She doesn't get it."

"Surely, you can't be serious?" Lance shook his head.

"I told you, stop calling me Shirley!" Eric shouted, grinning widely.

Drew knew how much Lance would give to hang out with his dad if he could, and he marveled at how his friend kept it inside right now. "But you're back!"

"Yeah, I'm back." Eric raised his hands in victory. "What are you guys up to? Have you ridden Odin's Beard yet?"

Drew and Lance glanced at each other. While they said they intended on riding everything, Odin's Beard was the one they were the most wary of. The thing flipped upside down while you were left hanging from a bar. That was nuts.

"Let me guess, no?" Eric smirked. "You guys, let's do it now. Get it over with, and you'll thank me later." Eric was fearless when it came to rides. It helped that his dad took him to Cedar Point in Ohio every other summer and he was a year older and two inches taller than the other two. He had experience.

"I don't know." Lance shook his head.

"I was going to get some cotton candy." Drew pointed to the

concession stand.

"You guys. Don't be wusses. We got this."

The gauntlet had been thrown down. Sure, Drew knew he could probably find some way out of it, but they would know it was a ploy. He might as well bite the bullet.

"Well?" Drew looked at Lance. "We said we'd ride *everything*."

Lance gritted his teeth and shook his head in resignation. They weren't going to put it off until the end this time and then say they ran out of time when they didn't get to it. "Let's go," he surrendered.

The ride was everything they feared and everything they loved. It was maddening and terrifying and thrilling and energizing. They got off and got right back on, and after that, the rest of the night became a blur. The Graviton, the Tilt-a-Whirl, the Scrambler, and the Roulette Wheel all blended into seamless streams of screams and howls of laughter. They were three boys on the edge of the world, flung over and tossed around and brought back on a strand of elastic mayhem. They lived as the lords of their own dominion, and the night was their sphere.

Until they went to the fun house.

The trailer that unfolded into the fun house was laughably small to most visitors over the age of eight, but there was always something creepy about it to Drew. It wasn't the wonky paint on the floor, or hamster-wheel room you had to climb through, or the clowns on the walls. It was the mirrors.

Sure, Drew would walk through just fine; he'd done it a hundred times. But there was something in those mirrors that always struck him as off. A single mirror was okay. Even a double one, though the infinite patterns of crisscrossed realities made him a little unsteady. The Hall of Mirrors, though, that was a totally different story. They lined the floors and walls and turns, and if Drew looked through them for more than a few seconds, he was hit with an unmistakable feeling that he was seeing something he shouldn't. There was a sense that another reality lay behind those twisted layers of glass, and as they compounded before him, he was witnessing the forbidden.

Drew knew this feeling didn't make any sense, so he never mentioned it to anyone. But as he trailed Lance and Eric, them both laughing at the strange turns and wild lapses in their sense of direction, Drew wanted to stop at the edge of the mirrored maze and turn back. He watched his friends walk in effortlessly and just knew he couldn't turn away. He had to keep going.

The lights blinked on and off as he stepped inside. Black lights illuminated him with glowing shoelaces and teeth. He tried to look ahead and follow his friends without focusing on the depths of the mirrors themselves, but there was a bluish shimmer that ran across the walls and drew his focus with it.

He walked in a straight line, or at least he thought he did, while off to the side, he saw trees—trees in the middle of the fun house? —which just didn't make any sense. There was lightning beyond them. But it wasn't raining at the fair.

Drew's stomach felt like it was filled with rocks. He stepped forward, noticing Eric's and Lance's voices had waned, and he realized he was all alone in the hallway. All alone and surrounded by trees.

They were the trees in his woods, the ones surrounding the stone tepee. They were grand and thick with needles, though there was a sensation radiating from them, a darkness deeper than the gloom between lightning strikes, and it tugged at Drew like shadowy fingers. The more he looked, the darker and darker they became, and under their boughs, Drew saw something when the lightning returned: eyes.

They were small, and they gazed up at him. Little eyes on little faces. The lightning crashed closer, and the thunder rattled the mirrors around him, and Drew saw their tiny bodies dressed in hides and carrying little spears and bows and axes. They were some kind of tribe, like little one-foot-tall pixies, things like the remains he had found earlier, and they were all staring at him.

Drew was hot. He felt sweat run down the sides of his face and down his back. The little things moved in the darkness, and when the lightning flashed again, they were closer. Some had raised their spears, aiming them at Drew. Some held their axes as if ready to toss. But stranger than their new aggression, stranger than the fact that Drew was even seeing these things in the middle of Lone Wolf, Montana, was that none of them looked alive.

They were standing, they were focused on him, but their eyes were dull and milky. Their skins were gashed and pale, grayish, and even green in splotches. They had split lips and blackening teeth, and it occurred to Drew as fear rose in his chest and urged him to scream that he was going insane. He was staring into a mirror and seeing things that were not real, and the next thing that would happen would be a trip to a mental institution.

Drew held his hands in front of him. If spears were coming, maybe he could block them from his face, at least. "It's okay, guys," he spoke, but they came closer, flashing in the light, preparing their weapons. He heard some kind of gurgled chant under the downpour of rain on the forest canopy. One hurled his spear, and Drew turned away, swinging his hand to block it—

"Drew?" Eric's hand was on his shoulder, shaking him. "Drew?"

Lance stared at him from a foot away.

"Yeah." That was all Drew could get out. The strobe light flashed, and the pixies were gone. The trees and the storm were gone. *It wasn't real?* He was going insane.

"Are you okay, man?" Eric asked. "You don't get seizures or anything, do you?"

"I—I don't think so." Drew didn't know for sure, but could that be it? Was that better than going insane?

"Come on." Eric led the way out. This time, they didn't leave Drew behind.

They went from the fun house back to the concessions, where they each got slushies. Sugar restored in their systems, they resumed their fun.

The pixies, though, didn't leave Drew's thoughts. Those seemed to stand in the shadows in the corner of his vision wherever he went. They crept inside the underbellies of the rides and watched him no matter how much he wanted to ignore their gazes.

Chapter Twelve

I T WAS IN THE LINE for the Roulette Wheel (for the second time) when it occurred to Drew that with such little time left before school started Eric should join them at his house this weekend. He wasn't sure yet if they'd be going into those woods like he had initially planned—not after seeing those pixie things—but they still needed more time to catch up and more bro time before they got sucked back in to the incoming web that school entailed.

"Eric," Drew pulled his friend's eyes away from a pair of high school girls who were walking by, "why don't you come over tonight? Lance is riding home with me. You can too."

Eric didn't hesitate. "Yeah, man. I gotta call my mom, though." He glanced at Lance. "Can I use your phone?"

"Yeah." Lance unlocked it and handed it to Eric. Being the only one of the three with a phone, he was used to it. Eric called and got the okay, and all three shared a feeling of triumph, knowing the rest of the weekend together was secured. They had been separated the last few weeks and would be again soon when classes and extracurriculars pulled them in different directions, but at that moment, they were the owners of their destiny. They celebrated with a selfie on Lance's phone, with the Roulette Wheel's bright neon sign high in the background.

"Oh, that'll be a cute one!" Maggie shouted from behind them in line. She laughed with her best friend Janet at her side, and Drew could only scowl as he imagined them both as a pair of cackling witches.

"Your sister." Eric tried not to smile. Drew and Lance both knew he had a crush on her.

"And Janet Green." Lance did not hold back his smile. He was like a little lost puppy whenever Janet was around him.

"Forget 'em, guys." Drew turned back toward the ride.

"Yeah, yeah." Lance tried so hard to look cool at that moment, like he wasn't yearning to get closer to Janet, to stare mindlessly at her curves.

"Lance," Eric asked, "you think we'll make the next group?"

Lance counted seats as the giant disc spun, with one side then the other rising and falling.

It looked more like a spinning top in its final wobbling throes before collapse than what Drew imagined a roulette wheel would do, but it was a blast, so he wasn't picky about it.

Lance moved to counting those in line ahead of them.

Drew watched the machinery below the platform. A giant arm with hydraulic pistons held the platter at an angle and shifted as gears spun and twirled the thing around. It was so fast and seemed so intricate as all the parts moved in sync. It made him wonder about the design of it all. Could he build a model of one out of gears and gizmos like the set he had at home that he had made an excavator with when he was younger?

He was trying to place where the parts linked and where the gears from the spinner told the riser what to do when he thought he saw something else moving around under there. It wasn't shaped like a mechanical part. It was more fuzzy and organic. There was some sort of animal under there.

"Nope," Lance said. "Two groups before us."

"Look at that." Drew pointed under the ride. "What is that?"

The shadowy shape shifted, almost floating over the components. The more Drew tried to focus through the gloomy underbelly and the ride twisted and turned, the harder it was to make the thing out.

"What?" Lance leaned over the orange caution tape that marked the edge of the line. "The gears and stuff?"

"No," Drew said, "there's something else in there. Like an animal or something."

Eric put a hand above his eyes, blocking out the bright mobile lights that lit the fairground. "I don't see anything."

"Did you see a gremlin?" Lance smirked. "Is something on the wing?" They had watched the Twilight Zone Movie at the start of summer, and it was obviously still on Lance's mind.

"Shut up." Drew wanted to say yes. After his experience in the fun house, seeing something weird under this ride only made him want to walk away, and quickly.

"The plane's going to crash!" Lance's voice rose and squealed. "We gotta get out of here."

Eric laughed. A handful of people in line stared with curious gazes.

"Shut up, Lance." Drew shook his head and looked at the riders, instead. It was hard. There was a nagging inside him. Something was cracking through the smells of kettle corn and sweet cotton candy in his brain, cracking the cool August night and tugging at his sense of safety. Something was telling him that what he saw under there was malicious and he needed to do something. But what? His friends didn't see what he saw. He couldn't tell the carnies to shut down the ride. Why would they believe a kid? He'd look as stupid and crazy as the guy in that movie.

Hopefully he was wrong. It was probably just his eyes playing tricks on him, right? Leftover hysteria from his delusion at the fun house?

The Roulette Wheel slowed and lowered itself flat. Riders disembarked, and the attendant counted as he allowed new riders on board. Drew, Lance, and Eric stopped moving forward with about thirty people between them and the front of the line. As the platter started spinning and the hydraulics heaved, it looked like Lance would be right again.

This time, there was a whine as the machine started up. It was high-pitched and shallow, but Drew was sure he heard it.

Passengers screamed with exhilaration as the giant disc reached full speed and rose up and down, tilting and undulating.

Drew's eyes went back and forth between the riders and the machinery. *What was that noise?*

There was a loud pop, and for a split second, Drew thought it was a firecracker. Then a stream of liquid exploded from one of the hydraulic pumps. It arched over the gears, spraying down the rest of the mechanisms, and the entire structure groaned loud and low. It was a tone that made Drew's insides sink and turn sour.

Something bad was happening, something worse than he could have imagined.

The ride attendant took a sip of his drink and stared at the rears of a pair of high school girls walking by in short shorts. People in line chatted and smiled and stared at the riders, waiting their turn. No one seemed to notice the spray or the groan, and it made Drew seriously wonder if he had lost it.

He couldn't have been the only one seeing this problem. Was he watching the work of gremlins like some kind of mental patient? It was real. It had to be.

He looked at Lance and Eric. They were talking about the next Marvel movie and whether it would be any good while they stared at Maggie and Janet.

"Guys?" Drew pointed at the ride. "You have to see that."

A low grinding noise rose over the hum of the engine as Lance and Eric turned. Lance frowned, and Eric's mouth slowly dropped.

"Dude!" Lance shouted at the ride operator. He pointed and screamed again, "Kill the ride!"

Some of the crowd turned to Lance. Most ignored him.

Drew grabbed Lance and Eric by the shoulders and pulled them backward in line.

"Stop the ride!" Lance shouted.

"Stop the ride!" Eric repeated.

They were almost to Drew's sister. She scowled at them as they neared, and a series of sounds crashed through the crowd's rumble. Another pop, but this one was as loud as a gunshot, a crunch as gears ran into each other, and a deafening crack as something metal snapped.

The crowd turned with a communal sense of terror. They knew what was coming was deadly, maybe from some prehistoric sense that only raised its head in life-or-death situations. There was a group inhale as their minds caught up to their senses.

The riders of The Roulette Wheel screamed, but it wasn't from joy this time. The wheel jolted, and they knew what was happening was not part of the attraction. The giant, spinning platform screeched as it rolled off its base, thudded onto the ground, and wobbled toward the center of the fair.

There was just enough time for the ride operator to turn toward his controls before the thirty-foot-wide disc's edge rolled over him with a crunch. Half of him lay outside the impact, leaving a leg, an arm, and half a torso that looked almost unremarkable, while the other half was crushed into a liquid-like paste under the topside-turvy steel.

Now, screams were reality. The onlookers caught up and joined the riders. Both on the amusement and in the stunned crowd, the howls of terror were thick and ubiquitous.

The rolling disc demolished three 4-H members who would have been next on the ride as those beside them turned and ran. They only made it a step before their legs were severed by the wheel of rolling death, and they watched the disc move on.

Maggie and Janet stared, dumbstruck, as Drew shouted at his sister, "Run!" She didn't move, and he let go of Lance and shoved her. "Go!"

Maggie turned to him. Her eyes were wide and her mind was yet to comprehend, and he grabbed her hand and pulled.

"Come on!" Lance grabbed Janet's arm, and the five of them

stumbled toward the center of the fair.

Screams were cut short as the massive disc crunched one and then another fairgoer under its massive weight. Then, like a tired toddler, it ran out of momentum and crashed onto its base. Three final souls found themselves victims: an elementary school girl completely crushed, a man in a cowboy hat whose legs were pinned under the steel, and a woman smacked in the head as the ride closed in on the ground, ripping her scalp from her skull.

The beast of metal was finally at rest directly where Drew and his friends had been standing in line.

Eric stopped, leaned forward, and puked between his knees. Janet stepped back, tripping over her feet, and fell on her rear, dragging Lance to the ground beside her. Drew held Maggie's hand, and they stared as two dozen riders screamed from their seats on the Roulette Wheel, begging to be let off.

That was when Drew noticed that Dean was one of those riders.

The two hours after the accident were lost in a haze of scurrying officials and crying fairgoers. *Accident* was what everyone was saying, but Drew knew better. But it wasn't like he could tell anyone without looking crazy or them saying he was in shock and imagining things. He might have been in shock—he had never seen anyone die in real life, let alone over a dozen—but he was sure of what he saw. He only told the police about the result, though, not the cause.

Dad was there as soon as he heard what happened and was let through the police line. Ambulances and fire teams were still working to free victims and corpses when the boys left in Dad's truck. Janet drove Maggie to her house, and Dean caught a ride with his friends once he was set free.

Lance had to plead with his mother not to make him come home and ruin the entire weekend. She worried that he should be rushed to counseling as soon as possible so his fragile little mind wouldn't be ruined by the trauma. He assured her he hadn't seen anyone die—a lie—and that he was nowhere near danger the entire time—another lie, but it worked.

Eric's mom was fine with them keeping to the plan of him spending the weekend with his friends. He heard the sounds of Rusty's Saloon in the background of the call, and he was pretty sure she was happy to not need to sober up and come get him if she didn't have to.

Dad was a little sketchy about bringing the boys over after such a traumatic event, but when the other parents agreed and Drew assured him it was best for them to be with friends right now, he allowed it.

None of them knew what to expect from the rest of the night, but there was a sense of hyperreality around them and a feeling that they had just witnessed something monumental. This night was something that was going to stick with them for the rest of their lives, and it wasn't ready to end just yet. There was energy, there was unease, and there was a sense that something was changing in the world around them, more than just the end of the season. They had to stick together. And they had to know where this weekend was taking them.

Chapter Thirteen

THE FIRST STOP FOR DREW, Lance, and Eric when they reached Drew's house was the kitchen. Yes, they had eaten at the fair, but fair food didn't count. They needed something then, after all the excitement, before they could even think of "settling in," as Dad called it.

Dad sat in the living room, where he had hooked up the TV while they were at the fair, and pretended to watch one of his reality shows about cops or rangers in the woods instead of eavesdropping.

"That was the grossest thing I've ever seen," Eric said.

Drew grabbed a bag of fries from the freezer and walked it to the air fryer on the counter. "Yeah." He pulled out the basket and loaded it with heaping handfuls of potato slices. "Did you guys recognize any of them? I thought that was Suzi Russell's dad that got squished at the end." Suzi was a grade higher than them and, frankly, always acted like the queen of Lone Wolf School.

"It was," Lance said. "That was her little sister too."

"Oh, man." Eric shook his head.

Drew slid the fryer basket into the machine and started it. "That sucks."

"Zoe Baker was on the ride," Lance said, a smile creeping in on the corner of his mouth. "I'd love to be counseling her right now." Zoe was the older sister of Tina Baker, who was in their class. But Zoe was definitely more *developed*.

"I bet you would." Drew shook his head.

"You'd counsel her if you could," Lance said.

Drew glanced into the living room. Dad was facing the TV. "Yeah. I guess I would," Drew admitted.

"Recognize anyone else?" Eric asked.

The fact was they knew half the crowd at the fair, but when they backed away and the machine went haywire, it was like the world had lost any similarity to real life. Those faces in line might as well have all been the same. The riders were more like a sea of generic faces than individuals. Drew hadn't even realized that his brother was on the thing, and remembering it now only made him fear what could have happened if Dean had been a few places back in line and not gotten a seat. Dean could have been there, squished, like those other unlucky souls—they all could have been if he hadn't made them move.

That thought lingered. If he hadn't made them get out of the way, Dad could have come to the fairgrounds and found all three of his kids and their friends dead. How could they have been so lucky?

But was he?

Since it all happened, he hadn't seen another pixie or gremlin or whatever it was in the shadows like he saw under that ride. So maybe he did imagine it all. But if he didn't imagine it, did that mean he could be responsible? Not that he made it happen, but if those things were there because of him? He thought of the bodies he and Dean had dug up and immediately remembered the myths of the old Egyptian tombs. It was said that anyone who invaded those tombs would be cursed. What if being followed by shadowy things was his curse? What if they continued to do it?

He didn't have much time to think about that because the air fryer dinged and the front door swung open. Drew emptied the basket of fries onto one of Mom's serving dishes, and Lance sprinkled way too much salt over them.

Dean came inside and closed the door. "Hey, Dad." He tried to hide his glance at the clock. It was 11:05, five minutes after he was supposed to be home.

Dad raised his eyes from the TV, also trying to hide his glance at the clock. "How you doin'?" He spoke softly.

"Cool." Dean shed his hoodie and walked toward the kitchen. Drew could see the look on his face: *get away from Dad before you get punished.*

"Dean." Dad raised his hand. "Come here."

Dean winced and walked back toward their father.

"Really? How are you doing?"

He shook his head. "I'm fine, Dad."

"Okay. I just know that it's been a crazy night. I'm here if you want to talk about it." He reached for Dean's hand and pulled him down into a hug.

"Thanks, Dad." Dean stood upright. "I'm just hungry. That's about it."

Dad chuckled. "Go on." Dean joined Drew and his friends in the kitchen, and Dad turned off the TV. He stood in the kitchen doorway and announced to everyone, "I'm going to bed, fellas. Try not to leave too much of a mess in here when you're done."

"Yessir," Lance replied.

"Sure, Mr. Kline," Eric said.

"Night, Dad," Drew said.

Dean dug through the freezer, looking for his snack.

As soon as Dad was gone, Lance blurted out, "What was it like, Dean?"

Dean pulled a frozen pizza from the freezer and set it on the counter. "What was what like?" He started the oven preheating.

"Dude. Riding on that thing when it went off the rails."

Dean looked at him, then to Drew. "These are your friends?"

"What?" Drew shrugged and shoved a fry into his mouth. He

winced at the salt.

"They want to know what it was like." He turned to Lance. "You mean, what was it like to ride a thing that was crushing people?"

Lance stared at the ground. "No. Maybe. I guess that's kinda morbid, huh?"

"I bet it was scary," Eric said.

Drew stared at Eric, who resembled a different person. The solemn expression that hung from his friend's face was strange—he wondered then if he had ever seen Eric not smiling.

"Yeah," was all Dean said. He unboxed his pizza and rearranged the pepperonis for cooking.

"You still think it was gremlins?" Lance asked Drew.

Before Drew could answer, Dean asked, "Gremlins?"

"He saw something under the ride before it went nutso." Lance bobbed his head back and forth to illustrate. "Eric and me didn't see anything, though."

Dean looked at his brother. "What are they talking about?"

"I don't know. It was dark under there. I just thought I saw something moving under there before your group got on."

"What did you see?"

"It was too dark to tell. But after seeing those little pixie people in the fun house..."

"What are you talking about?"

"I saw them, Dean. The things from the fort; but they were alive. I saw them at the fair, and then there was something under the ride— I thought."

"Pixie people? Those things are fake."

Lance stepped between the two. "What do you mean, pixie people?"

"My brother's delusional." Dean hoisted himself up on the counter and gestured at Drew. "Tell them."

Drew started with the skull in his room and explained their trip into the woods and the stone tepee they discovered there. They ate fries as he told them about the pile of skulls and the body they uncovered, and, with reluctance, shared what he saw in and after the fun house. The more he said, the more he agreed it sounded delusional. Yet the ride had broken. Something had done that, whether it was little pixie things or something else hiding in that darkness.

Drew was ready for his friends to call their parents to come and pick them up when Lance said, "It's in your room?"

"What?" Drew had somehow lost him.

"The tiny skull you found? It's in your room?"

"Yeah."

"Let's go see it."

It was a race up the stairs to Drew's room, leaving Dean alone in the kitchen. Drew rounded the bed to the desk, Lance crashed over it, bouncing to the other side, and Eric quietly shut the door.

"Is that it?" Lance pointed at the obvious skull on the desk.

Drew picked it up and looked into its empty eye sockets. He saw the creatures in the fun house inside his mind and tried to imagine what this one would have looked like in hides, with skin on its face like the others.

"Let me see." Lance moved closer.

Drew took a last look and handed the skull to his friend as Eric neared.

"Whoa." Lance slowly rotated the head in his hands as he adjusted himself on the bed.

"Look at that." Eric sat beside him.

Drew watched and turned the desk chair to face his friends.

"Dude, this is real." Lance's voice was soft.

"I think it is," Drew said.

"Let me see." Eric held out his hand.

"Just a second." Lance ran his fingers over the bones, the joints, and the eye sockets. "Dean thinks this was made out of clay?"

"Yeah, or carved or something. But there's no way. Not after seeing that pile of them out there. No way someone sculpted all of those."

"Let me see," Eric demanded.

As the thing left Lance's hand for Eric's, Drew saw the words forming in Lance's brain. "Let's go out there."

Drew rolled his eyes and gestured at the black window. "It's like midnight."

"So? It's your property, right? We're literally just stepping into the backyard."

"Pretty big backyard," Drew scoffed.

"Still—come on?"

"We gotta see this," Eric agreed.

"Yeah," Drew conceded, but the night was probably not the best time. Those things... at the fair, they liked the shadows. "I'm just saying that maybe we should wait for morning."

"You can't do that," Lance said. His voice was low. "You know that. You can't just show us something like this and then say, 'No, you have to wait eight hours to go outside.'"

"Seriously." Eric nodded.

Drew was stuck. They were right. They had to sneak out of the house.

Chapter Fourteen

A LITTLE AFTER MIDNIGHT, DREW leaned out of his room, checking the other second-floor doors. Mom and Dad's door was shut. Maggie's was shut, but she was supposed to be sleeping over at Janet's house tonight. Down the long hallway, Dean's door was wide open.

Drew watched for a minute, trying to decide if Dean was awake or not and how to proceed. He was lying on his bed—Drew could see his feet—and after a few seconds, the feet moved. Dean got up, wearing his headphones, walked across the room, and did something at his dresser. Then he returned to his bed.

This could be tricky. They needed to be extra quiet if they were going to do this without him noticing.

Drew turned to Lance and Eric and placed his finger over his lips. They nodded in agreement, and Drew stepped out of his room.

One by one, they crossed the hall, rounded the wooden railing, and tiptoed down the steps. They turned in the entryway, crept through the living room, and passed into the kitchen. Drew took two flashlights from the slowly building junk drawer, then they headed to the small mudroom at the back door.

Drew paused with his fingers on the knob and looked at his friends. There was a cold feeling trickling down his back. A battle between his urges raged: wanting to know more about the tepee, his desire to please his friends, and wanting to stay away from whatever caused the dark visions at the fun house and The Roulette Wheel. Was this really a good idea? Or was he just letting his imagination get away from him? He wished he knew. He wished he could say with a hundred percent certainty that the visions he had were just stress-induced bullshit or that they were real and he should be packing up to move again instead of going closer to a possible burial ground.

But that was it, wasn't it? If he wanted real proof one way or the other, he had to go. If he wanted to make sure he had the facts before telling Mom and Dad what he saw and that maybe they should be retreating back to the old house, he needed evidence.

Drew turned the knob, and the door opened with a soft whine and an influx of chirping from the multitudes of crickets. He stepped back, holding the door open as Lance and Eric stepped through. He took one last look into the kitchen and was about to go through the door when he saw a pair of eyes in the hallway, then the kitchen.

"What are you doing?" Dean slid his headphones from his ears and set them on the counter.

Drew searched the kitchen with his eyes. There were no answers to the question other than the obvious. "We're going out to the fort."

"At midnight?" His eyes bulged. "Mom's going to freak if she finds out."

"Why's she going to find out?"

Dean sighed and glanced back at the living room and up at the ceiling before shaking his head.

"It's in our woods," Drew argued without being prompted. "It's just like going in the backyard." He was happy to use Lance's logic.

"You think Mom's going to see it that way?"

Drew could feel his friends waiting outside. He felt the pull of the excursion in his bones.

"It won't matter if we're quiet. We won't be gone long, anyway." Drew could see his brother's hands tighten. He got that feeling again that Dean was trying hard not to be alone for some reason. "Do—do you want to come with us?"

Dean scowled and shrugged as if he were offended by the implication. Then he opened the junk drawer and grabbed a flashlight for himself.

"Yeah. Hold on." He came to the door wearing his hoodie and his shoes. "I'll tag along. Never know when you guys are going to need me."

Along the path, over the crest of the hill, and down to the lake, they walked with light steps and sealed lips. At the lake, the gentle lap of water against the shore and the creak of the dock were like screams compared to their quiet footfalls.

Drew watched the darkness, his eyes intent on searching every shadow for a tiny stalker. Dean eyed the water as if something might crawl from the lake, ready to have him on the menu. Lance and Eric giggled with gleaming eyes, the rush of tingling mischief needing some escape from their adolescent bodies.

It wasn't until they reached the edge of the woods that Drew switched on both his flashlights and handed one to Eric. Lance ignited the one on his phone, and Dean clicked on his own.

The forest was different at night. The greens were almost black. The overhead trees were an endless barrier of gloom. The crunch of needles underfoot and the intense smell of pine and sage were at the same time intrusive and soothing. And while Drew was growing more and more sure that there were things in the shadows at the fair, he was seeing none of them here. Or were they better at hiding in these (their) woods?

"This is all yours now?" Eric asked. He walked in the middle of the pack with Lance as Drew took the lead and Dean the rear.

"Yeah," Dean answered. "It was our grandmother's until now."

"Oh." Eric opened his mouth and closed it, realizing the inheritance was the outcome of her death.

Lance grinned as he shined his light. "These woods are creepy. And there's a whole little burial ground in there? Sounds like we should have a séance or something."

"A what?" Drew glanced back. "You mean try to talk to the dead?"

"Of course! You found skulls, right? We should try to talk to them—ask why they died, you know?"

"We are *not* doing a séance," Dean insisted.

"Well, yeah." Lance shrugged. "We don't have incense or candles or a spirit board. We'd need all that stuff. We could bring it next time, I guess."

"Count me out." Eric chuckled. "I want no part of talking to dead people."

"Really?" Lance seemed amazed by this. "We have, like, the perfect vehicle here. We have the skulls, proof of another race. We have death. We have these dark, creepy-ass woods. If we did a séance and got some ghostly voices on camera, we could be famous. Post it on TikTok and get, like, a million views. Make some money, get some girls..."

"Girls?" Eric seemed baffled.

"Yeah, from the fame and fortune. Girls love that."

"No séance," Eric repeated. "I don't care how famous we could get. I don't want to be around dead things."

"We're going to look at skulls. A tiny burial ground—that's dead things."

"Yeah, well..." Eric scanned the trees. He stared deep into the night beyond the shadows of the woods. "Maybe this is a bad idea too."

Lance slapped his hand on his side. "What? We sneak out, risk getting the double Ds here in trouble, and you want to go back before we even see the thing?"

Everyone stopped.

"You want to go back?" Drew asked. He understood what Eric was saying. Besides, the thing would be there in the daylight if they wanted to wait for morning. But he didn't want to go back, regardless of his trepidations. He wanted to find out the truth.

Eric looked back and forth at his friends. "I—I guess not. But no séances."

"No séances," Drew agreed. "Not until Halloween, right?" He chuckled, knowing there was no way it would even happen then.

"Right," Lance agreed.

"Shut up," Eric whispered.

"This way." Drew pointed left, where the ground sloped up. He felt the air grow colder as he led the way up the hill. Strangely, the cold was under his skin. It wasn't like winter cold where it hit the skin first, then muscle. This was like someone had injected ice water into his arms and legs, coating his bones and seeping into his muscles. It made him want to run home and bury himself in covers to warm up. But he couldn't do that.

He climbed between boulders and through trees. He stopped, the landscape feeling foreign all of a sudden as the flashlight's glow and shadows altered his view. He knew the fort was ahead and a little to the right, but looking in that direction, it seemed remarkably dark. It seemed unfathomably dark beyond the next set of trees, even with his light extended at the end of his outstretched arm. But he couldn't stop.

He moved toward the darkness, toward the mounting cold and creeping feeling that drifted up his calves toward his back. He passed the next clump of trees and noticed the quiet around him. No more crickets. He couldn't hear the lake's repeated swell and pull of gentle waves. Even his friends had grown silent.

Then, there it was, in his flashlight's failing light. He paused, and the others caught up and stood beside him.

"Is that it?" Lance's flashlight didn't help at all.

Eric bit his lip.

"That's it." Drew stepped forward. He noticed it wasn't the ground that was dodging the light—dead pine needles and dirt were clearly under his path—but the black rock structure seemed to repel the flashlight's cone. The stone was as dark as pitch, even as he stood beside the thing and crouched to crawl through the entrance.

"This is crazy," Eric said. He studied the walls and the way the stones met above. "I mean, how did this even form?"

"Magic." Lance spoke with an intentional tremor in his voice. "Or aliens. Like Stonehenge, right? Maybe it's a giant prehistoric sundial?"

"Shut up."

"What? You don't watch *Ancient Aliens*?"

"Just go." Eric waved Lance toward the passage as Drew moved inside.

"Alright, alright." Lance lowered himself to his knees and crawled. After Lance came Eric, and after Eric, Dean came through with a bundle of sticks in his grip.

"What's that?" Drew asked.

"You'll thank me." Dean passed the others and sat in the middle, forming something with the sticks. There was a flash as his lighter came to life, and the inside of the fort became illuminated in firelight.

As yellow light flickered, it highlighted patterns on the walls and ground. Not the rock itself, which still seemed to hold no light, but the layer of dust over it exposed the grooves and carvings, textures Drew had failed to see earlier in the day.

Swoops and swirls ran across the higher surface, reminding Drew of the giant rock formations he had heard about in South America, shapes so big you could only make them out by plane. These seemed to make animals and creatures, but not of a kind he recognized. One resembled a bear, but long strands, almost like dreadlocks, hung from its back. One looked like a bird, only its wings were backward and its head was upside down. Waves made things that seemed to be mountains, and more than one sun shone down from way above the rest of the drawings.

"You didn't say there were cave drawings!" The confined echo of Lance's voice was so loud the others winced. He shrugged and said, "Sorry. But that's so cool." He raised his phone and snapped pictures as he circled the room. He stopped when Eric grabbed him.

Eric pointed down. "Dude, you almost crushed it." A small skull lay under Lance's raised foot.

They both crouched down on hands and knees to examine it. Lance picked up the remains, and as Eric was opening his mouth to complain, he saw the pile.

"This is it?" Eric sat by the mound of small heads.

"Yup." Drew joined them, but not without scanning the darker crevices of the room for tiny beings. He squatted beside Eric as Lance's phone sang a jingle of beeps.

All three jumped, and Dean snickered by the fire.

"What's that?" Eric asked.

Lance held up his phone, showing an alarm. "A reminder. Mom said since school starts in a week, I need to start going to sleep earlier."

"One o'clock is earlier?"

"Eh…" Lance turned back to the remains, setting down the skull. He flicked at the dirt, uncovering what looked like an entire little person. Arms, chest, waist, all of it.

Drew watched the dirt get swiped away, and the bone body underneath forced him to remember the vision from the fun house: the tiny corpses, the tribe of them in tiny clothes with tiny weapons, and the ripped skin and oozing faces. They looked exactly like this thing only less decayed. Was this where they buried their dead once they could no longer function in the tribe? Or was the vision simply spurred on by seeing this? He had to find the truth. He didn't know what would happen if he was actually crazy. Would they lock him in a little padded room like he had seen on TV?

"Can you believe this?" Lance raised a tiny ax. It was exactly like the axes in Drew's vision: a small blade and a little stick tied together with sinew.

Drew felt a wave of heat come over his face. The stone walls seemed to swell and contract, and his breaths were heavy as they moved in and out of his chest. "Guys?"

They turned to him, and the fire flickered. There was a rumble underfoot, and Lance braced himself against the wall.

"Earthquake?" Eric asked.

They all looked down as, seemingly out of nowhere, a mist covered the floor. The fire disappeared, and Dean screamed. It sounded like he was far away, at the end of some tunnel.

"Guys?" Drew repeated.

There was no time for an answer before the ground vanished from below their feet and all of them were screaming. Falling and screaming.

Part Three

The Missing

Chapter Fifteen

ONNA OPENED HER EYES TO something that had to have been a dream. It was a cross between a fantastic world and a nightmare.

She was in a cavern of dark stone walls lit by hanging moss that glowed with a bright-green aura. There was a pool in the center, light-blue water that shimmered with an indigo iridescence. There were thousands of lights on the ceiling, pinpricks of white that twinkled like stars, and in the distance were offshoots from the cavern she was in, each lit with different colors of glowing moss or fungi.

Where she sat, however, was a world less wonderful.

Below and around Donna were hundreds of bones. She started counting the skulls and stopped when her eyes ran across the monster that had kidnapped her. He lay on his stomach a dozen feet away, breathing slowly. Between them was the monster's knife.

Donna needed that. Her hands were still bound. She imagined

she could look for a jagged bone and sneak off with it—it would likely do the job—but she didn't want to touch a single bone she didn't have to. Besides, she was naked from the waist down. If there was a better time to have a weapon, she didn't know when it would be.

She crept toward the knife on taped hands and bare knees. The slice on her sole burned. The bones below her knocked against one another, sliding around as she moved, and she prayed it wasn't loud enough to wake him. She just had to go a little farther and—

Donna settled on her knees and picked up the blade. She held the handle tight in her grip and backed away, her eyes on the man who had caused all of this. He was facing away, and his mouth and chin were coated in blood. His leg was bent backward at the knee, and the hand Donna could see was a mangled mess of fingers going in every direction. His chest moved silently, and Donna wanted so badly to climb over there and slice his throat. But she couldn't make herself do it.

She had to get away. She had to unbind herself. That was first. Maybe she would come back and get her revenge, but first things first.

She told herself she was being pragmatic, but she knew it was just as much fear driving her decision as it was logic. Just being so close to him made her tremble, even as she backed away. The man had kidnapped her. He was going to imprison her and rape her... probably kill her. He was likely the most evil person she had ever met. And she was still far too close. The idea of his eyes opening made her heart ache.

He groaned, and she froze. She envisioned the glee on his face when they were back in that little shed. She saw the sinister smile on his lips as he slid off her panties, and she held her breath.

He shifted slightly but didn't awaken. She let herself breathe and backed out of the field of bones. She stood and backed away farther as she cut the tape from her hands and ripped the strip from her mouth.

That was when she saw where they had come from.

Above the bone pile was a dark hole in the ceiling. Pieces of clothes and the limbs of bodies hung suspended from jagged stone extruding from the tunnel. She remembered falling into the pit. She remembered elbowing and kicking as they tumbled through darkness and his hands probed her. She remembered landing on top of him with a thud. Now she was here.

Standing, the room felt different. The ceiling was shorter, so short she could touch it with her fingertips. She ran her digits over the dots of light, and they came back slimy. Her fingers glowed with smudges of white illumination.

"What was that?" escaped her lips in a whisper, and ripples spread in the pool of water. Its surface vibrated as if some enormous monster had stomped nearby, and Donna had to scan the room to verify she was still alone. Something told her she wasn't.

It started as a low hum. It rose from the center of the room as if the pool itself was making the noise.

Donna shook her head and moved. She followed the wall around the room to the far side, where two tunnels led away from the cavern. She watched the bones below her captor rattle. He shook his head and lifted it, and Donna shrank into a shadowed spot between the hanging plant life.

She felt the cold, damp air over her bare skin, and she shivered. She saw the man's eyes as he searched the space. They were piercing. They were angry. He howled as he lifted his mangled hand and examined it. He wiped the blood from his nose and mouth, and Donna could feel the rage inside him from across the room. She thought about turning to run but couldn't move just yet. His angry eyes were searching the cavern, his gaze nearing.

The floor vibrated under her feet, and the pool of water danced in the tiny peaks of waves.

It was like nothing she had ever seen, but instead of piquing her curiosity, it pushed her harder against the wall. The man, the noise, the water, they were all things she should have no part in. They were all from a place she should not be. The combined atmosphere made her stomach draw in on itself. It made her heart beat harder inside a chest that felt hollow and cold.

Water shot from the pool, splashing across the open floor. It nearly touched Donna's bare feet, and something inside told her not to let it.

She pulled her legs tighter against the wall, and across the cavern floor, Donna watched the liquid drain into tiny holes she had not previously noticed. As it flowed down, the holes widened. It was like the floor was a sponge, soaking in the wetness, and those tiny holes grew into gaps nearly a foot wide. The sounds of scratching things came out of those holes.

Shadows danced over the openings. In the gloom within, darker things moved. They climbed toward the cavern. They clawed at their walls and shook themselves awake as they crested the tops of their crevices into the open air.

Donna couldn't help but gasp, a sound that reverberated across the room, even as far as her attacker. She slapped a hand over her mouth, but it was too late. His gaze was on her, and she saw his anger in the shiny reflections of his eyes.

He pivoted toward her over the bones. Pain and fury rippled across his face. He let loose a howling grunt, shifted his broken leg, and reexamined his twisted hand. He looked up as things emerged from the dozens of cavities across the floor.

First, there was fur, long and matted, with tufts pointed in all directions. Small arms clasped the edges of each hole. They were misshapen and floppy, with tiny clawed hands on the ends. Then rose heads that Donna, because of the darkness or their strangeness, could not identify. Snouts were long like rodents, but their fangs were twice what she would have expected, and though small, their faces bore an eerie resemblance to humans. Their tongues hung from between their jaws and licked at the air like snakes. But the oddest part came when their slug-shaped bodies emerged completely from their holes. They had no legs and slithered across the floor toward the pile of bones and the man responsible for Donna's abduction.

This isn't real. It can't be real.

Donna felt herself weaken. Her muscles were losing strength by the second from watching this, and her limbs were turning into jelly. The look of those squirming things, the realization that they knew when something hit that pile it meant dinner time—she was in the den of creatures she could have only imagined in her nightmares, and she needed to go.

They were headed to the pile, and he was backing into it, no longer focused on Donna. But what if she moved and got their attention? What if she made a sound and the entire room full of monsters came after her?

The options screamed from opposite sides of her brain: risk going now, or wait and hope they didn't notice her. Both ideas made her shrink. Her entire lower body felt numb, and she wasn't even sure she could move if she wanted to.

"Fuck off!" he screamed at them. They didn't turn away; they only moved closer. He passed the top of the bone pile and dragged his broken leg down the other side.

Donna couldn't see back there, but she guessed there was a ten-foot gap between the pile and the wall.

The last of the creatures was at least ten feet from her, heading away. She looked into the lighted tunnels and decided on the orange one. She stepped forward on tingling toes. The stone floor was cold on one foot and shot pain up the other as the slice in her sole screamed. She stepped over the holes the creatures had climbed up through, limping on one tiptoe and one flat foot. She reached the cave's mouth and took a final look back.

"Fuck!" the bastard screamed.

She couldn't see him. She only saw a mound covered in fur as those creatures slinked over the top of the bone pile.

She didn't wait to see what happened.

Glowing orange mushrooms hung from the walls and ceilings in clumps of ten to twenty. They lit the cave in an unnatural light as it widened and then thinned, making Donna feel like she was in some sort of enormous colon. Rocks littered the floor, making her constantly step over and around, trying her hardest to keep moving but also keep her feet safe. With two shoeless feet, one with a gash in its center, she didn't want to make it worse. She definitely didn't want to cripple herself further—she might run into more of those weird creatures.

She ducked under a low-hanging boulder, and the ground became wet. A small stream was running toward her, and the cool water felt good on her skin. It also made her question if the water was safe. Were there parasites in this stream? Was it like the strange pool in that cavern? What had made it splash and awaken those creatures?

She saw their furry, squirming bodies in her mind. She remembered the musky, damp scent as they crawled past her, the weird, snake-like appendages on their tops and the long fang-filled snouts. What were those things? She didn't see how they could exist and her have never heard about them.

The tunnel brightened as she moved, though mushrooms no longer grew. The light shifted from the orange of the fungi into a light-blue color. As she looked toward the next curve in her path, she saw a dream come true. It was so bright up there it could have only meant one thing: daylight.

She limped faster. The scents of greenery swelled. It wasn't like hiking back at home with the familiar smells of evergreen but more like the southeast, where she had hiked at summer camp as a preteen. There was a sweet, sappy smell, a hint of honeysuckle, and the embrace of a kudzu-like floral scent. It made her feel like warmth was coming. It gave her hope, which had been missing since that maniac had taken her. She imagined the strong southern heat she had felt that summer, and it didn't matter that it didn't make any sense for her to suddenly be in the South.

Donna didn't want to question how she got from a dreary Montana night to a warm southern day. She didn't want to know how falling down a pit and emerging from a cave could offer what she hoped was ahead. She just knew she was almost out of this cave and on her way to freedom.

Around the corner, Donna found a view that made her mouth drop open. She was not in the South or in Montana. She thought maybe she was in a dream or that she hadn't woken up from the fall, but the pain in her foot said otherwise.

Cool air rushed over her body, sending her into shivers. The scents were from the trees beyond the meadow ahead and those climbing up the mountains around it. The light-blue light was from the faint blue sun in the sky above. The stream at her feet was a branch of one passing through the meadow. All of this was wondrous and would normally have brought her awe. What made her teeth chatter and her stomach clench into knots were the dozens of twenty-foot-tall human skulls embedded into the sides of the mountains and overgrown with vegetation in every direction.

Chapter Sixteen

RANDY'S MOM CALLED FROM THE kitchen using her loud, insistent voice. Maybe he had been up there an hour listening to the radio, or maybe it had been five minutes; he wasn't sure just then. His attention had been on his copy of last year's 1998-1999 yearbook, Mandy Sloane's picture in particular. He wasn't sure why he had never noticed her before, but somehow, when she gave her book report on Friday, there was something about the twinkle in her nervous eyes that caught his attention. It was in the way she described the death of Cujo that made his heart jump inside his chest—and it had nothing to do with the dog.

"Randy!" Mom's voice was more shrill. If he didn't answer quickly, he would expect his door to fly open and some real yelling to begin.

"Yeah!" he screamed over Smash Mouth's "All Star" blaring on his boombox from the staticky top-forty station in Butte for the tenth time that day.

Though Mandy's photo was a year old, he still liked it. He wondered if she would give him a copy if he asked—he never would.

"Come here, Randy!"

He sighed and rolled his eyes. "Coming!" He closed the book and slid it under his pillow, a safe enough place until he came back.

The kitchen was thick with the savory scent of Mom's crockpot roast beef and potatoes. The oven exhaled the aroma of rolls, and a small pot of corn simmered on the stove—Dad always insisted on corn with his roast beef.

Randy leaned on the wall beside the phone and waited for Mom to finish dropping butter into the pot of corn and stir it.

She glanced at him, then peeked into the oven at the rolls. "Go out and get your brother. It'll be dinner time in a few minutes."

Randy checked the window. He saw the dock and the soft orange waves of sunset lapping against the shallow shore. It was a drought this year, and he hoped the snow this winter would fix it. Fishing in the lake this year was nowhere near as good as it was last year.

He looked at his mother sideways. "He's got a watch. He knows when dinner is."

"You know your brother gets caught up and distracted in his games. Do him a favor and get him up here. Dad's already grumpy today, and I don't want you boys yelled at for not being ready to eat."

He sighed and turned toward the mudroom door.

"Wait." Her arms were out toward him. He leaned in and hugged her. He could never resist smiling when she hugged him; it was like magic, and the fact that he had become an inch taller than her added to his grin. She let go and patted his back. "Now, go on."

She turned to check the crockpot, and he headed out the door.

There was a scream from someone having fun somewhere down the lake. There was a warm breeze, strange for this late in September, but a heat wave was passing through. Randy had heard Mom saying they were having an Indian summer, but he didn't get what she was talking about. The whole thing made him wonder if it was going to be a warm winter too. He hoped it wouldn't be too warm; he was really looking forward to sledding this year.

At the bottom of the path, Randy called for Bobby. It was an act of laziness, but he had to try. There was no way Bobby was going to hear him unless he was already on his way back up the path, but if he did, it would save Randy a few steps.

As he expected, there was no answer, so he headed between the line of boulders and into the woods with *Hey now, you're an all-star* unwillingly repeating in his head.

The shadows stretched over the forest, hiding almost everything but the path ahead. The red, dusky light of sunset was fading, and the long, dark arms of night were grabbing hold. Randy wouldn't admit it, but this time of day was always the creepiest to him. It wasn't the middle of the night like one would expect—there was darkness in the woods then, of course, but this was the edge. This was where the forest tipped from visible to hidden. It was when he knew things were waking up, things that were sleeping in the daytime, things that hunted in the darkness.

He approached the turn to Bobby's fort and wished he had brought a flashlight. He didn't need it just yet, he was sure he could get to the stupid stone structure and back home without trouble, but it sure would have made him feel a ton better.

"Bobby!" Randy waited at the edge of the hill. There was no response, and despite being sure that Bobby wouldn't hear him if he was inside his fort, the fact that he heard nothing back was both chilling and alarming. His heart was a motor inside his chest as panic rose. It was dumb. Bobby had been out there at night; he even convinced Mom to let him camp out in the stupid cave thing one night, and he was fine.

So why was Randy's blood rushing hot in his veins?

Why did he feel like centipedes were crawling across his neck?

Randy took a deep breath and headed up the hill. He passed the first series of boulders, the ones Bobby had named Gondor and Mordor, and heard pine needles rustle on his left.

Again, that was dumb to worry about. There were probably thousands of ground squirrels in these woods. But that specific sound didn't make him think *ground squirrels*. It flashed a memory into his brain of those little skulls Bobby said he found inside his fort. It made him think of little people hunting in his woods and sneaking up on him in the dark.

It was dumb.

"Bobby!" He noticed a tremble in his voice and immediately called again, lowering his tone. "Bobby!" Believing he had successfully called in a more manly way, he kept walking. That should have frightened away anything nearby, he was sure.

He turned his thoughts to Mandy Sloane. That would take his mind off the foolishness of getting scared in his own woods. Maybe Mandy would want to see his woods? Maybe she'd want to come hang out by the lake with him? What would she look like in a bikini?

He liked that thought, but it vanished as he passed under the boughs of the giant spruces that announced (or warned, he wasn't sure which) the presence of the stone tepee. It stood tall like it must have for eons, with only the faintest of the red sunset on its dusty coating. He told himself then he wasn't going inside that thing. Bobby could certainly hear him from here.

"Bobby! Come on! It's time for dinner."

There was no noise for a moment other than the brush of one tree's boughs against another's, then the quick steps of feet. It was like someone running up stairs and out of breath. A moment later, Bobby's head popped out of the passage leading into his fort. His face was bright red, even through the fading light, and his breath was heaving in and out.

"Go!" Bobby shouted as he climbed to his feet.

"What?" Randy frowned at him. "What are you—"

Bobby grabbed Randy's hand and jerked him along the path toward home.

Randy didn't know his brother was so strong. Bobby's eyes bulged as he pulled, and his muscles flexed. Randy had never seen him so worked up. Even when they wrestled on the living room floor, Bobby never seemed this strong. And because he didn't want to fall over, Randy ran along with his brother.

They dodged trees and rocks, moving by memory and instinct because the forest had become a wall of blackness beyond the few gloomy yards they could make out ahead.

"What's going on!" Randy struggled to keep up. Bobby was so fast it was a shock. He looked around, the fear within his brother seeping into him. While he only caught glimpses of the trees, the forest felt odd, closed in for such a large space. It was like the trees were narrowing their path, as if they were consciously trying to stop them from escaping.

That wasn't something that could happen. It was the gloom. It was the heaving breaths and the fear. That was it. Wasn't it?

Cracking sounds echoed down from the trees. A crash as a branch slammed into another. Rustling as if movement.

A cold wave shot through Randy. Was it a mountain lion? That was the only thing he knew of that could climb trees like that, that could hop from tree to tree. Had one targeted his brother for its dinner?

But there was more than that. It was more than one tree and in more than one place. The sounds of snapping limbs, the rustle of needles, the fast movement and shuffling along branches were coming from all around them. It was getting closer the longer they dwelled within the darkened woods, and Randy understood why Bobby was running—the feeling, anyway.

Bobby jerked him right at the bottom of the hill. They were halfway out. He thought—prayed, at least—that the edge of the forest would mean safety. If they could make it there, whatever this was would have to remain within the trees, wouldn't it?

He huffed. His throat burned. A new sound caught Randy's ear—soft, high-pitched voices from above. He couldn't understand what they were saying. It was another language, if it was real at all.

There was a shifting of debris along the ground before them. It was hard to see in the dark, but it looked like something was moving under the path, that as the trees creaked and moaned and inched inward, something else was slithering under the dirt and needles. Something was working its way in their direction.

"Faster!" Bobby's voice was raspy. He didn't have much left in his lungs or his legs, and Randy could feel him shake through his hand. They let go of each other and ran harder.

He's right, was all Randy could think. He ran faster, passing in front of his brother as his heart pumped in his ears.

He felt a strange sensation under his feet. The ground that should have been solid, should have been still, was flexible. It shifted under the balls of his feet and the impacts of his heels. All he could do was run harder.

After another minute, the trail opened up ahead. Randy's lungs ached, and his joints burned. His ears throbbed. He saw the line of boulders and the dock in the distance, and he strained even harder.

"Almost there." Randy turned his head and huffed at his brother as he moved. "Almost..." His hands were wet with sweat. His throat tasted like acid. He could feel the crawling things under his feet rise in front of his toes—they were trying to trip him—but he didn't stop. He lifted his feet higher as if running through a snowbank. He wasn't going to let them win.

The night air had finally cooled as Randy burst from the forest. He trotted along the string of boulders, the ground finally still beneath him, and he slowed.

"We made it." He stopped near the dock, leaning forward on his knees to catch his breath. "What the hell was that?"

Randy looked back toward the woods. The trees were no closer than they were on any other day. The forest floor was dark but motionless. And his brother was nowhere to be seen.

"Bobby?" Randy stood and turned in a circle, scanning every rock and boulder, every crevice where his brother could fit. He glanced at the dock—maybe he was hot and went to the water? "Bobby?"

Bobby wasn't there. Bobby was supposed to be right beside him, but he was gone.

Randy's stare shot to the woods. He took a step toward the trees, and his pulse rose. His hands clenched, and his legs refused to take another step. "Bobby!" He was in there. His kid brother was in there, and he had failed to bring him along. But worse than that, he couldn't go back for him. He just... Tears ran down his face as the thought of that language in the trees tickled his ears, as fear wrenched his guts at the memory of shifting ground and rustling shadows.

Hope shined for the briefest of seconds as he thought of Mom and Dad. They could fix this. They could go into the woods and bring back Bobby.

Randy burst into a run up the hill with the strangest notion in his head. He thought of a man who wasn't a man. It was a man made of foggy shadows. He crossed the yard and grabbed the doorknob, mouth open to scream inside for Mom and Dad to come now and help. He imagined a disgusting head on the shadow man, a face with no skin. He turned the knob and stepped inside.

The scents of meat, potatoes, corn, and rolls guided him from the mudroom into the kitchen. Mom and Dad were sitting at the table, loading their plates with food. Joan was slicing into her meat— she was never one to wait for the rest of the family.

Something tickled at Randy's brain as he took his seat. His mouth watered as he waited for the roast to come his way.

Mom glanced at him and then around the room to the door. "Where's Bobby?"

"What?" Randy's hand was out toward the meat. Was he supposed to get Bobby?

Chapter Seventeen

A FAINT SCREAM ECHOED FROM the tunnel behind Donna, and though she heard it, the sound would not register until she played back her thoughts later in the day. The sights ahead controlled her mind. The cool, damp air on her bare lower half added to the overwhelming sensation of otherworldliness because this was not Montana. This was likely not even Earth. So either she was having a dissociative break from reality or her attacker had dosed her with some really strong drugs.

She walked into the meadow, soft ground below her feet and grass tickling her shins and knees. She kneeled by the water and watched the blue shimmer twinkle as ripples in the current passed by, and she was overcome with thirst. She never would have done what she did next except she was sure this wasn't real. The entire world seemed to be some kind of a trip, and at that point, she felt like the best way to deal with it was just to go with it.

Donna leaned over the stream and let the tiny splashes tickle her nose. The thirst grew. Her tongue was drier. Her stomach contracted, begging to be filled. She pressed her lips into the running water and let the stream flow into her mouth with cool, light liquid that, in any other place, she would have argued was not water at all.

At first, it was sweet and bubbly, like the pink Moscato her mother used to like. But as it ran down her throat, the flavor grew a bite, and the consistency thickened into something closer to a milkshake. Yet her thirst remained.

She drank more, guzzling it down. She felt it on her lips and over her tongue. She felt it sliding down her esophagus, but it didn't seem to reach her stomach.

She tried hard, waving the water inside with her cupped hand. It splashed on her chin and nose and wet her shirt. And she was not filled until she pushed herself up from the stream and sat on the grass.

Donna watched the world around her change as her belly contented. The sky dimmed to delicate blue dusk. The mountains around her seemed to inhale and exhale, rising and falling with her breath. The branches of the nearby trees rippled and waved like the hairs of some giant beast on a gusty day. It was enough to make her chuckle to herself.

She had definitely been drugged; she knew it now. A fuzzy feeling of connectedness trickled down her arms and legs as the trees shed their leaves and needles. There was a groan as branches stretched outward and back in and what looked like mouths exposed themselves between the largest of the lower boughs.

She could only shake her head and grin as the leaves in one of the mounds bulged upward like a kid bursting from a forgotten fall pile and a creature the size of a dog emerged. Her grin dropped because this was not a fluffy neighborhood pet. It was splotchy, with matted fur in some places and bare, with open, puss-filled wounds, in others. As it crawled from the discarded leaves toward her, Donna saw more clearly.

Bulging eyes drooped from a squat, squished face as if they would fall from the oddly primate-shaped skull at any moment. Its mouth hung open, with several skinny tongues licking its face. Claws dug into the ground, and it moved slowly closer to Donna.

"No, no, no," Donna mumbled to herself. She backed away, and the creature followed her. It stood up on two feet for a moment, taller, the height of a small child, and she could see holes in its flesh, ribs peeking through dirty, crusted sections of fur and putrid skin. The distorted half-human face and the animalistic frame made her think a mad taxidermist had been at work combining various dead things into a horror of flesh and decay. And it was staring at her. It was studying her like a predator. All she could do was repeat, "No," and continue backward until her rear pressed into the scratchy bark of a tree.

She felt something in her hand and realized she was still holding the knife. She rotated it in her grip as the thing moved closer. She scanned the skeletal trees, the blue light over the gloom, and her breathing sped as she debated about what to do.

Run? Was this thing fast—could it catch her? Into the woods? Up a tree? Back into the cave?

Or fight it? She had the knife, but she hadn't been in a fight since she sparred in the jujitsu classes her dad made her take when she was twelve.

"You're too indecisive," Mom always said. "Learn to make a decision," Dad told her. "Which one?" Samantha Jane asked in her bedroom as they weighed their choice of colleges.

Yes, she was indecisive; yes, she liked to take her time making decisions, but the last twenty-four hours seemed designed to throw her into a crash course in decision-making, and she hated it. And whatever had been in that water was making things worse.

Fifteen feet separated her from that thing, and the space was dwindling. Its eyes dropped lower from its face. It crept forward on two legs, and its tongues slapped the rotted sides of its face. Its arms cracked as its paws split into mangy claws on fur-wrapped hands. But the worst thing was its eyes. They were human eyes. They stared through her with hunger but also with pain. It sniffed and eyed her wounded foot.

"Go away!" she screamed at it.

It was hard to tell from the cracked lips over the canine jaw, but she was pretty sure it smiled as it dropped back to all fours and burst into a run.

Donna howled. She spun to her right and ran into the trees. Her bare feet depressed the ground, every other step an instant of torture as her wound felt like it was tearing even wider. The earth gave, and the dried brush scratched. Swaying branches waved in front of her as she sprinted head-first into the denser bush.

Behind her, she heard it laughing. It was between a hyena and a wicked child, a cackle that chilled her.

She was hot, even in the cool, damp air. She heard her feet smack the ground and the creature's steps behind her. The tiny hairs across her body stood on end as the thing's gallop ceased and, eerily, she knew what was coming.

Donna jerked left and raised her knife. She saw it as she turned. It was in the air, claws reaching. It snagged her shoulder, and she felt the fabric rip and her arm burn.

Keep running or fight it?

She hooked her hand on the base of a tree, spun ninety degrees to her left, and sprinted again. She heard the thing slide in the underbrush, and it was galloping again. Chasing her again. Quiet—in the air again.

Donna screamed. She tried turning to her right and felt the rip of her shirt and then her other shoulder burned. There was a snap in the air by her ear.

Run or—

Pain in her leg, searing, jolting, tearing her to the ground. She rolled away and saw the thing over her. It paused to lick blood from its claw, then lunged.

Donna swung the knife without thinking. It made a crunching sound as the blade crashed through the bone on the side of the thing's head and sliced into its brain. Its jaws clacked together a hair from her nose, and she smelled its last breath as it collapsed on her chest.

It was a rotting smell. It was damp, spoiled meat and fungus. Fluids leaked from its nose as blood seeped from the tongues resting on her chest.

"Ahhhh!" she screamed again, this time from frustration. What the fuck was going on?

She shoved the beast to the ground and lay there looking up into the barren branches. Small things skittered across the bark. The dark-blue sky twinkled. Light-colored wisps seemed to race across the air.

What kind of world was this?

Tears ran from her eyes to her hair, and she covered her face.

No, she told herself. There was no time for that.

She sat up and stared at the creature, at its pus, at the rotting meat visible through its wounds. At the slime it had left on her shirt and legs.

Donna hesitantly grabbed the thing's skull with one hand. Its wet flesh felt ready to slide off the bone. She took the knife with her other hand, closed her eyes, and ripped it free. She ignored the disgusting sound it made and rose to her feet.

The mountains still swelled as she breathed. The trees still swayed. But this was no dream. This was not simply a drug-induced vision. The giant skulls on the neighboring mountains may have been looking down on her, but the pain in her shoulders and legs assured her it was all-too real. Whatever this was, it was happening, and she had to survive it.

She wiped the animal's blood from her knife onto its matted fur. There was another scream from the cave she had emerged from; this one she noticed. This one she smiled at.

Donna headed deeper into the trees as a sound like high-pitched singing came from the distant treetops.

He may have had one crippled hand and a broken leg, but James wasn't going to let those wounds be his death.

He knew what those things wanted as surely as he knew the bones he was crawling over were his victims from the past twenty-plus years. He would have bet Melody's bones were somewhere under there if he had had the urge and the time to dig down and look for them. And those things—those were essentially his pets at this point. He'd been feeding them all these years, apparently. But now he was being confused for food.

He would remedy that. And then he would find his escaped plaything. And he would make her pay for what she had done.

James snatched a bone from the pile as he stumbled to the cave's rear. It was an arm bone, and he had to yank it a few times to rip the remaining dried ligaments that secured it to its shoulder. He pulled himself to the back of the pile.

Bones clattered against each other as they shifted below him. They clattered louder on the other side of the mound, where creatures crawled and slithered and knocked each other around to get to their dinner.

His back met the wall, and where he should have felt fear for the army of things coming to clean his bones like the ones before him, James instead felt rage. How dare they come after him, the person that fed them for so many years. How dare that woman knock him down here. She was the toy, not him. She wasn't supposed to be able to do that.

His gaze went to the cave roof, where the tunnel had led them, dropped them, and abandoned them. The hole was at the highest part of the ceiling. There was no way he was getting back up there, definitely not with his hand and leg the way they were.

He saw the corridors across the cave, where his toy had gone. Maybe he would go that way. He was going to find her eventually.

He checked the other walls, checked behind him—no other exits he could see.

A furry-thing's head popped up over the mound. The face somewhat reminded him of Joe Turner, a kid from his elementary school days who had died in a car accident when his drunk of a father crossed the center line. He hadn't thought of that kid in years, but as the creature crawled down on his side of that pile, he couldn't help thinking that beyond the fangs and the slithering body, the face held a hell of a resemblance.

He was snapped out of that thought when a sharp pain tore through his broken leg. James thought it already hurt as badly as it could, but when an unseen creature planted its fangs in him, he was proven wrong.

He screamed and raised the bone. He brought it down with a crack on the creature's skull. His voice echoed through the cave. The sound of his own scream struck him like an alarm clock's shrill alert, stiffening his back and reminding him that he better get his shit straight or this was the end.

The thing's tentacles flailed around as he whacked it again. Its teeth jolted, clamping harder on his leg before they finally let go.

He heard a hiss gasping through jagged fangs on his right, and he turned and slammed the bone down on another. Joe Turner opened his mouth to take a hunk out of James's hide, and James shoved the bone hard into its left eye.

"Fuck you, Joe!" he screamed through a harmonic bend of anger and pain, and he raised the bone above his head. "Who's next?"

Chapter Eighteen

THAT FIRST NIGHT, IN SEPTEMBER 1999, Randy and his parents spent five hours screaming Bobby's name in the woods. Mom waited at the edge of the forest until dawn, until the sheriff came and agreed to organize a search party. The search started around noon, and no tree, bush, or crevice was left unexamined on the Kline property. By seven that evening, when the sun began to dip, with the exception of the depths of the lake, they had searched it all. The sheriff even had Tom Gentry, the town's septic system installer, open the lid on the tank and poke around in the house's sewage. It was embarrassing, disgusting, and led to nothing more than a sense of completion in the sheriff's report. Another dead end.

There was no blood trail, no footprints or tracks out of the Kline's woods. There was no sign of an invading bear or mountain lion. It was as if the boy simply vanished. Or snuck away himself.

That night was a quiet one in the Kline house. No one ate more than a nibble. Dad sat by the window and drank. Mom sat beside him, crying on and off. Joan hid in her room, and Randy sat on the back patio until Mom pulled him inside and sent him to bed. He was hoping to hear a noise from the woods or, at the least, stay out of his father's accusatory glares. He accomplished neither.

The next day, the search party expanded. Groups went in each direction around the lake and fanned out from the Kline property over land. By the end of the second fruitless day, there was talk of bringing in a dive team to check the waters and the FBI to do whatever they could.

On the third day after Randy's brother went missing, he was forced to go to school. He had lost interest in seeing or talking to Mandy Sloane. He sat with his head on his desk in every class, waiting for the last bell to ring so he could go home and search for his brother, because he insisted that his dad was right and it was all his fault. There was a nagging sense of guilt that he had been the one to lose his brother, and he needed to get back into those woods and find him. The more he thought about it, the more he believed it, the more he knew it was the truth. Despite the failure of the search parties, Bobby was in there somewhere.

Once he decided that, nothing else he did in school that day seemed to matter. It was like he was caught in a dream that he had to finish before he could rejoin the real world and accomplish his duty. There was a haze over interactions with people—they didn't matter. There was a shimmer over the desks and chairs and walls, even his teachers. They spoke in tones of echoes. They walked and talked and sat around in a world that seemed to vibrate. Their actions were trailed by streaks of muted colors—dead colors.

None of it mattered.

The last bell rang, and Billy Jacobs tried stopping Randy to share his condolences. Mary Swanson did the same by the west exit. He ignored them both, their voices sounding lost down the end of an empty tunnel.

He walked through town without stopping at the pool of black liquid leaking from under the butcher's door and filling the parking lot. He didn't stop for the glow tracing the windows of the apartment above The Gilded Lady. He ignored the tiny people in the trees that lined his road and someone shouting his name from behind.

At home, he found Dad drunk in his living room chair and Mom crying in the kitchen. It was pretty much where they would both live for the next two years until Dad left. Randy ignored Dad's stares and Mom's indifference. He dropped his bag in his room and headed toward the trees.

He was almost down the path to the lake when something fell on his shoulder, and he spun to see what it was.

Dwight Banks, who Randy hadn't seen since Dwight moved to Rock Bridge, two towns over, at the beginning of the summer, was standing in front of him. The sight grounded Randy in a way he wasn't expecting. The haze lifted, and his best friend since second grade stood before him with a compassionate gaze over his freckled face. It felt for just a moment that summer hadn't passed, school hadn't started, and they held the world, bright and ready for them to conquer, in their hands. The past three days had just been a nightmare—that's all. He just needed to wake up.

But then Dwight spoke. "Man, I just heard about Bobby."

It all came crashing back. The guilt. The sadness. The obligation to make the world right again. His lip quivered, and he had to shut his eyes as he pictured Bobby alone and frightened in some dark place.

"Randy?" Dwight was holding his shoulder. "What can I do?"

There were times when the three boys had spent what seemed like the entire summer running and jumping from the dock into the lake. Where Bobby tagged along behind them as they strolled through town, hoping to bump into Mary Swanson or Sheryl Perkins and make the afternoon into an impromptu date, after ditching Bobby, of course. There were what seemed like a thousand nights when they played board games in Randy's room or read comics on the living room couch when the parents were out. But now, in this cold world with Bobby gone, all those memories felt like they were from some other life that happened a million years ago. Today, Randy had to find his brother.

"You okay?" Dwight asked.

"Yeah." He nodded. "But I have to find Bobby."

"I heard there were search parties looking."

"They won't find him out there. He's in our woods. I know it."

Dwight nodded. "Can I help?"

Randy hadn't smiled in three days. He did now.

The feeling of being back in Lone Wolf was one Dwight had not expected. His absence had been jarring—trying to get to know a new town, navigating a new school, dealing with his little sister Abby's breakdowns on a daily basis over whatever bratty need Mom wasn't tending to—and his return left him more at ease than he expected. He had always felt stressed, tightly wound, in Lone Wolf, but even with those feelings coming back, they didn't really bother him. He imagined it was like someone going back home to a big city—they would have to look out for muggers, but those streets and the need to be alert would feel like home. And once he returned here, so did the peculiarities he had left behind.

Mom had agreed to bring Dwight and drop him off at Randy's while she took Abby with her to visit some old friends with the understating she would be back at seven to get him. That was almost an hour ago, long enough for Dwight to sit outside Randy's house and think—long enough for him to feel where he was.

There was the continuous sensation that he was being watched. Dwight knocked on the door when he got to the house, and when no one answered, he assumed no one was home. So he sat on the front porch to wait. While there, the sensation called him from every direction as it had when he lived there, like the watcher wanted something from him and he had better stay on his toes. When he lived in Lone Wolf, he had just grown to think it was normal, but after not feeling it for months, the return was... strange.

There was the smell, like something burning. Again, something he was used to before, but coming back, there was a nagging in his nose, telling him there was a fire somewhere in the distance.

The light was the most notable part. Sometime between crossing the McGregor County line and Randy's house, the landscape picked up a very light-blue tint. It reminded him of how people said everyone who lived this far north had a vitamin D deficiency from the weaker sunlight. While the sun itself wasn't dimmer than in Rock Bridge, he did feel cooler. He felt like the rays on his skin had less effect warming him than he felt at home that morning. It was almost like something was sucking away part of the light, stealing it from him.

These observations didn't make any sense, no matter what he felt or didn't feel. It was likely just his emotions, worry about Bobby and what his friend was likely going through. At least, that's what he told himself. That was what he reminded himself of as he and Randy approached the woods together.

"Why do you think he's still in there?" Dwight asked.

The daylight waned as they stepped beneath the canopy. The scents of pine, sage, and juniper filled his body with abundance, and the forest was no longer an external thing; it became something he was a part of simply by walking inside it. The needles crunching under him were just the sounds his feet made. The widening of his pupils to take in his surroundings was as much an autonomic response as yawning or blushing or his pulse quickening when his new crush, Julie Sanford, walked into their homeroom and sat a row away. As strange as the return to Lone Wolf felt moments ago, right now, he was where he was supposed to be.

"I just know he's in here." Randy walked slowly, examining each tree and shrub they passed as if it was the first time seeing them. "I can't really explain it."

Somehow, Dwight understood. Why would Bobby want to leave these woods, anyway? "So what should we do? Do you have a plan?"

Dwight saw the answer in Randy's eyes as their gazes met. There was no plan. There was only the knowledge that this was what they had to do.

As much as Randy wanted to explain his feelings to Dwight, he just couldn't. Yes, he and Mom and Dad had searched the woods high and low, and yes, a search party had been through there. Still, the feeling that Bobby was in the woods was the same as any other day when his brother would yell, "I'm going to my fort," and return a few hours later. It was like knowing your parents were home even though they were in their room or knowing your sister was there from the torturous scents of nail polish and hairspray even though you hadn't seen her in three days. If you could smell Bobby's energy, he would have said that. His brother was still in these woods.

He looked closely behind trees and bushes. He examined leaves and bark and debris in ways he never had before, noticing the dried-yet-sticky sap that flowed from the ponderosa pines and the little blue berries on the juniper bushes. He saw the dead limbs of tall pines that hung with an eerie warning to those who stood below. He saw the hundreds of footprints left by the search party and hoped they didn't trample away any evidence. But at the same time, he didn't think that mattered. Bobby was there, somewhere.

"Bobby!" Randy called. Dwight repeated him.

They kept moving, slowly but diligently. They passed the stone structure Bobby used as a fort, and Dwight climbed the nearby boulders and looked down on the small clearing. There was no sign of him, but they continued searching.

On the side of the hill, they stopped and checked out a cave. It wasn't very deep, and Randy had checked it the other day, but his heartbeat sped up anyway as they looked inside, and it ached as they found it empty. There were animal bones and hair, the remnants after a mountain lion had bedded down some past night. But no Bobby.

Randy wanted to scream in frustration. He called for Bobby instead, but without answer, the frustration remained. He was running out of time. He didn't know why he thought that, but he did. It was like a clock was ticking down the moments of his brother's life, and he had been tasked to stop it. But everywhere he looked, he found nothing.

Under trees, in bushes, in the gaps between brambles. Behind boulders, in caves, in the canopy above. None of them held a clue.

He had to do it. Randy howled into the trees.

Dwight watched him, frowning with concern.

Randy dropped to his knees. His stomach hardened into a rock, and his fists pounded on the earth. He just couldn't understand how this was happening, how his brother could come out here day after day for years, how he could be in his own woods, just playing his stupid little games in his fort, and go missing. Maybe worse than that...

Dwight put his hand on Randy's shoulder, and it did nothing to soothe him. But when Randy looked up, there was something new, something that hadn't been there before: a man-shaped shadow by a distant copse of trees.

Randy raised a hand, pointing across the shaded undergrowth. As his finger crossed the outline of the shape, it shrank into the gloom, and whomever it was was off.

"There!" Randy was up and running. He pointed into the empty gap where the shadow had been. "Stop, you!"

"What?" Dwight ran after him. Randy only knew Dwight was coming from the crunch of needles behind him, because he was *not* going to take his gaze from that spot.

"A guy! There was a guy over there!" His heart was pounding. He moved through the woods in strong, powerful strides. He pushed himself faster than he had run before, and then he was there, standing under the same tree that shadow had occupied. He smelled a damp rot that made him think of moldy wood. He wanted to curse himself for not getting there fast enough, for not spotting the man sooner, and then he saw it again, running down the hill on his right.

"There!" He pointed and took off again.

"What?" Dwight followed. "I don't see anything!"

"Just come on!"

Randy dodged trees and ducked under branches. He saw the thing moving and wasn't going to lose sight of it again. He leaped over a dead log, and his right foot slipped from under him. He slid across the ground over debris, rammed his foot into a rock, and rolled across the forest floor. All along, he kept his gaze on that shadow of a man.

"Jesus, Randy!" Dwight crunched on dead things and fought to keep up. They both rounded a large boulder, and he shouted, "I see it!"

The shadow slipped behind another set of trees, and Randy was no closer to it than when he started. But he saw where they were and where it was running. It was almost to the stone structure, to Bobby's fort.

"That way!" Randy shot to his right, down the steeper path. It was a harder run, but maybe he could catch up now that he knew where it was going.

"Wait! Shit!" Dwight let out a muffled groan. A thud. He was sliding down the hill, but Randy was sprinting full-bore toward Bobby's fort.

"Who are you!" Randy shouted as the decline lessened. He planted his foot on a rock and sprang ahead, only a dozen feet behind the shadow as it ducked inside the fort. "I got you!"

Randy skidded across the ground like he was sliding into home. He turned onto his knees and started inside the rock formation.

"Who are you?" he repeated, rage filling his chest. It was so absurd, what was going on, and he wanted it to stop. His missing brother, the chasing, the strangeness of this guy's shadowy shape—it all had to end. "Where's Bobby?" he screamed.

The inside of the structure was almost black to Randy's unadjusted eyes. There was only a moment where he caught a glimpse of the shadowy shape and received an impression that could not have been real—the face, the face was almost a skeleton. No skin. Raw, exposed eyes. Glistening muscle over its cheeks. Wet, open holes where a nose should have been. Crooked, blackening teeth shone through split, hanging lips. It was like a dead, faceless thing, but it was running—how could it—

That was when the world inside the fort went white. A burning smell flared in Randy's nostrils, and he pulled his head back, cracking it on the entrance roof.

His eyes fluttered, and when he regained his sight, the thing was gone. The shadowy, dead thing had disappeared into thin air. But the strange scratches on the walls glowed in a fading red light until they were as black as the rest of the wall.

"No!" Randy screamed.

Dwight crawled into the fort behind him. "Where'd he go?"

Randy slammed his fists into the ground again. He was so close, and he lost him, lost his only clue to finding Bobby. All he could do was scream.

Regardless of the thing being gone, he knew it heard him. It knew he was on to it.

Chapter Nineteen

DONNA'S LEGS WERE FREEZING. THE day was getting dimmer, though it seemed stuck in a perpetual blue dusk. She wished she had something, anything, to cover her legs and groin with. She debated ripping her shirt in half but wasn't sure if it would make her warmer or colder once she lost that extra layer and moved it down.

Even if she ended up colder, she knew she wouldn't feel so utterly exposed, so she decided she would have to risk it once she found a safe place to rest. But where would that be?

The trees and hills felt never-ending. The climbing and descending, the noises in the branches that she was sure meant something was following her—it was a never-ending haunt. The soft chirping of voices was ceaseless, driving her to go faster and faster with the hope that she would outrun them. But she didn't. And more than once, she wondered if they were going to drive her mad.

She couldn't decide on a place to rest for the oncoming night as long as that noise was right behind her. After the things in the cave and the one at the stream, she couldn't take that chance.

Donna pushed through a gap in the trees and found herself at the top of a cliff, hovering over the bank of a roaring river. Its rapids shone brighter than the sky as waves crashed against rocks and a stony shore on the other side. She clutched the tree tightly as her legs wobbled beneath her. She clamped down hard, desperate not to tumble in. She was cold enough already, and something told her that was freezing water, maybe a death sentence if she fell in.

This wasn't a place to camp, but at least it was something different. But where was she going to go? She could either follow the cliff up or downstream.

Donna scanned the river's path, and her breath hitched in her lungs. The opposite side of the water was not lined with rocks as she initially thought. It was lined with bones, giant bones that brought her gaze back to the surrounding mountains and the enormous skulls that formed cliffs and scaffolding for plant life. These were not quite that big, more like the remains of people thirty feet tall, but their size was alarming. The amount of bodies was alarming too.

One over the other, rib cages, arms, legs, and skulls all formed a mound that built the shore of the raging rapids. But more than the sight of the oddly large bodies, what grabbed Donna's attention was their faces—and their wounds. Legs and arms were cracked into long shards. Gaps cried from ribs where it was obvious someone had stabbed or crashed through them with swords or axes. Skulls held cracks and holes reaching from top to temple, from eye socket to jaw, from nose to chin, and each skull seemed to be howling in a frozen mask of pain.

She didn't know whether this was a battleground or a burial pit, but each vacant stare told her she wasn't wanted there.

But where else was she to go?

She pulled her eyes from the dead and scanned farther down the river until she saw the only path allowed: a bridge, probably a half-mile down though it was long before the stretch of death was completed.

"Okay." She breathed deeply and started walking along the cliff.

The noise of rushing water seemed loud at first, but as Donna moved and no longer heard the voices in the trees, she found herself relieved. There was something about those high-pitched tones that really got under her skin. She knew they might still be there, hiding below the white noise of the monotonous rush of water, but for the moment, she was happy for the distraction.

That changed when she reached the bridge.

It spanned a hundred feet above the raging water and enormous skeletons, but it was little more than moldy rope strung through rotting wood. It had rope railings and rope supports that spanned from bank to bank, fixed with wooden planks, and it reminded her of something from one of those *Indiana Jones* films her dad watched where the hero had to scale some decaying jungle construction. But she was no hero, and in its state of decay, this was barely a bridge.

The good thing, she discovered as she came close enough to touch it, was its size. The bridge was larger than she expected, likely made for those giants, and likely as old. Only half the planks remained properly tied to the structure, leaving huge gaps between some of the boards, but the boards themselves, though rotting and splintered, appeared large and strong—or they were in their youth, anyway.

Donna glanced back into the woods and imagined her captor somewhere in there. She hoped he was dead, that those things had devoured him like they must have scraped all the meat from those bones, but she didn't want to be so foolish as to assume that was the case. He could still be back there. Others, like that creature who had risen from the leaves, could be back there. Whatever was in the trees making those noises—though they had not harmed her yet—could come after her.

She felt pushed. This bridge did not look safe, and under any normal situation, she wouldn't have dared set foot on it, let alone try to cross it. But with all she had seen here, she had to believe her chances were better across the river—a decision she would regret later.

She thought back to those adventure movies, to the silly grin Dad would get on his face when he watched them, and she really wished he was there with her. She wished she could be sure she would get to see him again, and she took the rope railing in her right hand.

It was larger than her fist, and she couldn't wrap her grip all the way around it. The fibers were rough under her fingers but wet from the river's spray. She gave the rope a hard tug and heard it whine, but it didn't rip or break. She would have to trust it.

Donna lowered a foot onto the first plank and pressed down hard on it. There was a creak, but it held. She swung her other foot to the next plank, her arms stretched as far as they would go so she could grasp the rope railing on both sides. The whine of wood and fiber made her heart race. The next plank was two feet away, and she was pretty sure she could fit through the gap if she slipped. She had to put that thought aside as she tested the next board with a hard stomp, and she kept going.

One board at a time, she passed over the rushing water. It grew louder, overtaking the snaps and creaks of the bridge, which was both reassuring and unnerving at the same time. She didn't want to hear the constant reminders that her life was in danger, but she also worried that one of those sounds might have been the only warning she had if the bridge was going to fail. But it was out of her hands, and the more the sounds of the rapids consumed her ears, the more she was sure it wasn't just waves she was hearing.

Under the watery crash was the cadence of language. It thudded and hissed with consonance and sibilance, and images formed in her mind of beings crossing this bridge, fighting on it, and dying. These were the words of ghosts.

A third of the way across, Donna found her first gap of two boards in a row. She stood on the plank beside the six-foot gap, looking down at the racing water. It was cold down there. It was death down there. She knew if she was back in her world and fell into a river like that, she might have had a chance. She was a strong swimmer. There was no chance here. It was water like she had drank from that stream. It was water that got into your head if you touched it, and this water... this water was where *they* lived.

Her eyes drifted to the bones, their faces. She heard their screams coming from their fleshless skulls. She saw the river below running red with blood as they fought and the bodies fell. She smelled the rot once they were gone and the water ate at their corpses, bloating, seeping inside, breaking them down until all that was left was a barricade of lost memories.

She wobbled where she stood, her knees feeling too loose to hold her weight. She had to cross this. She couldn't end up trapped with them. That was where she would spend eternity if she failed. She had to get through it.

Donna took hold of the rope on her left, wrapping both arms around it. She stepped onto the lower rope that acted as a support for the rest of the planks. Her body shaking violently, she began crossing the chasm.

She stepped, hanging and sliding, and stepped. The entire bridge shook beneath her. The ropes, even as large as they were, dipped from her weight as she hung. Sliding. Stepping.

The voices called from below. They wanted her down there. They wanted her to join them. At first, she couldn't understand them, but as she reached the halfway mark of the plank-less gap, and the crashing water soaked her bare legs and bottom, as the ropes became slicker with water and fear, she heard the words.

Gasyn is coming. It's safe here. Join us. Flow forever. Gasyn is coming. Rot with us. Be with us. It's safe here.

Donna squeezed her arms tight over the side rope. She was frozen as they repeated their call. Thick, humid air soaked her tear-ridden face. The smells of mold and rotten meat wafting up from the ropes made her sick. Her teeth clamped hard.

"God?" She looked up into the darkened sky. How was she going to get through this?

Another voice broke through the din. It warmed her and frightened her as she saw who was standing on the plank she was aiming for.

"You can do this, Donna." It was her father. He was in his favorite lazy flannel with his graying beard almost hiding the collar. His words were calm and clear in her head as if they were more thought than spoken. "Keep moving. Keep crossing. Hold tight."

"Dad?" She couldn't help but question. She had to wonder if she was truly insane at this point. If she was having hallucinations, she had surely broken.

"Move," he insisted. "Now."

A short glance down at the rapids, and she was moving again. She squeezed the rail. She stepped and pulled. She wanted to talk to Dad. She wanted to hug him and feel his warmth. She needed that hug, even though she knew she would have been embarrassed by having no pants; she just wanted him to hold her in his arms, to surround her with his massive embrace as he had when she was little and she was scared of everything after Mom had gone. When she was scared something was going to come and take him too, so he rocked her through the wee hours of the morning without trying to leave her once. He would have forever been her rock if she had let him, and she damned herself for leaving.

Squeeze the rail. Step and pull.

She climbed back onto a plank. She was on a solid surface again, and she looked for him.

Dad was gone.

She had lost her mind. She was in some alien world with unbelievable creatures and skies and then him—she had completely lost it.

Tears ran.

"Keep moving." It was his voice inside her head. *"You can't stay there."* He sounded like he was ahead, but he wasn't there.

She felt herself convulse as the fear and sadness consumed her. She was never going to see home again. Even if she somehow survived this, she was never going to see the real Dad again, never going to get to live her life, go to college, have a job. She was in this terrible place, and she would die here.

Her stomach crawled deeper inside her, cramping, and she wanted to curl up and die.

"Keep moving," he said again. *"You have to. Please."*

She nodded. She had to. Do it for Dad.

Still holding the rope with white-knuckled grips, she walked on. She reached the next gap of missing boards, and she crossed it like she had the last. She listened to her father's voice, and she pushed herself forward. She ignored the sounds of the river and the souls below it, and she marched on.

She was almost to the end, suspended high over the wall of bones, when she encountered the last gap of missing planks.

Skulls stared up at her, wanting. Their battered faces called out. She looked into their eye sockets and saw them shift. She saw their teeth chatter.

Donna thought she must be seeing it wrong. She looked away and closed her eyes and looked back. They had moved. Some bones as much as a few inches. They rattled, and she heard it just below the crashing water. A jaw slammed shut, and the clack of enormous teeth sent shivers across her flesh.

She did not want to cross this gap. She didn't want to dangle over those hungry bones and—*Clack!*

She looked back at the way she had come. The bridge was so long. There were so many other gaps she had crossed. She couldn't do that again.

Clack! Another set of jaws slammed shut.

"Go," her father demanded. *"Cross now. Before your scent causes them to rise."*

Rise? What?

She didn't speak out or even question. She looped her arm around the rail, her foot on the cross rope, and she moved. Moved with her blood rushing in her veins and her heart pounding. She had to listen to Dad. Had to get out of there before they rose, whatever the hell that meant.

She pictured an army of skeletons three times as tall as normal men chasing her, and she moved faster. She saw them catching her and plucking her tiny legs and arms from her tiny body and eating her with their bare ivory faces stained red with her blood.

Donna whimpered and worked her way to the other side. She reached the next solid plank, and without holding the railing any longer, she burst into a sprint across the rest of the bridge. Cold, bare feet on cold wood, she ran until her toes touched earth, then she ran some more.

She ran past a row of dying trees and stopped as she saw what was ahead: a blackened field of jagged rocks that looked like acres of broken onyx shards.

Chapter Twenty

SALLY KLINE SAT AT THE kitchen table with a cup of hot tea between her interlaced fingers. She had heard the knock at the door when her son's friend Dwight came by. She cried to herself and ignored it. She had watched Randy and Dwight go down the path and into the woods. She wanted to stop them, but she knew what they were doing, and there was a thread of hope that they would succeed. She had weighed the cost of losing a second son against the miracle of getting back her baby, and she decided to risk it. Now, she watched them rush back up the path with wide eyes and fearful faces, and she knew her assumptions were right: the cursed thing had returned.

Since she was little, her daddy had told her stories about building this house. She always thought he was pulling her leg. That was what grownups did to kids. They told stories that stretched the realms of reality, pushed kids to believe outrageous things like Santa Claus or the Tooth Fairy, and then they expected kids to be truthful one hundred percent of the time.

Daddy loved to tell her stories, but some of his favorites were about when his daddy was building the house. He was only a boy at the time, but he loved to visit and watch it come together. The way he told it, a lot of the men who worked on the house were travelers—it was the late '30s, after all, and there didn't seem to be an end in sight to the depression, not in those parts, anyway. The travelers set up tents and made camp down by the low lake—there was a drought that year—with some of them opting for the privacy of the woods, the same woods where Bobby went missing.

Some of the travelers went missing here and there, and while the foreman knew travelers to be unreliable and prone to wandering off, he especially noted that it usually happened after Friday's payroll was dispersed, not in the middle of the week—when things were normal, that is.

There was talk of high voices and singing in the forest. There was talk of eyes in the shadows. Those yarns were enough to keep Sally from playing in the woods when she was small. But despite not really believing Daddy's tales as she grew bigger, those weren't Daddy's favorite parts—those weighed on her more.

The way he told it, it was a cold morning in the spring of 1939, and the house was almost complete. There were some shingles left to nail and a few walls still needed plastering, but most of the travelers were preparing to move on to another job on the opposite side of town.

That was when the murders happened.

According to Daddy, there were twelve men at the camp by the lake when they went to bed that night—only one dared sleep in the woods anymore. Seven men woke up the next day screaming. Four of the missing travelers were never seen again. The sheriff followed a blood trail into the woods and found the fifth. Daddy never said exactly how bad off the man they found was, but Sally knew from his face when he told the story that it was bad. So bad that the sheriff called it a bear attack. He said that was the only thing that could have done it. It must have woken up early from hibernation and was hungry—so hungry it dragged off five men before one fought back enough to get himself killed on the way to its den.

But Daddy didn't believe that. He believed the travelers who packed up and left that day, and they said it was a curse—a curse from the land of the dead.

Daddy didn't go into those woods a single time so far as Sally had ever seen. She didn't go in there either after how shaken he seemed—except that one time when Momma was sick, and she tried not think about that.

By the time she had little ones, the worry of it had all waned. It had just been a story after all—that, and the silly, faded memories of a little girl that she knew she couldn't trust.

"Mom!" Randy burst through the back door.

She barely moved from her spot at the table other than following him with her eyes. He sat across from her, out of breath.

"A monster—I mean a shadow—I mean a skeleton." He heaved breaths in and out as Dwight closed the door and joined them at the table.

Sally wished she had the energy to console him. It felt like it had been a month of sleepless nights and endless tears, and her body had lost all its power to do more than walk to the stove for her tea kettle and weep. What else mattered with Bobby gone? He was her baby.

"Did you hear, Mom?" Randy asked. His face pleaded for a response. "There's a monster out there. We chased it into Bobby's fort, and the thing—" he shook his head and glanced at Dwight as if his friend might have had a better explanation, then he turned back, "—it vanished. Like, it was there, a shadowy thing with a nasty skull for a face, and then... it was gone."

Footsteps in the living room. It meant Owen was up. All Sally could do was shut her tender eyes and hope he was going to continue being a quiet drunk instead of an angry one.

"Did you hear me, Mom?"

She opened her eyes. Randy's brows were high, his mouth open; he was practically begging.

"Go on to your room, Randy." It was all she could get out. The tears ran. Maybe Randy was telling the truth, maybe he was mistaken, but the idea of anything so horrific dragging off her Bobby only made her want to weep harder. It spawned something, and she didn't know whether it was a memory or a nightmare. It was dark, with shadowy wisps and a face she refused to look at. It hovered over her like a giant, and she had to shake her head to relieve herself from the thought.

"But, Mom?"

"Go!" Her voice broke as she screamed.

Owen stomped into the kitchen, his boots heavy on the floor. He opened his mouth to scream as well, then he saw Dwight and stopped with his mouth wide. "Go to your room," he told Randy.

Sally could smell the whiskey before Owen had opened his mouth. Once he did, the room was full of the scent.

Randy stood. "But..." He glanced at each of their faces and followed directions.

When Sally had the room to herself again, she sipped her tea and thought of baby Bobby racing through the house in his walker. He smiled so much in that walker. It used to make her smile. Now, she just hoped that thought would remove the image Randy had placed in her head. That, and the murders of 1939.

"She didn't even listen." Randy dropped onto his bed. Dwight took the rolling chair he had sat in a thousand times before when they used to have sleepovers and Dad refused to let them play videogames downstairs because he wanted the TV.

"She's pretty broken up about Bobby."

Randy shook his head. "So am I. So is Dad." He pounded on his bed. "But at least I'm trying to do something about it."

"Yeah." He turned to the window and watched a car stop outside and Randy's sister, Joan, get out of the passenger side. She laughed, then leaned back inside and kissed whoever it was. "Your sister's here."

"Big whoop." Randy sat up. "You saw it, right?"

Dwight spun back to Randy. "I saw a shadow. It was crazy the way it moved across the woods."

"The skull face—you saw that, right? Inside the stones?"

"No. I wish I did, but all I saw was a flash, and then just you."

Randy sighed. "I swear, it was like Skeletor or something, but he had eyes and nasty muscles on his face, and his head was all gross."

"So where'd he go?"

"What?"

"We chased him into Bobby's fort, right?"

"Right?"

"And then he was gone."

"Yeah."

"So where did he go? It sounds like what happened to your brother."

Randy didn't move. He didn't talk. Dwight was right. The whole disappearing-into-thin-air thing was just like what had happened to Bobby. He was right there to see it happen, too, and he had no idea how to explain it or what to do next. He knew two things, though: it had something to do with Bobby's fort, and they had to figure it out.

Chapter Twenty-One

THE LAND IN FRONT OF Donna was like a desert of broken, black glass. The ground sparkled over hills for a vast distance, with only small patches of dead trees and irregular smaller hills to decorate the landscape. But there was one thing. In the distance, beyond the crystallized ground and before the mountains at the end of the valley, there was light, flickering light, like dozens of fires.

Hope sparked within Donna for the first time since the gas station in Bozeman. There were people up there. Only people made fires. And they must know how to get her home.

She had to believe that. Anything else was unthinkable.

But how would she get there? The ground ahead looked like it could cut through the hardest work boots, and there she was, barefoot and half naked.

Donna looked around for anything she could use for clothes or shoes. The thought of slicing her feet on that desert floor and making her wounded foot worse made her cringe. She had to make something work.

Behind her were the barren trees and the rush of the river. The sounds of the dead had lulled, perhaps convinced of their failure. She saw dead leaves and needles and branches on the ground. She saw dead animals among the debris. She must have missed them in her rush to get away from the colossal dead.

The carcasses looked similar to the things in the cave, but she wasn't sure. It had been so dark there and so dark now. She glanced at the blade in her hand and wondered. She knew the natives used to make shoes from hides, but those were tanned. She shook her head. It wasn't like she had much choice.

Donna kneeled beside the trees and poked one of the dead, furry slug things with a stick. It was stiff, and its small limbs didn't move. Its smell was sour and pungent, like death mixed with piss. She poked another, and she wondered how these things ended up here. What killed them?

Her eyes went to the glass desert, then toward the river.

She didn't know. She just had to hope it wasn't some kind of disease she could catch.

A breeze came off the desert, and though it made her shiver, she was thankful it took some of the stench away.

She held the closest animal in one hand, ignoring the too-human face, and sliced into its long belly. There was a hissing sound, and Donna dropped it, ready to jump back. Had she mistakenly sliced into a live one?

It didn't move, and the hiss slowly faded. Maybe it was gas escaping? She had heard that gases built up in dead things.

She picked it back up and proceeded to skin the thing, sliding her blade between the muscle and the outer layer. When she was done, there was a ball of meat on the ground and she held something that looked like a furry purse. She imagined it was large enough to hold her foot, but she didn't want to try it yet. The idea of sticking her foot inside the thing before she had to was revolting.

She skinned another one. It smelled worse than the first—maybe it had been dead longer—and she had to fight the urge to puke. She stood there, staring at the two skins, and regrettably decided she wasn't done yet, so she skinned two more.

She wanted to go down to the river and wash her hands and the furs before she did anything else. The memories of those skeletons dissuaded her.

Donna's skin crawled. She was disgusted, but she did what she had to.

With two more slices, she created leg holes in one of the skins and inched it up her limbs until it looked like she was wearing a saggy pair of furry bikini bottoms. She trembled at the wetness against her bare skin, at the vile smell, and the knowledge that it was touching her intimate parts.

After a minute, she gritted her teeth and kept working.

One at a time, she slid a foot inside a wet, bloody skin. She firmed pieces of branches she had broken below them and used strips she had cut from one of the furs to lace her makeshift moccasins together.

If she wasn't ready to vomit over the ordeal, she would have been proud of herself. Even feeling nauseated, she was a little proud. She thought Dad would have been.

Her eyes on the distant light, Donna slid the knife into her shorts and picked up a long branch she had trimmed to use as a walking stick. She started into the black glass desert, forcing herself to believe escape was somehow possible.

Inside, she knew she was going to die in a pair of blood-soaked fur underwear.

Donna felt the ground crunch below her feet. She tried to step on the flatter, less-pointed rocks, but they cracked and rustled under the wooden soles of her hand-crafted shoes just the same.

The moccasins felt okay at the moment, surprisingly so. The wood was stiff, but the fur provided some cushion. She didn't know how she would feel at the end of the day, though she was sure it was better than she would have after walking across the jagged ground barefoot.

The elevation rose and fell, and rolling passages of craggy razors lay in every direction. There were heaps and lines in the earth, and Donna imagined primordial lava flows that hardened and then shattered into the hellscape before her.

There were bones there, as well, partial animal skeletons, some that resembled the creatures she had skinned—the partial nature made her question and look to the skies. *There must be birds here.* It was the only thing she could picture getting in and out of this place unscathed. Some monstrous kind of vulture, she imagined.

She remembered seeing vultures circle when she was ten and Dad took her hunting. Mom thought she was too young but didn't protest more than once. She knew how close Donna and her father were. It was like she always knew how they would need each other.

When she was thirteen and their truck slid on the ice and rolled into the snowy ditch, it could have killed all three of them, but Mom made sure her and Dad survived. Donna couldn't recall the whole thing, only bits here and there. She didn't know if it was a repressed memory or what—she kind of wished the entire event was repressed when thoughts of it came back. It always brought on tears.

She could see the snow drifting through the air. First, it was like light speed in *Star Wars*, where streaks of white were lit up in the headlights, flakes rushing at them. Then, there was the soft-yet-terrifying scrape of rubber on ice, and instead of the gentle rumble of the road below, there was slickness and sliding, and she was upside-down, and there were crunches of metal and glass, and Mom and Dad both screamed—her saying "Donna!" and him saying "Hold on!"

There was a gas smell, followed by one of burning plastic. Donna slipped through her seatbelt, landing on a glass-lined roof. Dad pulled his knife from his belt and leaned toward Mom to cut her loose. She shook her head and looked at him, her upside-down gaze meeting his, and she said no. She was wet with melted snow and tears, and blood leaked from a gash on her forehead. Her face trembled, but she was firm. There was love in that gaze, and she insisted.

Mom's leg was crushed between the door's steel frame and the collapsed dash. Her tears ran into her hair as she told Dad to get Donna out.

It was the last time she saw her mother, and the smell of gasoline made her sick ever since. The charred body was too grotesque to display at the funeral, and she swore she still smelled the gas through the casket. She thought she would always remember her mother's face, but now all she could remember were still images from pictures. They felt like real moments when she tried to remember the occasions when those photos were taken, but they were projections from the images, wishful thinking on her part.

She wondered if she might see Mom again soon. She didn't want to be pessimistic, but her situation was looking grim. She didn't think about the afterlife much unless she was thinking about Mom. She figured she would have been an atheist after the horrors she had seen her mother go through if it weren't for the fact that that would have meant her mom was truly gone forever. She could not accept that idea, no matter the grievances she had developed with God.

She stared at the sky as she walked. Trickles of glowing blue overlapped light-indigo lightning. They crisscrossed the sky like mingled webs and made no noise. If she wasn't so scared and disgusted, she would have found it beautiful.

The firelight glowed on in the distance, and she wondered how far it was, if she would make it tonight. It was probably miles.

She could do that. She was a relatively fit young woman. She could walk a few miles, even through hills of black glass if she had to. Even with a gash on her foot if she had to.

The image of Dad on that bridge came to her. She had to make it back to him. He had already lost so much.

There was another crackling of glass to Donna's right. Not close, but close enough to make her jump. She was supposed to be the only one out there, after all—the only one other than those monsters back there.

On the hill, a few hundred feet away, a figure stood. She couldn't make it out in the darkness, but it was shaped like a man. It stood as if watching her, and she panicked for a heartbeat thinking it was the monster who had grabbed her in Bozeman. But she remembered his leg was broken—this couldn't be him. It wasn't acting like it was there to help, either, though. And more than what it was doing, what it *wasn't* doing told her everything she needed to know. It wasn't waving or calling out to help. It wasn't running away. It wasn't doing anything but watching, like a predator careful of spooking its prey. And that told her to stay away, that the shadowy man was not good news. It gave her a feeling of darkness, true darkness, not just the dimly lit desert but the darkness of the soul. It was stretching from that shadow man and reaching out toward her, and she wanted no part of that.

She walked faster, her hand sliding into her pants and gripping the knife's handle. She glanced back, keeping an eye on him.

After a quarter mile, he had disappeared from his mound, but Donna knew he wasn't gone for good.

Part Four

The Strange Land

Chapter Twenty-Two

DREW GRABBED, BUT HIS FINGERS found little. Air blew past his ears, changing color and feeling damp. He was tumbling through a brown fog, listening to his friends scream, until he thudded against a dirt floor.

"Ow!" It was Lance.

"Ah." Eric.

"Mother—fuck—" Dean.

Drew lifted his face from the ground. It was hot and wet, blood streaming from his nostrils. The others were sitting, then climbing to their feet. Drew took his time, trying not to leak blood all over himself. He pinched his nose and leaned over the dirt floor.

They snatched their flashlights from the floor and peered around. The walls were almost as black as they were in the stone fort but covered in much thicker dirt. On top of that, on one side of the chamber, thick, woody vines grew over a gigantic mound of tiny skeletons toward the top. They grew up and into the fog. Opposite the burial mound, a single small passage led out. In the center, hot coals from Dean's fire sputtered out.

Drew could just barely make out the top of the fort through the fog. It was like the floor had somehow disintegrated below them, and down they came.

He pinched his nose tight and pointed. "How did that happen?"

"The floor vanished!" Eric shouted. "It was like a magic trick."

Dean held his hand to the back of his head and winced. "The floor gave out, that's all. We're inside some kind of structure, and the floor collapsed." He spotted the vines and tugged on one. Drew could see Dean's gears spinning and his brother assuming the leadership mindset he tried to avoid. "I'll climb up and go get a rope."

"You sure about that?" Lance asked. "That stuff looks rotten."

Dean didn't answer. He snarled as he took one vine in his hand and stepped on a knot where two strands intertwined. With one leg and one foot, he pulled himself up.

Drew watched, his nose filling with blood. He agreed those vines looked dried out and weak, but his brother was probably the best climber he knew. When they went to the jump park in Butte, he was always the fastest up and down the rock wall. So, he watched hopefully.

Another hand on a higher vine, his other foot on a higher knot, Dean climbed, and long creaking sounds echoed.

"Get down, Dean," Lance warned. "It can't hold you."

Dean lifted himself a foot higher, and the woody vegetation cracked and shattered across the wall. It ripped away from the caked dirt and black stone, and wood and dust rained across the space in a tidal wave as Dean tumbled down.

Drew felt dust and cold, humid air slamming into his face. Tiny bones and broken vines scattered. When everything settled, Dean lay on top of the burial mound. Miniature heads rolled into the center of the room, their judgmental eye sockets glaring at them all.

"Dammit!" Dean stared up, the net of vines no more. It lay in tatters over him and on the floor, and the walls stood unfazed and unclimbable. "Dammit!" He rolled to the floor, brushing bones and debris from his chest and lap. He cast an accusatory glance at the others—a *this was your bright idea* glare.

Eric picked up one of the skulls, shivered, and put it back down gently. "This was a bad idea."

"You think?" Dean stood and studied the high walls.

"How are we going to get out now?" Lance touched the wall. He rubbed the thick dirt from his fingers.

Drew pointed to the small passage in the wall. "This way?" It was barely taller than the entrance to the fort they had crawled through at the top, but it did lead out of the chamber. "Maybe there's another way up?"

Dean walked over and kneeled in front of it. "Let's hope so, or we're going to have to start taking turns screaming and praying that Mom or Dad come looking for us."

That thought made Drew shrink, the idea that even if they were screaming, no one could hear them from down there. Even if they were outside the stone structure, no one would have heard them, they were so far from the house. He didn't know if he had ever felt so distant from civilization, definitely not at the old house. They really were alone.

Dean started crawling through, and the others looked at one another, unsure of who should go next. Lance shrugged. Eric gestured at Drew, so Drew crouched and followed his brother.

The passage was black rock, as dark as the stone that made up the long-lost fort. It was wide at the bottom and triangular, rising to a point at the top, and the longer they crawled, the more the air felt damp and smelled of something rotten. The farther they crawled, the more Drew felt like they didn't belong, that they had found their way into a place that they should not have entered, and only sorrow lay ahead. It was a sense that, like the rot in the air, this place was for unused or unwanted things, dead things that didn't belong in the rest of the world. The sensation crept up from the floor through his fingers and knees, spreading cold and gooseflesh and making his insides feel loose and unstable.

It felt like they were crawling for an eternity. Eric stumbled and cursed—something Eric rarely did. Lance, in the rear, asked a dozen times, "You see anything up there?" and got the same response each time: "No."

As the length and depth of the tunnel and the continued darkness set in, Drew started to think the passage was narrowing. The geometry was changing, and the sides were getting closer to his shoulders. The ceiling was lowering over his head. He was pretty sure he couldn't turn around if he wanted to anymore—none of them could—and if they had to go back, they would have had to do it by crawling backward. It made his heart beat faster as he worried about the inevitable, that soon the walls would be squeezing his shoulders. Soon, he might have to crawl on his side, or he might even get stuck. God, what would he do if that happened?

He felt his hands trembling, but he was quiet. He didn't want the others to know he was scared. What if they were scared too? What if they all tried to back out and escape at the same time? They might crawl over each other and get stuck—they could die in this tunnel in a pile of squished corpses.

His heart slammed inside his chest. He stopped and closed his eyes, doing nothing but breathing. In and out. His lungs seemed small. The air was thin. It was like the breaths he took didn't fit inside his lungs, and his chest was just a small bag full of holes, and none of his breathing did anything but—

"Hey, I see something." Dean's voice broke through Drew's thoughts. "Yeah, there's something ahead."

Drew opened his eyes. Dean was several feet in front, so he hurried to catch up. As he did, a light-blue light began to brighten the passage. After another few yards, he could see Dean's silhouette over a blue background.

"I see the outside," Dean said. "We're almost there."

"Yes!" Eric called from behind.

"Alright!" Lance echoed.

Thirty seconds later, Draw watched Dean stand and step from the path. He saw a patch of grass and the trunks of trees.

When Drew's head emerged from the tunnel, he had never been so excited to stretch his limbs and stand up tall. He ran his hands over his arms and legs and took deep, full breaths, welcoming the air despite the strange smell. He didn't notice the ground that was moving under his feet or the oddness of the trees until Eric spoke.

"Where are we?" Eric was stretching much the same as Drew had, but his eyes were active as he took in their surroundings.

Though everything inside Drew told him they should not be there, he could not help but be awestruck by the alien environment. The trees swayed, their limbs flailing like those ten-foot-tall inflatable men at the car dealership in town. The sky was blue, but not the sky he was used to—it was an eerie blue, an unnatural blue. The sun was blue as well and took up so much of the sky he thought he could see the blue flames burning on its surface.

"What the shit?" Lance was not as impressed. He shook his head and sneered. "This isn't right. This—this isn't right."

Dean turned to the others. "Just settle down. I bet it's just like the northern lights or something, a solar flare making everything look weird. Let's just get home and hope Mom and Dad haven't noticed we're gone."

"Yeah." Drew didn't know what to say or even think, looking at that sky. He was just glad to have Dean there, that someone had an idea to get them through this.

"Northern lights?" Lance scowled.

"Shut up, Lance," Drew said. "Let's get to my house, and we'll figure it out then."

None of them really accepted the explanation, but it was something. It was a life preserver to grasp onto as they floated in this place of unease and unknown sensations.

The tunnel had let them out on the side of a hill, and since they had to climb a hill to get to the fort in the first place, Dean suggested they head to the right, along its base. It made sense to the rest, so off they went.

It only took a few steps before Lance said, "The ground is moving, guys." His eyes darted around and settled on a boulder, which he leaped on top of.

He was right, but he wasn't. The sight shook Drew where he stood, but he didn't jump up there with Lance. Eric did, and Drew kneeled for a closer look.

At first, it appeared there was a purpose, like the grass was contracting together. But it wasn't that. Everything was shifting on its own but as a single environment. The soil rose and fell—not a lot, just enough to notice—as if a giant was sleeping below the surface and they were walking over its snoring chest. The leaves and vines on the forest floor waved back and forth, back and forth. They moved like they were in a trance.

"Drew, get up here!" Eric shouted.

"I'm not walking on that," Lance insisted.

"What is it? Why's the ground moving?"

"Come on, you guys." Dean shook his head. He looked tired. "Or just wait here. I'm going home—do what you want."

"The ground!" Eric pointed at the writhing vegetation.

"I see it. And I think there must have been a gas leak in that tunnel or something because it can't be real. And look—" he stomped on the trail, smashing vine and leaf. "—it's not doing anything. It doesn't care.

"Listen, you can stay here if you want and hide on a rock. I'm going home so I can forget this whole thing happened."

Dean started walking.

Lance and Eric looked at each other. They didn't speak, but Drew knew they were daring one another to see who would step down first. It was Eric who broke and got off, careful to place his foot only on the breathing dirt and not the other floor vegetation. He joined Drew, and finally, Lance dared to come down.

With all three back on the ground, they rushed to catch up with Dean. They only got about fifty feet before they found a shore. It was a welcome sight until Drew realized it was not their lake.

There were trees that met the water's edge, where the vines dove deep under the bluish-indigo surface. There was something that could have been a dock at some time, but not in the recent past. Pointed pillars rose out of the water like sharpened stakes, and though the water gently lapped the land like their own shore, this didn't seem to make a sound. And the color was off. It was like—everything, Drew noticed—the colors of the world were all over-saturated. Blues too blue. The green in the trees too green. The water's shimmer across the surface and onto the nearby trees was almost like a sparkle.

Bigger than the doubt of this not being their lake was the growing dread of knowing this wasn't their world.

"Dean?" Drew wasn't sure how to phrase it. "This—we don't live here."

"That can't be." Dean shook his head. "We're just on some other part of the lake. We need to keep going."

Everyone glanced at each other, none wanting to argue, all wanting to believe he was right but knowing he wasn't.

"Come on. We just have to follow the shore, and we'll find home." Dean pointed at Lance. "You have a phone, right? Pull up a map."

Lance smiled. He unlocked his phone, and that was when his smile ended. "Man. Mom's going to kill me for breaking another phone." He held it up for everyone to see. The screen was a scattered mess of rainbow lines and squiggles. "Must have been the fall."

They all deflated.

Dean started them to the right again, along the water's edge, and they walked in silence until the chanting started.

Chapter Twenty-Three

D EAN WASN'T SURE HOW HE ended up in charge of this little party. Other than being the oldest, he had nothing to do with the trip. All he did was follow the others because he was tired of being creeped out, staring out the window and imagining the dead. Why couldn't he get that out of his mind?

He would have given anything to have spent the night away from home like Maggie—especially if Janet was going to be there, alive, that is. But instead, he was in his room, unable to sleep, and Drew and his friends had to walk down the steps, sneaking about as loudly as an elephant at a construction site.

He should have said no. He should have let them go on their little expedition all by themselves. But no, he didn't want to be alone.

Serves me right.

He held out a hand and pushed back a branch as he followed the shoreline. He waited for Drew to grab it and continued on. Either

Lance or Eric shouted as the other released the branch into his face, and Dean chuckled to himself. And he wiped his hands on his pants.

He figured he was high. He figured there was something in that cave that made them see everything like this, a gas pocket or something. He had done mushrooms with his friends last summer and hated it, swore to himself he would never touch them again, and even those visuals didn't look like this. But this had to be a drug. It had to. Even still, he didn't like touching things here. The moving floor, the wiggling branches that looked slimy—the smell—all of it gave him the creeps, though he wouldn't tell that to the others.

He tried not to look into the water. It was too much like the water in his dream. He knew if he stared at it too long his high mind would pull things from that dream, and... he didn't want to think about that. Best to stay focused.

He stepped over rocks and twigs between trees and avoided getting too close to the muddy water's edge. He listened to Drew and the others. They marveled at the colored sky and water. They talked about the creeping vines on the ground. It made Dean wonder: how could they all be having the same hallucination? Seeing the same colors? Seeing the same strange objects move? No, there was a simple explanation. One saw it and said it, and the others then hallucinated the same thing. That had to be it.

The shoreline seemed endless. There was no land on the other side, unlike their house, and Dean had to wonder how far they could have strayed from home. He didn't think it was that far.

His foot caught on a boulder, and he tripped, stumbled, and righted himself just before face-planting in the mud. There were chuckles and congratulations, and then singing.

Why was there singing?

It was high-pitched, and Dean couldn't recognize any of the words. And it was above them, in the trees. It had to be the gas.

And then Drew had to ask, "What is that singing?"

How did Drew hear it too?

There was more singing from the trees in front of and behind them. It was all around them. It was eerie and hollow, and the tone seemed to drill into Dean's mind with images that made him close his eyes and shake his head—and it made no difference. They wouldn't leave.

He saw dead people. He saw singles and groups and armies. There was a man plunging a knife into another's neck, raking the blade around until the head dangled from one side. And the headless man dug his hands into the other's eyes and ripped his tongue from his body. A group ran at another with clubs, and each body in the fight wore pale skin and had clouded eyes. Each fighter took blows that would destroy a man, and they continued tearing into one another. An army of men missing eyes and ears and split in places that could never be healed marched on another, heaving swords and spears and poleaxes in the air. They rattled under armor and chain mail, and their voices were broken and scratchy.

"Stop it!" Dean howled at the trees.

"What is this?" Drew was covering his ears; they all were. Tears ran down Eric's face.

"Come on!" Dean shouted. He waited an extra second to be sure they all heard, then he started running along the shore.

His eyes were open, but the visions were still there. A hairless beast Dean could only have imagined ran at a man and tore into him with its tusks. The man stabbed the beast in the eyes, and they fought, rolling down a hill, goring and stabbing, losing organs and blood, and yet they continued.

The trees at the shore ended, and enormous boulders formed a line, blocking the land. Dean was forced into the water, but that should have been okay. If he was away from the trees, he hoped he would be away from the singing and the visions.

His feet submerged, first in inches of water, and then a foot. His shoes soaked it in. It ran up his legs as he splashed, and his pants acted like a sponge. But he kept along the rocky shore, and like he hoped, the singing faded.

Thank god! The singing faded!

Another thirty feet and the boulders ended. An open beach presented itself, and the singing continued to soften. The visions dropped away.

Dean rushed onto the beach and looked back. Drew, Lance, and

Eric joined him, and they all fell on the wide dirt swath.

"What the hell?" Lance shouted. He sat facing the water and covered his face.

"That was horrible," Eric whined.

Drew said nothing. He sat, staring at the water, out of breath.

The water on Dean's legs seemed to crawl up his body. His entire form felt wet. His gaze went to the lake, and everything changed.

The sky turned to night. The trees he could see over the boulders dropped their leaves. The water glowed in a blue-indigo radiance.

"What's happening?" Eric called.

Dean didn't respond. His gaze was still locked on the water, and what was happening there didn't make sense. He had thought they were drugged already, but it was like the water was making some other hallucination take hold. And this one gripped his heart in fear.

From the glowing depths, someone was walking out. Only it wasn't a someone; it was more of a thing. It was as big as a house, and its head had a misshapen skull. Dean imagined it was what a buffalo's skull would look like, only ten times the size. When its body rose above the surface and Dean could see the matted, hairy shoulders of its six legs, he screamed.

"Run!" was all Dean could say as he spun up onto his feet, grabbed Drew's wrist, and took off from the water's edge.

There was a strange sound from the water. At first, it was distant, the noise of several people rising from a bathtub at once, a kind of crashing and staticky sound. Then, a rumble filled the landscape, and, while Dean had never been to the ocean before, the thing that came next made him think of a tsunami as it crashed into an unsuspecting city and crushed building after building with a wall of relentless water.

"What is that?" Lance screamed. Dean didn't look back, but he was sure Lance was following. Eric just kept yelling "No!" like the more he said it the more the strange beast was likely to listen.

Fans of dirt flew from Dean's wet shoes. Drew stumbled but kept moving. They crossed the beach and weaved themselves through a boulder-filled meadow that felt like a maze, all the time Dean knowing it was slowing them down. He had to hope the large rocks would slow the beast down too.

A roar somewhere between a bear and an air raid siren made the earth shake. Dean thought his ears were probably bleeding.

He still didn't look. He dodged one giant rock and then another, dragging Drew through. For some reason, a memory of them trick or treating some years ago came to him, where he pulled Drew along from house to house and had to hold him back from stepping into traffic when they visited the buildings on Main St. The thought of Drew getting crumpled up under a car terrified him that night, both because it would have been his fault and because, back then, they were basically best friends—that made him wonder what had happened and why, and he wished it was different right now. How could they die, crushed by some massive monster while being the furthest apart they had ever been?

The ground shook under their feet as boulders crashed into one another, the thing behind them smashing and clearing the earth in its path. Chunks of rock from the size of pebbles to beach balls soared overhead and rained into their path.

Dean couldn't stop himself from screaming. He gripped Drew's hand so hard he thought he might break it, but he didn't care, not if it meant they both got out of this.

The rocky ground opened to a clearer meadow, and while it meant they could run without obstruction, Dean knew that the beast could as well when it got there. They needed a better plan than just running because with six legs it was going to win, and they were running out of breath.

Beyond the meadow, he saw more trees, and beyond that, mountains, only those were not the mountains that surrounded Lone Wolf. It made him finally accept that he was not just in some drug-induced state. He was in a real place that was alien and unknown, and as he spotted kaiju-sized skulls peeking from the mountains, overgrown in vegetation, he understood this was going to be the hardest, most dangerous thing he had ever faced. And he had to get his brother out of there.

"It's coming!" Lance screamed.

Dean dared a look back. The monster was only a row or two behind them in the field of boulders, and with its strength and speed—it swung one of its massive limbs, and Dean watched as claws the size of a man shattered rock. He saw holes in its massive pelt where dark gray flesh that looked dead poked through, and worms the size of snakes wriggled inside its meat.

He would have vomited if he wasn't running. He wanted to.

The trees were ahead, and maybe they could make it to those. Dean didn't want that singing back in his head, but it couldn't be as bad as what that beast would do if it caught up to them.

"Ow!" Eric shouted. "There's something in the grass!"

Dean was so focused on the monster behind them he hadn't even thought about looking down. There they were, scattered across the ground, small balls covered in thorns like cacti, but these were black with red spines. He dodged a group of them and pulled Drew left through the meadow, where he saw what he hoped was their salvation—at least for now.

Where the grass met the woods, there was a hole in the ground, a cave sloping down with a rock formation above it. The way the boulders lay reminded him of a Flintstone house like the shape ahead had been built rather than developed naturally (just like the fort, but he wasn't going to think about that at that moment).

"There!" Dean pointed with his free hand. "Everybody in!"

He sprinted harder than he ever had at his school's Track and Field Day, harder than he ever had to make it to home plate, all while dragging Drew along. He scurried into the hole as the noise behind him was no longer filled with smashing stone but a thrumming of tons of muscle and bone against soil.

The others climbed inside. They ran into the scattered array of boulders, sticks, and strangely crafted items until the dim light from the outside left them in shadows.

The roar came again. Dean pushed Drew back into the darkness and covered his ears. They were hot and wet, sore from the noise, and he knew they had to be bleeding.

"Go away!" Lance screamed.

The world shook around them. Rocks fell from the ceiling as the leviathan slammed its clawed feet onto the structure above. A loud cracking sound, and part of the Flintstone roof crashed inward, cutting the light even lower.

"Back!" Dean pushed them all deeper into the cave as enormous claws pushed into the opening and swept dank, putrid air across the space like a wave. The tip of a claw grazed Dean's arm, and he felt his shirt rip and his flesh shrink away as if it understood the alternative.

It swiped again and stomped over the roof. They backed even farther into the cave. The entrance crashed inward until holes barely large enough for a small animal remained, and light came through in tiny slices of blue.

They were covered in dust and drenched in fear. They huddled against a wet wall as the creature finally gave up and retreated toward the water. They trembled as a group, Dean still holding them back, the rest clung together until he realized a minute later what he was doing and let his arms drop.

"Is—is it over?" Drew asked. He was covering his mouth and his chest.

Dean crept back toward the front of the cave and peeked through the gaps between stones. He saw the monster sway as it walked and smelled the disgusting must the thing had left behind. This time he did puke, leaning forward, the sick landing between his feet.

He wiped his mouth. "It's gone."

"Eric!" Lance shouted.

Dean could barely see through the gloom, but he could tell Eric was shaking. He hurried back. Lance held a hand on Eric's shoulder as if he could hold him still and fix him.

"It's a seizure." Dean patted his butt pocket, but he had no wallet—he had heard you were supposed to put it in a seizing person's mouth for some reason. Instead, he grabbed a stick from the ground and shoved it sideways between Eric's teeth.

After a moment, the seizing stopped. That was when someone approached from the darkness, short and his facial skin torn. He was missing an eye.

Only Drew turned at the footsteps, but they all faced the kid when he spoke. "He'll die unless you get the antidote."

Chapter Twenty-Four

"WHAT THE HELL?" LANCE SCREAMED.

Lance was sure it was a kid, but the kid was dead and somehow standing in front of them and speaking. His skin was rotting and patchy and peeling from his face. There was a hole where there should have been an eye, and the other one was muddied white. His body was riddled with missing flesh and exposed bone, and still, he was standing there.

"What is that?" Lanced grabbed Eric, who continued to shake, and pulled him along the wall, away from what he could only comprehend as a zombie. "Get away!"

Drew backed up, screaming toward the collapsed entrance; Dean backed up as well, keeping himself between the thing and his brother.

"It's okay." The dead kid spoke with a wiry, gravelly voice. He held up a hand in protest, bones sticking through the tips of his fingers. "I won't hurt anyone."

"Stay back," Dean warned.

The zombie kid did. He took a step away, returning to his darkened place. "I was just trying to help." His tone was down, almost a whine.

They all took a moment. None of them moved beyond searching the room with their eyes for a way out of this.

Eric stopped shaking, but he didn't open his eyes or speak.

Finally, Dean said something. "What are you?"

"Me?" the dead kid answered.

"No, the other zombie!" Lance shouted.

"I'm not a zombie."

"Then what are you?" Dean's tone said he was calm, but Lance could tell from the way he stood that he was ready to pounce if the dead thing came any closer.

"I'm just a kid."

"But you're dead," Lance said. "Dead people don't talk."

"Yeah." The kid nodded. "That's the funny thing about this place. Here, they do."

Lance just shook his head.

"No," Dean cut in, "there were tons of those little skeletons back in that other cave. They weren't alive."

"You mean the Zeetee burial cave? You came through there too? You're from Earth then! Like me!"

Lance didn't know what stole the words from him more, the fact that this kid said he was from Earth, the fact that he was implying they weren't on Earth anymore, or that the tiny skeletons in that cave were from a real people.

"Zee-tee?" Drew asked.

"Yeah, they're like little pixie people that—"

"Wait," Dean interrupted. "You came through here the same way? Through the hole in that rock formation?"

"My fort, yeah. He dragged me down. I think they were mad I was disturbing their burial mound."

"No." Drew shook his head.

Dean raised a hand for this all to slow down. "You're... Bobby?"

Lance sat against the wall, just thinking.

They had set Eric on the ground to rest, sliding Lance's folded coat under his head for a pillow.

Lance wished he could rest too. He knew he was tired, but it was all too much to take in, too much stuff screaming in his brain for him to settle.

It was Bobby. The weird zombie kid was somehow Dean and Drew's missing uncle. He was there. He was dead. And he was still alive somehow. All Lance could do was sit and watch as they caught up with twenty-five years' worth of family drama and tried to clarify what the hell this place was. That was the part Lance was interested in.

"So dead isn't dead here?" Dean asked.

"Well, it's not living, but it doesn't mean you fall over and stay still. Not until you rot so much that your pieces don't work."

Drew sat with his mouth wide open.

"And it's an alien world?" Dean went on quizzing him.

"I don't know about alien. I think it's a realm—like another dimension. If I was to guess, I'd call it something like Valhalla for the Vikings, or a Purgatory, maybe? I've only seen dead things here other than us—well, you guys, now. But they keep coming. Then they rot until there's nothing left."

"Purgatory? But not from Earth—so, like an alien planet's Purgatory."

"I don't know. I'm just guessing from what I've seen."

"That monster in the water..." Drew finally spoke.

"Oh, he's bad, but he's not the worst thing in that lake." Bobby glanced over at Eric. "But we really should get your friend that antidote. He'll die if we don't."

"Die... like you?" Drew said.

"Yeah. Like me."

Drew and Dean glanced at each other. Lance imagined them conferring telepathically, asking, *Can we trusty this zombie?* They must have decided they could, because they both rose, and Dean said, "How do we cure him?"

"We have to find a mushroom." Bobby pointed into the darkness. "I've seen it on the other side of one of the tunnels. Hopefully it's the right time of day for them to grow."

"Lead the way," Dean said. He looked at Eric and then Lance. "You going to stay here and watch him?"

Lance nodded. "I'll stay with him."

"This way." Bobby started into the darkness.

Drew turned on his flashlight. "Just to be clear, you don't have any urges to eat human flesh?"

Bobby let out a soft chuckle. "I wish I could eat anything. My stomach doesn't work. I guess it's 'cause we aren't supposed to be here—those other things can eat you. But you know what I would give to eat a cheeseburger again?"

Lance didn't know why, but he found that one statement incredibly sad. He sighed and stared at the pinpricks of light coming through the collapsed entrance, hoping to God he hadn't eaten his last cheeseburger, as well.

It reminded him of the beginning of the summer, going to Gino's with Eric and Drew before summer vacation really got into full swing. Gino's was their favorite burger place in town, despite the fact that his mom, and Drew's as well, hated it.

"There's nothing of nutritional value there at all," Mom would say, but when she was at work and he was allowed to roam downtown until she got off, he was free to eat whatever he wanted.

The air was sharp and warm, the perfect summer morning, when Drew met him at the library at eleven. The summer fire season hadn't started yet, and there was just enough heat to make the day enjoyable without frying you as you walked from place to place.

"Is this great or what?" Drew said. "Three whole months without school."

They sat under the shade of a tree beside the library entrance and watched the cars pass on Broadway.

"Three months without homework," Lance corrected.

"Three months without Judy Coon farting in the seat in front of me." Drew pinched his nose.

"Three months without Mrs. Halladay's cat-piss breath." Lance waved his hand in front of his mouth.

"Three months without Principal Samuels's poop stink when she greets you every morning."

"I heard she has a bag attached to her hip that holds all of her poop."

"Gross! Why would she want to keep it in a bag?"

"Detention."

"No!"

They burst into laughter, and Eric's mom's van stopped on the street, letting Eric out. He walked to the driver's door, and they talked for a moment. Eric pointed at Lance and Drew and rolled his eyes. Finally, he backed away from the car and yelled, "Bye!"

Eric's mom was a lot like him, a nice and generally happy lady, but she had a worry streak as long as Broadway itself. When they invented those smartwatches that let parents track their kids, she was the first person in town to buy one, and he was forced to wear it until he got teased so badly by Billy Martin and the rest of the seventh-grade class that he told his mom he would never go to school again if he had to wear it. She finally relented, but Eric always warned Lance and Drew that he had to keep in touch with her, because if he screwed up, he would have to wear it again.

In the end, she got what she wanted—she always knew where he was, and she didn't need an app.

Eric joined them in the shade, and they made a rough plan for the day. They would hit Polly's, the candy store themed after Mr. Reed's long-dead parrot, then the toy store and the weird hippie game store on the way to Gino's Burgers for lunch.

It was a similar plan to what they had done a dozen times that year, but now it was summer. It was warm, and the day was theirs. They could goof off and keep their eyes open for girls. They could take their time and know that responsibility was three months away. They were free that day, with nothing holding them back except themselves.

They each felt it, though none of them said it or even knew how to articulate it. Summer was now, and now was forever.

At Polly's, Drew got a three-foot-tall Pixie Stick, and Lance bought three rock-candy sticks. Eric bought a pound of fudge for some reason, and until they made it to Gino's, the jokes didn't stop about how much Eric loved hot fudge on a summer day, and how when he was older he would keep it in a bag on his side like Principal Samuels.

They each bought a quarter-pound cheeseburger at Gino's; The Brooklyn, Gino called it. Each of his burgers was named after some place back east, though most of Lone Wolf's residents didn't think Gino had ever been all the way to the coast. He did put on a Brooklyn accent every now and then when he walked the burgers from the kitchen and called out order numbers. Lance thought that was just so cool, the way he could turn it on and off.

But what happened that day that made it particularly memorable was still to come. It was what happened after lunch (combined with the cheeseburger) that brought that specific day to mind.

"Come on, let me have some fudge," Lance insisted as they walked back out into the sun.

"You don't want it," Eric said. "You're just ragging on me."

"No, I do, I do." Lance fought hard against his temptation to laugh. He was surprisingly good at keeping a straight face.

"Fine," Eric said, "but I don't want to hear it." He opened his bag from Polly's and unwrapped the wax paper. It peeled back with a slurp, and melted chocolate clung to the wrapping and nearly dripped with brown sludge.

"Ew!" all three of them yelled.

Eric grinned.

"Don't even think about it!" Lance screamed.

Eric gripped the fudge and held it up to Lance's face. Lance backed up, and Eric moved forward. Drew backed up, and Eric aimed the chocolate at him.

"Eric!" Drew warned.

Eric took a step closer, and Lance sped off. Drew was right behind him.

Eric chased them both, fudge pointed ahead. "Come get it! You want my fudge, don't you!"

They ran for half a block, and Lance turned right between the walk-up Chinese place and downtown's mini amphitheater. Drew and then Eric followed. They screamed as they entered the alley.

Blood seemed like it was everywhere. Organs lay across the ground, and something was tied up at eye level, split open and headless. The blade came down, slicing into the body, and the skin peeled back.

It took a second of staring, all three boys clumped together and the fudge slipping from Eric's hand to a splat on the ground, before Lance saw the head in the back of the pickup. It was a deer, or it had been, anyway. The side of its face was crushed, and meat and bone and a black eyeball hung in a clump from the side of its skull. It grinned with bloody teeth and a half-crushed jaw. Blood dripped from the truck bed in a pat, pat, pat, and for a while, that was all Lance could hear. Not the yell from Mr. Polson to get the hell out there. That one solid black eye, that one crushed eye, they both seemed to stare through him. They had something to say, but he couldn't understand what it was. Something from the other side of death that it wanted to tell him, and he wasn't grasping it.

It took Drew yanking on his shoulder and turning him away before he realized what was happening.

The rest of that afternoon was a soft blur behind Lance's vision of that roadkill deer being butchered. He ate his rock candy, and it was tasteless. They ran and played in the streets of downtown, got yelled at by the security at the walking mall, and spent more time in the game store and the toy store, but none of it was really real to him. It was like the day had been put on mute, but it wasn't until he was getting ready for bed that he understood why.

Lance yawned as he walked into his bathroom. He wasn't physically tired, but the day had been a mental drain. He was brushing his teeth, looking in the mirror, and his face became its face—the deer's face. His teeth were mangled and bloody, and his lower jaw was crushed and hanging from his cheek. His eyes were mashed into his head, and his skin and muscle were squished into bone fragments and clumped against a depression in the side of his skull.

He saw into his full, black eyes. He saw blood running down his bathroom walls and over his pristine white sink. He saw the woods with barren trees and a dark, blue sky. He saw arms of decay swinging and his own flesh turning gray and blotchy and dripping from his skull.

He was dead. He was somewhere he shouldn't have been, and he was dead and rotting.

He wanted to scream, but he couldn't breathe. And his eyes were not done showing him. He saw rotting things in the water and things of bone that moved and chased after him. There were creatures of fur and fang that cracked open and showed him their insides. He saw an army of giants with broken skin and mouths large enough to swallow him whole. And he saw Dad.

It was after he had first seen Dad in the house, after he had come to realize the haunting would be back from time to time, sometimes for the good and sometimes for the so, so worse. It had been a flip of the coin each time, whether he was going to get the feeling of a pat on the back and the pleasant smell of Dad's aftershave or the anger of a forgotten chore and the aroma of way too much Bacardi. But those darker moments were never purely Dad. They were like someone had taken his rage and amplified it, like there was someone else there, stabbing Dad and using that pain to drive him. And this time, he thought he saw that someone.

It was behind Dad's rotting face. Lance didn't know if Dad really looked like that after so many months in the ground, but he assumed so. As soon as he saw the rot, he knew which Dad he was going to get. Only this time, the shadowy haze around Lance's father was darker, and behind the image, Lance could make out the slimy, decaying skull within that black fog. It was hiding, smoke-like shadows swirling in front of it, but he saw the cheekbones, the gooey lidless eyes inside its sockets, and the deep, blood-red shine over it all. There was a shriek as it noticed Lance's gaze on it instead of his father. It jerked away, and Dad lunged forward, screaming.

Lance screamed back. What else could he have done but howl and fall backward, nearly landing in the tub. He scrambled across the floor, planting his back against the door.

When he dared to look up again, Dad was gone—it all was. All that remained was his toothbrush on the edge of the sink and the water running full blast.

Lance glanced down at Eric, on the cave floor next to him, and wondered—(*Purgatory*)—was Dad here? Was he wandering around in this horrible land with his flesh rotting from his bones like that kid Bobby? Was The Shadow Man?

Chapter Twenty-Five

DREW AND DEAN WATCHED BOBBY lead the way. There was a limp in their dead uncle's stride, but for a walking corpse, he was surprisingly nimble. What Drew couldn't overlook were the noises he made, or the smell—one of creaking yet slurping and slippery, one of rotting and decomposition, which further enforced the death all around them and the tickling chill up his spine. There was as little doubt that Bobby was dead as there was that he was still alive, and after only knowing zombies as bloodthirsty, brain-eating simpletons, accepting Bobby as a sentient, helpful individual was taking its time to solidify.

Drew guided his light around the cave, watching his step, but he couldn't help himself from studying the holes in Bobby's clothes where gray skin and wounds showed. He couldn't not notice the gaps in Bobby's hair where exposed bone shone through, despite not wanting to be rude for staring. But it wasn't every day that you came across a... a what? What would he even call what Bobby was? He wasn't a zombie or a ghoul. He wasn't a monster at all, just a kid whose body refused to die. He settled on *undead.*

The passage veered left, and they had to climb over a series of boulders and under a group of stalactites. Seeing the next section made Drew's mouth drop open. The wall was covered in clump after clump of strange, glowing, orange mushrooms. Their caps were thick yet pointed upward, and Drew was sure these must have been the antidote mushroom they were after, but Bobby walked right past them without slowing.

"What about these?" Dean asked.

Bobby glanced quickly but kept his pace. "Those? Those are poisonous. Definitely don't eat those."

There was a moment of silence where Drew thought about asking how he knew, then he remembered he was talking to a dead kid. Instead, the conversation turned to the past, the family, and his stay in this horrible place.

It wasn't comfortable, but they filled Bobby in on the last twenty-five years, his father leaving, and the death of his mother. They told him they were living in his house now and found his crawlspace and the skull—the Zeetee skull.

"Oh," Bobby said. "That's why you're here, I bet."

"What do you mean?" Dean asked. "We fell down a hole when the floor collapsed."

"You mean when the realms converged."

Drew and Dean looked at each other.

"The floor of that room was removed when the realms converged. When the convergence ended, the stone was restored. I guess you didn't wait around in there very long. The joining of worlds only lasts twenty minutes or so. Until it comes again."

"So we have to go back the way we came?" Dean said.

"Or sneak through one of the other convergence points."

"Why did you never come back?" The cave ceiling lowered, and Drew had to duck to avoid hitting his head.

"Once I figured it out, I was dead." Bobby led them right where the cave forked. "I think if you go through dead, you'll just be dead on the other side, not like I am now. I was afraid."

Drew hated to think what his choice would have been if he was in Bobby's shoes. How do you choose between being undead and just plain dead? He might have made the same decision.

"So, if we don't get Eric the cure..." Dean trailed off.

"He'd be like me." Bobby turned and smiled. Drew could tell he was trying to lighten the mood, but the rot in his teeth and the gashes in his lips showing gums and bone prevented it from being funny. "But you guys don't want to go back the way you came—the Zeetee are too dangerous."

"But you know another convergence point?" Dean asked.

"I think so." Bobby held his hand up to his face as the light inside the tunnel brightened up ahead. The exit. "This way." He went to the edge of the passage and kneeled, staring out. Drew and Dean kneeled behind him.

"What is it?" Drew whispered.

"Just making sure." Bobby stood and walked out into what looked like a valley floor made of black hunks of glass. The shards crackled under his steps as he walked left, and shiny strobes of light burst from under his disintegrating shoes.

"Making sure of what?" Drew followed him out and scanned the valley, looking for more six-legged monsters. He didn't see any. What he saw were dozens, maybe hundreds, of mounds made of the black glass-like rock. Behind him, the cave he was emerging from exited through one. Were all those mounds different caves?

In the distance to the right, he saw firelight illuminating an area. "What's over there?"

Bobby stopped and looked and shook his head. "You don't want to go over there unless you have to. It's bad. Trust me."

Drew nodded, and they all walked left toward a row of trees that bordered the desert. As they neared, Bobby held a finger to his lips. The bone-tipped digit and the torn skin around it made Drew's stomach clench.

They walked slowly through the barren trees to a cliff, where Bobby held up his hands, gesturing for the brothers to wait. Then, he descended down a narrow path.

Another cliff lay across from theirs, and Drew could hear water rushing. It was a river. The mushroom they needed must have been on its banks. He told himself he had to see it. What if he needed some of those mushrooms later for some reason?

He inched toward the edge, and Dean tapped his shoulder. He shook his head *No*.

Drew waved him off and held up a single finger. He just wanted a quick look; it wasn't like he was going down there after Bobby.

He saw the far shore and the river, rushing with faintly glowing, bluish-purple water. It crashed on rocks and roared downstream. As he moved closer, his side of the riverbank revealed what looked like white logs at first. They were piled and layered, intertwined, big and small, straight and curved, with sharp ends and ends that looked like—

Drew had to step back as his eyes settled on what he first thought was a large white boulder. It was not a rock. There were eye sockets and a nasal cavity. As his gaze went down, there were broken teeth and, as he looked closer, white, rotting tendons stretched across the joints and... It was a person. A giant person.

The skulls in the mountains registered in his mind. For some reason, even after seeing those, they didn't seem like they were real, just geological elements that looked like enormous human remains. While this wasn't nearly as big as those, it was easily five times the size of a normal person, if not larger. As Drew looked down, he saw it was attached to a body, and it was not the only one.

Yes, those were bones, not tree limbs, and while there were plenty of scattered remains, there were also full skeletons. There were bones he could easily identify now as arm or leg or hip or rib, but there were also whole sections of giants: rib cages attached to arms, heads and necks still clinging to their chests, and even entire bodies that had lost their skin and most of their muscle to time and preda-tion. They were broken and gashed and chipped. Faces with holes, shattered craters in ribs. And there were so many of them. Like an entire army. This was the remains of a battlefield of monumental proportion, and something told Drew it was related to that desert of black glass.

Drew leaned farther forward until he could see Bobby going down the side of the cliff. It was a tight path down to where the bones lay, and all Drew could think was that his uncle's brain had rotted. Those things looked dead, but their sheer size made them even creepier than Bobby. How could he go down there?

Then he spotted it.

Three corpses in, growing in what must have been the last bit of decaying ocular tissue, was a small patch of blue mushrooms. They were growing in its eye! And Eric was supposed to eat that?

If this worked, Drew knew he wouldn't be telling Eric where they got it until they were safely at home. As much of a positive guy as his friend was, Eric was not one to eat daringly. They had to threaten to expose his crush on Cynthia Nixon just to get him to try pineapple pizza—and he loved pineapple.

"What do you see?" Dean whispered.

Drew couldn't answer. His eyes were glued to Bobby as he reached the bottom and tiptoed over legs and arms and navigated through the massive piles of white. Drew wondered if Bobby had done this before, and it occurred to him that even though Bobby looked like a dead kid, he had been here for twenty-five years. He was actually in his thirties and probably knew this place better than Drew knew Lone Wolf.

Drew sensed Dean creeping next to him, and he turned. His brother's mouth hung wide, and he recoiled at the sight below.

"Those are..." Dean didn't finish.

Bobby reached the target skeleton and crept toward the head. Drew's chest tightened. There was something about Bobby's cautiousness that made his stomach rise. It dawned on him that Bobby wasn't being so mindful because he was creeped out or because it was gross. He hadn't warned Drew and Dean back for no reason. There was danger here, like so much of this world.

Are these things sleeping?

"What's he doing?" Dean whispered.

Drew pointed at the mushrooms with an unsteady hand. Dean scanned in the direction of his finger and squinted for a moment, then nodded in recognition.

Bobby made it to the head and reached over the enormous face. Apprehension burned inside Drew's chest, but at the same time that Bobby's hand clasped a mushroom, Drew had a vision of relief. Drew imagined Eric rising and Bobby leading them to a way home. He felt like after this they would be on the right path, and this nightmare field trip could be over.

Bobby transferred the mushroom from one hand to the other and reached for more. To Drew, the sequence was in slow motion. Bobby's hand hovered over a lower jaw with chipped teeth and an upper jaw that was broken between where the giant's lip and nose would have been. It looked like a King Kong-sized ax had bashed in the center of its face. Bobby reached over bands of light-gray tendons that stretched across the cheekbone, over the ocular cavity where the deflated eyeball fed the bed of fungi. He was about to grasp another mushroom when the worst thing imaginable happened: it moved.

"No," Drew whispered. His hand flew to his brother's arm. He knew he should pull back, get the hell away, but something made him stand still. There was a curious internal force that wanted to watch whatever was about to happen, even if it meant his own doom.

The giant's jaw snapped shut with a deafening clack. Its head shifted, and Bobby fell backward onto the bone floor. The head rose and turned, and it faced Drew and Dean as if its missing eyes saw just as clearly as any other being.

The giant's hand crashed against the ground and started pushing itself up, and Bobby rolled away, trying to stand. He locked eyes with Drew, and he screamed in his weak dead voice, "Run!"

Bones and beings across the white shore rattled and sat up. The mushroom-eyed giant reached its full height, and one of them— Drew wasn't sure which—released a roar so loud that Drew vibrated in its wake.

Dean grabbed his brother around the waist and lifted him. He said something that only came to Drew as muffled sounds, like speaking through a dozen pillows. Dean carried Drew toward the trees, and Drew looked back at the monstrous death behind them.

The giant was taller than the cliff. His head and chest rose over the embankment like an average-sized person standing against a railing.

Drew would have expected a thing like that to be slow, some lumbering thing that moved at a fraction of his speed. It wasn't. The thing never lost its lock on him, even as Dean hoisted him up and retreated, and in less time than it took for Dean to move a single pace, the giant had its hands on the cliff. Dean swung his leg in stride, and the monster of a man was climbing up onto the cliff, its mouth drooping open, ready to chomp on a meal it couldn't even digest.

More of those ear-shattering roars rose from the river, and while he would have thought he would have been worried about Bobby right at that moment—he was a flea at the feet of nightmare gods— the fact was, he couldn't even imagine what was happening down there. He saw the teeth as large as his arm, the hands scrabbling as the beast launched itself toward Dean and him, and all Drew could think of was what an eternity in that thing's decomposing gullet would be like. If it bit off his head and swallowed it, would he suffer as a suspended head with no means of movement, let alone escape, until he rotted enough to no longer be able to think? Would that be his torturous fate?

But Dean was moving. He felt Dean dip and stride, pulling them both away from the edge, just not away from the monster. The monster was gaining. The monster was twenty feet from being able to reach them, and as Drew thought this was probably it and their fates were sealed, three more heads rose. Three more giant, nearly decomposed bodies rose and secured their gazes on them. And as fast as the first, they leaped onto the cliff edge, climbing, launching themselves toward the brothers.

"Dean!" Drew called. "Dead! More of them!"

Dean shifted, dragging Drew in one arm and racing into the trees. The giant was even closer, maybe two breaths away, and he knew that as strong as Dean was, he couldn't save them alone. He burst from Dean's arms, and they raced at each other's sides.

They crossed the first set of trees. The ground was uneven here, with black roots that seemed to be rejecting the soil. Drew hadn't seen this on their way to the river, and if he had had more time, he would have pondered if they were even like that when he was going the other way. But right now, those roots were like hooks, ready to grab a foot as they passed over. They may have even been moving.

"Go!" Dean screamed as they met the second row of trees.

Drew could see past the next row and into the long, empty black glass beyond. He wondered what would happen out there once there were no barriers to slow the giants. Maybe they could make it to their tunnel, but the way it was gaining on him, he doubted it. The glass desert was where they would die.

The ground shook beneath them, and another wave of roars made their ears ring. The trees crashed and cracked with snapping sounds that could have been heard for miles. Hot air rushed past Drew, a strange sensation after the cold dampness of this world, and all he could think was the giant was about to eat him. It was the monster's breath as it leaned forward to sink its teeth into Drew's back, to nibble off his legs like Dad slurped the meat off a chicken wing.

He didn't feel his legs anymore. He realized that as he forced his body forward, they were these imaginary things below his waist that he had to pilot with only hope that they would listen and faith that they could comply.

Drew and Dean crossed the final group of trees together. There was a sting on the back of Drew's leg, and he thought maybe the roots had whipped him—but that couldn't be.

"Dean!" Drew called to his brother. "What do we do?"

The black glass crunched under their feet, and the trees cracked and snapped behind them. The firelight in the distance seemed so safe from here, yet so far away. Drew wanted to be there. He wanted to sit next to that fire and feel warm and relaxed. He didn't want to run anymore or be chased or smell the death in the air that had clawed at their nostrils since the fall. But they were doomed, weren't they?

"Wait," Dean said. The booming had stopped. The cracking of trees was no longer behind them.

Drew hadn't thought to look back. He only knew safety was ahead. He looked.

Four skeletons were turning away.

"Are—" Drew looked down, panting, remembering the feeling, the strange vision that this black glass was the result of what killed them. "They're afraid to come here."

Dean dropped his hands to his knees and leaned forward, panting. "Why would they be afraid."

Drew saw a great explosion. It reminded him of an atomic bomb, but he didn't think that was it. "Something happened here. I don't know." He wanted to sit and rest, but the ground looked like it would rip his skin to shreds if he touched it. He mirrored his brother to catch his breath.

They watched the trees for a while after the great beasts sank over the cliff, back to their resting places.

Then Bobby emerged. He limped onto the glass. He was missing one foot and walked on his stump. He limped past a shadow that seemed to be watching them, and then it was gone.

Drew had to shake his head to be sure it wasn't there. He couldn't be sure of anything in this weird place.

Bobby came near with frustration in his gaze. In one hand, he carried his foot. In the other, Drew could see a blue mushroom.

Chapter Twenty-Six

ERIC FELT HIMSELF TWITCH, BUT it was one of those feelings you get when sleep almost has you. He was in his bed at his dad's—or, he thought he was. The room was dark, and it smelled like garbage, and he thought he saw Lance there, and then... he was back at Dad's.

He had just gotten there. The summer was young, and Dad hadn't been too drunk over the first few days. That meant they were already off to a better start than last year when Dad got a DUI on the way home from the airport.

There was chatter downstairs—Andrea. She was making that dolphin sound she pretended was a laugh, the kind of noise that disrupted bats' radars, forcing them to keep clear of the county. Eric had really grown to hate that sound.

It wasn't the noise itself; it was more what that noise had come to represent.

He first heard it when he came to visit Dad on Easter. They were a new couple then; even so, she was already shacked up in Dad's bed and hanging on his every movement like a blonde-haired parasite. Eric was never one to judge a book by its cover, though, so he decided he would look past the dyed hair, the fake boobs, the mounds of makeup, and the clothes that tried to say she was eighteen while obviously being in her thirties. All that would have been okay if she was nice, nice to Dad and nice to him. But the laugh, even though he tried to ignore it, pierced through some sensitive layer in his brain that he didn't know existed. She did it when laughing, of course, but it also seemed to pop up when she was embarrassed or nervous or didn't understand what was going on—and when she was with Eric and his dad, that happened a lot.

Eric and Dad had their own way. They were smart-asses. They were sarcastic. They had a shorthand way of speaking that referenced comedies of the '60s, '70s, and '80s, which used to play on repeat on the television and both of them could recite line by line. Movies like *A Shot in the Dark*, *The Pink Panther Strikes Again*, *Police Squad*, and *Airplane!* created a slang between them that when everything else was falling apart through the divorce, when life seemed to be ending, gave Eric a sense that it would be okay, that his dad was still Dad, and whatever else happened, they'd get through it—even if they now lived in different states.

The trouble with Andrea started when Eric said, "Surely, you can't be serious," after Dad told him they had his favorite cookie-dough ice cream for Easter dessert, and Dad replied, "We do, and don't call me Shirley." Her expression was that of confusion. Seeing the smiles on their faces, she made the sound. It wasn't a real laugh because she didn't understand at all, but she wanted in. Not just in on the joke. What she wanted was to be between them. Because to her, there couldn't be something between them that she wasn't a part of.

Dad, seeing her confusion, vowed to play *Airplane!* that night. While Eric and Dad laughed, she surfed on her phone, then brought him drink after drink until the movie was over, and her wandering hands persuaded him to send Eric to bed so they could have their alone time. That was the last time she allowed a movie made before

1999 to play in the living room.

But now, that sound was resonating through the vents, ringing inside the metal like someone had given a toddler a tuning fork and they were bashing it right beside Eric's ear for fun. It made his head throb, and when he closed his eyes tight, he was back in that cave with Lance. He rubbed his temples and moaned.

Why did she have to make that sound?

He sat up in his bed and pulled off his covers. If he was going to be awake, he might as well go down and eat.

The smell in the air was part bacon and part not. Andrea had converted Dad to the mostly turkey stuff, and Dad had promised they would get some real bacon the next time they went to the store. When they went, Eric saw Dad put it into the cart, but by the time they got home, it had mysteriously disappeared. Either way, Eric was happy that he had another summer day to spend with his dad, and on the way down, he wondered what would be on the agenda. Fishing? Kayaking? Exploring on his dad's property and adding on to the tree fort they had started last summer?

At the table, he found his father with a drink he first thought was tomato juice until he smelled the liquor as he hugged Dad good morning. He didn't say anything, but it was jarring. Dad had always been a drinker, even to excess here and there (as the DUIs had proven), but this visit, it seemed to have been kicked into overdrive. Another clue emerged as to why when Andrea sat next to him wearing an untied robe, with her breasts nearly falling out, and a fizzing mimosa in her grip.

Eric picked up a piece of toast from the plate in the center of the table, avoiding the turkey bacon, and sliced a sliver of butter to spread. "What are we doing today, Dad? I was thinking maybe the tree fort could use a deck—we could even use it as a deer stand when I come back for Thanksgiving."

Dad tilted his head, considering. "That's not a bad idea, Sport." He sipped his drink. "Maybe—"

"Baby," Andrea's voice was half singing and half whining, "you said you'd take me into the city this weekend. I have to have a new dress for the Dickinsons' party next week."

She smiled as she glanced at Eric, and though her lips were bright, what he saw was something else. It was another image hovering behind her face, a skull with rotting muscles and glistening eyes, blood dripping down its front and hanging from its teeth. He saw a shadow suspended in the air behind her as if it was frozen before it could reach the floor.

Gooseflesh rose over Eric's arms as he watched that skull grin behind her, and Dad said, "Yes, I did say that." He patted Eric on the shoulder. "Why don't you stay here and plan it out, and we'll get started on it tomorrow."

Eric would do that. He would spend the entire afternoon drawing out the plans and measuring the fort and agonizing over each detail, but by the end of the summer, not a single new board would get placed.

There was a flicker over the breakfast table, and Eric was back in the cave, Lance beside him. It was cold there, and Eric wished for the warm summer to return. To be back at Dad's, even if he did have to deal with Andrea.

"It's gonna be all right," Lance said. "They'll be back soon."

When Dad and Andrea came home, it was dark outside. Andrea dropped a bag of cold fast food on the kitchen table as she helped Eric's drunken father into their bedroom. There was a look in her eyes as she glanced at Eric and said, "Here's your dinner, boy; don't bother us." The look said *See, he's mine.* He could see the bones behind her face, the shadow lingering around her frame, hiding.

Eric fingered through the bag: cold nuggets, no sauce, and old, hard fries. He tossed it into the trash, made himself a bowl of cereal, and sat in front of the television. He watched *Spaceballs* on one of Dad's old DVDs and tried to laugh. It wasn't funny this time, even when Lone Star dropped the giant statue on Barf's foot. Even when they made laser swords and insinuated they were dicks.

He didn't think he had ever not laughed at that.

He was trying to ignore the hurt in his gut, the sour shiver in his nerves at the fact that his dad had ignored him all day long and then gotten drunk and went to his room with *her.*

He didn't want to be mad at his dad. If truth be told, he was the one always making excuses for his father. When he didn't send the child support Mom really needed. When he didn't call or send a card on Eric's birthday. And now, when Eric got to spend the few weeks a year he was able to—the time they were supposed to have together—instead, he was left alone all day long, and he still wanted to make an excuse for Dad. He had already planned the trip into town, or it was all her fault. But inside, down where those feelings were rooted like concrete in his heart, he didn't believe it. And his heart ached.

The fact that Dad was letting *her* come between them made it hurt even more.

As Princess Vespa and Lone Star stood at the altar declaring their love, Eric hit the power button. The room fell from blue illumination into blackness, and he immediately felt cold. The warm summer air was sucked from the room, and a frigid, humid breeze blew over him. It smelled of rot, and he wondered where that scent kept coming from.

He stood feeling for the coffee table and the couch to guide him to the hallway and back to his summer room, but neither were there. His hands fell through the darkness as if he was standing in an empty space.

"Come on!" Lance's voice echoed in what sounded like a tunnel. "He's getting worse."

But Eric couldn't see his friend.

He walked forward, arms out. He would find the hallway one way or another, and then he could guide himself.

He dragged his feet as he walked. They were strangely heavy. And then they were wet, like he was walking through water. Then it was his knees. The hallway wall was no closer, but he was wet all over his legs. Cold and wet. Tired and cold and wet.

"Dad?" he called out. He didn't expect an answer; Dad was practically passed out as they stumbled through the living room earlier, but he didn't know what else to do.

Tired and cold and wet *and afraid.*

"Dad?" His face was wet now. It wasn't from whatever was on the floor. It was from tears. His chest pounded, his breath sped up, and he knew this was not his dad's house, and he knew this was danger, all of it—and Dad chose *her* over him.

There was a creak, a door opening, and light shone into the void, illuminating nothing. Her head leaned out. Her eyes, cold, lidless eyes surrounded in bone, shrouded in shadow, locked onto him.

"He's mine." She said it this time.

She came through the door and closed it behind her. She disappeared into the darkness, but she was there.

He could feel the water chilling below him, rising below him, her cold, rancid breath nearing.

"He's mine, and so are you." She was a disembodied voice, but she had power. That voice seemed to reach inside his chest, the shadow slipping through the darkness, and it gripped his heart. It held it tightly, and he felt pressure on all sides. His chest was full of shadow, and he was getting dizzy as its grip slowed his pulse.

"Dad..." His words were a whisper.

"Help him!" Lance screamed.

"Help," Eric breathed without tone. His heart jerked within the shadow's grasp, and sharp, stabbing pains shot from his chest through his arms and legs.

Throughout the years, whenever Eric thought about death, he never thought about the pain. Maybe it was because the few people he knew that had died, like Grandma and Aunt Simone, had gone in their sleep or in a hospital bed. He always thought it was just like falling asleep and then you would wake up in heaven. What he felt was not that.

There was lightning through his chest and limbs, a bright, burning pain that seized his skull and made his brain wish it was being fried—that would have hurt less. There was fear and anger and seeping mountains of sorrowful regret. There was mourning for everything he had missed and would miss because it was over. Maybe worst of all was the knife of betrayal that burned from his gut to the center of his chest, with his father at the handle.

Then he opened his eyes.

Chapter Twenty-Seven

DREW HEARD LANCE SCREAMING BEFORE he could see him. He didn't think he had ever heard Lance sound so terrified. It was bad.

He was following Dean as they raced through the tunnel, Bobby behind them, but when they heard Lance scream, it turned into a run. Drew took three steps before realizing there was no way Bobby could run, and he went back.

"Take these," Bobby said, placing the blue fungi into Drew's hand. "He needs to swallow them all."

There was a doubtful drop in Bobby's stare, and Drew knew then what it meant. Bobby didn't think Eric would make it. But Drew couldn't think that way. As one friend screamed and the other lay dying, he couldn't do anything but hurry. He had to have hope, and he clenched his fists and forced his legs to move.

"Guys!" Lance yelled. His voice was a siren. It pierced through

Drew's heart like a spear and drove him faster through the gloom, around the turn, under the lower-hanging stalactites, between the walls of the thinning passage, and out the other side.

Eric's head was in Lance's lap. Lance looked hopelessly down as Eric breathed short, rattling breaths. Dean stood over them, waving Drew over like a third base coach sending a runner into home.

Drew sprinted there and dropped to his knees. He froze in place as he looked down at his friend.

Eric's face was pale. Drew could see that even in the dim light. Tiny purple lines traced the curves around his eyes and stretched outward, poisoned capillaries, miniscule veins crying for aid. He was cold but sweating, shiny, yet his lips were dry and cracking.

The sight made Drew want to retch. His poor friend, the sickness, the loss he felt was coming no matter how hard he wanted to deny it.

"You got it?" Dean asked.

Drew had drawn a blank. Got what? What was he supposed to do? There was no way this depended on him.

"Drew!" Dean shouted.

His job clicked. *He needs to swallow them all,* echoed in his mind. He looked in his hand. Three tiny blue caps. These were all that stood between life and death. It was silly to think that something as trifling as these tiny things could save a life.

He closed his hands over one another and rubbed the mushrooms between his palms. He felt them roll and tear into smaller pieces. He held them over Eric.

"Open his mouth," Drew told Lance. Lance pulled Eric's bottom jaw down, and Drew dropped the ripped hunks of mushroom inside. "He needs to swallow."

Lance stared at Drew, and Drew stared back.

Lance's face was wrinkled with worry. "How do we make him do that?" Both boys looked up at Dean.

"Dean?" Drew pleaded.

Dean dropped to his knees and put his fingers in Eric's mouth, pushing the mushrooms to the back. He held Eric's mouth closed and began massaging his neck downward. Drew realized he had seen

Mom do that to their old cat Theo when he was dying and didn't want to take his pills.

Drew's fingers curled into fists. His teeth clamped together. He couldn't help but remember all the fun, stupid stuff he and Eric and Lance had done together and hope they would get to do it all again. The rides at the fair. Hiding Mrs. Ashleigh's chair when she left the art room. Joking about the girls they pretended not to like as they stared from across the lunchroom.

Why was he thinking about those things? He was being negative, acting like Eric was dying—Eric was not going to die. They would have plenty of years to tease each other about girls and have midnight snacks and drive cars and go to college. That stuff was going to happen. He just had to swallow, and it would all be better.

"There." Dean released Eric's mouth. It came open in an O shape like he was going to start breathing like a fish. Dean was right, the mushroom was gone from his mouth; now it just had to do its magic.

"Come on." Lance patted Eric's chest. "You ate it. Get better."

"Dad..." Eric whispered. His voice was throaty and dry.

The boys looked at each other.

"He's dreaming?" Drew guessed. "That's good, right?"

Eric's body began shaking again. It started in his chest and rippled out. His muscles flexed and released, flexed and released, over and over again, waves running from his core to his fingers. His mouth clamped shut, and bloody foam leaked from the corners of his lips.

"Help him!" Lance screamed.

They grabbed his arms and tried to hold him still.

"Get better, man," Drew whispered. His voice cracked. Tears ran over his cheeks.

Eric fell still.

They each took a deep breath.

"Help," Eric whispered, but he didn't inhale after that.

Drew looked at Dean.

Dean saw the helpless look in his eyes, and his hands twitched, not knowing what to do.

"Eric!" Lance screamed. He pushed on his friend's chest in a futile attempt at CPR. "Get up! You're not allowed to die!" He turned to Bobby, who stood in the darkness, cradling his severed foot. "You said it would fix him!"

Bobby shook his head. He stammered, "It should have. It—it must have been too many thorns." He looked each of them in the eyes. "I'm sorry."

Eric opened his eyes, but there was no breath in his lungs.

They were all called by the sounds of tapping and scraping from the collapsed entrance.

Part Five

An Empty House

Chapter Twenty-Eight

R ANDY OPENED HIS EYES TO a quiet house and felt strange. He still wasn't used to sleeping in Mom's old room, but more than that, he wasn't used to waking up without his children's arguing or yelling being his alarm clock.

He felt Emma to his right, first his hand on her back, then her chest rising and falling. But if he didn't know any better, he would have guessed the house was empty beyond the two of them.

Outside the window, a bird called. Emma let out a gentle snore. Somewhere down the road, he heard a truck's engine. Not a single sound from his kids or their guests.

He pulled back the covers, twisted, and dropped his feet to the floor. He slid on his slippers, a birthday gift from the kids, and headed for the bathroom.

His routine—teeth, toilet, and a little ibuprofen for the phantom pains that still prickled his missing fingers throughout the day—was something he did on autopilot. When finished, Emma still snoozing, he headed down the hallway.

He remembered Maggie was at Janet's house for the weekend, but due to the habit of checking every room he walked by, he poked his head into hers. The room was trashed—clothes all over the bed, boxes ripped open and waiting to be unpacked, dresser covered in makeup, knickknacks, and keepsakes yet to be put away. But it smelled like her, and that reassured him it was all right—she would get it clean, eventually.

He found Dean's room empty as well, a little curious for nine a.m. on a Saturday, but maybe he was downstairs getting breakfast. It happened like that sometimes.

He smiled at the tidiness of Dean's space. No boxes, no scattered clothes in sight, though he was pretty sure there would be some under the bed if he bent down to look. Dean was at the age where he wanted to do things with his friends at a moment's notice, and he knew his parents were always more likely to say yes if his room was clean.

As Randy's gaze moved from dresser to bed, it occurred to him how the room was arranged exactly like it had been in the old house, minus Drew's stuff, of course. Same organization of pictures, cologne, and trophies on the dresser, bed across from the window, diagonal to the door. It was interesting that the boy was able to recreate that layout, but Randy also hoped it wasn't a sign of some obsessive habit he would need to look out for. He wanted to move something and see if Dean fixed it when he came back later, but he resisted.

Drew's room was empty as well, and this time, seeing an empty room raised the hairs on the back of Randy's neck. There were three boys that were supposed to be sleeping in there, and it was hardly messier than Randy remembered it being last night on his way to bed—and where was the noise? Maybe Dean could be quietly eating downstairs, but there wasn't a single thing that group of boys could do quietly.

Randy turned and headed down the stairs, not noticing his heart rate was rising. He stepped on the entryway floor, his ears open and awaiting the sounds of kids, the sounds of dishes and breakfast—at least the sound of the television going. There was nothing.

In the living room, nothing. His heart beat heavier, now noticeably. He scanned the slice of kitchen he could see through the doorway as he marched in and looked around. No food—some mess from last night, but that was it. His gaze went to the window, to the backyard, to the lakefront and the dock.

He saw nothing but a calm late-summer morning empty of human involvement.

A flash hit him from somewhere inside. It was a sense of loss from so long ago, staring out that window and wondering if he would ever see Bobby again, wondering if it was all his fault—if this was all his fault.

But no, he was being silly. They were just a group of kids outside the house, probably doing something stupid, but it was fine.

He saw something in his mind that he could only place in a dream, running through the woods from something with Bobby. Something wanted them, Bobby, especially, and fear dripped through him like burning sludge that melted his throat, ate up his belly, and coated his insides. But this wasn't about Bobby. This was about his boys.

He was being irrational. He needed to just start the coffee and take a breath. He would calm down, and they would come walking in the door, probably soaked in mud from some game on the shore like he used to play with Bobby. He remembered the army men and G.I. Joes they had bought at the thrift store. They battled in the muck, and only the Power Rangers could save the day.

Randy took a deep breath, swallowed his anxiety, and started the coffee pot. He opened his phone and checked the weather: hot during the day, cool at night once again. He checked social media, and his high school acquaintances were discussing a new chain fishing store going up between the interstate and the lake and how it was going to kill Mike's, the local bait and tackle shop.

His heart barely slowed.

Randy grabbed the pot from the Mr. Coffee before it was close to done and poured a cup. He usually didn't like to do that—the first coffee through was always stronger and more acidic—but he had to finish this ritual. Coffee at the table made the world make sense.

He added French vanilla cream and two sugars and sat. It smelled good. He sipped and barely tasted it. He saw his mother sitting at the kitchen table, crying. And he remembered something else, a dream that didn't feel like a dream. It was surrounded by a fog—no, a shadow.

A Shadow Man.

Lightning shot through his system and yanked him from his seat. *The Shadow Man!* How could he have forgotten him? It was like the memory had been smothered, and it was climbing free from a mound of dirt like some B-movie zombie from a grave, like some magic had been hiding it and now it was wearing off.

He had told Mom about The Shadow Man, and she didn't want to hear it, but—as the memory unfolded itself inside his mind, he started to think that it wasn't that she didn't want to hear about it; it was that she already knew.

Another look outside, and he was running to his room to get dressed, shaking Emma and telling her the boys were missing. She barely understood a word of what he said and believed less. She got up as he ran from the back door into the cool morning air to check the woods.

Young Randy sat in his room with Dwight, thinking about The Shadow Man and Mom's reaction. It didn't make sense that she didn't care, but that wasn't going to stop him. The Shadow Man had something to do with what happened to Bobby, and he couldn't drop it. As much as he didn't want to, as much as it scared the crap out of him, they had to go back out to the woods and try to figure this out.

Dwight called his mom at her friend's house and arranged to stay the night before they left for the woods again. This time, they were more prepared—they thought, anyway. Randy had dumped his back-pack's books and schoolwork and filled it with flashlights, granola bars, and camping gear. They stopped at the shed, and Randy grabbed a machete from the gardening tools. Dwight opted for Randy's baseball bat from the sports pile.

The day was growing cooler as they hurried past the back door and down the path. There was urgency in Randy's steps, not for Bobby but because of Mom and Dad. There was something Mom knew, he was sure of that, and the last thing he wanted was for her to stop them. The same fear was true for Dad, not because he knew anything but because in his drunkenness, he was likely to give Randy a hard time just due to his pent-up frustration and impotence after not finding his son. What Randy didn't expect was when they reached the dock they found his sister, Joan, sitting there.

He tried to pretend he didn't see her and walk past, but she saw him and his gear.

"What are you doing?" She wiped at her eyes.

Randy was confused. He hadn't seen her for more than a few minutes since Bobby disappeared. She had been out with her friends or boyfriends or anywhere other than home. He definitely hadn't seen her shed a tear. She was crying over a boy or something; he was sure.

"Nothing." He couldn't explain it. Why even try?

"No, you're up to something. What is it?" She stood, and Randy could tell her entire face was red. Her eyes were irritated. It struck something inside him, and even though he was in a hurry—Mom could see them from the kitchen window if she was looking that way—he wanted to give Joan a hug. He hadn't hugged her any other time than Christmas or her birthday in several years; they just weren't close anymore. But he wanted to hug her now and ask what was wrong. But there was no time for that.

"We're uh—going to look for clues."

She smirked with a sour glare. "A thousand people have been through those woods looking for him, but you think you'll find something they missed?"

"We saw—" Dwight stopped when Randy raised his hand.

Randy shook his head and dismissed any care about Joan's tears. "At least we're doing something other than sitting around and crying about boys." He turned and motioned for Dwight to walk.

"Boys? You think that's why I'm crying?"

"I don't know why you're crying. You haven't been here since Bobby disappeared."

She covered her face, but Randy could see her turn a brighter red. He knew the tears were running now, and a sinking pit of regret opened inside his gut.

"I just can't, okay?" Her voice was broken. She turned toward the water. "I can't be here, or I can't stop worrying about him. I couldn't find a place to stay tonight, or I wouldn't have come home."

Randy couldn't help himself. He stepped forward and put a hand on her back. She turned and dove into him. He was three years younger, but at that moment they were exactly the same height, and she seemed to shrink even smaller as he put his arms around her shaking body and held her.

"Joanie, I..." He didn't know what to say other than, "I'm sorry."

They stood there for several minutes, long enough for Randy to be sure Mom would come outside and scream at them to get in the house, but that didn't happen. Instead, when their embrace broke, Joan said, "I'm coming with you."

Chapter Twenty-Nine

EMMA WAS DRESSED AND DOWNSTAIRS before she tried to understand what Randy had been saying. The kids were gone? So? That's what kids did. They wandered off and played and gave parents heart attacks. Was it weird that they were up so early? Yes. But that was no reason to believe they had somehow gone missing the way his brother had.

She found the coffee pot and poured herself a mug, then stood at the kitchen window, drinking. The lake *was* a beautiful place despite all of Randy's mother's crap being in the way. If they were to get their finances in order and make the place work, it might not be that bad. Although, the constant chill did bother her—and more so the longer they lived there.

It had been like a cool breeze when they moved in, the slight dip in temperature that made the hairs on the back of her neck rise. The next day, it was her feet that couldn't get warm. She put on an extra pair of socks while she was roaming around the house, and it didn't seem to work. It made her think of those dark winter days in the old house where just opening and closing the front door would make the room twenty degrees colder for a solid thirty minutes while the heater worked to catch up.

Today, the chill was invasive.

She thought it was the house but at the same time knew it couldn't have been. Her neck, her feet, those feelings followed her out the door to work and wherever else she went. This morning, it was in her chest, and she feared what that might mean because now the cold wasn't just cold—it was a nagging sensation that something bad was coming.

She was never a superstitious person nor one to believe in the occult or even premonitions, but this new chill was married to a sense of dread that though she could ignore, she found hard to. Especially when her husband was ranting about the boys being missing and a possible emergency.

What she needed was a distraction from all this. She needed out of the house and to get warmed up. This time, it was her conscience telling her it was a bad idea, but as she sipped her coffee, failing to warm her core, her nethers warmed with her plan. She knew where she was going. Whether James was answering the phone or not, she was going to go over there and have her way.

Emma watched the sun rise higher and the shadows shift. She climbed into her car, her tongue already tasting James's lips. It had been too long. Yes, it had only been a few days, but it was too long, and her fingers tightened around the steering wheel, yearning to grip his firm muscles.

Down the road and toward town, the green mountains looked down on her. She thought about the day James started at the realty office, when Kelvin McCluskey was showing him around and introducing him. Those eyes, she looked into those eyes and had to catch herself. It was like she fell inside them, the deep brown surrounding her the way his warmth would later that day when she was showing him her newest listing and explaining the way Kelvin worked. His bare arms around her bare chest in that empty home, the threat that the owner could come by at any time, the thrill of his hungry mouth as it searched her body, it was like she had been sucked into some fantasy she didn't even know she was dreaming of.

That memory made her quiver until she passed the baseball field at the community center—the one where Randy taught Dean to hit a ball, the one where Dean used to play Little League before he grew out of his passion for the game.

She couldn't help the sigh that followed. What if Randy was right—even a little? Maybe the kids weren't gone forever like he was running around and freaking out about, but what if they were in trouble? Randy's conclusions may have been bad, but the symptoms could have been correct. The boys, both theirs and their guests, all up so early on a summer weekend morning—it was weird. And them being gone.

No, it was just boys being boys. They get wild ideas and run after them. They were crazy—that was something she learned long ago. You couldn't try to rationalize the behavior of teenage boys, and this was just another instance of that. By dinnertime, they would all show back up, starving and demanding their infinite appetites be filled.

Still, there was something about it she could not shake. The intensity in Randy's eyes. She hadn't seen him like that in ages. The man seemed like he had been on autopilot to some extent for the past three years, ever since the accident with his fingers and the mounting hospital bills that the mill refused to pay. Then the layoff. Then his mother. She had wondered if she was ever going to see the old Randy again, and despite the reason, the fire in his eyes this morning was at once irritating and invigorating.

Though, his lack of fire was somewhat her fault, as well. She knew that. She pushed him away both before James and now. She wasn't what she could have been.

A coldness crept over Emma as she turned onto James's driveway. It chilled all but the parts she wanted him to touch.

This would be it. She decided that as she approached the house.

Yes, James drove her wild; yes, it was probably the best sex she had ever had; but she needed to stop. She loved her family—she needed them. But she needed James one more time. Just one more time she would have him, and she would enjoy it, and she would make it the best one ever, and then she would never see him again. After that, she would devote herself. She would turn her attitude around and fix her marriage. She'd work with Randy to make this new house into the home they always wanted, and when they sold the old house, it would be a new start for them financially. Maybe she could coach Randy, lovingly, and help him to find a new, better career.

Just one more time.

She parked in James's empty driveway.

Just one more time.

Emma turned off the engine and got out. There was no way James was missing too. Did that bastard shack up with some other woman last night? Was that why he wasn't here?

No. He must have gone to the store or something. Maybe he had a morning showing?

She pulled out her phone and typed: "I'm at your house. Where are you?" She clicked the little paper-airplane icon and waited until the message said it was delivered.

She heard a chime somewhere in the distance. James was there.

Of course he was there. He probably had car trouble and had it towed or something.

She went to the door and knocked. The shadows from the surrounding trees shaded the porch. Needles littered the deck, reminding her of the oncoming fall.

He didn't answer the door. She checked her phone. He hadn't texted back, either. There were no little dots—he wasn't typing back.

He was probably asleep. It was still morning, after all.

The idea took hold that she would sneak into his bed with him and surprise him. She imagined him lying there naked and felt her insides tingle.

But the knob didn't turn. Locked.

"Shit."

She texted again: "Where are you?"

This time, she noticed his notification chime wasn't coming from inside the house. It was coming from the woods.

He was in the woods?

"James?" she shouted into the trees. "Where are you?"

She stepped off the deck and noticed a path she hadn't seen before. It was thin, maybe just larger than an ATV track, and it led into a denser section of the forest.

"James?" She walked toward the path. "Are you in there?"

No answer.

She walked to the edge and looked into the thick gloom. She texted: "Hello?"

Indeed, the chime was ahead.

"Okay. Into the spooky woods I go."

Pine needles snapped below her steps. The forest scent filled her nose. Her eyes adjusted to the shadows, and yet the chill refused to fade. But neither did the heat. She needed to find him. She needed to resolve this urge and move on with her life.

The wind blew through the trees, and the air's gentle morning warmth was replaced with a shiver. Emma rubbed her arms as she walked and wondered. *What is James doing out here*

A bird cawed from high in the boughs above and then squawked as if in pain. Emma didn't look, but she did move faster.

"James?"

She texted: "James. I'm looking for you."

The chime was ahead, beyond where the path turned right, and through the trees, she could see a cliff. She knew James's property was expansive, but none of her visits had allowed for them to explore it. None of them strayed beyond the bedroom for the most part. This, she thought, could have been interesting if under different circumstances and if she didn't have the feeling she was being watched.

"James!"

There was rustling in the trees ahead and behind. More on the ground to her sides. It was in the debris, whatever it was, and she told herself it was a squirrel or a chipmunk. Maybe a rabbit—they were so fast when they ran it was hard to catch them. She scanned the forest floor, and while she saw a pile of needles shift, she saw no animals.

She rounded the corner, and there it was. James's truck lay ahead, and a little shack stood just beyond. She bit her lip, and trying to hide the waning desire, she typed "I found you" and tapped send.

The chime sounded through the window, and she frowned. The truck was empty. He hadn't gotten any of her messages. He had to be in that shack.

Ideas ran through her mind from a Unabomber-style shop for crafting explosives to a tool shed to a small smokehouse. She hoped it was the last and tried to fill her mind with fantasies of a woodsman taking her into his rustic work area. God, that would make all of this worth it.

Just one more time.

The door had no knob, just a latch that held it closed. As the woods rustled behind her and a line of prickles ran down her back, she lifted the latch and pulled the door toward her.

She stood there trying to make sense of what she saw as the vision narrowed around her. It couldn't be real.

A woman's clothes were on the ground, not a whole set, but she recognized jeans and panties for sure. A hole was in the floor on her left. Chains were attached to the wall, and she wasn't sure whether that disturbed her most or if it was the sight of a workbench covered in knives and pliers of different sizes and shapes.

There was no way this was real.

She shook her head, trying to use her body to convince her brain that this was not happening. The clothes on the floor hurt—maybe James was seeing other women—but the chains? The knives? It was like she had discovered some kind of torture room.

It sank in with a trembling wave. The room spun in front of her. This was not a joke. This was James's secret.

Memories flooded of moments she had ignored and pushed away. Times James had hurt her, either casually or in bed, when he was quick to apologize but his eyes never backed up his words and the smirk on his mouth whole-heartedly rejected them. She remembered those moments, and now she was sure he was smiling behind those words.

Emma's heart slammed into her chest as she realized what this meant. She had seen what she shouldn't have, something that was sure to doom her if he caught her there. His truck was right there, so he was somewhere nearby. He was going to walk up to her in his secret place and—her eyes went to the chains—back to the tools. It could end up being her restrained there. That may have been his plan all along. It still could be his plan.

She had to get out of there. She had to run to the car and get the fuck—

The noises in the woods shot toward her. She turned in time to catch a blur of fur racing along the ground. It shot up her leg, and pain ripped into her thigh.

Emma screamed, stumbling backward into the shack as another blur darted at her from under a pile of pine needles and dried leaves. It was the shape of a giant slug, but it moved like a lightning-fast snake. It was on her leg.

Hot pain shot into her other leg. Heat and blood, wetness ran. She looked down at her legs, not knowing what to do. She saw fur and blood and was afraid to touch either creature. They would turn their fangs on her hands if she tried to move them; she just knew it.

There was another blur. It was rushing from below James's truck.

She turned and jumped deeper inside the shack, slamming the door. Her foot twisted and caught on a floorboard.

There was nothing she could do as she toppled toward darkness. She thought of Randy as she fell into the hole. He was going to find out, and that might have been more terrifying than whatever was at the bottom of this hole.

Chapter Thirty

RANDY STOPPED HIMSELF FROM RUNNING. While he suspected that he knew where they were, he had to pray it wasn't true. He had to search as far and wide as possible before he knew for sure.

"Drew! Dean!" He stood at the crest of the hill and scanned the property. The lake. The dock. The grass and sparse woods to the right. Lastly, the trail of boulders leading into the woods, the path he knew he would be taking. "Drew! Dean!"

Nothing. No response from a kid or even another living soul. No birds. No vehicles on the lake. Other than the breeze cooling his limbs, he could have assumed time had frozen and left him alone on this hill.

"God, no." It was a whisper into the ether.

He walked down the path, eyes scanning, looking for any trace of evidence. A track, a candy wrapper, a crushed flower.

At first, the beaten-down trail showed nothing more than hard-packed dirt. At the bottom of the hill, though, there was a size-nine sneaker print in the dirt that he knew belonged to Drew. Another, twelve, Dean's boot. Both headed into the boulders, along with two more sets.

Randy wanted to drop to his knees right there. He moved forward instead, picking up pace as he went.

"Dean! Drew!"

Into the forest.

"Dean! Drew!"

Along the path and then up the hill.

"Dean! Drew!"

He felt the stare. It was watching him, The Shadow Man. He could feel it in his chest and in his guts. He had somehow escaped The Shadow Man last time, and like an idiot, he had handed his kids right to him. He wanted to cry.

"Dean! Drew!"

Those things were in the trees. He heard them scurrying up there on their dead feet, wearing the skins of those they killed, carrying their death in their bags and in their singing.

It trickled down from above, the words in that creepy language. He didn't want to know what they were saying. He just wanted them to shut up. But they wouldn't, not until they were ready to attack.

But he couldn't resist. "Shut up! Be quiet, you bastards!" *The blood. There was so much blood. The teeth, the skin…*

"Dean! Drew!" He felt cold inside, though his heart pumped hard. The shadows were like ice on his skin.

He reached Bobby's old fort and squatted by the entrance. The wind blew over him with a freezing, dank breath that smelled of decay. He spun, and he knew it was there, The Shadow Man. He couldn't see him, but he was there.

"Give me back my kids!" he screamed.

The next breeze sounded like laughter.

"Give them to me." It was more of a plea this time than a demand.

Randy crawled into the opening.

He could smell the scent of Drew's shampoo, of Dean's deodorant. His stomach clenched as he prayed he wasn't too late. He flicked on his flashlight and scanned the walls, the writing and drawings, and he remembered them all as if today was twenty-five years ago, as if he was sitting here with Dwight trying to figure out what had happened to his brother.

He crawled to the skulls at the side of the crypt. There was dirt and broken vines around the area. The kids had found it and messed with it.

His heart fluttered inside his chest.

"Fuck!"

He felt a laugh from the entrance and spun. His body turned numb, and he jumped. His gaze locked onto the glossy, lidless eyes of The Shadow Man, and his stomach dropped. His breath froze. He wanted to yell, but his body was too stiff and too still.

It had happened again.

Randy was quiet, Dwight and Joan as well. There was a feeling between them that covert action was required. It might have been a bit silly since there was no way that Mom could have heard them once they were in the woods and so far from the house, but Mom's demand that they go to Randy's room had been so intense, so angry, that none of them wanted to take a chance.

It created an atmosphere around them, a sensitivity to the woodland sounds that Randy might not have otherwise acknowledged. Within that, he noticed the lack of bug noises. He hated bugs, but he always heard them buzzing and bumbling about in the woods. He remembered someone saying that droughts led to multiple things, including snakes and frogs being hungrier—had they eaten all the bugs? Then, there were the cows that lived over the hill to the west. They were loud today, so much so that he would have thought they were roaming around in the woods with them if he didn't know any better. There was a screech from a hawk overhead and then the repetitive crunch of their steps on the forest-floor litter. All of these sounds seemed to compound inside his ears, and as they approached the rock formation, Randy had to close his eyes and focus to get his concentration back.

They reached the fort as the sun was about to pass behind the mountains, marking the start of dusk. A bluish-indigo shimmer fell over the woods, and the black rock ahead seemed to shine just a bit.

"This is Bobby's fort?" Joan kneeled and looked inside.

"It's the last place we know he was," Randy said. "And it's where we saw The Shadow Man disappear."

"The Shadow Man?" She looked at Randy, puzzled, and he explained what they saw, down to the last detail. Her response was, "You expect me to believe that?"

"It's true," Dwight insisted.

"Just..." Randy struggled with his words. "Bobby was in there. We start in there."

"Okay." Joan crouched and led the way. She was almost completely inside when she stopped. "What the hell?"

"What is it?"

"I was about to climb inside, and the floor disappeared."

"Disappeared?" Dwight scowled.

"What do you mean?" Randy asked.

Randy didn't think he had ever heard a sound like the one that followed his question. It was a guttural howl from the pit of Joan's belly as she jerked forward into the passage. Her knees and feet seemed to vanish as she took off, and without a thought as to what was happening, Randy charged after her.

"Joan!" He leaned inside the stone structure and saw what she meant. The floor had vanished, leaving a cloudy brown fog in its place. A ripple that looked like blue lightning ran across the surface, and just as Randy was about to call once more for his sister, the face of The Shadow Man rose from the mist.

Randy's mouth dropped. He saw his reflection in the slimy eyes that hung from the skull's face. There was a hollowness inside those eyes and a stench that ransacked the inside of Randy's senses.

He was never given the chance to scream. A shadowed claw appeared from nowhere, wrapped around the sides of Randy's head, and pulled.

There was ice in that grip. There was a feeling of bony tips clutching his skull as it pulled him. A vision of skulls and bones and decay set in as his body left the ground and shot into the hazy floor below.

"Randy!" Dwight watched the second person in thirty seconds dart into that hole, and he knew for certain that he didn't want to be number three. He took a step back, preparing to turn. He didn't want to run. He wanted to help his friend, but it was too much. Them vanishing into the blackness of that hole was too—

The face emerged from the doorway. It was the one he said he didn't see, but he had. He couldn't have missed it, couldn't get it out of his head if he tried. He had hoped it was all a delusion, hoped it could have been a mask of some kind, maybe, a kid's Halloween mask getting taken advantage of in the dark woods and dark—

It left the hole and rose inside a pillar of black smoke. It hovered toward him, eyes shifting inside their sockets, meat connecting the skull to its jaw, flexing and slackening, and letting the teeth chatter as they neared, and the hands of cloudy blackness reached toward Dwight.

Now, he did want to run. Now, all thoughts of helping his friend vanished in favor of saving his own life. If only he could. His legs trembled below him like the stalks of some strange plant, dead to the world, unresponsive, unknown to the sentient, just worthless sticks of meat.

There was a sizzle in Dwight's left ear. His hearing went fuzzy as the left side of his head started to freeze.

Then it was happening to his right.

He smelled smoke but didn't dare take his eyes off this floating monster to see what it was. Until the pain tore through his head, and he realized his ears were burning.

Smoke stretched from The Shadow Man to Dwight's head, where he knew without looking that the monster's digits were piercing his ears and burning him away with cold.

It was then that Dwight screamed. He would have guessed that it was even louder than Joan's or Randy's, but before he had a second to think about it, he was hoisted from where he stood and dragged through the air. He saw The Shadow Man's face in front of his own as they both soared into the hole, into the stone structure, and down into the floor of brown clouds.

On the other side of the fog, The Shadow Man was gone, but Dwight was still falling. He saw Joan covering her face and crying, Randy watching him fall, stroking his head, and the floor coming so fast.

Dwight thrust his arms ahead to stop his fall and watched his fingers fold backward as he slammed down and then rolled into a pile of bones and vines.

He screamed. Randy leaned forward onto his knees and howled at the floor. Joan looked into the darkened space and covered her eyes again, weeping to herself.

All Dwight could do was roll onto his back and sob. He watched the foggy roof roll into itself, against the wall, and back around. He shivered as he looked at his mangled fingers and wondered what to do. With his good hand, he touched his ears—holes in the top of each as if someone had melted through them with a blowtorch.

His breath hitched, and his eyes went to the ceiling, where the fog curled, and for some reason, he could no longer feel the floor at his back.

The echoes of screams pained Randy's ears, but his attention wasn't on them. It was on the brown, rolling ceiling fog that he, Joan, and Dwight were rising toward.

It wasn't like they were thrown or launched. It was like something above them with cold, hard hands—Randy thought of The Shadow Man but didn't see him—was hooked into their bellies and yanking them up. He felt like a yo-yo, first tossed into that hole, now jerked from it.

But why?

He wasn't given time to ponder the question as all three were flung into the cloud at the top of the cave, and though he expected to see Bobby's fort on the other side, he didn't. He saw trees.

They were suspended in the air for a fraction of a second before gravity took hold. They plummeted down, all screaming together, and Randy rotated his body to see where they were.

They were in the woods, his woods. The stone formation was to one side, and they were twenty feet up, sinking through the branches.

Dwight's howl shifted to pain as a bough thrust into his back and he rolled off and kept falling. Joan thumped, belly flopping onto the dirt and pine needles. Her breath left her, and she rolled and held her gut. Randy landed on the side of the stone structure and rolled down on his belly, then back, and repeated. He almost made it to the bottom uninjured until his head slammed into the boulder at the base.

Chapter Thirty-One

EMMA'S FACE SCRAPED AGAINST ROCK as she tumbled down the shaft. She flipped and felt a sharp pain as her hand slammed into stone. She flipped again and felt a hard surface ram into her back. She was about to cry when she saw the two furry slugs that had been on her rushing down the walls after her. They had been knocked loose, but they wanted more.

They were too far away for it, but she was sure she could smell them long before they were close. Damp fur, like moldy, wet dog and pungent, sour trash and rotting meat and fruit. They were just slightly slower than the rocks and dust they knocked loose while descending, but they were fast enough to make Emma realize that if she didn't die from her injuries, those things were going to kill her.

She pushed herself up, back against the wall, ignoring the pain that shot down her spine and into her legs. A flash went through her mind: did she have anything at all to defend herself with? A knife?

Even a key or a goddamn pencil? She thought about the phone in her pocket and knew that would be useless.

The darkness hid all but the silhouette of the things leaping at her. The tufts of fur in all directions, the whipping tails, the tiny arms, or whatever they were, flapping around. She knew their shapes were an understatement of the horror that was about to befall her if she wasn't fast, faster than she felt capable of at that moment.

It was instantaneous; pain tore up her leg as soon as the first thing landed on her. She beat the top of it with her closed fists, all she had, and felt it sting the bottoms of her hands. She kicked and flung her legs around, yet it held tight to her shin.

Inside the pain, she could feel its tiny teeth moving in and out of her like sewing needles. It wasn't just locked on like an attacking predator; it was chewing. It wasn't trying to kill her; it was trying to eat her.

In the panic and agony of the first attack, Emma had forgotten about the second creature until it landed on her forearm and dug its fangs in. Its needled teeth moved in and out, and she felt what must have been its tongues slurping her blood and prying at her skin and muscle.

She howled into the pit and saw white. Then, her vision seemed to disappear. Time and space seemed to vanish as she moved without thinking or feeling.

Emma turned and slammed the thing attached to her arm into the wall. She yelled at it with a war cry that she couldn't hear. It yipped, and she slammed it again. Its fangs sank deeper into her as she shoved it into the rock face, and she bashed it harder. And harder. She felt its bones crunch below the rancid fur, and she heaved her arm into the wall as hard as she could.

The thing loosened its grip, and its teeth slipped from the wound. Emma screamed once more and kicked at the wall. Her blood rained from her arm and slid down her leg, and she kicked harder and harder. She would break her leg against stone before she let this monster continue to bite her.

The thing on her leg may have yipped and cried like the other one, but she didn't hear it. She felt it slip loose, though, and she felt herself getting woozy and cold.

She was losing blood.

"Fuck," Emma muttered to herself. She raised her foot and stomped hard on each of her attackers two or three more times, listening for crunches under each kick.

She leaned against the wall and looked up. The top of the shaft was a dim circle, and dots fluttered across her vision. She had to do something about her wounds. She pulled her phone from her pocket and found it a shattered brick.

She thought about screaming for help, but who was going to hear? If James was around somewhere—and not killed by those things—she was obviously in his secret place. He wasn't going to help her. There was no love there; she knew that. Their arrangement wasn't based on feelings, not to either of them. It was, if anything, just a mutual transaction to satisfy their urges and nothing more. He wasn't going to help her. And she was too far inside his property right now. No one else would hear her call. Best to be quiet.

She wondered if she could climb up the walls and doubted it. She wasn't a rock climber even when she didn't have a wounded arm and leg.

Emma sank to the ground and inspected the torn flesh on her arm. She had no light and had to probe it with her fingers.

The skin was missing between the outer punctures of that thing's bite, and she could feel the strands of muscle that should have been covered. It had licked the skin from her arm in just that short period of time, and she wanted to puke. It made her think of the rows of needles on a lion's tongue ripping her flesh away, and she shuddered at what would have happened if she had been any slower to get it off.

She felt her shin, and when her fingers touched bone, she immediately jerked them away.

"Fuck!"

Deep breath.

She ripped her jeans, using the bitten hole to get started, then she wrapped and tied the material over her shin. She ripped the bottom of her shirt and wrapped and tied it around her arm. It wasn't good, but she prayed it would keep enough blood inside her to stop her from passing out. Then, the adrenaline faded. Then, the pain and the cold really set in. Finally, realizing the direness of her situation, she wanted to cry.

She heard Randy telling her that the boys were missing, and she shuddered. Knowing she would be considered missing soon as well, she wondered if she shouldn't have blown him off. What if they really were missing? And instead of helping, here she was in a goddamn hole. And what if she was never found? Or worse, what if she was? What if they find out about all of it? The affair, the scandalous sex in homes they were supposed to be selling, in the hotel, in the alley behind the office; what if it all came out?

Her heart sank inside her chest, and this time, the tears did come.

She thought about Randy's face when he discovered it all, and her gut burned with guilt. She never truly wanted to hurt him. She wanted him to be sorry. There were years between them where she just wanted to be recognized for the person she was and not feel like she was being taken advantage of by being shoved into a mother role. She wanted to be cared for and not shunned for being depressed and angry. So, yes, she snuck out. Yes, the spite inside her wanted him to feel something—she wanted to feel something—but not this. Not what this would lead to.

There was no escape from that now, though. Even if she found her way out of this hole, there was no explaining her wounds. Even so, she had to get back to Randy, to Drew and Dean and Maggie. But what could she do other than sit and hope help came?

That was unlikely. What she did hear coming was the scratch of claws on the shack's wooden door.

Randy looked into The Shadow Man's eyes, and they stared back at him. He was twenty-five-years older, but they were ageless. Blood seeped from the edges around the thing's sockets, coating the glassy ebony balls like tears. The bone and muscle of the thing's face shone in the gloomy light as if they had been polished and then coated with slime. Shadows moved like smoke around its head, around its entire body, making it look like some sort of ghostly grim reaper. It was hard to look at. Randy wished its face was only a skull, not the undead-looking head before him with meat still attached to bone and wriggling strands of muscle that seemed to crawl along the creases of white.

The stone walls surrounding them were a limitless black. They cast no shine and held no light. Within the walls of the stone structure, Randy and this demon were alone in time and space, with only the small path behind it to secure them to the rest of the universe.

Randy stared into that face, one he had amazingly forgotten and only seen in his nightmares since childhood, and somehow, his fear was pushed down by rage. That thing was there when his brother was taken. It was here as he worried about his sons. It had done more, he knew that, though the facts were hazy, and he would not stand still and let things be.

"Give them back!" Randy screamed. "I want my sons, now!"

"Blood for blood," echoed in the chamber.

Randy didn't have time to process the words. A wind blew through the enclosure, carrying the scent of the dried-up dead. It was moldy yet dusty, not pungent, but pointed. It pulled at the strings in Randy's memory, calling firelight, bonfires, and chanting in a blur of mixed energies and emotions. It made him sad, and it made him long for something lost. It called with tones of friendship lost and pages long since turned in the book of life, and it teased that his lack of control in the past had never been rectified.

There was a snapping sound behind Randy, and he spun. He was wary of taking his eyes from The Shadow Man, but something told him he better.

What he saw made his skin crawl. The pile of pixie skulls twitched, then their jaws snapped shut. *Clack!* There were at least ten of them, and they sprang open, then clacked shut once more. As they opened and closed, though, they were not stationary. They inched toward Randy.

"Give me my boys!" Randy howled. His stare darted back and

forth between the demon and the remains. Vines that had grown over the tiny bones stretched toward Randy.

Clack!

They were only feet away to his right, The Shadow Man equal distance to his left, and the exit of the structure straight ahead. He knew what The Shadow Man was threatening, but goddammit, he didn't want to give in.

"Please!" Randy howled, his voice cracking. "Please." Tears ran down his face, and the wind from the next snap of skulls blew past his back. The vines slithered across the ground. They wanted to tie him down, the skulls wanted to chew, and from the dirt where the skulls had rested, tiny skeletons brushed soil from their chests and began to rise.

If a fleshy skull could smile, Randy was sure The Shadow Man would have been doing it then.

"You can't scare me away!" Randy shouted. He turned and kicked, and two of the skulls rolled back to their homes, their jaws coming loose and skipping across the ground. He stomped on vines and kicked at another skull, and a roar shook the room.

Those cold, bony hands, Randy remembered them immediately as they gripped his head from behind. They chilled his entire being while kicking his heart into overdrive. He pictured the hands of death on him, only he knew that was giving this demon too much credit. This was a worker, not an architect. It was powerful, but it wasn't all-powerful.

But it was stronger than Randy.

His head could have been ripped from his shoulders, or that's how it felt as it happened; he was jerked backward, his body tagging along. He was yanked from the stone building, and the sides of his head burned from the cold. It was tearing through his scalp and chilling his skull. It was making his brain freeze, slow, and vibrating his thoughts like some trip from his late teens.

His body flew across the clearing and slammed into a tree. He felt the rough bark in his back as he slid down, tumbled forward, and hit the ground face-first.

The pine needles scratched his skin, and the tears made them stick as he raised his head, the phantom no longer gripping. His body was stiff, and every bone, muscle, and organ ached. His head felt like it should have been bleeding where the thing grabbed him, but his blood didn't run. There was no wound.

Randy climbed to his hands and knees and crawled shakily toward the opening. "Give me my boys!" he screamed.

He reached the opening and stuck his head through.

The Shadow Man was gone. The skulls and vines were resting. There was no passage to that other place as he knew there could be. There was only him and his failed attempts, now and twenty-five-years prior.

"Give me my boys." He sat on the ground just outside the opening. He wasn't getting in this way. He needed to find the Whisperers.

Chapter Thirty-Two

RANDY, DWIGHT, AND JOAN STOOD, battered and bruised, shaking and staring at the stone structure. Randy shook his head and stared at the opening. Joan backed away and stepped behind a tree. Dwight started limping down the path toward Randy's house, shaking his hand and rubbing his head.

"Come on!" Dwight called. "Before it comes back!" He massaged his reddened ears.

Randy didn't want to admit it, but Dwight was right. Whatever The Shadow Man was, he could have killed them. He was definitely strong enough to. He had played with them and tossed them out of there like they were nothing but toys. His wounds had seemingly vanished like waking from a dream, but that thing could be back at any time to give them worse than the warning they had received.

He turned and saw Joan watching him from behind the tree. A red scratch traced her jawbone, and she had a scrape on her forehead.

She was holding her stomach.

"Come on." He gestured at the trail home.

"But Bobby?" She pointed at the entrance.

"We have to find another way." It was all he could think of. He hoped it was true.

It took a few steps down the path, but as Randy watched the trees and the path ahead of him, he noticed a strange change. There were faint golden lines floating above the ground, debris that had golden marks on it, and, what gave him goosebumps, tiny golden footprints among it all.

"Do—do you guys see that?" Dwight pointed down, his finger circling around them and aiming at the various lines, splotches, and foot-shaped markings.

"And... that?" Joan pointed up into the trees. Tiny marks were on the boughs, places that looked like a tiny person had stood and gripped the branch and left golden handprints and footprints behind.

All Randy could think of was the tiny skull Bobby had found.

"This isn't right," Joan said. She ran toward the house, jumping over golden lines that crisscrossed their path. "No."

"Joan!" Randy ran after her, followed by Dwight. They raced down the slope and over the trail, watching the strange markings as they went. It was wondrous yet frightening, and Randy thought he understood. These things had been here all along. Somehow, though, they were just now seeing them.

He squinted, tracking the lines as they ran. Were the tiny people there now? If he followed the trails and markings, would it lead him to one of them? The thought was exciting and terrifying at the same time. What if he found one—a thing that was small and had a head the size of that skull? Would it—he remembered The Shadow Man, another skull, and a bigger fear evolved: how were they connected?

Out of the woods and past the trail of boulders, the golden prints almost all stopped. Some traces moved forward, but they were faded as if worn down or washed away by time.

Randy watched Joan run up the path to the house, and he was about to follow her when he spotted the lake, and he and Dwight both stopped in their tracks to stare.

The lake glowed with a bluish-purple hue as the sun fell behind the western mountains and lit the sky in streaks of red. There was something moving just under the surface of the water, leaving traces of gold behind it. It was the color of the trails in the woods, and despite a nagging pull in the back of his mind, Randy walked toward it.

"What are you doing?" Dwight shook his head and took a step back. He watched while Randy walked onto the dock that should have extended two dozen feet into the water if they weren't going through a drought. "You—you shouldn't go out there."

Randy only heard tones of concern behind him, not words. He crept to the end of the dock, something inside telling him not to give himself away to whatever that was.

He could see the golden line extend as whatever it was moved around the lake.

At the dock's end, he sank to his knees, his head tilting slightly as he watched, not only seeing where the line was going but also tracing it back to its source below the depths of the water.

Lone Wolf Lake was deep in some places but fairly clear, especially right off Randy's dock. The glacier and yearly runoff that fed it made it so cold your balls could turn blue even in the summer, but the water was so transparent that Randy could follow the golden lines going left to a shallow area along the shore below the woods. He couldn't tell where it started exactly due to the trees, but if he had to guess, he would have said it led to another place like Bobby's fort, but this one underwater.

"What are you doing?" Dwight hissed from shore. His arms were folded over his chest in a defiant statement that he was in no way joining Randy out on that dock.

Randy waved him off. He watched as the leading end of the golden line crossed the lake, swam up to the shore, and—he had to lean back as he watched—the thing that was making the trail crawled up onto the beach.

From that distance—the lake was about two hundred feet across where he watched—he couldn't tell exactly what it was, only that it was moving on four legs (or possibly more) as it clambered up the bank and toward a group of tall trees. It slinked, drawing its limbs up and placing them down like a big cat, and when it vanished into the woods, a tail swayed behind it.

Randy had to point as he moved backward down the dock. He couldn't lose it. It was a necessity, something inside him screamed. It was too important.

Cold ran down his spine as he replayed what he had seen inside his mind. He turned to Dwight. "Did you see that?" *What kind of animal could do that? Swim underwater all the way across the lake and then climb out and walk away?*

"No, I didn't see it." Dwight was shaking his head in denial, and Randy knew it. He hadn't seen that horrified look on Dwight's face since he borrowed Davy Winchester's VHS of *Return of the Living Dead* last summer and they secretly watched it after Mom and Dad were in bed with the volume so low they could barely hear it. That look was: *I wish I hadn't seen that, but I have to play it cool.*

"You did too! It was right there!" Randy forced himself back to shore. He pointed again, recreating the creature's path. "It came from the woods, swam across the lake, and got out over there—some kind of weird creature."

Dwight shook his head. "I think we should go inside." He glanced back at the woods as if The Shadow Man was going to rush out and get them.

"No." Randy was emphatic. "The damn Shadow Man won't let us go after Bobby; I'm going after that thing. I mean, look at that." He gestured at the golden lines in the woods and marks on trees, the line through the water. "It's related. And if it gets me closer to finding Bobby, I'm doing it."

"No. I saw it, okay? If that's what you want me to say, I'll say it. I saw it. But—it wasn't right. It was some kind of *thing.*"

"Yeah, so that's why we need to figure out what it's doing. If it came from where Bobby went—the other side of that brown fog— learning about it can help us."

"No. I'm not going."

"Fine. You can go wait in my room. I'm going."

"Going where?" It was Joan.

"I thought you were going inside?"

"I got to the door and saw Mom bawling at the kitchen table. So, I had to come back and see what dumb idea you were doing."

Randy scowled. "Dumb idea?" The look on her face reminded him of some Fourth of July past where they lined up across the yard from each other with bottles and bottle rockets, and Bobby watched from the edge of the house, uncovering his eyes between explosive pops.

"Yeah. Where are you going?"

Randy showed her the line across the lake and explained what he saw. Again, he was surprised when she agreed to come with him. "Dwight? You coming?"

He didn't want to. It was still written across his face. "Yeah," he finally answered.

Randy led them right, through the trees along the shore. He ducked under the branches he could see in the failing light and held his hand in front of himself for those he couldn't. They passed the Carters' place, the closest neighbor, then a half mile of their forest. Randy didn't know who the next neighbor was, only that they had a blond Cocker Spaniel that barked relentlessly from the back porch.

They passed two other houses, and by the time they reached the opposite shore, the night was only lit by a rising half-moon. Fortunately for Randy, the golden trail was still there, leading them into the trees.

Randy paused at the edge of the woods and glanced at Joan and Dwight. He wanted to make sure they were still willing to move forward but found himself scared to ask. The shape of the thing slinking into the unseen played in his mind over and over. The idea of a strange, six-legged monster made his skin crawl. He needed to go after it, but Christ, he didn't want to do it alone. What if they said no?

He didn't have to ask. Joan nodded, followed shortly by Dwight. They were going. Randy was never so unsure of what was happening in his life, but he was secure at that moment, strong at that moment, with them beside him.

"Okay." He turned and headed into the woods. He stepped quietly, following the trail through trees and around shrubs. The patch of trees was larger than it had seemed by the lake, but that could have just as easily been the darkness messing with his senses. Or the thrum of his heart against his chest—his mind telling him he was in the middle of something too big for a kid to get involved with or understand. But what else was he supposed to do? Dad wasn't going to leave his bottle to come look; Mom wasn't going to stop crying at the table, even if she did seem to know something. This group was all Bobby had.

The scent of fire cut through the cooling night. It was sharp and peppery, a bonfire or a camp maybe—but this wasn't camping season, not around the lake.

Beyond the next fifty feet of trees, Randy saw the flicker of orange light. There was movement. There were people—people?—in the direct path of where the golden trail was leading.

The menacing shape of that thing returned to mind. It was something that would have sent most people screaming. He would have screamed and run if it had come out of the water on his side of the lake. Yet there were others ahead. Had they not seen it? As they moved toward the firelight, Randy had to ponder this. Before their run-in with The Shadow Man and falling through that brown fog, they hadn't seen the golden markings—he wondered if he would have been able to see the creature before now.

They neared the edge of the forest, and Randy, Joan, and Dwight each stood behind a tree, studying the meadow ahead. They watched the fire and three people around it. They saw the golden trail leading directly into the blaze, and the animal... it was standing in the middle of the flames.

"What the..." Joan whispered.

There was a man and two women. They walked in a circle

around the fire, wearing red robes and chanting something that sounded like Latin. They each pulled a dagger from beneath their robes and held it to the sky.

The creature in the fire stood motionless over the coals as tendrils of flame lapped at its flesh. It indeed had six legs. It was the size of a cow but muscular, and each of its limbs had large, hand-like paws. Its hide was thick, patchy fur with gashes and holes where Randy could see its ribs and flesh within, and as the robed chanters spoke, the fire climbed up its fur, burning and smoking and sending new sparkling lines into the ether. These were not golden, like its trail; these were red.

They stopped chanting and screamed. Their howls rose into the night like pain and murder. They sounded like death, and Randy felt his entire body wrap itself in gooseflesh as if it could armor him against such things.

The creature joined their scream, and they plunged their daggers into it.

Blood ran, and the whispers started. The sound was something Randy could only have described as haunting. The voices of unseen whisperers were inside his head. They sounded like they were beside him, but no one stood there. They sounded like they were inches away, but the ceremony was clearly much farther, and despite the weather only being cool, it chilled him worse than a deep, snowy winter.

Each thread of flame rose higher over the beast. They dug their blades into its body, and its blood spilled onto the fire, acting like kerosene. Tendrils shot upward, tying themselves in knots around legs and clawing at the monster's flesh. The robed trio slashed and hacked, exposing organ and viscera. Pieces of the beast fell, and the fire flared. It howled louder, and from its burning flesh rose thick lines of red, sparkling smoke. It swelled into the sky above, and the three at the fire held their heads over the flames, breathing in the crimson strands.

"My god," Dwight muttered. He glanced back into the forest, and Randy failed to understand the expression on his face. It was fright, but somewhere between checking for an escape route and alert; was something behind them?

Randy looked back as well. The forest was lit by orange and red light that flared every time the beast let loose another howl. He didn't see anything back there except a twinkling in the distance—just for a moment—that kind of looked like eyes.

It howled again, and Randy spun back to the fire. His blood ran cold as he looked; the creature was staring right at him.

Its eyes were black and held the shine of a dead thing soaked in blood. Its face not only had no fur but no skin. It was meat and bone and reminded Randy of The Shadow Man. Not just reminded him of it—it was it, at least in part. The Shadow Man was inside this thing, burning, spreading itself into the air and into those people. And into his mind as the whispering repeated.

Fire flared up and over the monster. Red light and smoke burst out and upward, soaking the three and knocking them back on their rears.

Joan let out a yelp, and each robed figure turned and spotted them.

Those faces were burned into Randy's mind. He was so shocked at their stares that none of them registered as human, but they did register as a threat.

"Run!" He grabbed at Joanie's arm, but she was already spinning in retreat, Dwight too. They all turned without another word and darted into the woods, back along the golden line, around trees, and over rocks. They panted and hurried, and Randy's head pounded from the rush of whispers, blood, and fear.

They breached the other side of the woods and cut back toward home. They didn't stop running until they were halfway around the lake, out of breath, and the whispers had subsided. Joan leaned on a tree where she could watch for any followers. Dwight collapsed on the ground and held his face. Randy leaned on his knees and panted, his throat acid and his lungs on fire.

"What the hell?" Joan said over her heaving breaths.

Randy watched the sky above those woods where red plumes rose into the clouds above and seemed to turn them dark indigo. There was a howl from that direction, and he spotted another beast crawling from the water and into the woods, following the same path as the first.

"I don't know," Randy was finally able to say. "But I feel like we need to get inside."

"Yes." Dwight raised a thumbs up.

"Yeah." Joan released the tree, and they started walking toward home.

Images from that clearing flashed through Randy's mind. The creature, the fire, those faces. It hit him then who those faces belonged to. The women were Cherry and Frieda Lewis, the sisters that ran The Gilded Lady. The man was Sheriff Palmer, and that realization nearly halted Randy in his tracks. It meant the police had no intention of finding Bobby. It meant things all just got even more complicated.

Chapter Thirty-Three

A S HE RACED INTO THE house screaming Emma's name, all Randy could think about was his boys. He would have guessed Emma had gotten coffee, but she wasn't in the kitchen. She wasn't in the living room or the halls or the bedroom.

"Emma!" he yelled again, grabbing his phone from the nightstand. He unlocked it, cursing under his breath at the damn slow thing and wishing they had the money to get new ones and didn't have to rely on these three- or four-year-old devices. He opened the phone app and called her. "Pick up. Pick up."

She wasn't going to believe him. She wasn't here last time. She was going to blame him, though, and he was sure that he deserved it. He still didn't know why he hadn't remembered or why he was so hazy now, but he should have known something was off. He should have refused the house when he learned he had inherited it. Regardless of their financial situation, he should have known that the house his brother went missing from was a bad place to raise his family.

"Pick up!"

Her voicemail greeting played.

"Emma, call me now. I need to talk to you about... about the kids. Whatever you do, don't go into the woods. It's not... Just call me."

He hung up and called again. He texted her while it rang: "Call me! Please!" She didn't answer, and he didn't leave another message.

Randy walked out of the room and stood in the hallway, staring from room to room. His mind was racing. What to do?

The Whisperers, he had to find them.

He remembered another time; he saw tiny men with tiny weapons and faces of rotting flesh charging inside the house. He saw them raise their spears and axes and charge.

Randy shook his head. He glanced into Maggie's room. Thank god she was at Janet's house and out of danger. If he could only find Emma.

He remembered golden lines cutting across the woods and inside the lake, and... there was more, but it wouldn't come. He remembered Sheriff Palmer and Cherry and Frieda Lewis. The way their faces gave him nightmares.

"The Gilded Lady." But Cherry and Frieda Lewis had disappeared soon after his brother went missing—or did they? It was fuzzy in his mind, but he knew for sure they hadn't been around town for the last twenty-plus years.

Sheriff Palmer, though... he remained in office until the late 2000s and, if Randy remembered correctly, retired west of town. He vaguely remembered talk of the sheriff investing in dot-coms and making a lot of money—his property was supposedly quite a ranch. But there was more to it than that, Randy was sure; he just couldn't see it through the clouds in his brain.

Something made him think that if he could see those gold and red streaks right now, he'd see one pointing all the way to Sheriff Palmer's place.

Regardless of what had happened and what he could and couldn't remember, Palmer was the only Whisperer left. He had to go out there and question him.

Randy tapped the image of Emma in his contacts list, and he listened to the phone ring. *Where is she?*

No answer. Again.

"Emma, I'm headed to the old sheriff's house—Palmer—it's on Old 300, west of town. I think he'll know something about what happened to the boys. Call me. *Please.*"

Emma stood in the pit, staring up into the faint light above, and the sound of scratching echoed and repeated.

Scratch, echo, scratch, echo.

They were coming, she had no doubt. The teeth and claws of the furry bodies at her feet assured her of that. The walls of the shack were thin plywood. The door was wobbly, held in place by six or eight tiny screws. Those things would either squirm under the door or chew their way through the flimsy wood, and she would end up with what were essentially garbage disposals in fur raining down on her.

She trembled and patted her arm. The bleeding had lessened, but it hadn't stopped. Her leg throbbed around the wound, though she felt nothing if she tapped on the exposed bone. She wondered if she would be able to keep her foot if she was lucky enough to get out of there.

They could smell her blood up there. She was sure of it. They were predators, and predators had keen senses of smell. They smelled her and would not stop trying to get to her until they found her.

If only she had a weapon.

She had nothing on her and didn't expect a hole in the ground would have anything, but she bent over to look regardless. At that point, even a large rock would have been better than nothing.

The ground was dark, hard to see. Emma crouched and moaned as her torn flesh screamed at her. She felt along the ground, finding dirt and stones, then a rock the size of her fist, which she set by her foot for safekeeping as she kept looking.

She brushed against the body of one of the animals and yanked her hand back. The hole already stank of rotten meat; she didn't want it on her hand as well.

She searched around the thing and, finding nothing, moved on.

The scratching seemed to move faster, and that alone made her heart jump, but to make things worse, she heard a second sound. It was a ripping sound. It was the sound of wood being torn from the wall or door and a hole growing under the consistent attack of fang and claw.

She moved faster, as well. Her hands swept over the dirt, and she found another stone, and another, all about the same size as the first. Nothing bigger. Nothing sharp or pointed. She couldn't stop there.

Emma found the second beast, and this time she didn't restrain herself from touching it. If monsters were going to come down there and devour her, did it really matter if she smelled?

After pushing aside the body, she searched the ground where it had sat. The funny thing was the ground where the carcass lay was not as solid as the rest of the pit. There were hard spots, worn ground that was either compressed dirt or the start of a huge boulder—likely why they stopped digging if this was initially a well like she imagined—but there were other spots where her hand went down and kept going as if she was reaching into another room.

For the first time since falling into this pit, her heart leaped for a good reason. Another room? If she could get through there, maybe there was another way out—maybe a weapon or a way to block herself off from those monsters.

But the hole seemed fixed in place. As much as she pushed or pulled on the ground beside it, she couldn't dig through or make it any wider. The funny thing about it, though, as she ran her fingers along its edge, she found it was wider where the animal had sat and seemed to trail away, ending in a line.

"No," she mumbled to herself. "That doesn't make any sense."

She had an idea, but—no.

Emma went to the other creature, the one she refused to touch at first, and pushed it aside. She felt blood on its flank. It was cold. Then, she ran her hand over the ground below where she found it.

There was another hole. A-fucking-nother hole.

She felt around the gap, still barely larger than her hand, but it was bigger than the other one. And she decided she would use this one to test her theory.

Flinching, Emma grabbed the nearby carcass and found the face, where its fangs were exposed. That was where it was leaking rancid-smelling blood into the pit. She put the mouth on the ground beside the hole and stepped hard on the little monster. It squished under her feet, and she heard the sound of wet, sliding meat, followed by the sound of wetness on rock.

She dropped to her knees and checked.

She was right. The spots on the floor where the thing's blood leaked now had holes. Three of them, smaller, beside the first one. Three! She could barely get a finger through, but they were there. The blood had opened a door to the cave below.

There was a sharp, squealing sound in the room above. The scratching was worse. Emma imagined a fanged mouth coming through the door, and as if to answer her image, it stopped, and a chewing noise ensued.

She was out of time. She knew that.

Emma grabbed both disgusting little bodies and faced them down beside the small and larger holes. If this worked, she might end up with one large hole—at least, that was her hope.

She jumped. There was a squishing noise and several small pops. She felt the ground wobbling below her feet, and she heard a loud squeal from up above. And another. And up in the shack, way up there, the scratching and chewing ceased.

"Fuck." She let the breathy word drop from her mouth and jumped. She squared her feet directly over those carcasses, and her soles slammed flat on top, working to make every last drop of blood squeeze through.

The sound of wetness erupting from those creatures' bodies was almost like a slap, like she had burst a damn that was holding back their blood, and it exploded out of their mouths and up over her feet. The ground below opened like cracks in the top of a frozen lake, and she plunged into the hole, with nothing but air below her.

Emma dropped through a brown fog, and it washed her face in moist, death-scented air. She wondered for a brief second if she had made a horrible choice as nothing broke her fall. Had she dropped from a room into a bottomless pit? What if she fell so far that the fall killed her?

Something slammed into Emma's back, and before she saw what it was, she understood she was sliding. She was sliding down a smooth rock surface. She wasn't going to collide with the ground and splat like she was worried about. But just as that fear was assuaged, she slid over the side of a cliff and crashed down onto a pile of shifting rocks.

Pain from a dozen tiny impacts rippled up her back. But it was over. She wasn't falling any longer.

Emma lifted her head and searched the room. She was in a cave with glowing fungus on the wall, and below her... they weren't rocks.

"Emma?" it was a voice she recognized. A male voice.

She didn't know if she had ever been so happy to hear a familiar sound, and she spun to see who it was.

Her jaw hung open, and she couldn't speak. Something that only somewhat resembled James was moving toward her.

Part Six

Across the Dark Plain

Chapter Thirty-Four

DREW HAD TO STEP BACK from his friend. Eric was rising, but as much as it looked like Eric, it wasn't him. His skin was pale. His eyes had a slight haze of white. And he wasn't breathing. He was dead, but he was getting up.

"It worked!" Lance screamed. "He's okay!"

"It didn't work." Drew took Lance by the shoulder and pulled him back.

"What do you mean?"

"He's dead, Lance!"

"Guys?" Eric reached for them. "I feel a lot better now." But his expression didn't second the statement. His expression was one of curiosity, of questioning what exactly was going on. He held his hands in front of his face, examining it.

"I think we need to leave." Dean stepped between his brother and Eric. "Look." He pointed at the collapsed cave entrance, where tiny people were crawling in through the gaps in the boulders.

Drew shuddered. Fear clung to his skin like a thousand baby spiders. It was them, the people from the shadows at the fair; their heads were the size of the skulls he had found; their bodies were the same as those buried in the stone fort. But the way they walked and the decomposing nature of their flesh was what made him shudder. It made his fingers twitch.

They climbed through the entrance with the grace of athletic warriors, even as some were absent an arm or leg. Their bodies were falling apart, with slashes in their skin, stitches sealing their guts in, and bones and muscles extruding from elbows, shoulders, and cheek-bones, but they came forward relentlessly while holding axes, spears, and bows.

"The Zeetee," Bobby yelled.

To Drew's surprise, Bobby wasn't encouraging everyone to leave; he was charging at them with a large branch fashioned into a club. He swung it low to the ground, crushing the tiny people in its wake. They splattered against the wood or flew into the nearby cave wall. Bobby kicked with his stumped leg. He smashed his club into the rocks they were climbing through, smearing their insides along the stone.

But it wasn't enough. They seemed to be spilling into the cave at a fantastic rate. They chanted as they slid inside. They sang in a high-pitched tone from the other side, and as Bobby swung again at the new wave, several on the right drew back arrows and fired. Others heaved their spears.

Drew looked at Dean as arrows the size of toothpicks and spears as long as pencils stabbed Bobby across his chest and neck. The question in Drew's gaze was silent and understood: *How do we help him?*

Dean scanned the ground, and from the overflow of stones and boulders from the entrance collapse, he lifted a large rock and tossed it at the siege of pixie things. It crushed two immediately and rolled, taking down three more.

Drew picked up the rocks at his feet and tossed them into the fray. Lance and then Eric joined. Wave after wave of stones cracked the heads of tiny people. Some were crushed but kept crawling anyway, broken hands and feet, some with shattered and severed limbs, but they wanted Drew. They wanted Dean and Eric and Lance. There was determination in their tiny, dead eyes, and the unwavering aggression reminded Drew of some zombie flick. They kept coming as if a primal force like hunger was powering them, even as their bodies were pulverized and destroyed.

The singing dimmed, and even with arrows and spears in his face and limbs, Bobby kept swinging and pounding. There was a layer of mashed meat and bone by the cave entrance, and another Zeetee climbed inside and exploded against the ground as Bobby's club came down over it.

The cave became thick with the stench of rotting Zeetee. It was like moldy, green meat that had been sitting in the trash for weeks, waiting to be taken out, and it twisted Drew's stomach into a knot. Still, he heaved rocks.

"Jesus, they keep coming!" Lance screamed.

Eric howled and pitched stones like fastballs.

Dean looked for the larger stones, the ones that would crush with a single toss.

A Zeetee somehow made it all the way to Drew's feet. It hopped on one of his legs and swung its ax into Drew's flesh. The blade ripped through Drew's sock and sliced into the side of his ankle. He lifted his other foot and crushed the thing under his heel. It was harder than he expected, but when he felt the head crunch and pop, he knew it was done.

It took several minutes, but finally, they stopped crawling through the holes, and the singing died. Bobby gave one last crack of his bat across the pile of mangled Zeetee corpses, and he joined the others.

"We need to go," Bobby warned. He knocked his club on the ground, letting the clinging carnage trickle free.

"But we beat 'em," Lance said.

"Only for now." Bobby pointed at the pile. The mass of flesh quivered and slowly separated, reorienting itself into piles. "You can't kill Zeetee." He yanked the arrows and spears from his chest and neck. The wounds didn't bleed or close or do anything. They gaped, allowing Drew to see even more of Bobby's insides. "They'll attack again as soon as they reform."

"Fuck." Lance's mouth hung wide as he watched the brain by Drew's foot crawl back into its skull and the flesh seal back together.

"That's not possible," Eric said, backing away from the carnage. "They were just..."

As Drew watched Eric shrink into the tunnel, he was conflicted. That cold white flesh, those dead eyes. He didn't know what it all meant. Bobby seemed to be helping them, and Bobby was dead too, but he was still unsure if they could really trust him. Could they trust Eric?

"That's sick," Dean said, picking up another rock.

"You can't kill them." Bobby said. "Only time can. When they've rotted away so much that they can't move or think, they'll get laid to rest at their burial grounds. Until then, they hunt and do what The Shadow Man says."

"And keep coming back?" Drew asked.

"Yeah." Bobby picked up a bag made of some kind of fur and gestured with his severed foot for them to move. "We can talk more after. Go."

Drew knew he was right. He nodded at Bobby. "Let's go, guys." He ushered the others onward, glancing back at the shifting piles of flesh. He saw bones snapping back together and muscles threading themselves into systems. They would have to do it all over again if they didn't hurry.

He started down the tunnel, hissing as his weight fell on his injured foot. He wished he could crush the one that caused that wound again; his foot hurt.

Bobby took the lead and guided the group in a different way than they had gone the last time. The rest didn't speak much until they reached the opening. As they walked from the tunnel into the outside world, there was a sound like crashing water.

Lance watched as Eric walked in front of him, and Drew's words echoed in his mind: *He's dead.*

That didn't make sense. Granted, so much of this place didn't make sense. Saying Eric was dead when he was obviously up and walking around made the least amount of sense. Sure, their uncle was dead and walking around, but what did they really know about that guy? He was dead when they got there. Eric wasn't. And they were going to get home, regardless of any of that bullshit, all of them, alive.

The waves of tiny people returned to his thoughts. The crushed little things, the brains and guts and cracked bones. And they just kept coming. There was definitely some voodoo happening here. Before, he didn't know if they had somehow crashed onto an alien planet or something, but now he was sure; there was magic here.

He glanced back at Drew and Dean. Their faces were as serious as he felt. He looked past them as if he could see the cave back there, as if those things were already on the hunt for them again. He didn't see anything except darkness, and what did that mean?

They turned a corner, and the ground beneath Lance's feet vibrated. He heard the distant sound of crashing water. He wished he had faith in where Bobby was taking them, because he just wasn't sure how much more of this he could take.

Something in his chest fluttered as he recounted it all. Falling down that hole, racing through a forest, being chased by that giant monster, Eric almost dying, and then those pixie things... Oh, and the ride collapsing at the fair. How could so much happen so fast? He just wanted to be home. Home, in his bed, where he could pull up his covers and forget all of this.

"Wow," Eric said in his usual optimistic tone. Leave it to that guy to almost die, have to fight off zombie pixies, and still be positive.

As he neared the exit, though, Lance saw what was out there. He had to force his lips closed not to say wow as well.

Drew thought he had seen a waterfall before, but that was nothing like this. That was a miniature model of a waterfall compared to this.

It was him, Dad, Dean, and Maggie—Mom had to go to some real estate convention in Denver—and they were visiting an old friend of Dad's from school who lived in Custer Falls. Since the falls themselves weren't in the city proper, they went for a hike in the national park and eventually found it.

It was a strange trip, and Drew didn't understand the point at all. Dad was walking in the front with his friend, and their eyes never stopped moving, as if they were looking for something. They talked quietly, and when Drew asked what was going on, Dad just said it was grownup talk.

Drew hated that. It was like they didn't think his brain worked. He could understand things. He understood that the entire trip was stupid and that he would rather be back at home playing with Lance and Eric than in the middle of some dark and spooky woods.

Then they found the falls.

Water dove from a hundred feet up, and a rainbow shone across a cloud of spray where the falling river impacted the lake. It would have been beautiful if it wasn't for the sense that they were being watched.

Drew turned to ask Dad, and Dad was gone. Dean was there, so he asked him. "Do you think we're alone out here?"

Dean glanced around. Maggie sat on a log by the lake's edge and leaned back like she was sunbathing. The shore was desolate all around them, even across the water on the other side.

"I don't see anyone," Dean said. He walked to the beach and picked up a stone to skip.

Yeah, Drew didn't see anyone either, but he couldn't shake the feeling. He had it sometimes back home, mostly on his way to school when he had to pass Lone Wolf Lake, but that feeling of being watched had mostly subsided until they were there. But Dean was probably right. They were alone.

He joined Dean at the water's edge and picked up a handful of his own stones. He sorted through them, deciding which were better for tossing up and splashing and which would be better for skipping.

He uncovered one that was hefty and pointed on all sides and couldn't postpone throwing it. He wrenched back his arm, tossed it up and out, and watched for the splash.

That water, the expanse of murky blue green, caught his stare in a way he didn't expect. He thought he understood in a split second that it wasn't a person who was watching them; it was the lake itself. There was a shape under that surface, a shadowy, black image that made him think of a face. It opened its mouth, and its eyes locked on Drew. He swore it was about to say something when his stone crashed into the water with a *ploop* and a splash that rippled halfway to shore.

The face disappeared, and he didn't see it again that day. But he wasn't looking for it, either—he tried his best not to focus on that water and was grateful when it was time to go because he didn't think it was gone, just hiding, and he didn't think it was the only one under there.

Drew didn't truly recognize what he was feeling at that lake until now—it was the sensation of death, of the hundreds of lives taken when the downstream dam was built and the valley filled and ranchers didn't want to leave their lands. It was the construction workers who died during the project. It was the fishermen and hikers and wandering travelers who had vanished over the years and somehow ended up in the lake below those falls. Their souls seemed to roam and swim in those frigid waters the same way others did here. Only here it felt like there were thousands held in the spray erupting from the falls hitting the river. Thousands below the current headed downstream, searching for feet to pull under and join them.

The water was falling from so high it could have felt like a deluge from the heavens. The cliff face where Drew and his group exited rose three or four hundred feet up, and the river below the falls roared and rushed downstream like nothing Drew had ever seen. He was shocked by the beauty and the chilling, unnatural knowledge that this was not just water. It was, indeed, a river of souls.

Amorphous beings glimmered in streaks of red and orange below the water's blue-indigo shimmer. They howled just under the crash, where neither a single word nor a solitary voice could be isolated, only the chorus of lamentations as they passed.

The river flowed with a forest on the other side and a bleak, hard-crusted, glass landscape nearby. There were ridges and black hills and something sparkling over the barren land. It too gave vibrations of lost souls, and Drew felt trapped, with nowhere to go other than dying himself.

He was overwhelmed. His chest felt full, not wanting to rise or fall for breath. Something was clawing at his soul, calling him to join the others with a desperation that there was no hope of finding a way back home, and he would be stuck in this land of the dead forever. He knew then that he needed to just dive into the river and let fate have him.

Drew began the walk toward the water's edge. The sounds ahead broke apart almost joyously. He started to hear individual voices in the melody of souls. They called him closer. They called him by name to dive in and join them.

There was a murmur behind him, but it didn't register. They were noises from the old world, and those sounds didn't matter.

He saw the infinite loneliness of his own life in his mind. He saw himself with no one and no love, and it was bleak and draining. He saw the never-ending flow ahead, a current of togetherness and joined sorrow. It was the path that he wanted, and all he had to do was keep walking.

"Drew!" It was Dean's voice, but Drew paid it no mind. Dean was part of his old life, not this new path. Maybe Dean would even join him one day once he realized this was the only release from the endless dread of the living.

Drew reached the edge. He marveled at the colors, the streaks of light that folded into the waves and swam in threaded overlap, singing, racing the endless race. There was a unity he needed, and he so much wanted to join the choir.

One foot out, he leaned forward.

"Drew!"

Hands grabbed his shoulders from behind and yanked. Drew struggled to get through them. He slammed onto the ground, his back kicking up dust and his arms and legs flailing.

"Let me go!"

Then Dean was in his face. He was screaming words, but Drew couldn't hear them. Was he sitting on him? Straddling him?

A hot, stinging hand on his cheek. His head jerked to the side. His hands were on Dean's neck, trying to choke him—his brother...

"Drew!" It was Eric.

"Stop, Drew." Lance.

Tears ran from Dean's eyes, and the sounds of the singing water turned sour. The screeches and howls of torture replaced the symphony he had desperately wanted to join. High-pitched and angry, it cut into his ears with hot, painful daggers.

"Dean?" He dropped his hands from his brother's neck and reached out to grasp his shoulders. Sorrow dragged on him from every direction. He cried. The promise of joy had faded, and it felt like rot was growing inside him.

"Dean." It was all Drew could say as the tears kept coming. The loss of eternity shattered his heart, but his brother's smile began mending it.

"Get away from there!" Bobby shouted.

Drew glanced at the water's edge. Translucent, bony hands reached toward them. They grabbed Dean's ankle and pulled.

Dean screamed. Drew watched his face contort and knew it wasn't a scream of fear; it was a scream of pain.

Eric, Lance, and Bobby grabbed Dean's hands and pulled. Drew scurried from underneath his brother, wrapped his arms around Dean's chest, and pulled. As they all heaved, Drew saw why Dean was screaming: a translucent, bony foot was coming out of the bottom of Dean's shoe. The thing wasn't just trying to drag Dean into the water; it was ripping his soul from his flesh.

"No!" Drew shouted. "You can't have him!" Burning regret filled him. It was his fault Dean was so near the water.

They pulled together, dragging Dean's body from the edge, but the thing held tightly onto Dean. It wriggled and turned, determined to keep its prize.

"Keep fighting!" Bobby let Dean loose as the others kept pulling, and he drew what looked like leaves from his bag. He rolled them between his fingers and sank to his knees by the ghostly form. He held up his palm to his lips and blew hard.

Crumbled pieces of leaf floated against the wind and drifted through the ghost's face. It screamed even louder, as if cursing Bobby through pain, and released Dean's foot.

Drew, Dean, Lance, and Eric tumbled away from the shore and scrambled to put distance between themselves and the water. Bobby rose and took a step to join the others when a streak of red, crystallized light darted from the current and pierced his chest.

The light faded into nothing, and Bobby screamed as he shuffled toward the others.

Chapter Thirty-Five

DONNA COULDN'T TELL HOW LONG she had been walking across the glass desert. Her joints ached, and she was fairly certain her feet were both bleeding inside their disgusting shoes. Her cut foot was angrily throbbing, and the sky hadn't changed a shade since she drank from that stream and the world fell into night. The good thing was she was getting closer to the firelight ahead, and that kept her in motion.

While the ground still consisted of giant chunks of black glass, it had grown hilly. The village, or whatever it was, was up high, a few rises and falls away, and with each rising step she took, she groaned and pushed and prayed these people could help her.

Donna stopped at the top of the next hill. She sat on a black boulder, careful of where and how she touched it. She checked the wounds on her hands, paper-thin slices where she had made the mistake of touching one of those glass rocks earlier. The bleeding had stopped, but the cuts still stung as if someone had rubbed salt into them. She lifted her feet, hoping to lessen the throbbing on her soles. She wanted to remove the disgusting shoes (not nearly as much as she wanted to remove the rancid fur around her waist), but she knew she would never get them back on again if she did. The soreness would multiply as soon as she removed all the pressure those things gave, and putting them back on would have been a nightmare.

The firelight danced above the structures a few hills away. She could see the individual lights from where she sat, and she was pretty sure they were lighting up an encampment of some kind. There were noises that she thought were voices, deep, masculine voices, maybe deeper than even her father's, which had always amazed her. He could sing the lowest melodies when they used to sing Christmas carols together. His booming voice would vibrate within her chest as they sat together by the tree and drank cocoa on Christmas Eve. Every year, they did that. And this year, they wouldn't.

Tears rushed from Donna's eyes. She covered her face and leaned forward. She felt the edge of the boulder cutting into her shorts, and she ignored it because nothing could hurt worse than this. This was a burning dagger in her gut.

She had insisted on going off to college. She had insisted that she was ready to be on her own, and his idea of doing a year in the local community college first was insulting. He was just trying to be helpful, trying to let her build up to the independence she craved, and she cursed his suggestion, practically mocked him for it. She ached now, thinking of his face and wishing she could take it back.

She hadn't been ready to be on her own. The year hadn't even begun and she had been taken against her will. How could she have been so dumb?

She would never hear his voice again, never sing on Christmas Eve with a warm, cocoa-filled belly, snow across the property and coating the trees, and them smiling at each other in warm contentment, knowing that the world was just right. It wasn't. It would never be.

Donna looked into the alien sky and screamed. She shivered as tears wet her neck and shirt. Then she noticed the voices in the encampment ahead had quieted.

They heard her.

Was that good or bad? She had focused so hard on getting to the light, hoping for help, that she hadn't really thought about whether they would actually help her. They might, but what if they were as dangerous as the things in that cave or in the forest or the skeletons?

No, they had to be good. They would be willing to help her. She knew it. There had to be some good people in this place.

As Donna watched and listened, she saw two of the light sources move, one on the right and one on the left. They hadn't moved in however long she had been trekking there, but now they were—now, after hearing her scream.

Chills ran across her skin, and she burned with shame for the position she had put herself in. As much as she wanted to hope those people were nice, she felt it in her gut that they weren't, and she had walked directly to them and announced her presence.

The flames on each side of the camp spread farther apart—they were being carried. Voices echoed again, this time shouting. The flames started down the hill toward her.

They were looking for her.

Panic and shame fluttered inside and forced Donna to her feet. She pushed up too hard from the boulder and sliced a new gash in her left hand.

"Shit," she hissed at herself.

She debated what to do. She could run away, though she had no idea which way to go. She could try to hide and hope they didn't see her; maybe she could even get a glimpse at them and see if they looked welcoming. She could try to sneak past them into the camp and look for supplies. She was dying of thirst and so, so hungry.

She deemed one idea brave, one cowardly, and one a suicide mission. But she wasn't sure which to do, and she hated herself for being so indecisive. She chose to think about it another way: which path would Dad take?

She nodded and wiped her face. He may not have been there, and she may never see him again, but she had him in her heart. She would carry him.

Donna moved her feet carefully, avoiding the sharper boulders, and headed toward the camp. She planned a path between those two lights, and though she couldn't tell what was over the next hill, she was sure Dad would know what to do, so she would too.

As Donna moved closer, ducking behind one boulder and then another, she heard them on her left and right. They talked, she guessed there were between two or three in each group, and their language made her want to curl up inside herself and hide. It was guttural and grumbling. Their deep voices vibrated the rocks around her, even at a distance. She hoped so badly that she had made the right choice.

She only moved when they were talking and held still between words. She could hear the shattered crystals of broken glass shifting and grinding under her steps even when she was as quiet as could be. She knew they would hear it too if she wasn't careful.

Then, there was a moment that made her heart want to leap from her chest. They all stopped. None of them moved on the right or left. None of them spoke. It was the closest she had gotten to the ones on her left, and she could feel them. She could smell what she thought were their breaths, damp fumes of musky air carrying a scent of rotten fish and molded vegetables.

One of them sniffed the air, and Donna panicked. Her stomach cramped, desperate to expel the boiling bile inside. Her mind raced to understand what they might smell. Yes, she was wearing rotten furs on her feet and waist, but with breath like they had, could something rotten stand out? She hadn't showered in too long, but it was cold there; she wasn't really sweating. The only other thing she could think of was—she pressed her hand into her chest, the bleeding hand she had cut on the boulder a few minutes ago—exposed blood.

She knew sharks could smell blood in the water from huge distances, and bears and mountain lions could track prey from their wounds. Could these people do that? Was she their prey?

It had occurred to her before she started this way that these people could hurt her, even kill her, but she hadn't imagined that they would want to eat her. The thought made her skin crawl, and she pressed her wound harder to her shirt, hoping by some chance that she could mute the smell.

They grumbled again on the right, then the left. A second later, she heard their footsteps and talking. They were moving away, farther from the camp. She had done it. She had slipped past them.

A flood of relief hit her. She closed her eyes and relished it as their steps moved slowly farther. Then she took a chance. She didn't think she should, but again, she thought: *What would Dad do?*

Donna slowly rose from her crouched position and looked out over the sea of jagged boulders and obsidian crystals. She spotted the group on her right, and she trembled from head to toe.

While not as large as the skeletons by the river, these people were huge, twice the size of a human. They wore furs that looked like what she had on and carried weapons like tribesmen. But more than their size, what terrified Donna was their skin. They were dead, with the skin of the dead. Patches of broken rot, bone extruding, chunks hanging. If they hadn't been talking, she would have thought of them as giant zombies.

This couldn't be real, she told herself. She had to be hallucinating. But she knew she wasn't. Just as the creatures in the cave looked unreal, as the strange trees and the skeletons in the river had, this seemed so far from what she knew as reality, but it was, in fact, real.

One of them turned to the side, and she felt her bladder swell. She was about to burst, but instead, she dropped back down and held her muscles tight. She had to live—a devastating cascade of images passed through her mind of zombie movies, of being bitten and turning into one of them. That couldn't be what happened here, but Christ, she just didn't want to know.

Donna stayed low, as close to a ball as she could squeeze herself, and they kept moving farther away. She imagined what was inside the camp—what would giant dead people have that might help her? What provisions would they need?

She tried to dispel anything helpful, trying to convince herself she should turn and leave, but the dry sandpaper texture of her tongue convinced her otherwise. She was in a desert. There had been no food or water over the miles she had passed, and who knew how many more miles she would have to go before she found any. If there was even a chance that they had water, she had to take it.

Die in the village or die in the desert of dehydration? She pondered. *Dad would keep going.*

She straightened up enough to move, and she snuck forward.

The encampment had twenty-foot-high walls made of stacked black stone. Donna found it incomprehensible that it could have been built without ripping workers' hands to shreds. But here they were. Torches were mounted along the perimeter, and though the entrances weren't manned, she stared at the flickering lights and knew they were just as much her enemies as those giants' eyes.

The talking inside boomed. The tones weren't as focused and serious as had come from the creatures that were hunting her, but they still terrified her. She heard laughing, and that struck her as odd. These monstrous things were there, dead, and still living their lives? They were dead and laughing? What an absurd place she had found herself in. But if they were laughing, they were distracted, and that gave her a better chance.

She moved along the side of the wall and peeked farther into the camp. A dozen of them were crowded around a fire, men and women. They sat on boulders, and other than their grotesque appearances and massive size, they reminded her of what could have been a Viking village a thousand years ago. There was a table fashioned of dried-up logs, with weapons on one side and another with what might have been pottery. That was her goal.

She started to sneak through the entrance but froze when she caught a glimpse of their faces.

While their bodies looked human, though twice the size, their faces could only have been described as human-ish. Their eyes were too close together, and those that had noses had smushed snout-like things that would have seemed more appropriate on a pig than a person. Their teeth were wide and jagged, filling their grins in such a way that it surprised Donna when they were able to fully shut their mouths.

The worst part, though, were the things that stretched from their cheekbones and chins. What looked like tiny arms with hands of three or four claws extended from each cheekbone and each side of their jaws as if ready to snatch up food and shove it into those huge, terrifying mouths. Only, since they weren't eating, the small limbs opened and closed as the creatures talked, reminding Donna of how people sometimes talked with their hands.

There was a pop from the fire, snapping Donna from her thoughts, and she realized how exposed she was in the middle of the exit. She focused on the table lined with pottery (*that's what Dad would do*) and moved toward it with measured steps until she was able to crouch behind a boulder and take a breath.

Let there be water repeated in her mind. Food would have been wonderful, but something told her she didn't want to know what those things ate. Just water—that would get her several more miles across the desert. That would be enough.

She judged there was fifteen feet between her hiding spot and the table, but now she could also see it was at least six feet high. There were two crudely built chairs, though, one on either end. She would have to go for those.

Donna glanced over the boulder at the fire. The booming voices of males and females talking over each other, arguing yet joking— Donna thought anyway—continued heartily. This was her chance, if she truly had one.

She crept to the chair, held tightly to the dry, splintering wood, and pulled herself up. She saw the bowls and plates and gagged at what looked like shredded meat, bones, and entrails and then spotted what looked like a pitcher. She couldn't see what was in it, but hope bloomed inside her that it had to be water. It was beyond a minefield of atrocious, decaying, dead things, but it had to be water.

She climbed onto the table and stepped carefully over plates half her size and around bowls that could have served as tiny bathtubs. Her heart pounded as she took one last look at the fire and pushed down her sense of climbing dread. She crossed the distance with such focus that by the time she reached the first pitcher, she couldn't remember half the journey. But that was okay. She was about to reach her goal, despite the growing urge to flee, despite the feeling that everything was about to turn to shit.

Donna's lips were cracked, her tongue stuck to the roof of her mouth, and her cheeks felt glued to the sides of her teeth. She needed this sip. She needed to guzzle it down. She knew her thirst was endangering her, but with the prize right in front of her, her body began screaming for hydration.

She gazed down into the first pitcher. It was easily the size of a barrel, and it stank of mold and something else she refused to identify. And it was empty. *Fucking empty!*

She refused to believe it; she had come so far. The next one had to be full.

Donna slipped around the first pitcher, hiding behind it as she moved, and perched beside the second of the three. She leaned over the end and smelled something so vile she had to jerk away before she vomited into the thing. She breathed in and blew out, but the sour scent was hooked to the inside of her nose, and below that, she knew she smelled alcohol. Whatever that nastiness was, it was their party drink.

Shit!

One more. She squeezed her hands into fists and promised herself the next one was it. The next one would make risking her life to do this worthwhile. She had to believe that. Other thoughts were screaming, and she had to ignore them. They told her to jump down and take off, that she had run out of time and was about to be caught and end up a desiccated body for them to plunder and devour.

She needed water too badly to listen.

Donna rose behind the third pitcher and gazed down. It was liquid. It shined dimly in the night. She didn't smell the rancid scents of the last two containers. This was it; it had to be.

She reached inside with a cupped hand and scooped a portion out. She raised it to her face as tears wet the corners of her eyes. This was it. This was what she was risking herself for. Only, as her hand rose above the edge of the pitcher and the firelight shone over it, she saw that what was in her hand was not clear, not even slightly. It was deeply dark. It was thick, and as her nose took in the odor, she knew what it was.

It was blood. It was a pitcher full of blood from the things they had caught and killed and eaten.

Her world crashed down around her. There was no water in this desert. These giants drank the blood of their prey to hydrate. And she was in the middle of their camp. On their table, like one of their dishes.

Donna stumbled back from the pitcher, letting her fingers part and the crimson liquid run down to the table.

Her life was over. She knew that now. She was not going to survive this place, and she was going to be eaten and drank like one of her ancestors would have done to a rabbit or pheasant had it been dumb enough to wander into their camp.

Her foot caught on a plate, and she fell back onto a pile of gnarled bones with strings of tendon hanging like torn threads on a well-worn shirt. She shuffled to get up, and her hand went through a pile of something slick and gelatinous. And as all this happened, the bones and plate rattled and clinked.

She hurried to her feet and set her gaze on the fire. More pairs of eyes than she wished to count met hers.

She remembered once finding a dead squirrel in the horses' water trough back at home. It had been a dry summer, and it must have had no choice but to risk diving in and drinking from the trough or dying of thirst. And then it was trapped, drowning in the very thing it needed to survive. She had felt so sad for it. And now she was it. She was in the middle of this camp, looking for life, and what she found was death.

Chapter Thirty-Six

THEY MADE IT THIRTY FEET from the river before Drew, Bobby, and Dean collapsed on the ground. Lance and Eric stood above them, worried, glancing back at the waterfall, then the tunnel they had surfaced through. Drew didn't need to ask why; the fear of those dead little pixies was written across their faces.

"Where do we go?" Lance asked Bobby. "I'm sure they'll be here any second."

A cold wind swept across them, blowing dust from the barren ground and whispering with the lost voices of the dead.

Bobby pointed away from the river into the black glass desert, toward the flickering light in the distance. It was closer here than it had been the first time Drew saw it, and he wondered just how those tunnels worked to make that happen.

Bobby winced and pulled his arm close, cradling it over his chest. They all stared at him. By his left collarbone, there was a hole through his body—from that shaft of red light—and the edges around it seemed to be rotting away as they watched, decaying in front of their eyes like some kind of time-lapse video.

"Jesus, Bobby!" Drew scooted closer. "What is that?"

He shook his head and clutched his bag. "First, we need to move." He pointed with his good hand, again into the desert. "They won't follow us there."

Dean climbed to his feet. "But you said not to go to those lights."

"And we won't. But the only other conduit back home is past those lights—unless you want to go back through the Zeetee and dig our way out of the tunnels."

Dean looked at Drew, then Lance and Eric. "No. We'll head toward the lights."

Drew stood and held out a hand for Bobby. He and Dean got him up on his one foot and stump, and Drew tried not to flinch at his uncle's smell.

"Now, let's go." Bobby limped ahead and leaned on a black boulder as the ground shifted from dry, brown dust to shiny obsidian. The chattering of small voices echoed from the cave. They all looked back and then hurried into the glass wasteland.

About a hundred feet of black glass separated them from the riverbank when the Zeetee emerged from the tunnel. Despite all of the little people stopping at the edge of the glass desert, their anger still chased. They howled and shot arrows. They threw spears into the gap with no way of reaching Drew and his party, and they howled into the endless night to someone only they appeared to see.

Drew made himself look away. He was afraid that Bobby was wrong, that they may decide to venture into the desert even if they never had before. The images of their broken bodies reforming in that cave haunted his thoughts, and he had to block them out, look ahead, and blindly have faith in his uncle. Still, though, there was a sensation that even if the Zeetee weren't following, something was. Something was listening to the Zeetee's scornful wails, and they were not in the clear. They wouldn't be until they made it home.

They marched ahead at the speed of Drew's one-legged, undead uncle while constantly scanning the world around them. Dean limped as well, his foot aching from where they tried to steal his soul by the river. Drew felt along his nose, trying to decide if it was broken from the fall back in the stone fort. It seemed like the pace finally gave them their first moment of rest, where they could actually reflect on where they were and what they had to do, and none of them liked it.

Eric felt his chest, his neck, and his wrist, all the places he had learned in Scouts to check someone's pulse. He found that he had none. He was breathing—somewhat, at least when he consciously forced himself to so that he could talk. He was moving. But his heart had stilled, and now that he had the time to focus on it, he was start-ing to panic.

"Guys." Eric's voice was thready and shaking. "What am I going to do? I'm... I'm really dead."

"You're not dead," Lance said. "Look at you walk and talk. We just have to get you home—to a doctor. You'll be okay."

"Walk and talk?" His voice was louder, annoyed. He pointed at Bobby. "You mean like him? Is that all he needs? A doctor?"

Lance gazed at the ground. "They'll fix you. I know it."

Drew didn't know what to say. His heart ached for his friend, but he didn't know how to form that pain into words or how any of those words could help anything. He stared at Bobby's back, at the growing hole through his chest. Bobby had been here twenty-five years, dead and rotting. Drew had to wonder how bad it was—did it hurt? And then he had to ask.

"Bobby?" Drew walked ahead, closer to his uncle where he hoped Eric wouldn't hear. "Is there a fix? If you went back home, I mean."

Bobby shook his head. He understood exactly what Drew was really asking: *Was there a way to help Eric?*

"I don't think so," Bobby spoke softly. "It's just a feeling, but whenever I stand near a conduit, I get it. It tells me that if I go through there, I'll be leaving this—" he gestured at his animated form, "—this magic that keeps me moving. I get the feeling I won't be moving anymore if I go through."

"So you went there? You tried to get back?"

"I stood at the edge, and I stared into it for a long time—maybe days, I couldn't tell—just trying to decide. That was after this happened." He opened his shirt, exposing a hole over his heart.

Drew could see it behind rotted skin and cracked ribs, a gash the size of one of the Zeetee's spears. He understood then the rage back in the tunnel, the anger Bobby moved with when he smashed those little things to bits.

"I couldn't risk going through. Not if my fears were true."

Again, Drew didn't know what to say. He had never known his uncle other than the few memories Dad had shared here and there, but as they walked together, he felt the weight of a lifetime missed. He imagined living in a cave for years, dodging the Zeetee, that monster in the lake, and the river of souls. Bobby was alone that whole time; he lost it all. He lost the experience of finding a girlfriend and growing up, lost his mom and dad and brother and sister.

Drew glanced at Dean. He felt a little warmer knowing Dean was with him. He also felt guilty that he was responsible for Dean being there.

Eric rushed ahead of Dean and Lance and walked beside Bobby. Drew didn't know if Eric had heard their conversation or just found an urgent need to know more. Bobby was the only one of them who knew what it was like to be dead—or *undead*—after all.

"I am dead, aren't I?" Eric didn't frame it or try to get out of it. He trembled as he spoke, but he wanted the real answer, and Drew admired that.

"Yes," Bobby said. "Your body is dead. By some magic, this place lets the dead walk."

"So, are we like the Zeetee? If you smash us..."

"No. The Shadow Man protects them until the decay gets so bad they can't move. Then they go somewhere else."

"Like heaven?"

"For these things—maybe? From what I can tell, this place holds the dead of some other realm. And for some weird reason, there are conduits that break through to ours."

"What do you mean, Shadow Man?" Drew broke in.

Bobby turned. "I guess you haven't seen him. I've only seen him a few times, but they've always been by the gates or around the Zeetee. He's like a guy made of shadows, and his face—"

"It's a skull," Lance interrupted. He had crept up on the other side. "A nasty skull."

"You've seen him?" Bobby said.

"Yeah. I thought it was my dad." Lance looked out into the black glass wasteland. "My dad haunts my house sometimes."

"I don't know anything about that. But I'm pretty sure The Shadow Man guards the conduits. I think he gets to decide who comes through and who doesn't."

"He's like the bouncer," Dean said.

Drew turned to him—he hadn't realized Dean was also listening.

"I guess." Bobby shrugged and winced at the pain in his shoulder. He pointed to a group of rocks ahead. "Let's take a break."

Lance looked back. "I don't think they're following."

"We'll be safe until we reach the village." Bobby sat on one of the boulders. "Careful. Every edge of these things is as sharp as a knife."

The others maneuvered themselves into sitting. Only Dean cut himself, grazing his palm when his ankle failed him at the last second.

Bobby set his severed foot beside himself as he dug into his bag. He removed what looked like a pile of fungus, a couple of bones, and a strip of fur.

"What about, like, a defibrillator?" Eric said.

Bobby motioned to Drew with his severed foot. "Can you help me?" Then to Eric, "What's a defibrillator?"

"Yeah." Drew did not want to touch the dead limb, but he had a strong sense of obligation at that point.

"I need you to hold it where it goes, under my ankle."

Drew did as he was asked. He tried to only look as long as he had to, ignoring the curling skin and the smell of oozing decay from Bobby's flesh.

"You know," Eric said, "the thing with the paddles. They put them on your chest and yell *Clear!* and then shock your heart into beating again."

Bobby smashed the fungus between his hands and smeared it on both his foot and his ankle, covering the wound and several inches on either side. He stuck his fingers inside the wound and wiped the substance on both severed ends as if he was using some strange form of crazy glue. He placed a bone on either side of his foot, somewhat like a splint, and said, "Okay, hold these in place."

Drew held the foot with one hand and the bones with the other as Bobby wrapped the fur around it all like gauze for the undead.

"What do you think?" Eric said. Drew could hear the hope in his voice. It was teetering on the edge of something Drew couldn't bear to know the depths of. "Could they shock our hearts into pumping again?"

Drew slowly set Bobby's foot on the ground and stood. As he rose, he caught an unwanted glimpse of the hole in Bobby's chest, and the sight made him stagger. It was larger, maybe twice the size. The rot had moved so fast that ribs were exposed. As bad as that was, part of what shocked Drew was that even the clothes Bobby was wearing, while in terrible shape after all these years, were disintegrating along with his flesh.

Bobby looked at Eric and sighed. "Maybe if that machine was there when you died. But at this point, I don't think so. I know this is hard, but you'll need to accept it. We are dead. Only the magic of this world is keeping us going."

"No." Eric shook his head and backed away. "That's not true. There has to be a way. Like those pixie things. If magic's keeping us going, it can bring us back."

"You don't know everything," Lance shouted, and stood. "There could be a way." He walked over to Eric and put a hand on his shoulder. He was clenching his jaw and blinking hard, obviously holding back tears. He stood in front of Eric. "We can figure this out, even if that guy didn't."

Drew reached into the empty air toward his friend. He thought about Eric missing fairs to come, missing dances, even though they always agreed they were dumb. He thought of them missing each other as the future years went by if what Bobby believed was true and the magic ended beyond the conduit. He reached and wanted to hug Eric, but Lance already was. So he stood and wished again that he knew what to say. How to help. But he didn't.

A few hills from where they stood, fires burned over a small village, and Drew turned and watched the flames dance. That was when he heard the deep, booming voices of someone ahead.

Chapter Thirty-Seven

REW WAVED AT THE OTHERS, then cupped his hand over his mouth to illustrate *Quiet!* He scanned the hills between himself and the firelit village, and as a head rose over the crest of the next hill, he ducked. He waved toward the ground for each of them to follow suit, and they did, with wide eyes and panicked faces. There they were again, another horror in this crazy land of the dead.

Dean raised his head to peek. He immediately lowered himself at the sight of the monsters ahead. Giants, but dead and strange faced. He gestured for everyone to huddle together.

"What are those?" he whispered, his eyes locked on Bobby.

"Some kind of giant," Bobby whispered back. "They're from the village, and they will eat anything they catch. That's why the desert is so desolate. They must be looking for something." He rose and peeked at them. "I was hoping to avoid them, but at least it's only three. They aren't very smart, just big. Maybe we can find a place to hide until they pass."

"Or we run back the other way," Lance said.

"You see how long their legs are? They can walk as fast as we run. Better to hide and be quiet."

Lance scowled and checked with Eric.

Eric nodded reluctantly at Bobby. He was even more pale, and his eyes seemed duller. "I—I don't know how fast I can run."

"This way." Bobby stood in a low crouch and walked diagonally between the path of the giants and the village. He moved remarkably well on his patched-up foot. He still wobbled but was moving much better.

Bobby guided them down into a crevice and waved for them to follow. They went down the hill, Bobby then Drew, Lance, Eric, and Dean at the rear. Each raised their head every few steps to see where the giants were, and while Drew knew they shouldn't all be doing that—it raised the risk of being spotted—he couldn't stop himself. His heart felt like it was in his throat, and his insides were tight and squishy. He didn't think he would be able to survive not knowing where those things were.

The giants grunted and talked in voices that sounded evil. The things hanging in front of their faces made Drew think of crab legs waiting to snatch food and shovel it into their mouths. They were so big; those little arms alone were probably enough to grab him, and then it would be all over.

They reached the bottom of the hill and climbed up the following one, hiding behind one boulder and then the next. They passed the giants and continued in between the monsters and their home. At the apex of the peak, Drew could see why they had to go that way.

Their destination had been hidden in the gloom. Beyond the village was a great rock wall leading into a canyon. It shone in the dark, its ebony walls glittering with indigo sparkles. Sneaking past the village was the only way in, and in was the way home.

Drew nudged Lance and Eric and pointed. Lance's face wrinkled with worry. Eric seemed happy as if having another destination fueled the little bit of hope he needed to move forward.

The next thing Drew noticed from this vantage point was that there were more of the same loud, booming voices inside the walls of the village. They spoke and laughed—the monsters actually laughed, and for some reason, Drew found himself wishing they laughed more like the villains in the old cartoons he watched when he was little, not this. This felt more real. It reinforced the idea that those things were just mindless beasts that looked something like men. If they were as evil as Bobby said—eating anything they found—and they had laughter that sounded real, even for their deep and disturbing language, it was worse. Those cartoon criminals never actually hurt anyone. They locked heroes up and made threats while they preached world domination, but Drew never felt like they were in real danger. Real laughter from real monsters ready to serve you up over a fire was real danger.

It was at that moment that a horrible quiet passed over the entire area. All sound ceased from inside the village walls. The roaming giants stood motionless. Bobby raised his hands and forced everyone to be still so they could be as quiet as the rest. Then, a scream pierced the silence.

It cut through the damp, putrid air, telling Drew three things: (1) that was a woman in trouble, (2) she was a real woman, not one of those giants, and (3) as the roaming monsters turned and ran toward their village, he might get through this terrible black desert alive.

"That was a girl," Eric whispered.

"Yeah," Drew agreed. "Like, a human girl."

Bobby glanced at the village, and then back to the others. "Whoever it was, she's not going to make it. We need to pick up the pace and get past the village while they're all inside."

Eric faced the village as another scream, this one a shrill howl of absolute terror, came from inside its walls. "We have to help her."

Lance threw up his hands. "It's a town of giant monsters, dude. What are *we* going to do?"

Eric stood tall and firm in front of the rest of them. "If she's a human, we have to at least try. How would you feel if it was you, and we just said, 'Glad it ain't us,' and moved on?" He turned and headed for the village.

He was right, and Drew knew it. He didn't know if they could rescue the girl—they were giant freaking monsters in there!—but they had to at least take a look and see if it was possible.

Drew went after him. The rest followed.

Chapter Thirty-Eight

THOSE HORRIBLE EYES WERE FOCUSED on Donna from across the village's common space; the murky deadness, the cloudy swirls of white over decaying ocular matter scanned her, and she felt them imagining how she tasted. They were like her old cat Gypsy, a calico stray she found in the barn during a mid-January snowstorm and brought inside. She was feral but too tired and malnourished to fight. She became a friend as she put on weight and recovered that winter, though the tops of her ears had to be removed because of frostbite. She was almost tame, except when she spotted a mouse or a vole. Her eyes would lock—just as these things did now—and she would wait, perfectly still, until that prey animal moved. Then she would pounce.

That was what Donna was now. She was prey, frozen in place, knowing she was caught and they were readying themselves to pounce. There was only one thing she thought she could possibly do:

create a distraction.

She fought the urge to duck and hide, the urge to turn and run. She would have to do that soon enough, but right now, she had to hope and pray the lessons she learned from her magician's trick book at ten were still valid.

Donna shifted her weight to her right and moved at a snail's pace until she was behind the middle pitcher, the one that stank the worst. She placed a hand on the pitcher with blood and stretched the fingers on her other hand between the empty pitcher and the middle one. When she was ready—once she had taken a deep breath and knew this was her only shot—she pulled on all three as hard as she could.

The pitchers started to topple, and giants sprinted toward the table.

Donna let out a scream as they moved, then forced herself to go with the plan.

The blood pitcher, being the heaviest, hit the table first, splashing crimson in all directions. She ducked as it sank, pushed it, and dove into the empty one. All three pitchers rolled along the table as a wave of thunder raced across the camp under the charge of giants.

Donna felt the rotations, and if her stomach wasn't already ready to blow, the barrel roll would have done it. The sound of pottery on wood resonated as the pitcher followed the others. Her head was pressed against the clay, and the sounds rattled in her brain.

And then it wasn't as loud. She hoped it meant the blood pitcher had rolled off the table, then it was even quieter in her head. The second pitcher had dropped. Her world went silent as her pitcher rolled off the edge of the wood. She had a moment, just a moment, to enjoy the peaceful stillness inside her weightless vessel. It was like floating, and she imagined this was what space must feel like.

Before she had time to come to a conclusion, the roar of a half dozen giants found her ears. The pitcher slammed into the hard-packed ground below the table, and as the pottery burst into a thousand pieces, a few dozen of them poked and prodded at her sides, back, and then head. A large chunk of hardened brown clay lay on top of her.

Donna scrambled to get free of the broken pitcher and scanned the ground for where to go. She could see the openings in the village wall ahead and behind. She could see a few black glass boulders. There were huts on the left that looked as dead and ready to collapse as the giants, and then there was the fire and the group of monsters running at her in front of it.

Her feet felt glued to the floor as she tried to decide what to do. She couldn't hide behind a boulder, not with them chasing. She might be able to hide in one of the shacks, but they were so far away she wasn't sure she could make it. The village exits were way too far, but it would have been best to get out.

Two of the giants seized the table and lifted. They tossed it to the side, exposing her to the enormous things. They were so close they could probably swing and grab her, and all she could do was run. So she did.

She didn't know which direction she had chosen until she faced front and found she was headed toward the gate. Then three giants, the ones she had been avoiding beyond the walls, stepped inside.

Donna skidded to a stop. She couldn't get past them.

She darted right on instinct alone. She heard a rumble and watched a giant stumble and fall that had been following and couldn't turn as sharply as she had.

The huts were ahead. They were made of rock and dried wood and a fuzzy substance on top that, as she looked at it, she understood was made of something like the animal skins she was wearing.

A giant stepped from the doorway of the middle hut and charged toward her.

Donna cut to her right again. There was another booming crash as a giant landed hard on the packed earth. She turned to see where she was going and caught a glimpse of the other exit. That was where she would aim, and if she kept getting them to fall and slow down, she could make it. She just had to keep her wits about her and keep running. They were only big, dumb—

Her feet rose from the floor. She had lost contact with the ground. A split second later, she felt the grip around her waist and arms, and she looked down. She was in a single hand. Its massive fingers were locked around her like that poor lady in *King Kong*. There was nothing she could do and nowhere to go, and as the thing turned her toward it, made her confront it, face to face, her bladder let go. Her heart beat as fast as a hummingbird's. Her lungs pushed air in and out so quickly her head became light, and spots of black, white, and purple danced in her vision.

The small, clawed arms swayed in front of the monster's face. They curled in toward the beast's mouth again and again as if they were welcoming her into his maw.

She wanted to scream, but she hadn't the breath. She wanted to run, but her feet were so far off the ground. She wanted to break free, but its hands were wrapped around her like the clawed arm of an excavator. She had no escape, only fear and her choice of how to accept her end.

Donna's gaze locked on the monster's. She saw it dead but envisioned it alive, an alien thing living a primitive existence somewhere she couldn't imagine. She knew it used those gigantic hands to kill and survived as barely more than an animal, and she prayed.

"Please?" she whimpered. "Please, let me down. Please, don't hurt me."

It looked at her curiously. It grabbed one of her arms between two fingers and let her hang as it took the other arm and held her spread wide. She dangled as the monster examined her.

"Please! No!"

She wasn't getting through, and the giant swung her close to its face and sniffed her with its giant pig-shaped nose. Its tiny facial arms grazed her up and down as it took her in. Other giants neared and looked on.

Donna wept. She had to look away. At the sky. At the walls. Beyond the gates to what should have been her freedom. There, she spotted something strange: a group of kids beyond the gate, hiding and watching her from behind a boulder. She wanted to be there with them. She didn't understand how there were other humans here, but maybe they knew the way home.

Her thoughts were cut short as the giant took her by the waist and pulled on her left leg until it ripped from her hip socket.

She screamed like she didn't know she could and watched in

astonishment as the monster placed her leg on its tongue, the tiny arms stroking it as it went into its mouth, and then it chewed.

She heard crunches as its teeth cracked her bones and a gulp as it swallowed. She felt cold as she streamed blood from her hip down onto the black ground.

Donna blinked and was somehow outside herself. She didn't feel the pain. She looked down, following the blood with her eyes, and the entire scene was hard for her to understand. Why any of this was happening was hard to understand. She was just a college kid from a small Montana town. This type of thing didn't happen. It had to have been a nightmare all along. It was impossible. And from deep in her gut, a laugh roared from her mouth.

The monster must have liked the taste of her leg, because it immediately grabbed her other leg and ripped it from her body.

Donna snapped back into her head and howled as the monster handed her limb to its tiny arms and they rotated and aligned it with its lips. She felt her legs screaming in phantom pain as that thing sucked on her severed thigh.

The monster to the left shouted something, and Donna was passed to that next giant. It turned her upside down and gave her entire body to its four waiting facial appendages, which held her to its lips as it sucked from her gushing wounds.

She thought this must be what a crayfish would feel if it was alive when people sucked out its insides. It was like a vacuum removing her blood and sucking her flat. She felt pressure and pain, and thankfully, a few seconds later, her vision turned black.

Donna didn't know how long it had been when her eyes opened. All she knew was when she tried moving, nothing worked. She saw the monsters above her. Was she lying on the table? One placed something in its mouth—it was her arm! She tried to scream, but there was no sound from her mouth. Another giant slurped up something that looked like spaghetti into its massive hands. Another held—*God, no!*

She recognized a small tattoo of a butterfly on the ribcage, and she tried to scream again. And it occurred to her as she watched, unable to move—how could she scream with no lungs?

It put her chest into its mouth, and she heard it crunch.

Lastly, one picked up her head, and she watched its mouth grow ever larger. She watched its massive brown teeth close in on her face, and there was a crack and a pop, and she was no more.

—Or at least, she was there no more.

She felt rushing all around her. She was together with thousands of others, slipping and sliding, moving with a current and drifting wherever the path took her. She heard them moan and howl, and then she felt the all-consuming burn of the liquid around her. She howled with them. She howled without a mouth or body, only an essence that screamed to escape, or at least drag others in to join her.

Chapter Thirty-Nine

REW HAD TO COVER HIS mouth to keep from screaming. She had looked him in the eyes, right in the eyes, from over there. He had connected with her for that moment, and then... the way she hung from the giant's grip, the way it plucked her leg off like you would pluck a grape from a stem; it made him want to shout and cry. And then it ate her legs! When the other one took her and started sucking her dry, Bobby put a hand on Drew's shoulder and ushered them away.

There was nothing they could do to help her, not at that point.

Drew walked in the line: Bobby, Eric, Lance, himself, and then Dean, all of them shaking and glancing back, all of them mourning for that poor girl. Drew had to wonder if they could have saved her if they had gotten there faster. He wondered who she was and if she came through the same *conduit* or, maybe, the one they were heading toward? If she came through that one and the giants caught her, maybe this wasn't a safe path. Maybe they needed to go a different way?

He glanced at every rock, at every darkened spot in the gloom, at every step. It seemed this place was filled with nothing but things that wanted to kill you. He doubted that they were going to get through them all. There were just so many, so many creatures and so much death.

When they reached the tall walls and thirty-foot gap that marked the start of the canyon, Bobby stopped them. He looked each of them in the eyes. "This is a dangerous path. We need to be careful here."

Lance pointed back at the walled village. "If this is dangerous, what was that?"

Bobby's eyebrows raised, and he winced. The rot in his shoulder had reached his arm, and the limb was barely holding on. "That was just how this realm works. Ahead? That's another story altogether."

Dean leaned in. "What do we need to look out for?"

Bobby winced. Drew swore he heard a crack as Bobby's arm shifted lower.

"This canyon isn't like the other places we've been. In there— the rules of this realm seem to shift. It's a path where reality slips and folds, and the creatures that live within... they're just as bloodthirsty as those things," he glanced at the village, "only they're used to the shifts in there."

"I don't get it," Lance said. "What do you mean, *shift*? Obviously, you've been in there before."

"And I barely made it out. You'll see what I mean. Just..." He paused. His face contorted in a rictus of pain, and his arm crackled and dropped from his shoulder. It hung from a slim strand of flesh connected to his armpit.

"Bobby!" Drew reached for him, but Dean held him back.

Bobby clenched his teeth and with his good arm ripped the other from its pendulum. He groaned loudly, and the others were frozen, silent. He looked at the limb longingly and dropped it on the glass floor. Even detached, whatever new rot that infected Bobby kept eating away at the severed-limb's flesh.

Bobby met the others' wide eyes and open mouths. "Just be quiet and quick, and stay out of sight. And we should get through this."

"Bobby, your arm?" Drew said. He looked from his uncle to the limb and back. He watched the flesh on his uncle's chest sizzle as it dissolved. "You're being eaten away."

"Honestly, it's about time." Bobby smirked. He didn't say it, but he looked grateful. His brows raised, and he smiled.

All Drew could think about was how hard it must have been for his uncle to suffer here all alone. And then to finally be found.

"Let's just get you guys home."

Dean remained at the rear as they marched into the canyon in a single-file line. He scowled as he stepped over Bobby's arm. It seemed like this trip had just been one giant nightmare, and he hoped to God that Bobby was right and this truly was the way home.

It had been one dreadful thing after another since they got to this place. The fall, the forest, the beast in the lake, the giant skeletons, the tiny people, the giant zombie things... it seemed to be going on forever. And Drew's friend Eric—the poor guy. He felt like shit thinking about it. He knew he wasn't the designer of this quest, but he was the oldest—that meant he was responsible. And he hadn't been. He walked out into the night with three younger kids by his side, and now one of them was dead—walking around, but dead. That idea made him sick. But more than that, it scared him. He was scared for Drew.

The fear stretched several ways, and it was hard for Dean to wrap his head around it all. He was afraid of what Drew was going to have to deal with when they got back—what all of them would have to deal with, but especially Drew—losing a friend, and he was sure Drew would get blamed and blame himself for it. His brother was a sweet kid; there was no way it wasn't already eating him up. And he was afraid for his brother physically. This place had death around every corner, and it just kept coming. Add to that Bobby's warning when they started into the canyon.

It was all so much.

And Dean was tired, ready to pass out. He was sure he would if he had more than a minute to sit and rest. It was after midnight when they snuck out of the house, and they hadn't taken a real break since. Not that he would want to sleep here, but still.

His eyes were heavy as he crossed into the canyon. The walls of the passage were thirty feet apart, and though the outer edges were black glass, the same as the desert floor, once inside, they were something different, something that felt off. The surface was still dark and shiny, but as Dean looked closely, it wasn't glass. It was black, porous lava rock, and it was wet. Something was seeping from the holes in the wall, and the wetness was making it shine. It put a thought in his mind, one of a shadowy thing with a face that didn't stop smiling, and he wanted to rip that thought from his mind. But he couldn't. It hung back there, refusing to leave, hovering as he measured his surroundings.

Between the walls were long boulders. They were as tall as a person, and the way they sat across the path, they made a sort of maze through the space. It made Dean wonder just what was hiding within those twists and turns and dead ends. What kind of *shifts*, as Bobby put it, were coming?

All he knew was that looking into the dark maze of boulder-strewn canyon ahead filled him with dread. And he would be on his toes every step of the way to protect Drew, no matter how tired he got.

Lance walked with clenched fists. He did not like the tall, black walls on either side of them—not that he liked anything since coming to this living hell-world—but the sight of the oozing liquid that coated them from as far up as he could see to the canyon floor made him shiver. It was gross, and as much as he was curious about what it was, he knew he would regret trying to find out. It was only going to get worse. This place only got worse the longer they were there, and he knew this canyon would be more of the same. The farther they went into it, the worse it would get, the more he would know that they weren't getting out of this.

Sure, he put on a good face for Eric and Drew, but he was aware of the truth: they were going to die here, probably before they reached the end of this path.

Didn't they see that girl get literately pulled to pieces? Didn't they see Eric die? Christ, Bobby just lost his arm. And here they were, headed into another dangerous place where—

Lance stutter-stepped as a shape seemed to glide across the enormous boulder on the left. It was a flutter, like a sheer piece of black fabric slid over the rock and slipped away—a shadow.

But then it was gone, and he kept moving.

He was so tired, and his eyes were playing tricks on him.

He watched the wall on the right. There were caves up there, high above them, and he hoped nothing was in there. He glanced at the other side and saw caves there as well. He was about to open his mouth when he remembered Bobby's instructions: "Be quiet and quick, and stay out of sight." They were moving at a good pace, and no one else had said a word yet. He hoped the boulders covered the third part: stay out of sight.

They moved from the right side of the path to the left, around a small boulder, and to the side of another larger one. It felt good to be less open, but now they were almost right next to the wall and exposed to the caves above.

Lance's eyes went from cave to cave. The shadow drifted across the wall from one to the next just behind where he stared. He turned and watched, trying to track it, and it was gone. It was like this trick of the light was just out of focus—or was he too tired to deal with this?—or was it hiding from him?

He stared hard, watching a single cave. He swore if he just stayed concentrated there, it would come back.

What came was something different.

It was a face in the darkness, just inside where the gloom made that world everlasting night. But this face stood out, and he recognized it. It was broad and square, chiseled, with a five o'clock shadow and deep-brown eyes. It was scolding him with its gaze, and Lance felt like he was four years old again. He had pulled the chocolate milk from the fridge and taken it into the living room to watch *Paw Patrol*. Then, he accidentally dumped the entire gallon onto the carpet. It was a chocolate marshland, and his feet splashed and slipped all over the floor until Dad came in. The scream from his father lasted inside his memories longer than any *I love you*, and as he saw that face in the cave, he felt it coming again. The scream was going to make him scream back, and he'd have to run the other way, no matter what the other guys were doing. He just couldn't stand it.

Lance stopped and covered his mouth. "No." It was a whisper chasing his shaking head.

"Lance?" Eric asked.

Dad's mouth opened. The scream was coming. He could feel it. It would dig into his guts and rip apart his soul the same way those monsters did to that woman.

"Lance..." Eric stood in front of him. He looked up at the cliffs and then stepped between Lance and the wall.

"Dad," he whispered, with Eric blocking his view of the cave.

But Dad wasn't there. And as much as he was afraid of that scream, he realized that he wanted to hear it. He wanted to hear any bit of Dad's voice that he could.

He missed it so badly.

Tears ran from his eyes, and he thought he saw something. But it was only a shadow. A shadow of a skull-like face in that darkness.

Eric wished he could do more for Lance, for all of them. The longer he existed like this, the more he knew he wasn't going back, and the more he saw things he wished he didn't.

As the tears ran down Lance's face, Eric was sure he couldn't share what he was seeing. It was hard enough for them as it was.

The Shadow Man's face was everywhere he looked. It reflected in the oozing wall slime. It stared down from the caves above and from the sky. It was omnipresent, like some helicopter god that refused to give them an inch of space.

Eric fought with the question: was he going insane? Were these things real or were they a byproduct of his mind starting to rot inside his head? How could he tell the difference?

"We need to keep moving," Bobby whispered to the rest. He glanced up at the translucent shadowy skull in the clouds—or, at least, it looked like that to Eric... "It's not safe here."

Eric needed to ask, but not near the others.

They moved one at a time along the path through wet boulders and bleeding walls, and Eric rubbed the side of his head. He could feel something slick, but not with his fingers. As he rubbed his scalp, he understood it was deeper. The slickness was inside his head. Inside his skull. Was his brain melting?

No. Bobby said something about this canyon messing with people, *shifting.* That was what this was. It was messing with his head.

He forced his hands to his sides and looked ahead. The canyon seemed endless. It went on into the gloom, on and on above the scattering of boulders, and Bobby just led them forward.

Why is Bobby doing this? It was something he hadn't asked himself before, but now, it struck him as odd. If this really was Bobby, maybe he was doing it out of some sentimental attachment to his lost family, but he didn't even know Drew or Dean. What if this wasn't Bobby? What if it was some random undead guy and what was waiting at the end of this path wasn't an exit but a trap? Maybe The Shadow Man waited ahead, and Bobby was looking for some reward for his trouble? To get his arm and leg fixed the way The Shadow Man fixed the Zeetee.

He shook his head. He shouldn't be thinking such things. They weren't helpful.

Still, though. His stomach curled inward, and a rotting belch pushed its way up his throat and over his lips. He looked up to blow the gases out, and he spotted something strange.

The Shadow Man was gone, but other shadow beasts had come.

They flapped their wings and soared in long strides above the canyon. They looked like nightmare things, dark, translucent beings with multiple tails and skeletal faces with single eyes yet long snouts of fang and horn. Limbs whipped from their sides and fluttered in the wind, but as they passed one another, these limbs would clash and strike like barbed whips.

It had to be another delusion, right? It had to be his dead brain inventing images for him to fear, not real beasts that were only half inside this reality.

He watched one turn and descend. It was ahead of them and swooping down, gliding through the canyon, and then it was coming right at them. He stopped and watched in stunned silence. It was such a strange delusion because it was going to disprove its existence as soon as it passed the others unseen.

"What the hell?" Dean shouted from the rear of the line. "Look out!" He was pointing up ahead. He was pointing at the flying thing. It was real, and it was changing as it approached. It solidified from shadow into flesh, and its open maw screeched so loudly they had to cover their ears as they hugged the boulders and cringed.

Eric felt the wetness on his shoulder as he pressed himself against the stone. Bobby cowered in front. Drew was nearly flat against the ground. Lance was just a little higher, covering his head with his hands.

The beast snapped its claws at Eric as he ducked lower. The sound was like stone on metal, a hollow clanging sound that ground as the claws slid across each other.

Eric turned forward and was about to speak when another set of claws seized Lance's shoulder right in front of Eric's face. He just had time to see blood seeping from the connection as Lance was jerked out of sight, screaming.

"No!" Eric hated himself as another set of claws found Drew and lifted. Drew howled, and Eric knew he should have mentioned the beasts as soon as he saw them. He thought they weren't real. He thought—

Daggers ripped into his shoulder and lifted him from the ground. "No!"

He saw them grab Bobby and Dean as he was yanked toward the heights of the canyon walls and dragged into an enormous, gloomy cave. The beast screeched, and that was all he could hear as the darkness shifted to bluish-purple light and hungering shadows crept toward him.

~ 289 ~

Part Seven

The Whisperers

Chapter Forty

RANDY LEANED AGAINST HIS HEADBOARD, and Dwight and Joan sat on opposite sides of his bed. It was a meeting he never thought he would have in his room, and definitely not about this subject.

"What are we gonna do?" Joan brushed her damp hair behind her back. She had insisted on taking a shower as soon as they came inside. "Those people by the fire have to know something."

"We have to go to the police," Dwight said. His fingers twitched over his pants pockets, not knowing what to do with themselves, especially with Joan in the room and the knowledge that she had just been in the shower fresh in his mind.

"I know who they were. The police can't help us." Randy stared at the ceiling, still trying to put it all together because it just didn't make any sense. "It was Cherry Lewis and Frieda Lewis, from The Gilded Lady, and... Sheriff Palmer."

The other two's mouths dropped open.

"Sheriff Palmer?" Joan repeated. "No way."

"I know what I saw. They stared right at us, and I saw their faces."

"No." Dwight shook his head. "You gotta be wrong."

"I'm not wrong."

"That means—"

"It means the police won't help us. It means they won't find Bobby because, at the least, the sheriff is in on it."

All three were quiet for several seconds.

Finally, Joan spoke. "So, what do we do?"

Randy thought for a moment and finally said, "We start with the safest option. We go investigate the ladies at The Gilded Lady first and see what we find. They live in that apartment above the shop. Maybe we can sneak in and figure something out."

"I wish Mom and Dad would help," Joan mumbled.

"Yeah." There was no hope for their help. Mom was still in her own world in the kitchen, and Dad was a few sips from passing out drunk in the living room. "But they won't. We both know that."

She sighed.

Randy scooted down the bed and put a hand on her knee. "We may have to do it ourselves, but we'll figure this out. We'll get him back."

He really wanted that to be true. He hoped it was, but he needed her to believe it most of all. The way she reacted at the docks was still with him. He thought she was going to have a complete breakdown over Bobby. He couldn't let that happen. He had already lost one sibling.

She leaned in and put her head on his shoulder and cried. He held her there until she sat up. "I'm sorry." She got up and walked to the door. "Tomorrow morning, then." She wiped the tears from her eyes and steadied herself. "Right?"

"Right."

Randy lay in bed, exhausted and unable to sleep, staring at the ceiling. He had chatted with Dwight about the Lewis sisters and the sheriff and about how hard it was going to be to get to the bottom of this, and though he was certain they would figure it all out when talking to Joan, now he wasn't so sure. And that nagging uncertainty was eating at him.

What if they failed? What if Bobby wasn't just missing? They looked like a bunch of witches around that fire—what if they killed Bobby or turned him into something unrecognizable?

And that thing—that monster—it swam. It ran and had claws. What if the Lewises could control one? What if they had it as a pet or something? They wouldn't actually be the safest ones to investigate if that was true.

But behind all of those other thoughts was the question of The Shadow Man. They may have identified some townsfolk who were involved, but they still had no idea what he was or how he could expel them from Bobby's fort like that. He was a sickening kind of monster, one that seemed to Randy worse than the beasts because something worried him that The Shadow Man could pretend to be just as much a human as the Lewis sisters and the sheriff could. The face of bone and meat, that non-corporal shadow of a body, screamed demon. And demons could just as easily slide into people as Randy slid into his pajamas.

He turned to his side, where he could see out the window. He saw stars and the handful of streetlights in town. He could see Dwight in his sleeping bag on the floor, and he just didn't feel comfortable, so he rolled the other way.

He saw over the bedroom rug into the empty hallway. It was dark. There was a faint murmur from the living room TV, and he wondered if Dad would go to bed tonight or sleep in his chair like the past few nights.

His eyes were heavy, and though his mind still had questions to ponder, they fell closed. Until there was scratching behind him. A sound of tapping on wood and a ripping noise mixed with the faint whistle of the wind through the open window.

Randy turned, and at first, he wasn't sure exactly what he was seeing. There was movement on his windowsill. The screen was flapping—had it been ripped?—and something was crawling through. Whatever was happening, there was a tiny golden trail forming on his screen, his windowsill, and—was it going down the curtain?

That didn't make sense. He had obviously dozed off and awoken to something that his sleepy mind didn't understand because he was starting to think those were tiny people climbing through the window and crawling across his sill, tiny things with pale faces and scrunched noses, and they were walking toward Dwight's sleeping head. And they were carrying little axes and spears.

"What—" His voice was groggy, but it was enough to make many of the little people look up at him while the three closest to Dwight continued toward him, raising their spears and axes as they closed the gap.

An understanding crashed into Randy: the golden trails, the tiny people—their heads specifically. They were from Bobby's stone fort. The Shadow Man had sent them, and they were here to hurt them.

"Dwight! Get up!" Randy threw back his covers and jumped from his bed toward the hallway. He grabbed his baseball bat from the corner next to his closet and raced around the bed.

"What?" Dwight's eyes were closed. He faced the bed, and they were almost on him.

"Dwight, get up! Quick!" Randy ran between Dwight and the window, and he felt the air move by his ear. He scanned the ground and saw a tiny thing raising its spear to throw.

Without a thought, Randy slammed his bat down on top of it. There was a wet crunching sound, and a series of high-pitched words came from the window.

"Jesus!" Dwight was sitting up, his feet still in the bag, and he was pushing himself toward the foot of the bed, with little monsters following him. Closing in on him. "Randy!"

After a series of tapping sounds, a half-dozen arrows the size of toothpicks were sticking out of the sleeping bag. Dwight screamed.

Randy swung the bat at the things on his sill. There was a *whap*, and they soared across the room and slammed into the wall. He ran toward Dwight and brought the bat down hard, thumping on the carpet and crushing two of the things in one swat. The remaining little creature raised its ax and ran toward Randy. He stepped back and swung again, and that one squished into a broken pile of flesh beside the others.

There was a shriek.

"Joan!" Randy spun and headed toward the door. Dwight jumped up and pushed the bag down his legs, tried to step, and fell hard on the bedroom floor. Before Randy left the room, he saw Dwight fighting to get back up and free his legs.

Randy rounded the corner and, mid-stride, took in the room. Joan stood on her bed, an arrow in her shoulder and a cut on her forehead. She swung her feet, unsuccessfully kicking at an advancing pack of five tiny people.

In the dim light of Joan's room, Randy could see them better— their torn and rotting skin, their pig-like noses, their decaying and disgusting eyes. They reminded him of some B-grade horror movie with little Claymation monsters he would have watched late at night while Mom and Dad were sleeping. But these were real and hurrying at his sister despite her awkward footwork that looked more like bad dancing than an attempt to defend herself.

Randy raised the bat as he neared the bed and swung wide. He crunched through four of them and just clipped the fifth. The ones he hit flew across the room, tumbling through the air like mangled toys, their limbs flopping at unnatural angles. The one he clipped spun and flailed on the bed. Dark-red blood ran from its arm, and when it stood back up, the limb hung limply. That didn't stop it from picking up a tiny ax in its other hand and charging at Joan.

Joan yelped and leaped off the bed.

Randy shifted his weight, raised the bat high, and brought it down as hard as he could on the ax-wielding thing. He felt it crumple into a pile of meat and bone through the handle, and he scanned the room for more.

"Randy, come on!" Joan was just outside the door, with Dwight by her side.

Randy searched the room one last time and retreated to the door. He slammed it shut. They raced toward the stairs, and he yanked his door shut on the way. They hurried through the house, down the steps, and into the living room, where Dad was snoring in his recliner and the room smelled of whiskey.

"Dad!" Joan shook him by the arm.

It took several shakes before he opened his eyes and five minutes of Joan pleading before he agreed to stand up and look in her room for the intruders. When he did, he found nothing, and his tirade shook the house.

Dad went to his room that night.

Randy searched both bedrooms for any traces of tiny people and only found fading golden tracks. They were gone.

He slammed and locked the windows in both rooms. All three decided to sleep in the same room, and they took shifts staying awake to look out for the zombie-pixies' return.

Randy leaned on the wall, his eyes on the window and his hands gripped around his bloodied bat. He watched what looked like shadows shift behind the windowpane, and he thought about Bobby. Poor Bobby, wherever he was. He glanced at his sister, in his bed, and Dwight in the sleeping bag, now on the opposite side of the room, closer to the door. It had taken them a long time to fall asleep, and Randy didn't blame them. He wished he could sleep, as it seemed that dawn was forever away.

He needed dawn. He needed a reprieve from the anxious feeling in his chest for himself and his sister and friend and the growing sensation of dread for his brother. He needed to do something about all of this. It was the only way he was going to feel better, to make his loved ones safe. He had to wait for daylight to wake them up so they could visit The Gilded Lady and get to the bottom of this.

He gripped his bat tightly. It squeaked under his fingers. He was going to get answers at The Gilded Lady, one way or another. He imagined he was going to have to threaten the Lewis sisters to solve this, but he had no idea just how dangerous those ladies would be.

Chapter Forty-One

"I DON'T SEE YOUR PARENTS' CARS," Janet's mom mentioned as they pulled up to Maggie's new house on the lake. "Are you guys going to be okay here alone?"

The car stopped, and all Maggie could hope for was that Mom and Dad took Drew and Dean with them so she and Janet could have some time to themselves before Drew bugged them and Dean drooled over her friend. She picked up her backpack and grabbed the handle.

"Mom was talking about getting some necessities for the kitchen the other day, so I'm sure she'll be back once she's done shopping." That was a half-truth—what Mom actually said was she hated the house and wanted to replace everything—but she didn't care. The important thing was to placate Janet's mom so she didn't object to leaving Janet over. It was bad enough that the weekend was cut short because the woman's boyfriend bought them tickets to some concert in Missoula; she didn't want to spend the last free weekend before school alone with her brothers.

"Okay," the mom said as Maggie opened the door and climbed out. "But call me if you have any problems." That was directed at Janet, who slid out next, with her small green backpack in hand. Janet had a history of *having problems*, or as most of her friends called it, *being a diva*, which was why her bag was stuffed with all of her necessities, including facial scrubs and creams, fingernail treatments, her daily skin care regimen, her daily hair care needs, her vitamins and supplements—most only known of from TikTok reviews—and a massaging machine for her feet, arms, and neck. And if any one of the items was found missing over the course of her time away from home, she would not hesitate to get her mother on the phone and have a replacement delivered immediately. It was not something Maggie enjoyed about her friend but something she had grown to accept because in almost every other aspect of their friendship was joy—until the fair accident last night.

Every hour following the event had been spent with Janet either crying because it could have been her that got crushed when the ride went rolling off its track or with Janet on some high horse saying she had been blessed by God, and God didn't want her to die. Maggie could agree that they were lucky, maybe even that God wasn't ready to punch their tickets just yet, but she wasn't ready to say it was thanks to some cosmic phenomenon where the fate of the world was at play and Janet was saved because she would one day become a prophet or something.

But it was traumatic. And that meant they had to sort through it and support each other, even if it was a pain sometimes. Maggie just hoped the change in scenery would help to snap Janet out of her deus ex machina complex and let them get on with regular stuff, like planning their senior year out properly. That wasn't going to get done all by itself.

"Okay, Mom." Janet spoke in a dry tone and followed Maggie inside as her mother drove away.

Maggie glanced at Janet's mom as she turned onto the main road and hoped for the woman's sake that Janet wasn't missing anything, because if that call came, she was in for a three-hour ride back from Missoula to soothe her child's needs.

They crossed the entryway and headed directly for the kitchen. It was almost lunchtime, but what Maggie really had her mind set on was the tub of ice cream that she knew was in the freezer. Only, when she opened the door, the tub was gone.

"Those little shits!"

"What?" Janet set her bag gently on the counter.

"There was cookie dough in here. I know for a fact there was."

"You really want to eat ice cream with less than a week to burn off those calories?"

Maggie hadn't thought about it that way. She did want to look irresistible on the first day of school, really show those boys what they had been missing all summer. But a spoonful or two wouldn't have hurt. Probably.

"I guess you're right."

"They probably did you a favor."

"Yeah, but they're still little shits."

Janet laughed. "Of course they are."

"Fine." Maggie closed the freezer and opened the fridge. She snagged a bag of baby carrots and a small container of dip. "Let's go to my room, and when Mom and Dad get back, we'll make them order pizza or something."

Janet grimaced.

"Okay, okay, salads."

"Better."

Bag and snack in tow, Maggie led the way to her room.

"The new house is cool." Janet didn't mean it, but Maggie was glad she was trying.

"It's okay. My room's a bit bigger, and the lake is nice."

"I need to see the lake. I brought a suit. Can you get towels?"

Maggie wasn't really in the mood to swim—she definitely wasn't in the mood to have Dean ogling her friend—but she guessed that was one of the things she would need to learn to deal with living on the lake. She wanted to be a good hostess, after all.

In her room, they munched a few carrots and changed. Minutes later, they were down the path to the lake and laying out towels a few feet from the shore. In the distance to the west, they heard a boat and someone yelling. Someone else laughed.

"This is actually really cool," Janet said as she lay on her towel. Her suit was smaller than the bra and panties she normally wore, and it made Maggie feel a little apprehensive about hers, a more modest pair of swim shorts and a petite top. She hoped Janet wouldn't think of her as a prude or immature. She felt like it was a kid's suit.

"I need to get a suit like yours, I guess, if I'm going to be living at the lake," Maggie conceded.

"Yours is cute," Janet lied. "I mean, it's probably better for paddle boarding and stuff—do you have one of those yet?"

Maggie felt a cold flush. She couldn't afford one of those, but now, living here, she was sure she was going to be asked if she had any of the toys water people owned.

"It's on my list," Maggie lied. "Definitely by spring, when it gets warm again."

"Cool." Janet pulled her sunglasses over her eyes and set her head down so her whole body could get sun.

Maggie did the same, pulling her shirt up to her breasts so her belly could tan.

Minutes passed under the soothing lap of gentle lake waves against the shore. Another boat passed their inlet in the distance. Maybe a jet ski? Maggie wasn't sure of all the noises yet. What she was sure of was the feeling that began to creep over her.

It started in her toes, a cold feeling as if the water was rising and slowly dousing her. But that was dumb; she didn't even open her eyes to check.

Then it reached her ankles and trickled up her calves to her thighs, to her hips. It climbed up her spine with tiny tickling fingers, and as it did, she felt coolness creep over her arms, down to her hands. Her whole body wanted to shiver but didn't. She clamped her teeth and told herself she was being stupid. She was lying on the shore on a warm morning with her friend, and then there was a scratching sound in the trees to her right.

Probably a squirrel. It *was* a forest over there.

There was something about the feeling and the sound together that made a thought click inside her mind. It was a recognition that even though she hadn't turned and looked, she knew what was happening: someone was watching them. Someone was peeping from the trees.

Dean! It had to be her brothers or their pervy friends hiding over there to fill up their spank banks with images of Janet and her half-naked.

She sat up quickly and spun to the left, expecting to catch them crowded around a tree or a boulder, eyes wide and freaked out after being caught.

There was no one there—not that she could see, anyway.

"What is it?" Janet didn't raise her head or even open her eyes.

"Nothing. Just thought I heard my brothers. I guess it was just a squirrel or something." Maggie lay back down and closed her eyes. The uneasy feeling refused to leave, but she remained still. She listened. If her stupid brothers were around, she was going to catch them one way or another. She just had to wait.

A bird cawed off to the right. The lake calmly brushed against the shore and lulled. And again.

There was another noise on her left. It was them; she knew it. She just had to play possum a little longer, let them get a little closer. Then she would catch them.

Rustling in the pine needles and dry grass. Whispering, but it didn't sound like two boys. There were more than two voices, and they were high-pitched.

What's going on here?

As quickly as she could, Maggie spun and stared toward the woods. The whispering ceased. An army of tiny people stood there, maybe ten feet from where she lay.

At first, Maggie thought it was a trick. How else would you explain between ten and twenty little mutant people staring at you? They had to be plastic or ceramic, like little lawn gnomes, only these looked like tiny zombies with pig noses.

For the first few seconds, her assumption made sense. They were all still. Obviously, Drew and Dean had somehow snuck over and placed these things while her eyes were closed to frighten her. She wasn't going to give them the satisfaction.

"Ha ha, guys," Maggie shouted toward the trees, then the house. "I would have thought you could do better than that."

"What?" This time Janet did lift her head and look. "Creepy. What's the deal?"

That was when the one in front tilted his head to the left.

Maggie tilted her head in return, wondering how a ceramic statue could do that.

Another statue did the same. Another turned its head from Maggie and looked at Janet.

"Why are they moving?" Janet asked. She sat up.

That feeling in Maggie's spine electrified her. It screamed in her ear *Get up and move! Now!*

"I don't know what those are," Maggie said. She backed off her towel and rose to her knees. "Dean! Drew! This isn't funny anymore!"

Two of the gnomes looked at each other, and the high-pitched whispers resumed.

Janet stood. "I don't like this. Let's go inside."

Maggie was about to agree when a small stick flew past her face. She followed it with her eyes as it arched and descended, crashing into the front of Janet's bare thigh with a quiet *thuck*.

Janet screamed. Blood ran over her knee in a trickle.

"What?" Maggie screamed.

The group of little people launched themselves toward Maggie and Janet. Instead of whispering, there was a chorus of tiny war cries as they came.

"Run!" Maggie screamed. She moved, and another tiny spear soared past her.

Janet took off, running faster than Maggie despite the spear in her leg.

The air whined, and buzzes like tiny bees flew past Maggie's head. reached the path up the hill, and she felt a sting in the back of her leg and another on the back of her head. "Ow!" she cried, and kept running as another sting found her other calf.

Janet howled as she raced to the top of the hill.

Maggie felt her legs getting numb as she climbed the path. It seemed like her body all around those stings was losing its feeling. She ignored it and glanced back. The little army was rushing after them. They were nowhere near as fast as humans, but they were coming at a good pace, and something told Maggie that if she didn't outrun them, she would be done for.

She groaned and pushed herself up the hill.

Another sting, this one in the back of her arm. The numbness was almost to her toes, and Maggie worried what would happen when both legs were completely numb. Would she fall? Would she die? What would those things do to her if they caught up?

She looked up the hill for Janet. Her friend had crested the path, and she could barely see the top of her head. With the numbness spreading, Maggie wasn't sure if she could make it all the way to her house. She needed her friend.

"Janet!" She couldn't see Janet anymore. Janet didn't answer back. Bees buzzed past her head. "Janet!"

Her left arm had no feeling except for her fingers.

Janet heard her name but kept running. The pain in her leg said those things were serious, and as much as she loved Maggie, she loved herself more. If that meant those things took Maggie and she lived, she just had to assume that was how destiny worked.

She tore open the mudroom door, stepped inside, and slammed it shut. She felt for the locks as she stared out the window and sealed herself in the kitchen.

"Jesus! What the hell was that?" She felt herself up and down, yanked the miniature spear from her leg, and realized she had left her phone down there with her towel. "Shit."

She wasn't going back down there. But how was she going to call Mom to come get her? Hopefully she hadn't left town for her concert just yet.

Maggie's phone! That was it. She remembered Maggie leaving it in her room because she was too scared to take it near the lake and get it wet. For once, Janet was thrilled to have a poor friend.

She ran through the kitchen, her knee throbbing from the wound. Blood streamed down her leg and left a trail across the house as she moved.

Up the stairs and down the hall, into Maggie's room. She shut the door and looked at the knob—no lock. Were they so poor they couldn't afford locks on their doors?

She groaned as she spun around to look for the phone. She thought she saw Maggie put it on her nightstand, so Janet circled the bed, stopping between the mattress and the window.

"Shit!" the phone wasn't there.

There was a ripping sound to Janet's left. As she spun to see what it was, she remembered there was no AC in Maggie's house and that the windows were open. She cursed Maggie as a one-eyed thing—all she could identify at that moment was the eye and the teeth—soared through the window and sank its fangs into her wrist.

If she had to describe it, she would have said it was like a cat, only made of shadows. The only part that looked solid was the skin-less animal head ripping into her arm, tearing away flesh as it shook its jaws back and forth. The rest was fuzzy, as if half of the black beast was in this world and half was somewhere else.

Its tails snapped as they changed direction. The whipping tendrils on its back sliced the skin on her belly and whipped at her eyes. The legs clawed into her elbow, holding on as she screamed in pain and shook her arm up and down and left and right, none of which seemed to help.

She howled. How was this happening to her? She saw her blood leaking from her arm and the gashes in her belly, and beyond the thought of how ugly those scars were going to be, she wondered just how much blood she had. Could she lose that much and be okay?

Janet raced for the door, her arm out to the side. Blood spattered with every step. She needed help. Maybe Maggie was back and would help her? She would pretend that locking the back door was a mistake. As she passed Maggie's dresser, though, she had another thought. She raised her arm high and slammed it down on the giant piece of ugly, archaic furniture, animal-side down.

There was a screech as the thing collided with wood and then a crunch. The pain was immeasurable as claw and fang sank deeper, then released. Janet drew her arm back, relieved at leaving the beast behind.

She stood there for a moment, calculating. Her thoughts came slowly as she caught her breath. Was she safe now? She still needed a phone. She heard her blood patter on the floor and watched it drip, drip, drip in large blobs. She needed a bandage. She needed to find another room to hide in and call Mom.

When she took a step to escape the room, she saw another one. It was just outside the door. Its bony jaws opened. If jaws could aim, she would have said they were aiming right for her.

Janet's next thought was the window. Maybe it was clear now, and she could get out that way.

Her eyes swept past the dresser, and there was a clicking sound as the smashed beast's body shifted and plumped, crackling as its bones realigned. It stood up and squatted, ready to pounce.

"No!" This couldn't be happening. Not to her. Bad things didn't happen to her. She just had to get away, to get to her mom. Mom would make it all better.

Janet took off toward the window. There was a soft series of thuds, a galloping of feet on her right and behind her. She grabbed the window frame, desperate to fling herself through, and hot, siz-zling pain ripped into her back.

Her fingers instantly stopped working. She couldn't grab or pull on anything. She could only curl her hands to her chest as whatever was in her back seemed to be running—running in place and digging into her spine and nerves as she sank to her knees and fell on her side.

She gagged, and blood bubbled up from her throat, over her lips. Her legs twitched and flicked out and in involuntarily. The second creature walked, almost sauntering, in front of her. It seemed to sniff at her with its skinless nose, examining the scratches on her belly.

Janet could only cry. She whimpered, but no words would come. She was forced to watch as the beast in front of her gripped her wound and spread it with two legs, then dug deeper with the other two. There were only a few quick slices, and the thing was inside her.

As it dug through her body, all Janet could think was that she hoped Mom had a horrible time at the show.

Chapter Forty-Two

B Y THE TIME THE SUN shone on Randy, Dwight, or Joan, each of them had woken with a start more than once. The night was short between the attacks and the morning, but it felt like a lifetime of worry and fitful attempts at sleep.

They slid on their clothes, eyes on the windows and ears attuned to the others. They ate a few swallows of Cap'n Crunch and Honey Nut Cheerios, and they were off on foot toward The Gilded Lady, Randy's baseball bat clutched securely in his grip.

Between the three of them, none carried themselves with the confidence Randy would have liked. They were determined to get to the bottom of whatever was going on, but after witnessing that fire and the burning creature and the whispers, with the attack from those weird little people, they were on edge, all of them. They watched the bushes on the sides of the roads and the branches of trees. They didn't look at each other when speaking. And what they spoke about was procedural: breakfast, crossing the street, what time the shop opened—not a word about the plan, what kind of weird magic was happening, or what the women may do when they showed up at their door. It was fear holding them back. Randy was sure.

He stopped the group at the corner of Poplar and 9th Avenue, two blocks from their destination. "Are you guys ready for this?"

Dwight didn't speak.

After a few seconds, Joan said, "We have to find Bobby. So, yeah."

Randy faced Dwight. "If you're not up to this, you can hang back. We don't have a choice; he's our brother. You do."

Dwight shuffled around a bit. "I'm coming. What do you think's gonna happen? You think they'll talk to us?"

"I don't know. Maybe they do. Maybe they have an army of those little people in there." Randy raised his bat. "We won't know 'til we get there, but we'll learn something."

Dwight looked around. "Wish I had one of those too."

So did Randy. If only he had an extra bat. "If anything goes down, get behind me." He scanned up Poplar and then 9th. Traffic on this side of town was light so early, and not a single car was out. "Okay."

He led them up 9th, and they stopped at the locked door of The Gilded Lady. The sign in the window said *Closed*. They opened at nine, and as Randy checked his watch, he saw it wasn't even eight yet.

"What do we do now?" Dwight asked.

"This way." Randy headed right, into the alley beside the building. There was a parked minivan there, and a door. Faint, red glowing trails led from the front doors of the minivan to the door on the side of the building. The upstairs windows held a light golden glow around them. Randy aimed at the door with the end of the bat. "Their apartment."

"That red stuff…" Joan pointed.

"Like the fire last night," Dwight added.

"Yeah." Randy raised his fist to knock on the door. As his knuckles rapped the first time, he noticed the red wasn't just a trail, it encircled the frame, following the outline around with a loop circling the knob. It was a strange sight, and he hoped he wouldn't have to discover what that was all about.

There was a collective inhale between the first and second knock. Randy felt his bowels clench, and he tried to calm himself. It was going to be okay; they were just a couple of middle-aged ladies—nothing to fear. It crossed his mind that maybe he shouldn't doubt his senses as the door creaked open and Ms. Cherry Lewis stood in the doorway.

She was a pleasant-enough looking woman, and Randy had always thought she seemed like a typical knitting-circle type. A little shorter than him, with gray hair, a few streaks of peppery black not-withstanding, she was a mildly plump and usually smiling woman. As she shined that usual smile toward Randy, his friend, and sister, she said, "Good morning," and Randy couldn't deny there was something else behind that smile today.

Behind her in general.

It was a red-edged shadowy haze that seemed to float in the air at her back. It swirled and rippled just enough to make the smoky edges twist and turn with the alley's incoming breeze.

Dwight took a step back, and Randy felt him retreat. Joan shifted where she stood, but she didn't back away.

There were waves of cold coming from inside. Each washed over Randy in the blink of an eye, and as they did, the red edges around Ms. Cherry Lewis flickered. Whispers drifted from the open door, spoken by none, which crept into Randy's mind. The red trail around the door flickered. The glimmer of daylight in Ms. Lewis's eyes flickered with a red hue.

Randy realized they may have made a huge mistake by coming here like this, and there was a flood of fear in his mind when he understood that the next words out of his mouth would determine their future.

"What did you need?" the woman asked. Randy swore there were red sparks between her teeth when her mouth moved, and the whispers paused as her words sounded.

In the split second that followed, Randy remembered every one of Bobby's birthdays, every Christmas, riding bikes around the lake together, playing pranks on their sister, building those damn models, and the face Bobby made when he was five and skinned his knee and Randy carried him to the house for Mom to fix it. Each one of those memories weighed as much as a house. Each one pulled at him, screaming that Bobby was gone and this lady was responsible. They wiped away the hesitation in his mind, whether for the good or bad, and pushed him to act.

Randy lifted the bat up sideways as if he was about to bunt and darted forward, ramming it into the old woman's chest. As he passed over the threshold, he felt himself cross a field, an invisible wall that red magic had made, and it tingled on his skin like static electricity walking over him. But he wouldn't stop for that. He wouldn't stop until he was sure this lady was going to talk.

"Randy!" Joan screamed.

Cherry fell back onto the steps leading up to her apartment, Randy following her down, the bat pressed firmly against her chest. Joan followed them inside.

Randy stared into her eyes and saw that red magic flutter around. Her face flushed, and she was about to speak, and he knew he had to talk now or he might lose his courage.

"Where's Bobby!" he screamed into her face.

Cherry's eyes crossed and rolled back into her head. For a second, Randy wondered if she was having a seizure. He pictured her getting wheeled off in a body bag and himself in handcuffs, the cops charging him with murder.

But it wasn't a seizure. It was the start of something else.

Whispers filled the stairwell. They seemed to be coming from everywhere. From the old woman, from the stairs themselves, from up above in the apartment and down below in the street. They spoke in a language Randy didn't understand, and they layered over one another in a chorus of voices, more voices than he could pull apart to count.

"Where's Bobby?" Randy repeated.

The stairway was lit with webs of overlapping red strands. They crawled across treads and risers like electric strings.

There was a boom from above. It shook the stairwell and

dragged Randy's eyes up. At the top stood the other Lewis sister, Frieda, her gray hair alight with crawling red trails. Her eyes were drawn back into her head, and her hand shot forward.

What happened next would have haunted Randy for the rest of his life if he was able to remember it. It sent a shock through his system that he didn't know how to react to—only respond to without thinking.

From Frieda's hand erupted what first seemed like another strand of the same red electricity that crawled over the stairs and surrounded the door, but as it descended over the steps in a continuous bolt, it widened and solidified. As it passed over Randy's head, he saw it take on the properties of matter or, more precisely, blood.

It was liquid, but it was solid. It was a beam, yet it was flowing, thick and viscous, and the end of it went through the door, wrapped around Dwight, and yanked him inside the building. It pounded him into the wall, and as he dropped, his eyes rolling backward into his head, the door slammed shut and the blood went for Joan.

Her mouth opened to scream, and it covered her entire face in a swath of thick scarlet.

That was when Randy acted without thought, because thought would have only held him back. Thought would have had him on the floor crying at the madness and ferocity of the evil encompassing his sister. Thought would have brought more fear, fear of now, fear of pain, fear of future repercussions.

Somehow, he knew, and he trusted his senses.

Randy pulled the bat away from Cherry's chest, raised it over his head, the end of the barrel pointed down, and rammed it into Cherry's face like a battering ram. There was a crack the first time, and then a scream inside the chorus of whispers. She didn't open her mouth, but he was sure when he brought it down the second time her voice was in there too.

That time, the crunch was wet. There was give below the bat, and the webs of red lines over the stairs died. Frieda's long tentacle of blood lost its solidity and dropped from the air, splashing over Randy, the stairs, and what was left of Cherry Lewis.

A scream of inaudible words carried down the stairs from the second-floor landing. The whispers were still there, but they were muted. There was still energy flowing over Frieda's face and teeth, but it was more of a light orange. The shadow was there behind her, and the orange tips of its swirling fog looked almost like fire to Randy's worried eyes.

"Joan!" Randy shouted. He didn't take his eyes off Frieda Lewis. He knew there was only a moment before her next move. He raised the bat to his shoulder, ready to swing at whatever came. "Joan? Are you okay?"

"Yeah..." Her voice was weak.

"Open the door. We need to go."

"Dwight... He's knocked out, I think."

"Drag him out."

Joan groaned. "It won't open!"

The whispering witch at the top of the stairs was doing it. She was keeping them locked inside with whatever that red shadowy power was, and the longer he waited, the harder he knew it would be to leave.

He jumped over Cherry's body and started up the stairs as fast as he could.

"Randy, no!" Joan screamed.

He had no illusions that Frieda was going to be harder to deal with than Cherry had been. Cherry wasn't expecting him to charge at her. Frieda Lewis, on the other hand, was staring at him, glowing, and though they had dimmed, the whispers around her only seemed to be growing louder.

He was almost to the top when she raised her hand and pointed it at him—the same hand that had spawned a twenty-foot solid limb of blood. She screamed, and the whispers pounded in his head. They raged on his skull like a torrent of whitewater. Her eyes were completely red and glowing in a way he didn't think was possible other than on toys and Christmas lights.

He was almost in range, about to swing his bat, when her hand jerked and contorted. The skin around her fingers sealed together, and their tips hardened and elongated. It only took a second, but in that time, her hand became a fanged muzzle that shot toward Randy's throat.

He shifted and swung, bringing the bat down hard on her hand. His foot tripped over the top stair in the maneuver, and as she screamed and darted to his left, he landed on the top floor.

Joan hurried up the stairs behind him.

Dwight shook his head and climbed to his feet. He yanked at the door, pulling the knob with all his weight.

Randy pushed himself up and watched as the second Ms. Lewis stumbled, pivoted, and stared back at him as she turned into something only his nightmares could have imagined.

Her hand snapped toward him like a chained dog. Her other hand cracked and reshaped itself into a similar fanged orifice, only with more teeth. Her tall body creaked and slurped as she collapsed toward the ground, and her face curled into her chest. Her torso split open like a flower, welcoming her head and exposing her pumping lungs and beating heart.

Joan reached the top and screamed.

Frieda's chest sealed shut, and a new head sprouted from her back. It was slippery with blood and formed around shadow and crimson lightning. It had a beak, with fur and wet feathers surrounding six bulging eyes. It took just a second to tear the clothing from her flesh, and then it charged at Randy on four mouthed limbs.

They snapped as she moved, biting the air and carpet and piercing the whispers with loud clacking sounds. She jumped, aiming a muzzle at Randy and another at Joan. Those eyes, those wet, bulging eyes, seemed to watch everything in the room at once.

Joan spun, covering her chest and face with her arms and squatting on the stairs. Randy leaned back and swung his bat with everything he had in him.

There was a crack as Randy's lumber collided with the woman's beaked face. Her fanged hand flew past his cheek but caught a shred of his shirt and dug a red line into his shoulder. Her other hand missed Joan, but as she flew over the top step, over the stairway, her mouthed feet snapped at Joan's leg, taking a chunk of jeans and a two-inch strip of skin with them.

Frieda flew over tread after tread and put her hands down in front to catch her fall, but they crumpled as they touched. Her bones snapped, her beak cracked as she rolled onto her new face, and when she passed her dead sister, her skin seemed to release. The seams opened up on her deformed hands and chest as if the magic could no longer keep them sealed.

Dwight screamed, and suddenly the door opened.

The whispers faded to nothing, and every trace of red magic faded from the room.

Joan cried at the top step.

Dwight called from outside the door, "Come on! Let's go!" but Joan sat with eyes closed and fists in balls.

Randy watched the two humps of Lewis sisters for several seconds, sure they were about to leap to their feet and come at him again. When they didn't, he crouched beside Joan.

She heaved as her chest rose and fell, and tears slipped past her eyes.

"Joan, it's over." He placed a hand on her shoulder. "Look."

She shook her head and wailed.

"Joan, we have to go. Please."

"Home?" she eeked over sobs.

"Home, yeah. Let's go home."

She peeked through slitted eyes. She connected with him, searched the upstairs, then looked at what she must have been dreading: the bodies on the stairs.

"Come on." He stood and offered his hand.

She took it, and they moved slowly down. She didn't look at the bodies; she focused on the bright outdoors ahead.

Randy looked the Lewis sisters over, making sure they wouldn't leap into some surprise attack like horror-movie villains were prone to do.

Cherry was motionless. Blood seeped not only from her crushed face but from within her clothes as well.

While Frieda didn't move, Randy was less convinced she was dead. As he got to the bottom of the steps, though, and he could see through her open chest, he was reassured. Her exposed lungs lay still, flopped over her stringy-haired head. Her heart hung motionless in the gap, and all of her blood seemed to have emptied on the stairs, making it impossible to step around it. Above it all, that beaked head stared at him. Those eyes, all of them, seemed to watch as they passed through the door and shut it behind them.

Randy's skin felt a strange kind of prickle all over. His fingers trembled with the knob in his hand. It was guilt, and it made his legs weak. He knew he was just acting in self-defense, that he had just come to ask questions, but with a bloody bat and two people dead, the feeling was like a brick in his stomach. He knew he had to do what he did, but that didn't help, especially while Joan held herself, contracted in fear. They were still two lives, and he took them. And though he knew the Lewis sisters were dead, he couldn't resist the nagging feeling that he would see that evil again.

Chapter Forty-Three

MAGGIE SLAMMED INTO THE BACK door, barely able to stand. The knob didn't turn.

"Janet!" She looked through the window and saw no one. "Let me in!" Tears ran down her face, and her body shivered. "Janet!"

Her friend wasn't coming. She didn't want to believe that, not after the years they had known each other and the love she thought existed between them. But there it was. Her best friend in the world had left her to fend for herself with two legs that she couldn't feel and an arm that was as useful as a hanging slab of meat.

"Shit!" she cried, and limped along the side of the house.

She glanced back, expecting to see the little army cresting the hill. She didn't, but she couldn't trust that. They were sneaky, and she knew that even though she couldn't see them, they were somewhere right behind her.

Around the corner, up the side of the house, then to the front door, she wobbled as she went. She looked like a drunkard on a night out, and as much as she hated Janet at that second, she prayed she was okay.

Thank god the front door was open. Maggie limped through the entryway, locking it behind her. She staggered into the kitchen.

"Janet? Are you in here? Are you okay?"

The numbness was climbing over her hips. It was climbing up her arm and into her chest.

Maggie grabbed her phone from the counter and wobbled to the steps. "Janet?" She shoved the phone into her bathing suit and used her good hand to steady herself against the railing as she moved up step by step. She reached the top and started down the hallway to her room.

She froze. She didn't see Janet, but she saw enough. A pool of blood ran from under her bed and was creeping out of her room.

If her legs weren't already numb, they would have gone that way now. She dropped to her knees in the hallway.

"No, no, no."

Then, there was movement in her room. For an instant, there was hope. Maybe Janet was okay despite the lake of blood. Then she saw a face that numbed the rest of her in an instant.

Its one eye locked in on her. The shadowy legs propelled it toward the bedroom door, and Maggie knew what it wanted from that stare. It wanted her dead.

She scrambled backward and around the corner. She saw the stairs, Drew's room, the bathroom, and the closet. She did the only thing that made sense to her, racing on hands and knees into the bathroom, spinning, and slamming the door behind her.

There was a thud and a crack as she locked the door. She fell backward on the floor as that thing clawed at the wood. She reached for her phone while the numbness took her chest and climbed toward her head and her good arm.

It was gone, no longer in her bathing shorts. Franticly, she spun and spotted it. It was by the door. The screen was cracked.

"No." Her voice was a whisper.

On her side, she pulled herself around and picked up the phone. She could barely see what was on the screen, but she thought it was unlocked. She thought she hit *Phone*. She thought she called *Dad*.

Randy watched the sky darken as he drove through Lone Wolf toward Old 300 West. He passed The Gilded Lady and flashed with memories that he barely recognized as his own. There were scenes of red lights and blood. Of monstrous things and Whisperers. It didn't make sense, yet he fought to understand it, and the more he tried to remember about that week when Bobby went missing, the less any of it made sense. But he knew those memories were real, even if he couldn't quite piece them together yet.

He remembered searching the woods and finding nothing, and then he remembered finding The Shadow Man. The man Mom said didn't exist. And then, the next week, he was searching the woods again.

There were memories of little creatures in his room and Dwight and a fight, and then there were other memories of the same night, yet they were playing cards and reading comic books. The overlaying thoughts made him want to bang his head into the steering wheel until only the right ones revealed themselves.

He passed the fairgrounds, where a crane held the broken ride up and investigators wrote on pads while the carnies that were left stood around and worried. It occurred to Randy how coincidental it was that his boys went missing the day after the tragedy at the fair, and perhaps it was no coincidence at all.

He passed Emma's office and scanned the parking lot for her car. It wasn't there. The lot was practically empty, as he would have expected on a Saturday morning. So where was she?

The speed limit past Traction Avenue raised to forty-five, and Randy found himself going sixty. He turned left onto Old 300 West at the sign for Custer Falls and Helena, and he gripped the steering wheel so hard it squeaked under his sweaty fingers.

He racked his brain, hoping to remember anything useful from twenty-five years ago, but everything was just so jumbled up. There was a creature in the lake, and there was a bonfire. There was Dwight and him playing Uno in his room with Joan, and Dad went out and got them pizza and a DVD from Mountain Video. It was a late night of movies and then video games after Dad went to bed, and then the Lewis sisters and Sheriff Palmer's faces in the firelight, and red traces of smoke and energy, and tiny creatures covered in blood.

But in all of those memories, the sheriff was the constant. He was there when they searched for Bobby. He was at that bonfire. He was on the street when Joan and Dwight were—his brain hurt, trying to remember so much at one time. But regardless of what he could or couldn't recall, he knew that Palmer was somehow related to The Shadow Man. That bastard knew what happened to Bobby back then, and he had to be able to help them find Drew and Dean now.

Randy passed mile marker 12. The turn was almost there. He found himself wishing he had some backup. Emma, Dwight, Joan, all of them seemed like they should be there to help.

The fence line on the right side of the road changed from barbed wire to wood. After another quarter mile, there was a turnoff where he was met with a tall pair of ranch markers, tall posts joined with a drooping log over their top. Hanging in the middle was a metal plate with the word *Palmer* laser-etched through the center, with a pine tree on either side. There was also a locked gate below the sign.

Randy couldn't remember just how Sheriff Palmer had come into money. When he was a kid, the man was just a regular guy who lived in town a block from the police station and drove an old pickup when he wasn't on duty. At some point in the years following Bobby's disappearance, that changed, and then he retired from the sheriff's office, out here.

Randy spotted a video camera on the left ranch marker and kept driving. Though he wasn't sure of the details, he didn't think Palmer was going to be happy to see him. He drove another hundred feet and pulled onto the shoulder, then he turned off the car.

He took a deep breath, trying to clear his mind. He had to do this right. He needed to surprise Palmer, and he needed the upper hand when he did. He didn't have a gun in the car, and he wished he had grabbed his pistol from the safe, which was in some box in his bedroom. But he had something else.

He popped the trunk of the car and pulled the small duffel bag close that held the winter survival stuff they replenished every year. It held things like emergency blankets, flares, Hot Hands, and, in this case, what he was seeking: a utility shovel and a hatchet. It wasn't a gun (*or a baseball bat*, the thought rang in his mind), but he would make them work.

He shut the trunk and scanned the road for cars. With no one coming, he climbed over the fence and headed into the woods that lined the property.

There was a smell in the air as soon as Randy crossed onto Palmer's land. It wasn't strong, but there was a clear metallic scent that reminded him of something he couldn't quite put his finger on. It gave him chills as he passed under branches, seeking out Palmer's home. He had known this was a dangerous undertaking, but the chills warned of more than that. There was something here he truly didn't want to find.

After a long walk through spruces and pines, Randy found a large clearing containing the main house, a large, detached garage with three bays and what looked like an apartment above, and another building that he couldn't identify. It could have been a barn, but it was sided with dark-brown wood that matched the color of the main house. All three structures sat on a circle like a private cul-de-sac. Between Randy and the buildings was a gap of grass and decorative stones, a few hip-high boulders, and a scattering of tall blue spruces.

He scanned the windows and driveway for the ex-sheriff and started across the gap.

He didn't know if he ever felt so exposed. There he was, trespassing, walking across open ground with a shovel and hatchet, with nowhere to conceal himself and his sons' lives on the line. All he could do was move fast and watch out.

He paused momentarily at the few small boulders halfway across the lawn, looked at each window, and kept moving. The image of The Shadow Man hung in his mind as if that demon was there watching him. Maybe he was, for all Randy knew. He sure felt like he was being watched, even with no sign of Palmer or security cameras. But he was no expert. Cameras could be so small today they could have been mounted in the pine cones and he wouldn't have known.

The third, unknown building was the closest, so it was the first Randy stopped at. There were no windows, and when he went around to the front, he found only a large locked door. That metallic scent was strong there. It was like it was leaking from the cracks around the door, and the entire building made Randy's nerves tingle. Whatever was in there was bad news, and he wanted no part of it. He just hoped that Palmer wasn't in there too.

Next was the garage. One of the large bay doors was open, and Randy slipped inside to check it out. He found a fully restored 1969 Camaro SS that must have been repainted in flawless red with white stripes. There was also a blue 1982 Corvette that looked just as pristine as the Camaro. In the third stall, Randy found Palmer's trademark red-and-white 1985 Ford F150 with just as much rust and just as many dents as he remembered. He figured there was some part of Palmer that wanted to hang on to his roots despite the money he had come into.

But where did all the money come from?

There was a stairway to Randy's right that he followed up to an empty loft apartment. It was well appointed, with leather couches, fine china, and a bed softer than any hotel Randy had ever stayed in, but no clues. He would have to try the main house.

He slipped out of the apartment and back down the stairs. He was about to step onto the garage floor when his phone buzzed inside his pocket.

The sound seemed to fill the silence of the room, and panic gripped his chest. He fumbled the hatchet into the same hand as the shovel and pulled the phone from his pocket. The screen read: *Maggie.*

He declined the call and thanked God again that she was out with a friend and not at home. He shoved the phone in his pocket and calmed himself.

It was just a quiet vibration. No one heard my phone. I have to keep going.

Randy padded to the open garage door and peeked out. The sound of footsteps on asphalt pulled him back. It was him. It was Palmer. Now was his chance.

He listened to the footfalls as they approached from the house. He held his tools tight even as his body wanted to shake. This man knew what was happening and how to get the boys back. Randy had to do this right because if he screwed up, they could be lost forever.

He held himself against the wall beside the open door and waited. If Palmer came in, he would be in the perfect spot to bash him on the head with the shovel and incapacitate him.

But Palmer didn't come in. He walked past the garage toward the other building that Randy couldn't get inside. Randy had no choice but to lean out of the garage and watch.

Palmer stopped at the door to the third building. He took a key ring from his pocket and unlocked it.

The metallic scent hit Randy as soon as the door was cracked. It was like the smell didn't need wind to carry it, just the ability to be let loose. That scent rolled around in Randy's brain, and as hard as he tried, he couldn't place it. It was like blood, but it wasn't. It was like the ozone from a spark, but it wasn't.

Palmer stepped inside and shut the door behind him.

This was Randy's chance. He could follow Palmer inside or, worst case, if he locked the door behind him, Randy could wait and smack him on the way out.

It was now or never.

Randy hurried across the asphalt, careful not to drag his feet or make more than a minimum of sound. He reached the door, and the odor from inside made his brain buzz. There was something so famil-iar about it—it ate at his nerves, not being able to identify the source. It was creepy and dark, and he didn't want anything to do with it, but he had to go in there. The feeling in his gut was to turn and run, to find another way to help the boys, but he just couldn't do that. He was here. He had to make it count.

He turned the knob; it wasn't locked. He pushed softly, com-manding the door not to squeak.

The inside was dark. There was no sign of Palmer anywhere, and

Randy realized he was holding open the only source of light in the room, making himself the target if Palmer was watching.

He closed the door as quietly as he had opened it. He turned back to a shadowed interior, his hatchet and shovel braced in his hands. His insides twitched and twisted, screaming at him to run. He felt sweat drip down his neck.

Randy took a step forward, and blinding light overwhelmed his eyes. Coldness stretched through his limbs. Before he could see anything, he heard someone rack a shell into a shotgun's chamber. All he could do was raise his hands and wait for his eyes to adjust.

As the room slowly came into view, he wanted to scream at the gore before him. His fears only worsened as his phone buzzed once again and he was helpless to answer.

Chapter Forty-Four

RANDY'S BLOODY BAT DRIPPED AS he, Joan, and Dwight crossed the street. He was tingling all over, Joan looked straight ahead without saying a word, and Dwight hummed a song over and over again that Randy couldn't place, though it had a kind of nursery-rhyme melody.

What Randy felt right then was a buzzing that he wasn't sure would ever stop. The sights of the Lewis sisters hung in his mind like a tapestry from Hell. Those organs, their muscles, the way Frieda stretched and changed shape, the way Cherry's head seemed to crack like an egg. The images, the feelings of how their flesh bent and crunched, the sounds of it all, were like a voyage into madness and back again.

The three of them had been through a battle. They still had the sheriff to find and interrogate, but right now, their humanity told them they needed to rest and regroup before they were dragged down into Hell permanently.

Blood wet Randy's hand, and he wiped it on his pants. He wanted to cry. He wanted to scream. He wondered for a moment whether Bobby was even worth this, this feeling of sickness in his gut for the carnage he had endured. Of course, yes, he had to get to Bobby, but what was the cost going to be?

They had walked half a block from the Lewis' place before a car jumped the curb right in front of them. It was a white blur; everything happened so fast. Then Sheriff Palmer was running toward Randy, his massive hands open and grabbing.

At that moment, with the lights flashing on the Lone Wolf Police Department cruiser and the sheriff's badge shining in the morning light, Randy didn't see the man who knew something about Bobby. He saw the police, an authority that could take him and his life if he misbehaved. He saw the murders he had just performed and Palmer's hand as it hovered over his pistol.

The thought occurred to Randy that he could turn and run. He was covered in blood. He held a bloody bat. There was no way this could end up in his favor if Palmer took him to the station. But as he weighed that option, he spotted Joan. She sank to the ground, her rump crashing into the sidewalk and her hands up over her head. She was giving up. She wouldn't run, and he couldn't abandon her.

Randy dropped the bat. It hadn't hit the ground yet when Sheriff Palmer grabbed him, pulled his arms behind his back, and went for his cuffs.

The bat thudded on the asphalt and went into the sheriff's trunk. Randy, Joan, and Dwight were put in the backseat.

Randy watched from the rear of the squad car as trees passed by. He wondered how long he would be in jail for. Would he be an old man when he was released? Would he ever even be released? What about Joan and Dwight? No, he couldn't let them get punished. He was the one covered in blood; he would take the blame and say they didn't know anything about it. They were just on a walk together, and he went crazy and did it all on his own.

He hoped they would buy that.

With his confession decided, he could finally see what was going on outside. They weren't headed toward downtown. The police station was in the opposite direction. They were headed toward the lake.

Randy looked to the front of the car at the sheriff. The guy was driving calmly, patting his hands on the steering wheel to the beat of whatever country song was on the radio. The radio... He had been so far inside his own head that he didn't even realize the radio was playing, the cop's window was down, and he was driving like he was out for a leisurely trip to the lake.

What did that mean? Did the sheriff not care that Randy had just bashed the Lewis sisters into red pulp? Or was he going to handle this the old way, Frontier Justice as Randy had heard it called, where there was just the sheriff, the rope, and the tree and no one else to say a peep?

He couldn't let that happen to Joan and Dwight. He had been the one to swing the bat.

"Excuse me?" Randy's voice was cracked and weak.

The officer didn't answer.

"Sheriff Palmer?" Randy was louder this time. In the rearview mirror, the man met his gaze. "Please, sir, my sister didn't have anything to do with what happened. Neither did my friend here. I'll take all the blame, sir."

Palmer just smirked.

"Randy," Joan hissed, "what are you doing?"

He whispered to her, "We aren't going to the station."

She looked out the window, realizing for the first time since getting in where they were. "Sir," she spoke over the music, "where are you taking us?"

He smirked again.

Randy watched the houses and trees and sat up, shocked, as they turned down his driveway. What was this guy doing? Was he going to punish Mom and Dad too? Was he going to make them watch as he hung their children?

The sheriff parked behind Dad's car and got out. He walked to the door, knocked, and waited like he was there for a social call—just any other day, stopping at the Kline's house for a slice of pie and a glass of lemonade.

When Mom answered, Randy went cold all over. Panic flooded through him, and the world faded from view beyond his mother's face. It was wet and red from crying. Her eyes were puffy, and she held a bunched-up tissue between her fingers. She had been at the table weeping for Bobby. She probably didn't even notice that Randy and Joan had gone. Now, here they were in the back of a police car.

Palmer pointed at the cruiser, and Mom's gaze followed. She closed her eyes and bowed her head, then nodded.

Why was she nodding? What was she agreeing to?

She went back inside, leaving the door open, and the sheriff walked to the car. He opened the door and said his first words since they were placed in handcuffs. "Get out."

Get out? Why? What's going on? Randy thought these things, but his confusion stopped them from reaching his lips.

The officer stepped behind Randy and slid the key into the cuffs. They went slack and were off, and Palmer pointed to the house. "Now, get inside. Your momma wants to have a word with you."

A word? Did he not see the blood? Didn't he know about the Lewis sisters? Was he insane, or was Randy?

"Go on." He waved his hand, gesturing at the house, and Joan stood from the car. Then it was Dwight's turn. Again, he waved them toward the house, and as they walked to the door, he got in his car. He actually turned up his country song and backed his way down the driveway.

"What is going on?" Joan asked. Her voice was weak.

Randy had no idea how to answer that. All he could bring himself to do was find Mom. Maybe she had the answers.

She was in the kitchen, the room she seemed to never leave since Bobby disappeared, and as soon as the kids walked in, she commanded, "Sit."

It was a tone Randy had only heard a few times in his lifetime. It was stone, unwavering, and immutable. She was not to be denied.

He took the seat beside her, Joan the next one, across from Mom, and Dwight the one on her other side. Each of them squirmed in their places, unsure of what was coming and unnerved by the hard intention in Sally Kline's voice.

She looked into each of their eyes. There was regret in hers. There was pain and there was compassion. Randy saw a decision had been made, and this was the follow through.

"Put your hands on the table," Mom told the three of them. "Palms up."

They each did as they were told with puzzled expressions. They glanced at each other knowing no answers would come from the woman.

He knew there was no point, but logic got clogged somewhere in Randy's chest as he blurted, "We didn't mean it, Mom. We were just trying to find Bobby, and—"

"Enough." She said one word, and that word said it all. It wasn't loud, just her normal volume, but with the same stone tone that told them there was no other way than hers. She would not hear any more, no matter how much this pained her, no matter how much this would hurt them.

When Sally Kline was a young girl—back when she was Sally Jeffreys—she had listened to her daddy. It was he who told her never to go into those woods, who had told her the old stories about the travelers and what happened when the house was being built. She could have lived her entire life following those directions had it not been for the day her momma was lying in bed with pneumonia and the doctor told her and Daddy to prepare for the worst. He had said *the worst*, but those words didn't sink in right away. It took Daddy sitting her down in the living room and blankly telling her—he was in as much of a daze it seemed as she was confused—that her momma was going to die.

She was going to die? How was that possible?

Momma never got sick. Not in all nine years of Sally's life did she ever remember Momma even having a cold. But now, the first time it happened, she was going to die?

It just—it didn't make sense.

"Sometimes these things just happen," Daddy said.

No. No, they didn't.

Sally didn't know if she was more angry or sad or worried. She couldn't settle on sad or worried because to do that meant to accept what Daddy was saying, and she could not accept any of it. Other than anger. That one seemed to bubble up okay: anger at Daddy for telling her these things, anger at the doctor for trying to make them believe it all, and anger at Mommy for lying in that bed and letting it happen.

"She's not gonna die," Sally told her daddy, her tone much like the one she would use toward her son years later at the kitchen table.

"Honey." Daddy put a hand on her shoulder.

"No!" Sally spun and ran from the living room through the kitchen and out the mudroom door. She crossed the grass and went down the hill toward the lake. On the way down, she spotted the place she was never supposed to go, the place where she knew Daddy would be upset if she went.

She turned left and ran as hard as she could. The chilling, dusky air was harsh on her wet, tear-soaked cheeks. They burned, and she didn't care.

She ran between the boulders and up the path into the trees. She sobbed as her feet pounded the ground, and for some reason, she turned left. It wasn't that something was calling her, but something did make her want to run that way, up the hill and to a strange arrangement of rocks.

Sally stood there looking at the tall structure, tears racing down her face, and she felt something she had never felt before. There was something in those rocks that she couldn't see or hear, but she knew it was there.

It spoke inside her mind. *"Why are you crying?"*

She thought she was crying before, but what came next would leave all the crying she would do for the next few decades to shame. It rocked her from her belly through her chest and made her burn and clench inside as her eyes ran like faucets for her mommy. She fell to her knees and covered her eyes.

Then someone was rubbing her back. His hands were cold, but it felt nice. Something about it made the hurt hurt a little less.

"It's about your mommy, isn't it?" the voice in her head said. It was lower this time, and though it was only inside her mind, she could feel her body vibrate as if that bassy voice was being projected from below the ground. *"She's sick, isn't she?"*

She nodded, and he rubbed. She knew she was probably being rude by not looking at the man, but she just couldn't raise her face from her hands.

"What if I could help her? Make her not be sick anymore?"

It was like the wind ripped through the woods and cut through her clothes; it was so cold, but she felt none of that. What she felt was hope. It didn't make sense. Mommy had been sick for almost a month, and it just wouldn't leave. The coughing and wheezing came day and night. How could this person help her?

She didn't know the answer, but something about his hand on her back told her he could. It was like that hand was pulling all the sadness from her body and telling her it could all be okay if she listened.

"How?"

"Just say yes."

She looked up and saw him.

At any other time in her life, she would have screamed and ran. She might have thought about it then if that hand wasn't there, calming her, telling her he could fix it. If Mommy's life wasn't on the line.

"Say yes?" she whispered.

As the years passed, much of her went on to think that that day never happened, at least that part of it. It had just been the silly fantasy of a little girl. Her mother had just turned out to be lucky and overcame the cough and pneumonia, and they had so many good years together after that. So many good years until he came back.

Blood for blood.

Sally's eyes went from child to child to child. She saw that sadness in Randy's eyes, and she felt it. She wanted Bobby back too, but it wasn't going to happen no matter how many Whisperers he beat with his bat. If only he had been taken instead. He was never as good as Bobby.

She saw the worry in Joan's eyes. Her little girl would never have understood. She didn't think Joan had ever loved anyone as much as Sally had loved her dying mother.

She saw fear in Dwight's eyes. He had no idea why he was there, and she would help him with that. They would all feel much better very soon.

Sally stood over the table, a kitchen knife in her hand. She looked at those upturned palms and smiled because, at least for them, this was about to be much easier.

She plunged the blade down three times into three palms. They screamed, but they couldn't move. He made sure of that.

She drew the sign on her table, connecting their blood, calling him, with his hands guiding hers as she moved.

He stood behind Joan with his outstretched shadowy arms, and he asked, "Are you ready to say yes again?"

Why shouldn't she? The cost wouldn't come due for another twenty-five years.

"*Blood for blood.*"

Chapter Forty-Five

S THE LIGHTS ROSE IN ex-Sheriff Palmer's third building, the blood seemed never-ending. It flowed around and between the beings on his right, through invisible veins, into one atrocity and then the other. Their limbs and organs were mashed together, making what could have once been two creatures into one. Randy saw a single thing that made him understand exactly what he was looking at: the beak.

Randy knew Palmer had said something, but the words were just noise under the rush of fear and revulsion. That beaked head looked at him with several glossy, gray eyes, blind eyes of what was once called Frieda Lewis. She wasn't dead like so many had thought, and now he remembered that morning. Instead of gone, she was a mangled stream of muscle and organ wrapped around what had been her sister, Cherry Lewis. They twisted around each other's bones, their viscera intertwined and their limbs protruding in every direction. It was impossible to tell where one woman ended and the other began, but one thing was clear, though neither had working eyes, they saw Randy. Both Cherry's crushed head and Frieda's beak pointed at him as if they were waiting for something, and Randy sensed that they were eager for it.

"Drop the hatchet!" Palmer repeated.

Randy heard him that time. Dropping his one real weapon was the last thing Randy wanted to do, but when Palmer stepped between the monster and Randy, raising a shotgun toward Randy's head, all he could do was comply.

The weapon made a clank as it hit the ground. Randy didn't see it. He couldn't remove his gaze from the Lewis sisters.

"The shovel too," Palmer demanded.

Randy's hand fell open, and the shovel clanged on the hard steel floor.

"Good." Palmer motioned to the right with the shotgun. "Now, sit."

Sit? Had he really just said that? After getting caught and having a good look at that monstrosity ahead, Randy didn't expect more than to hear that shotgun ring.

There was a chair against the wall to his right, and slowly, without taking his eyes off the others, Randy moved and sat.

"I feel like this is déjà vu for you, isn't it?" A creepy smile crept over Palmer's face. Randy always thought the man looked like he was hiding something evil, but now he saw it all. He wasn't hiding it—it was who he was.

"What's that supposed to mean?" Randy said. He let his eyes leave the others, only briefly, as he took in the room.

Below where he had been standing was a pair of steel trapdoors that must have led to a basement or something. The walls were all solid and shiny; Randy couldn't tell if it was plastic or metal, but as his eyes shifted back to the Lewises, he assumed it was to clean the spilled blood more easily.

Behind the sisters was what he could only think of as a nest. It was a pile of fabric, layers and layers, covered in dried blood, making it look shit brown.

Below the sisters was something odd. It was metal, like the doors, but it was lined with black scorches as if someone had built a massive fire there in the past.

"What I mean is," Palmer lowered the shotgun to his hip and continued, "twenty-five years ago, it was your brother, and now it's your kids. Shit, if I didn't know better, I'd think you were the most unlucky sonofabitch this side of Montana."

Randy locked eyes with him. "What is going on? And how do I get my sons back?"

"Oh, Randy." Palmer tilted his head to the side. "I guess you might not remember it all. But I bet you remember them?" He nodded at the Lewis sisters.

They lurched toward Randy. Their limbs slurped as they passed over one another, and there was a squeak as their flesh skated across the metal floor.

Randy wanted to puke. He had never imagined such a grotesque thing could exist, let alone live.

"They remember you," Palmer said. "I actually think hating you may have helped keep them alive over the last few years, knowing this day was coming."

"What is going on!"

Palmer held out his hand, motioning the sisters to stay back. "What's going on is the payment of debts. You see, your momma owed a debt, and your brother paid it. Then, she owed another one for having the mess you made cleaned up. And your sons are paying that."

"No, no, that doesn't make any sense. You did this! I saw you at the fire. You made my brother go missing!"

"All we did was siphon some of the power off when it happened. I don't choose who goes through the conduit; only *he* does. He chose your brother, and he chose your boys."

Randy found himself caught in the middle of a panic attack. He was here, hostage, and—"The Shadow Man. You have to talk to him. Tell him to let my boys out!" He felt wetness on his cheeks. The tears were heavy.

"A soul was promised. He's not going to give it back." Palmer reached into his pocket and pulled out a pair of handcuffs. He stepped toward Randy, and Randy wondered if those were the same ones he wore as a kid. "Tell you what, though—you can ask him yourself in a bit." Palmer slapped a cuff on Randy's wrist and pulled it back, then he yanked the other arm around and locked both hands behind the chair.

Randy opened his mouth to speak, but nothing came. Hopelessness filled his heart like sludge, and he felt his body deflate. He suddenly remembered the table in his kitchen and Dwight and Joan and the blood drawing in the center. The Shadow Man had been there. Mom had summoned him—*Dear god, Mom was in on this?*

The sisters retreated to their nest, and Palmer reached down and pulled up the steel doors in the floor. They opened into a hole that stretched deep under the building.

A wall of grief slammed into Randy. His mother had betrayed them. It was true. She had helped make all of this happen. Bobby, Dad leaving, Joan breaking down and disappearing, leaving them the house, and now Drew and Dean—he would never see them again, just like Bobby. His heart had been cracked open, and everything he loved was falling into the abyss. Even Emma was nowhere to be found, and he had to assume The Shadow Man had taken her at this point. At least he still had—

His phone beeped. It was a voicemail. *Maggie!* She had called him. Christ, was she okay?

Palmer pressed a button on the wall, and part of the ceiling opened up above the scorched, black floor. He began piling wood over the charred markings—he was going to start a fire.

Randy pulled at the cuffs as Palmer built and lit the logs. Flames grew high, and the room grew hot. Palmer put on a hood and began chanting. Randy couldn't understand the words, but he recognized the sounds. It was the same chant he heard in that clearing when he was a boy. That night, when he saw their faces by the fire.

He felt himself back there, standing by the trees and peering, the fear in his veins from the sight of that creature, and the knowledge that if it saw them, it would rip them to shreds.

That fear followed him as he felt what was coming. The death that was coming.

A disgusting gurgling sound came from the nest in rhythm with Palmer's chant. It sounded like a man with a wet sock in his throat; it was one of the Lewis sisters, saying the words like they were gargling with their own insides in their mouth. They climbed out of the nest and joined Palmer by the fire. The darkest, thickest smoke went up through the hole in the ceiling, but the smell of blood and old, rancid flesh hung on the gray haze that filled the room.

Randy flinched as whispers echoed and flashes jumped inside his mind. It was death expanding, flashing, burning on that bonfire so many years ago and flowing into the sky as strands of red light and smoke. There was no fighting the gurgle in his stomach. He needed to puke, his body refusing the sights and sounds being forced on them, the knowledge that death was right around the corner and it was leaching into the ground and walls and air, clawing at his skin, calling his flesh and his soul.

The whispers, they dragged those memories closer as they tunneled inside his brain. Chasing The Shadow Man through the woods, getting tossed like he was nothing, the attack in his room, bashing the Lewises with his baseball bat—he could feel the blood on his skin like it had just happened.

He saw Palmer there chanting, and Palmer wasn't Palmer. He was a bag of flesh on a frame of bone that was waiting to be taken by the wrath of time and the soldiers of inevitability. He was being held together by nothing but simple mechanical processes, the beating of his heart, the intake of air, the energy carried and burned by cells. That could only last so long, and the unstoppable forces of entropy would take hold. All would become none. None would spread and devour. As it was, it would be again.

Red light shone in streaks from the hole. It lit the room as splashing sounds lifted from below. It was being called. It was coming, and red smoke preceded it.

Randy shook his head; he had to free his thoughts. They were an invasion from somewhere he didn't want to know and didn't want to feel anymore. They were invaders of everything, and they would not relent.

A grumbling noise. Splashing gave way to scratching. Scratching led to crumbling earth and rocks clattering as they trickled down into water.

He saw the Lewis sisters. He saw through them. Their twisted, mangled bodies deconstructed inside his mind, and he could see clearly which parts were Cherry and which were Frieda, but it didn't matter. Their flesh was all the same whether they were intertwined in this enigma or set apart. Death was seizing them like it was the rest of the room before it took the land and the planet and the universe entirely. Each sister would rot, and he saw it before him. He saw their skin dry and shrivel and turn green as their insides leaked and tumbled to the floor. He saw their bones topple to the ground only to be picked up and gnawed on by animals and microbes, broken down into dust, and broken down again into nothing but particles of floating emptiness.

They would all be gone soon. He knew it.

It was with that revelation of his own emptiness, of his own body decomposing in front of his eyes and his flesh melting into the ether, that his system revolted. Chills cramped every inch of him, and his empty stomach expelled globs of bile up over his lips and onto the floor.

He trembled as the beast grabbed hold of the ground ahead and lifted itself from the pit.

It was worse than his misty memories had shown. Six limbs pulled the great beast up and toward the fire. It glanced in Randy's direction, and he saw into its eyes—so many eyes, more than a normal being should have—and the three chanted louder. The whispers screamed in his mind. It turned to the fire. The flames illuminated its dark and matted fur, the fur of a dead thing. There were dozens of patches in the coat where fur was missing, many missing skin as well, and those seeped with a thick, slow-moving pus.

It snapped its jaws, and a *clack* shook the room. It walked with hands instead of feet on the ends of those legs, each with fingers and claws scraping the ground and letting loose a deep scratching sound against the steel that pained Randy's ears.

The sight alone was enough to make Randy tremble, but as it

stepped into the fire and the tendrils of flame licked at the fur, the smell made his stomach lurch again. Its fur burned, releasing red smoke and lines of energy, and it continued striding into the fire. It stood up straight in the middle of the blaze, and flames crawled into its open wounds, singeing muscle and bone. It howled with their chant, and as it did, many of the rising red lines turned, and instead of lifting into the sky, they circled Palmer and the Lewis monster before diving into their mouths.

Palmer rose above the ground. The Lewis sisters floated. They both glowed, the red light inside them shining through and bathing the room in bright, pink illumination.

As Randy watched, he wasn't sure if the next thing that happened was real or his imagination. What he was seeing made no sense, even if he did have a memory of it from so, so long ago. It all seemed like a madman's dream, and he was caught in the middle of it.

There was a rumble below the chanting. It shook the ground below his chair. He saw the light shine bright from the pit and then a shadow blocked it. And then it was him.

The Shadow Man rose from the hole, but unlike the beast, he was not climbing; he was floating. He rose like a fairy or an angel, a thing of magical providence that had no right coming out of that hole. His shadows swirled and shifted, and his figure was indistinct as he floated, just a disgusting head, a skull with meat and wet eyes and teeth. And then he landed.

He touched the floor, and though he was still shadow, he was firm. His smoke seemed solid somehow as he approached Randy. He even seemed to be smiling, and though he had no lips, Randy was sure he was.

The demon glanced at the event by the fire, and the red light and flames glistened over his shiny skull and musculature. He turned back to Randy and walked toward him.

Randy struggled with his cuffs and pushed against the seat. They didn't budge, no matter how close The Shadow Man came or how much his wrists hurt from resisting. The closeness made his skin crawl. It felt like a thousand millipedes were crisscrossing his body, each dragging slimy limbs and leaving trails for the next to overlap.

He felt ice in his hands and feet. The room seemed to shrink around them as the demon stopped just feet before him and tilted his head, looking Randy up and down.

"*You are persistent.*" The voice was deep and resonated inside Randy's head. "*So, maybe I will let you deal. You just have to say yes.*"

Part Eight

The Canyon

Chapter Forty-Six

D ARK AND VIOLET, THIS PLACE was everything Drew didn't want to deal with anymore. Slick rock walls surrounded him, creating a path ahead over a floor of layered bones. The hole he had been dropped through was behind him and at least twenty feet up. There was no getting out that way. The ceiling was open to an ominous night sky high above the walls, and the darkness seemed to watch him, even absent eyes.

He felt truly alone.

Drew's shoulder ached from where the flying thing had carried him. He rubbed it as he stood, leaning left and right while fighting for balance on the shifting mass of remains. Ahead, across more bones than he could count, there were glowing mushrooms on the walls that led around a curve. He didn't want to go that way, but he didn't want to stand on this pile of death, either.

A cartoonish idea came to him about building a ladder from all these bones to climb up to the hole he was dropped through, but that wasn't realistic. What got him moving was the fear that whatever left these bones would eventually be back.

"I've gotta do it," he told himself.

A whisper came on a breeze from the hole above. "Go." It was a cold, damp gust that made his hackles rise, not just from the word or feeling but also from the smell. There was an odor that reminded him of the worst of morning breath and oral decay. It was a whisper from something hungry that wanted to play.

Drew took a step forward, and the bones behind him rustled. They clattered lightly. Was something there?

With that sound in mind, his second step was faster, as was his third. He lost his balance as the bone he stepped on with his next pace rolled and sank, and he had to hurry with the following step to keep from falling. It started to feel slippery beneath his feet, like the bones were wet, and that rustling sound returned. It was closer, like it was following him. Then again on his right and left. The bones on each side shifted. Something was moving below them; he was sure of it.

He had to move faster. Whatever was down there must have killed all these things. And now it was after him.

Another twenty feet of remains lay between Drew and the passage ahead. His heart pounded and his chest burned, and he was just so tired he could hardly stand it, but he moved.

Drew watched the bones, and he ran. They were all sizes and shapes, none that were human. Some were small and curved, some almost spirals. Some were pointed, some were flat. There were so many skulls, shapes that he feared what they would have looked like in life. There were so many it was hard to understand the number of lives that were lost here.

Then, several of them began to stand on end.

They pointed toward the ceiling like the start of a small picket fence. He jumped over a row, and another stood, this time pointing toward him. He leaped over them, and as he landed, the next section felt softer under his feet. He looked down as he ran, and the bones mushed together like clay.

His shoe started sinking, and he leaped. There were only a few feet left, but he splashed as he landed, his shoe sinking through liquid bones to the rock floor below, and a sea of white surrounded his ankles and shins. It was cold and thick, and as he tried to jump again, it felt thicker, like chewing gum that was worn in and malleable.

It stuck to him and held him there. He was only a foot or two from the end, but it refused to release him.

"Let go!" Drew leaned forward and clawed at the bare ground.

In the sea of bones behind him, a hump rose. At first, it was only a rise and fall of what was now a consolidated mass of white. The edges contracted from the walls, and enormous eight-fingered hands rose from the bony muck. They were the combined substance of white with gaped lines where the bones joined each other. They were bone hands made of multitudes of bones, and they stretched and gripped the walls, pulling the rest of its being up.

Drew only saw the thing rising for a second and went back to fighting. He didn't want to know what that thing was, only to get away. But it was getting harder and harder. The white goo holding his foot was retracting and pulling him. The floor provided nothing to hold onto. There were no boulders, and as hard as he stretched, he couldn't reach the walls. All he could do was claw impotently at the ground as he was dragged toward whatever that beast was.

Arms, shoulders, and a head followed the bone hands from the muck. It revealed itself as something of a bug-headed beast with large, clumpy eyes and thick, horn-like hairs that stood from its skull and arms. Its mouth widened into four flaps, each segment lined with row after row of fangs.

Drew tried not looking back, but he couldn't resist. He saw the beast open and close its mouth, and the flaps rippled like waves, exposing hundreds of teeth. All Drew could think of was how they would grate his flesh from his bones without even chewing.

His mind shuddered as he imagined that. His skin and organs ripped to pieces in that thing's maw, and his bones added to its collection. It repeated in his thoughts again and again.

Without realizing it, he was no longer fighting to back away. He was shaking while being dragged across the rock.

He screamed. His voice echoed against hard walls and yelled back at him from down the passage ahead.

From the monster's skeletal chest, another bulge appeared, this one pointing from the sternum toward Drew. It was like the end of a barbed tail, and it grew longer and sharper.

There was something about that tail that snapped Drew out of his scream. Maybe it was the way it reminded him of a scorpion, and maybe it was just the overflowing fear that that thing was going to plunge into him. Regardless, the idea occurred to him that even though he couldn't grab anything, he might have something in his pockets to help. It was a long shot, but he was frantic for anything at that point.

The rock floor scratched his back as he searched. He found a receipt for his wristband at the fair. He found a few coins and a folded clump of dollar bills. In his other pocket, he found a foreign object that he had to pull out before he recognized. He couldn't believe that he didn't immediately know what it was.

He raised a simple ballpoint pen into the air and slammed it down at the mushy white mess around his feet. It made a hole and only a hole, but as he stared at the stretched marshmallow-looking stuff and the gap beside his foot, he was drawn into a frenzy.

Up and down like a frantic needle in a tattoo gun, he pounded the pen into the gunk. He made a hundred small holes, and though they were tiny, the more he made, the more he felt the white goo weaken.

"Yes!" he hissed to himself. He wiggled his feet and pulled, and the barbed tail stretched from the white beast. It rose ten feet above him.

Drew had to make the next few seconds count if he was going to avoid being stabbed. He stuck his fingers in the holes and ripped the white material back.

He was out of time. He spun and yanked and clawed into what he could of the cave floor, and he pulled his feet with everything he had.

His feet ripped free as the tail cut through the air. He jerked and hoisted himself up and ran. The tail's tip echoed with a *crack* as it slammed into the ground and tossed chips of stone floor into the air.

Drew huffed as he took off toward the passage and its glowing mushrooms. He rounded the corner and heard what sounded like a train behind him.

There was a long, straight path lit by fungi and a wall of darkness beyond. Drew heard a crash as the white thing behind him rammed into the narrow turn. It scraped and clattered as the bony tail raked against the walls, trying to hook him.

An immeasurable silence struck, and Drew stopped halfway down the path and looked back. The monster and its tail were gone. He leaned on his knees to catch his breath, but the breathing that caught his attention was from the shadows ahead.

Drew froze in place. He glanced back again—still clear, but he was sure whatever that thing was would be waiting for him if he returned to the previous room.

"Who's there?" he shouted into the darkness. He didn't expect an answer. He didn't know what he expected, but it wasn't what came.

Into the gentle light of phosphorescent fungi stepped Dean.

Drew's heart leaped, and he ran forward. His arms spread wide as he approached his brother. "Dean!"

But Dean didn't answer. He didn't widen his posture to accept Drew. He just watched as Drew came closer. He stared with bulging brown eyes and opened his mouth.

As Drew came within the last few feet, he noticed a horror in the dim light of that skinny passage.

Dean's teeth were long black fangs. His eyes were red in the center and not black. He leaned forward, turning his head, opening wider, and Drew skidded to a stop just feet before him.

The center of Dean's face split open vertically from his top lip to his scalp. It was like his face no longer existed, and only a flower of thin black teeth remained.

Drew understood this wasn't his brother, but part of him still felt like a crater had been dug into his heart. He pictured the real Dean being split open like the thing in front of him. But the sight of those teeth, they slapped him sober, and a scream bubbled up from the pit of his insides and belted into the small gap between them.

The sound of Drew's voice probably did nothing, but it looked like a trigger because no sooner than the sound left his parted lips, the Dean-thing reached forward with fingers that were no longer the color and shape of human skin but instead were slippery tendrils like something from the sea, and their tips bulged with their own pointed little barbs.

Drew may have been caught mid-scream, but he still moved like his life depended on it. He dropped back and low, pivoted, and spun. He sprinted toward the mush monster's cave, still screaming at the top of his lungs.

One foot at a time, he propelled himself forward, not caring that the other beast was probably in the next space. He didn't know what he would do when he got there, but he had to get away from the Dean-thing.

He was almost to the corner. He was anticipating the bone-beast shoving its tail at him at any second when his feet erupted in pain, and he fell face-first toward the floor.

His hands barely caught his fall. He was yanked toward his brother, again caught by the feet. But this time, with each yank, he felt agony. It was a burning, tearing pain. With each yank, he felt muscle and skin rip. He turned, and the Dean-thing had not moved. It was in the same place; only its finger tendrils stretched across the gap.

Drew leaned toward his feet and yanked on the tentacles gripping his ankles. He pulled, and barbs jabbed into his fingers. He drew his hands back, and they bled from rips across his palms and digits. They burned, and at the same time, he could no longer feel or control them. They were useless flapping things whose only sensation was that they were on fire.

"No!" Drew called.

The Dean-thing turned and walked into the blackness. He dragged Drew as Drew screamed, helpless to do anything else.

Chapter Forty-Seven

EMMA WAS JARRED AWAKE WITH a sharp pain in the back of her head. The ground was moving below her, and the sky was an indigo-tinted night. She was being dragged.

"What—" She lifted her head and looked around.

Her legs were raised, and someone was dragging her by her feet. "Let go!" She jerked her legs loose. Her escort turned to her, head tilted.

"Fuck!" she screamed as she saw his face and scooted back along the ground.

It was James, or it had been. What stood before Emma was barely something that could be considered human anymore, and had it not been for the odd smirk that was so commonly on the man's face, she would not have recognized him. Above his mouth, there was no skin. He had covered everything north of his nose with fur. There were holes for eyes and where his ears should have been. His chest was bare and torn and somehow stitched up with hair. The same matted fur pelts that he wore on his face had been sewn into gaps all over his flesh like some human-animal Frankenstein's monster. She could see through gaps between flesh and fur into his muscle and, in some places, bone. One of his arms was half skin and half pelt, and the other was even worse; it appeared he had sewn foreign bones into his arm to reinforce it.

"What?" He watched her with one eye. The other was nothing but a dark pit below the fur, and Emma noticed the smell of rot all around them. "You don't like my new look?"

She scooted back farther, her eyes wide and her mouth trembling. What was she supposed to say to that? He was—she didn't know what he was now or how he was even alive like that. Or how she got on the ground after being dragged... The fall came to mind, those animals, and his shed. Whatever was going on with James, she wanted no part of it. He had already been a monster unbeknownst to her, but now she could see it from the outside.

Emma rolled to her stomach, lifted herself on her hands and knees, and prepared to run. Pain ripped through her leg, and all she could do was scream and fall. Her face hit dry grass and dirt. She tasted it in her open mouth and wanted to puke—its smell of rancid decay was as wretched as the air. She tried to get away from the pain but couldn't. She rolled onto her back, but the agony remained, and she saw why. He was stabbing her in the calf with a sharpened bone.

"We're together," he said calmly. "Don't you know that?" He flashed the smirk again.

She clawed at the ground, pulling herself away, and he twisted the bone in her wound.

"Together," he repeated. His tone was growling yet somehow detached like he was talking to himself and she just so happened to be there with him. "Now, come along." He removed the bone but watched her intently.

As much as it disgusted her, Emma watched James, judging his intentions. He was like a statue, and had she not known he was sentient, she might have thought he was nothing but a strange Halloween prop. She weighed the idea of running again and saw her blood dripping from the end of the bone in his hand. He might have been sickening, but he was fast, and he had a weapon, which she did not.

Then there was the shadow.

It was part of him, and it was separate. It followed his form but levitated just above and just behind him. It was fuzzy around the edges, like smoke, and if she looked really hard, she could see another face behind his. But that couldn't have been, because as soon as she blinked, that other face was gone.

Regardless—as she ran through the scenarios in her mind: kicking him in the nuts, poking him in the eye, stomping on his feet— none of her options were a surefire escape. He was bigger. He was faster, especially with the aching hole in her leg. He had the weapon.

"Come on," he said. "We don't have all day. People are waiting."

"What people?" Her thoughts were idiotic. She imagined a party where they walked in and friends jumped out and yelled *Surprise!*

"You'll see when we get there."

At least that meant he wasn't planning on killing her right now... a little relief, but not much because that was if he was telling the truth. From the way he looked, she couldn't rule out madness.

"Fine." She leaned forward and slowly climbed to her feet. She would follow along, for now. "You didn't have to fucking stab me." She studied her foot. She was bleeding, but it wasn't bad. He must not have hit a blood vessel.

"You used to like it when I stabbed you." He grinned a sickening smile, and half his teeth were stained red. The sight sent shivers down Emma's skin. "Now, let's go." He motioned forward to a path between a cliff wall and a group of dead trees. "And don't try anything. I can run faster than you. Besides, something tells me you'll be interested in our destination."

She scowled and limped ahead. The odor struck her like a brick as she passed him. It was a mix of the decomposing flesh she had already detected and the damp mustiness of a mangy dog.

Her stomach heaved, but she continued on, tempted to run when she stepped with her good leg and wishing to lay down when she stepped with the other one. She looked into the trees and felt them looking back. They were bare, but she could sense that they weren't dead, not quite. She looked at the sky and knew it wasn't her sky. She hadn't been sure what she was looking at when she was on her back, but now she knew it wasn't the Milky Way-covered night it should have been.

"It's not our world," James said. "It's something very special. If only I had realized that sooner…" He seemed drawn to melancholy, as if he had missed out on something and dreaded it.

"What do you mean *not our world*?" She wondered if she could get him distracted by talking. Maybe then she could find a way to escape.

"Look at it. It's a magical place. Look at me. Dead is not dead here. Dead is just another state of things."

She glanced back at him. He looked like an insane person; no one could walk around in the condition he was in without being insane. They would be screaming and howling in pain, crying for a doctor, not fastening hides to themselves.

But as her eyes took him in again, her body shuddered. He was not just wounded, as she had thought. His wounds, now that she could see them more closely, as her mind wasn't in pure panic mode, were not recoverable. There was no way he was alive looking like that.

She went numb in the knees, and she had to fight to stay upright. It was real. Rolling waves of gooseflesh passed across her.

What had she gotten herself into? Why did she go to his house? Why had she betrayed her family to begin with? If she was in Hell, did she deserve it? There was a huge part of her that said yes.

"H-how?" She had to look away.

"I don't know that. You may as well ask a bumblebee how it flies."

"And you're…"

"Not alive anymore. That's for sure."

She didn't speak for several steps as the thought settled in her mind. If she was in some Land of the Dead, did that mean everyone there was dead? Was *she* dead?

Emma put a hand on her neck to feel for her pulse.

He chuckled. "You're alive. For now."

She breathed deeply. "So, is there a way back?"

"Of course. But why would you want to leave? Look at me. I'm dead, but I'm still alive. How could anyone walk away from this type of immortality?"

Immortality? She wasn't sure that was the word she would have used for how he looked.

They walked in silence for a long time, following the rock wall. Emma felt the cold wind on her skin and shivered. She wondered if she would ever see home again. If she would ever see Randy and the kids. She hated herself for being so dumb to come look for James. She hated him because she had wanted him even though she knew it was like hating a donut because she was hungry. She had been a stupid, horny idiot.

Yes, she had been angry with Randy—it seemed like she would always be, like those feelings of unappreciation and lack of recognition from all those years ago would never truly go away even if she wanted them to. Even if she desperately wanted to forgive him and move on with their lives.

She should have told him so. The burn of guilt drove through her. She should have yelled it at Randy. "I'm still mad at you, but I want to fix this!" But she hadn't. And here she was. No matter how much she regretted it, she didn't think she would ever have a chance to fix it. She was going to die in this place, and they would find her vehicle at James's, and they would put two and two together. Randy would know. Maggie and Dean and Drew would know. She wouldn't even be able to say she was sorry.

Tears ran down her cheeks. There was no fixing this. Yes, he said there were ways out, but with the armed zombie behind her and the wound on her leg, she was sure she couldn't make it.

The wind sounded like whispers. Emma wasn't sure what they were saying, but she was sure those were words.

The woods on her right cracked, and the boughs of trees that cluttered the way bent back. She froze. A mist washed across the newly exposed path and vanished into the woods. There was something down that path, and she didn't want anything to do with whatever it was.

The whispers grew louder.

"What are you waiting on?" James snapped. "Didn't you see the way open up for us?"

Without thinking, she turned toward him. The shadow was back, but only for a flash. It was just enough time for her to see its skinless face with raw, disgusting eyes. It slid behind James, and he shouted, "Go!"

Emma reluctantly started down the new path. She sensed the trees pulling themselves back with the same fear that drove her forward. What was whispering into James's ears was commanding them. That would have been a stupid idea on any other day, but here she was in a strange place, and it was what made sense to her.

The ground was softer here. Her feet sank into the earth like walking through mud. But she saw no mud. The ground below her path was made of stone, yet it gave with each step, sinking at least an inch and rebounding as she moved on.

The whispers faded and returned, and the mist blew across the trail once more, but this time when it had passed, there was something new ahead. It had just been a path into the woods, but now, directly in front of her, was a ring of stones about six feet wide.

There was something to that ring. It wasn't a fire ring or a garden ring. It was something else. Emma moved closer until just a few feet away, when James said, "Stop."

The whispers. They tickled her ears, and this time she was sure she heard, "Come."

There was a rustling below the trees on the other side of the circle, and from below the branches, a creature crawled. Its skin was bare, and cuts and bruises ran across its flesh. If they were back at home, she would have thought it was a hairless cat; but when it crawled into the ring and lay down, she saw it had six legs, and from its squished-looking face hung the arms of an octopus.

It lay down and stilled itself as others came from the left and right. They marched over the rocks and into the pit and curled up beside the first. Another and another crawled through. Many had blood on their feet and running down their legs. Some were missing parts of their face tentacles, and some dragged their organs from open wounds across the ground and into the ring.

When nearly the entire floor of the strange stone ring was filled, they stopped coming, and the most horrid thing Emma had ever seen stained her eyes and ears.

There was a howl from inside that circle. It was a howl from each creature together in a twisted harmony of pain. The only movement between them, though, was a trembling that befell them all simultaneously as their skin proceeded to melt from their bodies. It ran like creme-colored syrup down their limbs and onto the floor of the ring, and as they continued to twitch, their muscles turned to liquid as well. It was crimson tissue, then paste, then a runny solution mixing with their skin. Then it was their organs, and the yawling stopped. Then their bones. Their entire communion bubbled in the circle like an enormous boiling soup.

James said, "Now you."

"What?" She gazed at the pool of melted animals and then at James. "What are you talking about?"

"Go." He raised the pointed end of the bone at her.

"So I can melt away into nothing, like them?"

He moved closer, pressing the point into her back. "You're going in there. Either you walk in or I stab you to death and throw you in."

He pressed harder, and she had to move before the point jutted through her skin. She stood at the edge of the rocks. Steam rose. The smell coming from the thick air above the pool was vomitous. She felt the bone in her back and a hard hand on her shoulder. She immediately knew she should have ran. She could have at least tried, but now, he was holding her with a grip that felt like stone.

She raised her wounded foot and let it hang over the pool. The sound of those animals' screams reverberated in her mind, and she prayed she would die before the pain was that bad. She thought about that liquid flowing into the wound in her leg, and she shivered.

"Enough," he barked from behind her.

There was pain in Emma's back, and she was falling forward. At first, she thought she had been stabbed again. She would have been pleased with the revelation that she hadn't, except there was nowhere to go but into the bubbling animal soup.

She splashed down, her hand and then her face. She expected it to be hot. She expected to catch herself below the soup's shallow surface. Neither were true. It was freezing, and while she had seen how shallow the ring was before the animals entered, her hand kept going and going. Her face splashed into the disgusting mess, was soaked by it, and she kept sinking. She reached out and thrashed, and not only was there no bottom, but as she tried to swim to the top, she only sank deeper. It was like some invisible force was pulling her down into the depths of a disgusting darkness.

Her breath burned inside her chest, frantic to leave. She held it tight as she sank, knowing that would be her death. She thought her lungs were going to explode after a time. She had to let it out. Her arms flailed for a grip on anything to pull herself up, but she was alone in this mire.

Her air left in darkened bubbles. She gulped in sludge, and she was happy she could neither see nor smell. She gagged and forced it back up as her lungs protested, and she sucked it in again because there was no other option. She vomited and convulsed, and every-thing in her sight turned white.

So this is death, she thought, and she sank deeper. And deeper. Until the darkness was no longer wet, and she felt herself falling.

Emma slammed into the ground so hard that the fluid spewed from her lungs. She coughed and vomited under an indigo night, clutching at the dirt, just happy to be on land.

James kicked her in the side. "Let's go."

Chapter Forty-Eight

LANCE CLOSED HIS EYES DURING the flight. Part of him was grateful for this journey to be over, even if it meant through death by these monstrous flying beasts. But when his back hit the ground, he opened them wide. Bobby had said these canyons shifted things, but this was more like a completely altered reality than what he would have called a *shift*.

The sky was a bright gray, and he was no longer in a canyon. There was no rock of any kind other than the pebbles in the weedy dirt below his feet. But he wasn't in a normal world, either; he hadn't been transported home. What stood before him were layers of doors covered in writing. Red, blue, white, wood-stained, every kind of door you could imagine was in front of him. They blocked his path in every direction, overlapping each other and, as he understood it, making him choose.

The writing on each was a passage from a book Dad had encouraged him to read in the year before he died. One had a paragraph where Santiago fought the great marlin, struggling to keep his energy up in a days-long battle. There was a passage where Victor's creation argued that as a living creature he deserved a chance at happiness, at love. On another door, Dr. Dyer warned against further exploration into the desolate cold of the southernmost continent. Another was a description of murder and dismemberment leading to insanity and auditory hallucination.

It was like someone had been there with them. Or in Dad's head. Or in his head as he read and reread and worried for his father. As he scanned over his pile of books once Dad was gone and was at least grateful to have those.

But why were they here, and why were they on these doors?

He had to choose one. He couldn't stay here forever, so he chose Santiago's door. It opened onto the crashing surf of a Cuban beach. There were no fishermen and no boats, but there was a dock.

Lance walked out onto the sands and glanced back. The door he arrived through was gone as if it had never existed, and in its place was a bright-green tropical jungle.

It was the strangest thing Lance had seen outside of a dream. And it looked and felt and smelled so real. The sand moving under his shoes, the scent of the ocean, the salty breeze on his face. If it was fake, it was the most realistic fake experience he could have imagined.

He walked out to the dock, looking around and seeing no one. Not on the water or down the shore. No boats or surfers or fishermen. There were no animals, either. He would have thought there would have been seagulls or something. He had never been to a real beach, so he wasn't sure what should be there, but there had to be more than this.

Lance took a breath and shook his head. He was alone, and he was exhausted. Drew and Eric and Dean were nowhere around, and he had no idea where to go or what to do. He certainly wasn't going into that jungle. The woods at home were one thing, but that jungle seemed like a whole other deep, dark danger. He might try walking down the beach and seeing if he could find anyone, but he was just so tired. First, he would just have a seat and rest.

Over the soft, pillowy dunes and then the harder wet sand, he walked until he reached the beginning of the dock. It was old and weathered, once a solid white, now it was more of a gray, with worn-in cracks and strips of residual paint here and there. It was about eight feet wide and stretched out over the breaking waves into the deeper blue.

He started down the dock, feeling the wood creak and flex under his steps. The ocean was all that he heard, and even though he knew this place wasn't right, that he wasn't really in Cuba, he was somewhat awed by his surroundings. He thought of taking off his shoes and letting his bare feet dangle over the edge once he reached the end. He wondered if the water was cold like it was in Montana or warm like he had heard the Gulf was. Those thoughts left him as he reached the edge.

While the scene around Lance could have been a real one by most accounts, when he looked up, there was a cold grayness that didn't feel anywhere near earthly. It gave him the sensation that someone was watching from above, and as he looked around into the vastness of the false Caribbean, he started to wonder what monsters may reside under its depths. Things more deadly than Santiago's great marlin, and possibly worse than the crying souls back at the waterfall.

And he had walked out into the middle of it. All alone, with only the sea around him and a thin strip of rotting boards as a pathway back to safety.

What had he done?

He didn't need an answer or any justification. He spun and ran back toward shore. Weirdly, at the beach side of the dock, there was no more beach. A hundred feet ahead, there was a boathouse and the rocky edge of a lake. The boathouse was old and battered, sun-bleached, much like the dock, a once-white relic of an age that was no more. And in the window of the upstairs loft was a shadowy figure that looked out at him as he ran.

Lance stopped. He looked for the eyes of the being in the window and saw nothing. He squinted, hoping for anything that would clue him in about the onlooker's identity, and saw nothing but darkness. Was he racing toward friend or foe?

Without giving him time to answer, the wood under his feet cracked and bent down toward the water.

"Shit!" Lance jumped forward. The boards there cracked as well. He fought for his balance as his heart sped, and he started moving fast.

The calm sea below the dock came alive with frustrated frenzy. The waves picked up and crashed over the dock's edge, and a cold wind whipped at him from the ocean.

He was running toward the shore, but running toward what? Slices of water erupted between boards, and Lance found his feet slipping on the wetness. In his next step, his foot went through the wood, its splintered edges scratching his skin, and he barely stopped himself before his entire leg was underwater. He heaved himself up and stepped again, and as if teasing him, it cracked in half but bore his weight.

He screamed with irritation. The shore was still fifty feet away, and the dock and sea were mocking him. The wind chilled his ears nearly as bad as a winter storm, and with it came the putrid stink of rotten fish. Splashes on his right and left called his gaze, and in the water, he saw dozens of marlin.

They were long and majestic, with swords as long as one of his arms. But unlike the great fish in the Old Man and the Sea, these beasts had more than just their rostrum to stab and slash with. They also had long black fangs which they snapped as they leaped and splashed back down into the water.

"No." Lanced told himself this wasn't right, and his legs went wobbly. There had to be fifty of the giant fish around the dock, and one false step could send him down to meet them.

"Lance!" It was a call from the boathouse. The shadowy form was still in the upper window, but in the lower door stood someone who couldn't be. Dad was dead. But there he stood. "Run, Lance!"

He saw Dad in the coffin. He saw Dad in his house, floating and screaming with billowing black smoke behind him. He saw Dad in the living room chair by the lamp, a book in his hands, and his eyes scanning the pages.

Which Dad was this? The Dad that used to sit him in his lap and read to him, or the one who screamed and haunted him? Was it the angry Dad from the garage or the encouraging one from under a lamp in his living room? Or was it neither? Was it a trick of the shifting canyon?

The dock cracked behind Lance, and splinters burst into the sky. A sword swung from the water, hovering above the planks, and the dock itself began sinking behind him. Those fish wanted him, and he was going to get skewered and ripped to pieces if they got him. Whatever Dad that was ahead, he was right. Lance needed to get to shore.

Lance resumed his run, begging his feet to step lightly. Each touch of his sole to wood was a gamble, a wager between breaking through, between life and death.

Board after board, it held his weight, then a sword pressed on his ankle between strides. It cut through his sock, and he stumbled. But he kept running. A few more steps and a sword was rising as his tread was falling. It pierced the tip of his shoe, and his toes screamed from inside. It was searing pain up his entire foot. The saltwater splashed his face, and he tasted the sea. The monster pulled at him, sword clinging to sole. It dragged him across the wood, and the snapping sound of evil marlin jaws clacked in anticipation. He had no choice but to rip his shoe from his foot so he could keep running.

He was leaving a trail of blood. He didn't have to look back to see it. He could feel his foot pulsing with every step. He heard the fish calling in high-pitched howls, the smell of blood exciting them, the taste as it dripped in the water even more so.

"Come on!" Dad called from ahead.

God, he so wanted that to be him. The kind Dad that encouraged him to learn the guitar and loved seeing the weird creations he built with Minecraft mods where he could use gears and widgets and ship parts to engineer the world around him.

At twenty feet to the boathouse door, he saw the brown eyes and the eternal five o'clock shadow his father seemed to always wear.

Could it be him?

The pain in Lance's feet and the pounding in his chest made him want to think yes. He needed something to go right. Since Dad's death, it all seemed to be going wrong. He didn't want to admit it to his friends, and definitely not his mother, but it was just one thing after another. Now he was in this hell. Now he had lost Eric too. He could be stuck in this strange world, and... he just needed one good thing back in his life.

Please let it be Dad. Somehow.

There was a crack from overhead. Lightning crashed into the roof of the boathouse, leaving a rooster-shaped weathervane glowing red on the highest ridge. The gray sky was darker with over-cast anger. The puffy cotton of one cloud electrified another. Rain pelted the sea and the dock, splashing Lance as he took another step and another.

There was a whine from the water. It made him think of a cranky toddler who wasn't getting his way. There were only four or five more steps until he would be at the door, but that fact seemed to make the fish below furious.

One leaped from the water, soaring over the dock, its sword searching for flesh, and crashing into the waves on the other side. It howled as it flew, and Lance could see its teeth grinding together. Grinding as if his flesh was already between them.

"Hurry!" Dad screamed. He leaned from the boathouse door, hanging on to the inside frame. "Time's almost up!"

What did that mean?

Another fish shot from the water, and Lance thought it was going to stab him in mid-air. He jumped forward, and by nothing but luck, only the edge of its pectoral fin grazed his back. The spot was first cold and wet, then as the beast slammed into the surf, it was hot. It had cut him. He was sure.

Rain came down like a wet sheet, covering everything from Lance to the dock to the boathouse in a thickness that seemed unreal. It was almost like he was swimming, it took so much effort to move—so much effort that he was out of.

Lightning boomed so loudly the entire world shook. He felt it in his feet. He felt it in the air around him as much as he felt the elec-tricity hum around the boathouse ahead and from the waters below.

There was another wail, and just before his final step, a sword stabbed up through the dock, crashing through wood and swiping toward him.

He dodged to the left on his good foot and pivoted toward safety. Dad held out his hand, and Lance took it.

The old man pulled Lance hard, jerking him from the unbalanced stance in the tropical downpour through the door and into the building.

Too many things happened in that second for Lance to compute them all at the same time, and his mind seemed to switch from one to another until the sequence was complete—and even then, he was more fuzzy than he would have preferred.

There was the feeling of his father's grip. It was the type of thing that never left a boy. The groves in his hand, the way he was gentle yet full of a power greater than a boy could hope to master until he was a man. The grip around his hand and a second on his shoulder that guided him out of sea-bound danger and into the safety of shelter was unmistakably Dad.

In that moment, it was him, and Lance knew it.

Then there was the smell. It was some kind of Calvin Klein scent Dad must have started using in his teens and never let go of—it was on his clothes and books and chair—and it was here. But there was more. There was the smell of this new place. The salty, fishy smell of the outer sea was in there, but there was also a sandy, sawdust smell. It was the odor of a shop class in the back of a fish market where the moldy dumpsters' stink behind the building was leaching inside through the walls. It was a shifting sea of scents that caused Lance to be homesick at one moment and just sick in the next.

But the last thing that registered before he was completely inside and Dad yanked the door shut was what he saw. On the floor within the boathouse's wooden walls was a marlin. But it was dead.

It took his eyes settling on it for the smell of its rotten, fishy flesh to force his gut to gush upward with bile. He caught it before he puked on the floor, but it burned, and the carcass's rancid odor made his vomit taste of fish as he pushed it back down.

It was a mess of bones with patches of skin on the top. The

internal organs rested on the floor, flopping over the rib bones and nursing a squirming pile of maggots and a hovering cloud of flies. It was the last thing he expected to see inside, after his father, of course, and as Dad leaned against the sealed door and the rain battered the roof, Lance spun around to examine his dad.

His hair was grayer. His skin was looser as if he had been aging after his death.

He nodded and stared back at Lance.

"The Old Man and the Sea." Dad smiled. "I should have known you would pick that one. You always loved the idea of the ocean. I wish I could have taken you."

Lance arranged himself in a sitting position. He wanted to jump up and hug his father, but between the pain in his foot and the still-lingering doubt, he couldn't. Not just yet.

He winced as his gaze passed his bare foot and the back of his other ankle. Blood ran from both in steady streams. He didn't know what to do with either of them. He didn't have a first-aid kit, and just the sight of the blood on the bridge of his foot made him tremble. He didn't want to look closer, worried he might be missing toes.

"Let me help you," Dad said. He stood from the door and took a step toward Lance.

Lance pushed himself backward. He wanted that to be Dad, but he just wasn't convinced. Not like he wanted to be. He had seen Dad's body at the funeral. He had seen Dad's ghost. Sure, everything that happened over the past few minutes was convincing, but he needed more.

Dad raised his hands and stopped. "You don't trust me. I understand that. I guess I wouldn't trust me either, if I were you." His face wrinkled as his tongue searched the gap where he had a tooth yanked the year before his death, a habit Lance remembered well. "What can I do to prove I'm me? You definitely need some help with that foot."

"I don't know." Lance shook his head. He wanted so much to trust this man. "How did you get here?"

"I don't know that. I couldn't tell you where here is. The last I remember, I was driving, and there were screeching tires, and here I am."

"That's convenient."

"Yeah. I guess it is."

There was a creaking sound, then a banging on the wooden floor from below. The marlins wanted them. They had waited, but only for so long, and it seemed they wanted up through the wooden boards that separated them from the ocean below.

Dad held out his hand. "Let me help you."

Lightning boomed, and the entire building shook. It was deafening, ridding them of the sound of rain and the banging of swords for what seemed like minutes. The building felt like it was made out of paper under the impact, and Lance could see the entire structure collapsing into the sea below if they didn't get out first. There was a single door on the other side of the building, past the enormous fish carcass. That was where they had to go, and he would need help to get there.

Lance held out his hand, and Dad took it. He pulled Lance up and draped Lance's arm over his shoulder.

"Here we go." Dad started them toward one side of the fish, and its sword skated across the floor at their feet. "Shit!" He jumped and pulled Lance away with him, the sword barely missing them.

Lance screamed, and Dad pulled him close.

The fish swung its sword again, this time rocking its whole bony carcass and wobbling toward the father and son. There was a thick sloshing noise as the thing's organs dragged over each other and scraped the wood.

"Other way!" Dad called.

Together, they staggered back and toward the other wall. Swords banged from below. Rain clattered against the roof. They raced on three legs, and Dad put his hand on the door's handle.

He groaned, his mouth dropping open, as a slurping sound came from his gut. The bloody tip of a sword pointed from his belly toward Lance.

"No!" Lance screamed. He peeked around Dad and saw the dead thing's body in a broken and remodeled form. It had shifted its bones to make its fins longer, and it balanced with its head firmly impaling Lance's father.

Muffled, wet sounds came from Dad's mouth. He pulled the door open and flung Lance through.

Lance's rear hit the wet dirt as rain immediately soaked his face. He saw the pain in Dad's eyes, the clenched muscles in his face. The sword ripped sideways through his gut, dragging viscera from a gaping hole.

Lance didn't know if the rain was too loud or if Dad was too weak, but he couldn't hear what Dad said. He read his lips, though. They said *I love you* as he slammed the door and sealed the giant fish inside.

"Dad!" Lance climbed to his feet and shrieked as the pain in his toes returned. He banged on the door, screaming, "Dad!" but it wouldn't open.

A sloshing sound came from the sides of the boathouse. Marlin were walking up the beach, whipping their swords from side to side.

"Dad!" he called again, but he knew it was pointless. All he could do was run. He had to before the others reached him.

He cried as he limped into the jungle.

The shadow in the upstairs window watched him go.

Chapter Forty-Nine

EMMA SLOSHED THROUGH THE MUD and water. Stalks of something like grass and hard, petrified stumps jutted up from the murky bog. Her wound was caked in the mess, which she prayed was just wet dirt, but the rancid smell over the slime-topped water told her it was much worse than that.

James was behind her with the pointed end of the bone at her back. He jabbed her with it every few minutes to remind her he was there and likely to give himself a little laugh at the same time. She didn't need the reminder. She was terrified as it was, and she wasn't going to forget the bastard who was forcing her through this hell.

She did, however, let her mind drift in hopes of some part of her escaping. It was somewhat hard for it not to happen as the weariness from blood loss made her mind light and the walk through the sludge reminded her of part of her life she tried to avoid every day.

She was eight, and the piles of pizza boxes, bags of garbage, and ill-fitting clothes lined the walls of their family trailer. It was a pattern that repeated throughout the home. Her brothers had tried to keep their room clean at one point—there were three of them in that little room, after all—but Momma kept piling in the trash as long as there was empty space on the floor. Emma and her six-year-old sister, Patty, tried to manage the piles in their room, at least to keep them from falling on them while they slept, and most nights it worked unless the mice were too active and toppled them over. It was a daily routine that they had all become used to over the years, though the one thing they could never get used to, or get rid of, was the smell.

It hung on them, even when they were out of the house and at school. It was part of their clothes and stuck to their skin. Rotting trash and mold, and even though she took baths twice a week, she was never able to get the stench of urine off her body. Maybe it was the mice or the bugs, she didn't know.

Emma was in her room with Patty that day, and they were alone in the trailer. Even though she didn't want to, Patty begged over and over again to play hide-and-seek.

"No peeking!" Patty slipped from their bedroom as Emma covered her eyes.

"I'm not!" Emma yelled.

The door shut, and Emma started counting. The trailer was a standard double-wide, but for some reason, they always counted to thirty as if the place was so big they needed the extra time to hide. While Emma didn't uncover her eyes until she was done, she did start counting quite a bit faster after she got to ten—it was just taking forever. Finally, she got to thirty and shouted, "Ready or not, here I come!"

She took a quick few seconds and started her search by checking her room. She didn't think Patty was in there, but doubling back and hiding under her own covers was something Patty would do. She was a clever little thing.

But she wasn't there, so Emma stepped out into the hall. "I'm gonna find you!"

She went right and peeked inside their brothers' room. Huge

piles of clothes obscured her vision, then a mound of cans, another of empty Lunchables containers.

"I'm coming!" She stepped into the room and followed the path that navigated from the door to Clyde's bed. It varied from an inch wide to six, depending on where she stepped. Clyde's bare mattress was on the floor between a pile of dirty magazines and grocery bags of who-knew-what, probably their trash that at one point just got tied up and stacked as they became full. There was a brown comforter that covered half the mattress and also had a Patty-sized lump in the middle.

"Got you!" She jumped on the bed. There was a thump, but the fabric sank with nothing underneath. Startled roaches fled from below the grocery bag heap. "Hmm."

She checked around the rest of the room, finding nothing in Jacob's or Chester's beds. Patty wasn't behind the piles of old school papers or broken toys.

"Okay." Emma nodded and went back to the hall. "I'm going to find you!"

She tiptoed through the slim gap in the hallway where a path between Momma's old, soiled clothes and trash from dinners past piled high on either side. She was getting anxious now. She didn't just want to find Patty; she wanted to jump and scream, "I found you!" and scare the pants off of her. The game wasn't her favorite, but she had to admit that, like most games, once she got into it, she desperately had to win.

She followed the path that circled the living room, squeezing between mountains of broken and dismembered baby dolls and half-used makeup cases Momma had found at the dump on her weekly trips. She passed the stack of used microwave-dinner cartons and plates and ducked to see if Patty had squeezed behind Momma's chair and the bags of used cat litter that lined the wall. But Patty wasn't there.

She scanned the room, the heap on the dining room table, and the garbage below it, and she didn't see her sister. She knew Patty was in there somewhere. The only place left was...

Emma cracked a grin across her face that she was sure made her look like the Joker. Patty had to be hiding in Momma's room. They weren't supposed to go in there, but if she was and Emma didn't go look, it meant Patty won.

You sneaky little booger, Emma thought as she slowly opened Momma's door.

The smell in the rest of the house was bad, but it was something Emma had learned to live with. For the most part, she could tune it out or almost forget it was there, and it only really bothered her when she came home from school or was out of the house for long enough that the smell cleared her nose.

But Momma's room was different. It was worse. Way worse.

There was a wall of odor that made her step back when she opened Momma's door. It wasn't the same garbage rot stink that so much of the house had. There was another layer of sulfurous vapor and a deep haze of molding meat. Emma had smelled something similar the time she found a dead mouse under her pillow, which she assumed she accidentally smushed in her sleep some night before, but this was so much heavier.

There weren't any paths in Momma's room. There weren't really any discernible piles, either. The floor was a lake of trash, and every step was through layers of discarded clothes, food, wrappings, or collected items from the dump. As Emma stepped inside and looked around, her feet sank through the clutter. They balanced on trash, not able to touch the floor, yet she was up to her knees or higher in refuse.

She had learned to wear socks over the years to protect the bottoms of her feet and guard against bug bites—the bird mites were the worst—and as her feet sank into the crevices and pushed down layers, she felt them soak through. She heard whatever was below her feet squish, and liquid ran between her toes. She wanted to scream but resisted the urge; she needed to find Patty and take her by surprise.

The next step was over something hard, and she was thankful for that. The next let something small scurry over her foot, and she hurried onward. The next step let her climb up onto the bed.

She breathed a sigh of relief and ran her fingers over Momma's hard, crusty blanket. It moved and crunched under her touch, but as she suspected from its shape, Patty wasn't under there. But she was in there somewhere; Emma was sure of it.

She scanned the lumps on the floor, the nightstand, the dresser, the mountain of mystery in the corner. None of that really stood out to her. What did was the half-open closet. It was dark in there, so she couldn't really see the inside, but if Patty squeezed through, she could have been hiding behind the door.

Emma didn't shout, *I see you*, though she really wanted to, and instead crept off the bed. She smiled so big—this was going to be awesome—and she hardly noticed the cracking sounds and skittering noises of tiny claws around her. Her eyes were on that open doorway, and her focus was on the quietness of her steps as she neared and outstretched her hands toward the gap.

She still couldn't see into the darkness in the back, but she saw the climbing stacks of the hoard as it drew back into the gloom. She poked her head inside, convinced she would see her sister, but it was too dark. The best she could do was scream, "I got you!" as she leaped into the blackness.

Emma didn't know which she felt next, the claws or the teeth. Her hand slapped something furry that fell into a thousand pieces. She tripped on something in the dark closet, and one after another, a thousand times, tiny scratching things trampled over her chest and face. She screamed, and teeth sank into her arms and legs and cheeks. Burning, rending sensations enveloped her flesh. Mid-scream, something fell into her mouth and bit her tongue.

That was the last thing she could take. Her body switched from stunned terror to uncalculated action.

She spun over and spotted the dim light outside the closet and scrambled on hands and knees, crushing small, greasy furry things under her weight and feeling their bodies pop and poke her fingers and palms and knees. They scrambled over her and bit with horrified fear, probably as bad as hers, and hot wetness leaked from everywhere on her body.

She realized how loudly she was screaming as she ran from her mother's room, blood, scrapes, bites, and crushed mice stuck to her clothes; even three or four babies dangled, caught in her locks.

Patty screamed and emerged from behind a pile of tin cans as Emma ran through the kitchen. The blood and fear made her call 911, and as she waited for help, she cried, no longer fearing the mice but fearing what her mother would say when she came home.

That was the last day Emma spent in that trailer. After the hospital and the interviews with Child Protective Services and her mother's refusal to clean the trailer, Emma went to live with her aunt on the other side of the city. Years later, she wouldn't invite her mother to her wedding, let alone allow her kids to visit that horrid place. But the memory would live forever in her mind, no matter how hard she tried to bury it. Even as she waded through this odd bog, it was inescapable; she had no choice but to drift back to that place, to whatever wet garbage she had been forced to walk through.

But now, the sloshing under her feet almost made her smile. It was a ridiculous feeling, but something about that memory, as bad as it was, reminded her that things could get better. As disgusting as it was, walking through this muck that held the stench of death, things had to get better. She couldn't help but think the mud under her feet was a slurping mass of decaying meat—the smell was so similar to some of the nastiness in Momma's room, it had to be— but her mind, whether on the verge or already broken, was sure something better would come. Even if that better thing was her own death.

She stepped on what first felt like a smooth stone, and then another. She was gaining height, rising from the murk, and up ahead through the fog she saw the ground rise from the wetness, only it wasn't ground. It was an island of heads.

Some were nothing but bone, small and large, giant even. Some still had strips of flesh attached, skin of different colors, some coated with fur. They shook as a rumble made the entire swamp vibrate. The skulls under her feet went loose, and she slipped, splashing down into the thick brown water and catching herself with her hand.

The island of heads split down the middle. Skulls and rot rolled and splashed into the bog. From the ground came a dome larger than a house. As the bottom of the muck shifted beneath her, her strand of hope fled once more. As the dome rose to nearly thirty feet high and she recognized what it was, she prayed there would be such a thing as death, because this thing, this head of some underground giant, looked like it wanted to swallow her and digest her while she was still alive.

It was a humanoid skull, but only in the loosest sense. At three stories tall, its three rotting eyes were larger than a man, and they were locked on Emma and James. It had no nose, but strips of horizontal flaps that circled its cheekbones that must have served that function. Its mouth was triangular, and as it split in four directions, exposing green, moldy teeth on the inner walls, it blew a gust of sour air from its ten-foot-wide throat.

Emma knew what it wanted. It was presenting itself, expecting them to obey as an offering of some sort. She saw this monster living in a swamp of its own creation and understood. It wasn't as much of a bog as it was a pen, and she had been sloshing her way through its excrement. And now it wanted to be fed.

The familiar feeling of a bone in her back returned.

"Go!" James pressed harder.

Panic struck Emma. As much as she had thought she would welcome death, with it staring her in the face, all she could think about was the loss of everything that was her. She may not have been happy with who she was lately, but she couldn't just be deleted forever.

If she had been asked, she would have said her final thoughts would have been about her children, but they weren't. What ran through her head were memories of her moments alone, drinking wine at the kitchen table and enjoying the peace and solitude. They were of her lying in bed with Terry Hudson in her early twenties, where they would take ecstasy and not leave the room for the entire weekend. But those thoughts only lasted for an instant, and she rose to her feet and began to sprint away from James and the giant head.

She made it two steps. The blunt end of James's bone slammed into the side of her skull, and all she saw were flickers of white.

She was wet, being dragged again by her feet. Her head was

soaked in the swamp. It was banged on the beach of skulls. It was dragged over the slimy wetness of the inside of the giant's mouth.

He was taking her in.

They traveled into its throat, and as its mouth snapped shut, she wondered how much it would hurt to be devoured.

Chapter Fifty

WHILE ERIC WAS STILL GETTING used to the idea of being dead, one of the things that he knew for sure was that the concept of pain still existed. The hole in his shoulder from that bird-thing's talons ached like hell, but since he wasn't really bleeding, being dead and all, he wasn't sure what he should do about it.

The cave he had been dropped into resonated with walls of deep indigo. It stretched out ahead and around him with pillars of the same purplish stone, while shadows hid crevices and nooks below overhanging outcroppings.

Eric looked behind himself, wishing there was an easy way back to his friends. He didn't want to do this alone, whatever this was. But he had seen his friends get carried away. Whatever they were facing, he would bet it was similar. Hopefully, if he could get through this, he would find them again. *Hopefully.*

He started walking, his gaze searching the path ahead and the shadows around him, which seemed to creep just a little closer with each step he took. There was a tremble in the stone floor below his feet, and Eric stopped. He stretched his arms out to balance himself as the walls melted away and trees grew around him. Mountains rumbled up in the distance. The ground sprouted grass around his feet, and tiny pinpricks of stars lowered into the deep-violet sky.

Everything had almost stopped moving when he realized where he was. The land around him was his father's. The woods around him were where his treehouse should have lived, and as he stared into the pines, a cautious corner of his mouth rose. There was a structure up in the trees ahead.

He knew he shouldn't believe any of this. The whole thing was some kind of a setup. He had just been in a cave, and now he was in a forest—his dad's forest. It wasn't right, but it felt real, so real he could smell the pine and soil through the damp, moldy air that con-sumed that weird world. He wasn't at his dad's, but it looked damn similar, and he needed to know what was going on ahead.

He clutched his shoulder and headed into the trees. The feeling that he was being watched pressed into his mind as he walked, but he didn't let it deter him. He had to know what that was ahead. Had his dad built the treehouse after he left? Was it a present for his next visit? Or an apology for not doing it while he was there?

That didn't make sense. He tried telling himself this wasn't his father's land, that this was some sort of manifestation of that place. His heart didn't want to hear that. He needed to see this. He needed to know that his father cared after he abandoned Eric so he and his girlfriend could go on some vacation, after this journey, and espe-cially after his lack of sleep—and his death. He needed to see that Dad still loved him.

There were animal calls coming from the trees. They could have been squirrels and chipmunks. They could have been something vastly different. He didn't have the mental space or the time to care. There was a pressing urge to go deeper into the woods as he passed tree after tree, and the need to find Lance and Drew faded as he went.

He closed in and could see without obstruction, and his jaw

dropped. It wasn't just a deer blind converted into a treehouse; it was a masterpiece. It was more than he could have imagined.

The boards that had been nailed to the tree that they had used for a ladder had been replaced by a real wooden ladder. The blind had been removed, and a room that had to measure at least ten by ten had been constructed in the branches. There were walls and wood siding and a window on each side. The roof was sloped from front to back, and at the top of the ladder, Eric could see a trapdoor to get inside.

He ran to the tree. He climbed the ladder, flung the trapdoor open, and pulled himself up and inside. His shoulder hurt as he rose into the treehouse, and he didn't care. This was his treehouse, something he had wanted for so long, and here it was. Nothing was going to stop him from getting inside it.

The trapdoor slapped shut with a bang, and for some reason, he got the feeling he should lock it. It was a creeping feeling that chilled his arms as he turned and examined the door. There was a lock, an old chain that would have been at home on a front door to keep out unwanted visitors. He didn't see any harm in it, so he went with his gut and slid the lock into place. It didn't make him feel more secure, but that didn't matter because he had a new treehouse to explore.

The three walls that weren't against the tree each had an open window, and in the gaps between windows were posters of *The Pink Panther* films, *Airplane!*, and *The Naked Gun*. There was a table in the center with a pack of playing cards and stacks of poker chips. In the corners leaned BB guns and Nerf guns. On one side of the room was a shelf filled with *Mad* and *Cracked* magazines like the ones his dad kept in his office, and on the other was a trunk that Eric knew had more wonderful things.

Happiness swelled inside him, nearly overpowering his trepidations. He knew this wasn't right, that it couldn't be real, but he couldn't dismiss the longing he had to just have his dad back to himself after how possessive Andrea had become. The idea that his dad had not only built this place but filled it with joyful items that they could share was so overwhelming that Eric wanted to jump and scream. He wanted to hug his father.

As the pain rippled through his shoulder in a wound that would never heal, he was reminded that he would never have that chance again.

All of that joy drained away, and each item within the treehouse suddenly felt like a monument to something lost.

There was a cracking sound outside. Someone was walking through debris and snapping sticks underfoot. The sound sent a jolt of fear down Eric's spine. What was out there was dangerous—he knew that—and even though he was already dead, the instinct to protect himself was just as strong as ever.

Eric dropped to his knees and crept toward the center window. He raised his head slowly, hoping not to be seen by whomever it was. It didn't work.

Below the treehouse, staring up at his window, was a cowboy, only not a normal one. He was dead, like Eric, with grayed and rotting skin and pale, decaying eyes. But more than that, his face wasn't quite human. His rotten nose showed what must have been the base of pig-like nostrils, and his tongue flicked three forked tips over his long, black fangs. He wore a tattered blue shirt and leather gun belt, and his right palm's snakelike fingers waved in the air above his pistol's grip.

"Shit," was all Eric was able to say before bullets started flying.

Dean ran through the woods, chasing after Drew. It felt more like a dream than real life because every time he thought he was getting close, Drew seemed to slip around another tree or boulder, and then he was twenty feet away again.

The woods were just like at home, other than the darkness and the lingering smell. The canopy was thick with pine, and the floor was covered in needles and twigs. The ground rose and fell, and in the distance on his right, he was sure he heard the lake lapping against the shore. If only he could catch up to Drew—he just knew Drew was going to hurt himself, and it would be his fault. He was the older brother. He was the guardian when Mom and Dad weren't around.

"Drew!"

They were running uphill. They raced through a stand of dead trees that seemed to stare down from far above. There were stares from old ones, long gone but still hovering and still hungering. Dean could feel their desire, that they wanted life again so they could lurch forward and devour him and his brother. All he could do, though, was run and yell, and he did both as hard and as loud as he could until they passed another boulder and Drew darted inside the enormous black stone formation.

Dean ducked and dove inside. His heart beat so fast, and his lungs pumped so hard. His focus was on Drew, but maybe he should have thought more about his actions. But how could he? He had to catch up to his brother. It was when he reached for the dark ground inside the structure and found none that he doubted.

He fell. The cloud of brown fog surrounded him momentarily, and he expected to slam into the ground of the chamber at any second. He waited for it, just wishing to catch up to Drew. He had to.

There were too many times that he had failed as a brother. There were too many arguments in the old house when he wanted peace and solitude, and because they shared a room and he couldn't have it, he took it out on Drew. There were too many times when Drew just wanted to play with his older brother, his hero in many ways, and Dean just blew him off. He didn't want to feel like a baby playing baby games. He was a big kid and needed to act like one, and playing baby games was humiliating. There were so many names: loser, retard, baby, doofus, mamma's boy, and all of them stung Dean as he remembered the looks on his brother's face when he said them.

He didn't want to admit it because it was sappy and lame, but he loved his brother. It wasn't just because it was his job or because they were family; it was just who they were. When things were good, they made each other laugh. When no one was watching and the pressure was off, they had fun—or they used to. He owed it to Drew to get them back to those moments, not the bad ones.

The pain came. His ribs howled as he landed on a bed of rocks at the bottom of the chamber. He groaned and rolled over and caught a flash of Drew darting from the room into the small passage.

"Drew!"

He scrambled on hands and knees into the tunnel. He watched Drew from behind as he fought fruitlessly to catch up and didn't. They came through the end of the tunnel, and Drew was off into the woods, and as Dean followed, he saw that the woods here were different than last time. There weren't dead trees filled with singing Zeetee; these were woods like back on Earth.

It didn't matter. He had to catch up.

They raced past pine after pine until they reached the edge of a small clearing where a treehouse stood. On the other side of the clearing, a strange zombie cowboy was raising his gun.

Lance jumped over one vine and then the other. He ducked under spiny palm fronds but missed one, and it split the skin across his forehead. He stumbled and pierced his palm on the prickly trunk of a malicious tree while trying to steady himself.

"Ow!" He freed his hand, wiped the blood seeping into his brows, and kept running.

His palm throbbed. His forehead was wet, burning agony. He stepped on something with his bare foot every few seconds that felt like a knife. There was crashing and snapping foliage behind him, and he ran as fast as his tired legs would carry him. He had never thought of swordfish as such savage beasts before, but he was in some world where nightmares came to life, and he couldn't think anything was impossible anymore.

It seemed like as soon as he accepted that absurdity, each new tree that came into view was different than those of the Cuban coast. He ran past several more, and the landscape changed from a tropical rainforest to the evergreen pines and spruces from the mountainous northwest. It sparked a feeling of hope, of getting back to his mother, to his home.

Then he saw the cowboy.

The wooden treehouse wall burst with an explosive flower of splinters, catching Eric on the cheek. He covered his face as another shot blasted through the floor and another through the side panels.

"Stop!" He rushed backward and looked away. "Stop!"

He wanted to ask why, but he knew too well why. This place was a nightmare and only existed to torture him. It wasn't enough that he had been poisoned; whatever was in charge of this mayhem wanted to give him the gift of his most desired thing just to rip it away—just to torture him. And he had no recourse except to scream and cry.

He could do one thing. It was dumb, but he could do it. It was one small thing he could control, and maybe, by some miracle, it could work.

Eric crawled to the corner as splinters rained across the room. He picked up the BB gun resting against the wall. He shook it and heard the rattle inside. It was loaded.

This may have been the dumbest thing he had ever done, but he was already dead and he had to do something.

He cocked the lever forward and back, clicking it into place. He waited for the next shot to shatter his wall, and after he felt tiny shards of wood on his shoulder, he popped up and spun into the window. He lined up his shot and pulled the trigger.

There was a hollow, springy sound as the toy gun fired. It was almost silent after the deafening reports of the cowboy's pistol, but Eric couldn't help but be proud when he saw his shot land.

The cowboy's clouded left eye burst like a water balloon, spraying milky-white goo across his cheek and up onto his eyebrow. It seeped into the pus coming from the cracks in his dead skin, and the cowboy sneered as he fired his next shot.

The bullet didn't rip through the wooden shell of the treehouse this time. It sailed through the open window and burrowed itself into the bottom right side of Eric's neck.

Eric spun and fell, thumping onto the floor. He swore he heard the cowboy laugh as the shots resumed making his hideout into Swiss cheese.

"No!" There was a voice outside he thought he recognized. Despite the pain in his neck, he had to climb back up and see.

The bullets paused as Eric looked out. He saw Drew running at the cowboy. What the hell was he thinking? That dead sonofabitch was going to cut Drew down like he was nothing.

"Stop, Drew!" Eric shouted, but he knew it wouldn't do any good. He cocked his BB gun and aimed at the cowboy. He fired as the cowboy did. His BB hit the side of the zombie's hat—meaningless. The cowboy's bullet drilled through Drew's head, leaving a cloud of blood and brain behind it.

"No!" Now Dean was charging from the woods. Again, another fool running at that damned cowboy.

Again, Eric cocked the toy rifle as fast as he could, aimed, and fired.

This time, his shot was better. His BB impaled the other eye, sending the dead man off balance, away from the treehouse.

But the cowboy had fired too. He stumbled into the woods, yelling something Eric didn't understand, and Dean dropped to his knees, grabbing his stomach.

Dean wasn't exactly sure what had happened other than his legs stopped working and there was a wet, gushing feeling in his gut. He was on his knees, and there was Drew lying face down ahead of him.

The cowboy—*Fuck!*—the cowboy had shot Drew!

Dean crawled toward his brother. His gut ached, and it was hard to make his legs follow directions, but they would do it, goddammit, he would make them do it. He wasn't going to be stopped. He was going to get there and help his brother.

Tears ran heavy down his face. He didn't accept what was ahead even though he knew enough to fear the worst, even though his mind knew it well enough to stream tears like a river.

Drew was motionless in the forest debris. His arms were by his sides, and a hole in the back of his head exposed skull and brain. But Dean couldn't stop. He had to move closer. He had to help, somehow. He had to do something.

Dean grabbed Drew's arm. "Get up, man," he whined. He shook

Drew's arm, and he sat. He pulled Drew toward him, ignoring the gore that toppled from his brother's head. He turned Drew, closing the gap to give his brother one last hug, only... Drew had no face.

It wasn't that his face was blown away—his forehead had a gaping hole from the cowboy's bullet—it was that his face was blank. The entire surface that should have held Drew's eyes, nose, and mouth was a single, flat plane of skin.

This wasn't Drew. It was like a walking mannequin shaped like him.

All Dean could do was chuckle as he released fake Drew. But the laugh hurt, and he had to grab his stomach.

"Drew!" Eric ran from the bottom of the treehouse.

Lance walked slowly from the other side of the clearing.

All three kneeled beside Dean and the fake Drew when screams from the real Drew called from somewhere in the forest.

It seemed like Drew had been dragged forever. There were caves and rocks, and now he was over a forest floor. The barbs in his skin burned, and each time he hit a bump or tried to move, they seemed to dig deeper into him.

"Just let me go," he cried.

They went from the woods into a clearing. Familiar voices shouted.

"Stop it!" It was Lance.

There was a thud, and Drew looked. The fake Dean had wrapped Lance in the same barbed tentacles and was pulling him closer.

"Ah!" "No!" It was Dean and then Eric. The slimy things had enveloped their arms and legs and punctured their flesh.

"Let go!" Dean shouted, then, "Drew? Is that you?" There was both pain and relief in his voice.

They all shouted as the fake Dean started walking once more, dragging all four side by side into the trees.

Chapter Fifty-One

THE ROOF, THE FLOORS, THE walls were all flesh. As Emma's wits returned to her, she gagged at the world around her. She was being dragged through the insides of a monster. They were long past the mouth and throat, somewhere in the main body of the thing. James's steps were wet. They slapped the soft ground, and the liquids running through Emma's hair were thick and odorous, smelling like digestive biles and acids. And oddly, they glowed, lighting the way for them.

"Let me go." She barely got the words from her mouth without vomiting. "I'll walk."

James stopped and scowled down at her. His flesh looked worse than it had outside this living tunnel—grayer, and even in the wetness, he was chalky. She wondered if the gastric juices were taking a toll on him.

He dropped her feet and clenched his bone weapon with its

point aimed at her. "Go on, then."

She raised her palms to him in submission, then slowly stood, making clear she had no intention of running. She was up for less than a second before he nudged her with the point to get moving.

She limped ahead, her wounded leg hurting even more than earlier. The infection had to be getting bad.

Her feet splashed as she walked. Every few steps, she kicked something in the mess below. She only looked once to see what it was. After identifying a bone with flesh attached, she decided not to look anymore.

It was a while before they stopped. Neither of them spoke, and the endless twists and turns of the tunnel made time and distance hard to calculate. But then they found the cavern.

It was thirty feet tall and immeasurably wide. The floor was deep with the same glowing fluids as the tunnel, and the shore of a luminous lake was scattered with remains in various stages of digestion. All of this room was coated in thick mucus.

James rammed her in the back again, and she stepped down onto the shore, her foot sinking into the mucus.

"Where now?" She held her hands up in supplication, making sure he knew she had no intention of escaping.

He pointed to the center of the lake. She wasn't sure how this was going to work, because he didn't look like he could swim in his condition and her leg was probably going to fight her tooth and nail, but she knew what happened the last time she tried to argue. She just had to hope this wasn't where she died.

Emma stepped into the lake. It was hot and stinging as it touched her skin. She pictured it eating her away, but she kept walking.

Splash, slosh. James followed her.

The liquid quickly rose to her knees and then her thighs. It was up to her hips when the edges of the lake fogged over, moving in to cover the surface in a wavering mist.

"What's happening?" she asked. He didn't answer.

The glow dimmed and the fog thickened. In a matter of seconds, she could see nothing of where she was going, only the blueish hue of the fog.

Her legs stopped stinging, and they grew cold. The depths receded, it grew darker, and after a few minutes, the fog drew back. When she stepped from the liquid, it was stone below her feet instead of flesh, and she was standing in the middle of a canyon. They had been transported. She didn't understand how or where or why, and it didn't make any sense.

"What are we doing, James? We've been walking forever. What's the point?" This time, she was sure she heard him chuckle.

"You're about to see."

They passed a line of boulders that followed the canyon walls. There was flapping above, and Emma saw ghastly beasts flying that would haunt her dreams if she lived through this. They walked a little farther, and then she heard them.

They were screaming. "Let me go!" "Stop it!" "Leave us alone." She was sure she recognized at least two of those voices, and her legs carried her before she even had time to think. Strangely, James didn't try to stop her.

She was running. It was an ugly run because her leg hurt so badly every time she put any weight on it, but she would not stop herself. That was Drew and Dean. Her kids were here! *Goddammit, why?* She didn't even know where *here* was, but they shouldn't have been here. Not in this horrible place.

"I told you you wanted to come!" James shouted as he walked.

She paid him no attention. She rounded the next line of boulders and heard the screaming from a cave to the left. She ran inside, around a turn, and stopped in another canyon. This one held a ring around four boys and some sort of monster that forced them in place with whips or something.

"Let them go!" she shouted as she dropped beside Drew and took hold of the bindings wrapped around his arms. It was slick and cold, yet as she tried to undo it, she felt a sharp pain. Something on this slick tendril stabbed and tore at her finger.

She shouted and looked closer. There were thorns on this rope, and—pain racked her chest as a tentacle slammed into her and tossed her back. She collided with the wall and fell on her ass.

The room spun as she took in what was in front of her.

The kids were lined up in a circle. Drew, then Lance, then Dean, then Eric. They were all restrained by the tentacles of the thing in the middle, and that thing made her tremble as she got a better look. It was twice the height of a man and had no arms or legs, only an endless supply of those thorned tendrils. It made her think of Cousin It from *The Addams Family*, only twelve feet tall with tentacles instead of hair. And it had her kids; it was squeezing them and hurting them.

She felt her chest bleeding from that thing's strike, and even as the kids cried, all she could imagine was what it would do to them if she tried to free them again.

"Mom?" Dean called to her. "Is it really you?"

"Yes. It's me."

James turned the corner and stared at them all with a big, nasty grin on his gray lips. Emma thought she saw a twinkle in his eye through his fur face mask.

"I—I think I'm shot, Mom," Dean said.

No. She shook her head. That couldn't be. It was one thing for her to be trapped here, it was another, horrendous thing for her kids to be. She deserved it—she knew that. They didn't.

She couldn't see the wound, but she could see the blood. His stomach was drenched in even more of it than the rest of him. She had to do something to save these kids, and she had to do it quickly—or Dean was sure to die.

"It's going to be okay, Dean. We're going to get you all out of here." She had no idea how she was going to accomplish that, but she would. She was done being selfish. That was what got her into this mess to begin with. Whatever it took, she was going to get her kids out of this.

"Ha!" James shouted from his corner. He came closer to the kids and squatted. As he looked at Drew, the tentacles tightened, and blood ran from Drew's wounds onto the rock below him, and the rock glowed.

"Get away from him!" Emma screamed.

"Okay." James nodded and shuffled to his side until he was

squatting beside Lance. The tendrils tightened around the boy, and he screamed. Blood flowed onto the rocky floor.

Below the boys, the entire circle glowed. The dark stone floor became a light yellowish-orange as if it was fire itself. It lit each child and their agonizing faces, and it lit the thing holding them. Its shiny, slick skin was damp. Tendrils draped its frame with an outward, billowing presence. Even without seeing a face, Emma could tell it was watching her, and she dreaded what would happen if it lifted those tendrils and exposed its real visage.

"Good." James moved beside Dean, and the tentacles around him pulsed. Blood seeped into the ground, and light flickered around them all.

Emma shook with rage. "You bastard," was all she could get out.

There was no blood when James kneeled beside Eric, and while Emma thought that was strange, she saw his pale complexion and the gashes in his shoulder, and she understood. Her heart sank for him.

The ground brightened to almost white. The walls shone with the same light, and James stood, raising his arms into the air like some evangelical preacher calling up to God. Red strands of energy rose and twirled from the circle, and above them all, another circle appeared like a floating fire of gold and red.

James was quivering as he turned to Emma. "He's coming."

Emma's mind spun between fear and panic. She wanted to get up and run. She didn't know who *he* was, but she didn't want to be around when he got there. But how could she run with her boys in pain? She was never the best mom—she knew that—but she couldn't just leave without finding some way to help her sons.

There was a crackling sound, and the boys all screamed.

"Mom!" Drew called.

The words were agony in her heart. She reached out and, remembering the pain from that thing's thorns, she pulled her hand back. She covered her face, hiding from it all.

"Help!" Lance screamed.

"Mom, please!" Dean cried and coughed. He spat a glob of blood onto the floor.

The flaming circle above pulsed, and its red strands widened into thick ribbons. James brought his hands together, clutching the pointed bone in both hands, and he moved between her and Drew.

"Mom. Please help." Drew stared into James's sole eye as James raised the bone and adjusted his grip. Drew saw what was coming. "Mom! Help us!"

Emma's eyelids cracked, and when she saw what James was doing, everything before her crystallized into a single action. She leaned forward, propelling herself to her feet. She launched her body at the man who had been her lover, her hands spread and her legs wide apart.

He didn't know what was coming and couldn't prepare. The thing in the middle moved, but that was later. When Emma collided with James, her legs wrapped tightly around him. She had a flash of the dozens of times she wrapped those legs around him in ecstasy, and while this time it was different, she was determined for it to bring her joy in the end.

One of Emma's hands shot up and grabbed his hands tightly; the other dug into his face, ripping the fur pelt away and clawing at the wet, mushy places where his eyes and nose once lived. She dug into everything soft and fleshy, rending away chunks from his sockets and skull.

James screamed and teetered. He tried swinging the bone down at Drew, and she reeled his arcing weapon inward. It plunged into his gut, and James leaned forward, howling and blinded. But she didn't let him go. She knew he was already dead. This may have hurt him, but that didn't mean it would stop him.

She dug deeper into his face. She wrenched the bone, twisting it inside his wounds as he screamed. She bit into the side of his head, and he rocked forward over Drew.

"Mom!" Dean howled.

She couldn't look over there. There was no way. She had to focus on what she was doing for them to have at least a chance.

"Up there!" Dean called, but she still didn't look.

The tentacled monster's arms rose toward the fire above. It

reached for it, and again, remembering its blow, Emma thrust herself forward by rocking James over Drew and into the Cousin It.

There was a squeal as they slammed into the tentacled beast. Its limbs spread wide and seized both James and Emma, and she saw something that would have frozen her with fear had she had time to process it. Between its separating limbs, she saw its face. There were a thousand teeth and more eyes than she could count in a lifetime. There was a look from within that being of knowing death and beyond; inside it was a magic of pain that she could only fathom. As she and James pushed it over the boys and onto the floor, its arms enveloped them both, and she embraced the pain and kept working.

"Something's happening!" Lance shouted.

It was. She knew that. She had no choice but to make it keep happening and hope she had made the right choice.

As the tentacle barbs sank deeper into Emma's body and wiggled and ripped, she dug her fingers into James's grip and seized the bone. His hands went tight on his wound, and he screamed at the torture in his face and his belly and the barbs ripping his flesh. He did not fight her.

There was a tearing sound as the tentacles rent and swung then released and rewrapped themselves over her. She felt cold inside her pain as her insides were exposed to air and her warm blood fled her body. That didn't stop her. She finally had a plan, and she had to see it through. Her boys deserved that. They deserved to have their mother do one good thing.

The monster let loose a horrible squeal as it squeezed them all. The kids wailed, and Emma looked into the eyes of death, knowing it was planning hers, and she jabbed the sharp end of the bone deep into the monster's face.

She felt its eyes pop as she scraped and bashed harder into its soft and fleshy organs. It squealed louder, and her ears rang. She drove the weapon deeper, and the creature flung a tendril around her neck and yanked it wide. Her blood fountained from the left and right, and the world grew darker and colder. And still, she pushed the bone harder into that monster.

The tentacled thing slowed. It stilled. And in one last act of defiance, it flailed all of its limbs at once. Emma flew backward into the rock wall and heard a crack from inside her head.

She didn't know what happened next. She only knew she was freezing and that there were screams all around. In the distance, she heard the rushing of a river. It was calling her. It was getting closer.

Part Nine

The Way Home

Chapter Fifty-Two

THE SKINLESS SKULL IN FRONT of Randy's face held the same perpetual grin as it had so many years ago. In the woods when he first saw it. When they went back to Bobby's stone fort and were tossed away. When Mom summoned the thing into their house like it was just some normal guest. The shiny tendons that flexed and trembled as it moved and talked revolted him. Those lidless eyes that never stopped staring into his soul enraged him. The endless swirling of shadowy smoke made Randy want to swing. The more it hung before him, the more his hate overflowed inside.

"*I can take her now.*" The Shadow Man spoke of Maggie. "*She's only inches away.*"

Old Sheriff Palmer and the abomination that was the Lewis sisters paid no attention. They chanted and howled at the creature in the flames. They took in the loose strands of red magic that floated from the bonfire, and they changed. Palmer's wrinkled skin seemed to tighten. The intertwined organs of the sister monster unraveled, and Cherry and Frieda began to pull apart from one another.

But with all this madness in the room, it was the kids that Randy was focused on. It was Drew and Dean and Maggie. The Shadow Man said he could take her, and that was like a cold hand around Randy's heart. She was supposed to be at Janet's house, not at home. But he knew the evil bastard was telling the truth. He could take her like he had Drew and Dean and Bobby.

"What kind of deal?" Randy finally answered.

"*Blood for blood. That's always the deal.*" The deep, grumbling voice of The Shadow Man resonated inside Randy's head over the fire and the screaming and the chanting. It was in his mind and in his ears. "*The next born of your clan will be mine, and you can keep your daughter.*"

"You just took my sons! You want more of my family?"

"*One was promised. One was providence. They are both mine now.*"

Promised? What was that supposed to mean? His entire body ran cold as he remembered sitting at the table with his mother, sister, and friend. He remembered the blood and the demon appearing. The Shadow Man had wanted a deal then... and Mom said yes. She had done this for the magic to wipe his mind and protect him from the sheriff. She had promised that demon another kid, and now it was his sons being punished. She had covered up for him with the Lewis sisters and Sheriff Palmer.

It was like a wave of ice ran over his entire being. He had known his mother was cruel, that she would have preferred it was him that was taken and not Bobby. He knew the sharpness of her words and the anger deep within. This revelation, though, that she had doomed his children while saving him and his sister, made his mind reel. That she could have done something kind for him while dooming his son and then cementing it by willing them to live in her home after her death—it clamped his mouth shut and brought tears of so many mixed emotions.

This was both of their faults—his for leaving his room and fighting with the Lewis sisters, and hers for cursing their family again. And now, The Shadow Man wanted another. *Another!* But what choice did he have?

Maybe he could deal? Maybe they could figure out a way to move away from Lone Wolf before Maggie had a child and it was doomed to be taken? He thought of Mom's will. She had made his family live in the house. It was the only way he could inherit it. If there was a way to escape, wouldn't Mom have done that?

Had she even tried?

No matter what way he twisted this situation in his mind, he came back to the inescapable conclusion that he had to take the deal. He couldn't rush to the house and protect Maggie. He was caught. It was his fault again, and this was the only way to save his daughter today. There would be years before another child (his grandchild) would be taken. They would figure out a way out of this before then.

The Lewis monster screamed and pulled her two abdomens apart. There was a cracking sound as bones snapped and reformed.

"I want my sons!" Randy shouted. "You can't have them. It wasn't their choice. Take me instead."

"*Blood for blood,*" the demon said. "*A body was promised. A body was taken.*"

"You took too much!"

Randy would have sworn the demon smiled even wider. He looked behind The Shadow Man at the hole it had emerged from. That hole led to the other place. It was where Bobby had been taken and where Drew and Dean were. He swore he heard screams coming from that hole. Human screams—*Was that Dean?*

If the demon wouldn't give them back...

"Blood for blood?" Randy said.

"*Blood for blood.*"

"My daughter will be safe?"

"*Safe.*" The demon nodded.

Randy felt the cuffs fall from his wrists. He put his hand forward to shake. The Shadow Man's smoky arm swung toward him, passed over his open hand, and blood somehow leaked through the skin of Randy's palm—through the scar he had forgotten the source of.

"*A deal,*" the demon said. His cold, shadowy finger touched the drop in Randy's hand. It felt like ice as it sucked up the small pool.

"Good." If Maggie was safe, it was time for him to save his boys.

Randy drew back his hand and rolled from his chair, grabbing the hatchet on the floor. He swung it hard at The Shadow Man, cracking the monster on the side of the skull. The demon screeched inside Randy's head as blood sprayed onto his hand, but before he could pull back his hatchet and swing again, The Shadow Man vanished in a puff of smoke.

Randy ran for the wall where Palmer had leaned his shotgun. Palmer, who must have heard the demon's cry, saw him running, and immediately it was a race. It was a race Randy could not lose. He gave his legs everything he had. He reached as he came within two steps, and he felt something snag his foot. It jerked him backward, and he was going down, but he refused to stop.

"No way!" Palmer yelled. He was climbing up Randy's back.

There were still three feet between Randy's hand and the gun. He wasn't going to make it, so he did what he could.

Randy spun from his belly to his back, twisting and dropping the old sheriff to the side. He wasn't free of the man, but he could do what he had to. He swung the hatchet fast and hard.

The reflection in Palmer's eyes shone bright as the steel hatchet blade plunged into his face. Randy noticed that the man had no more gray hair as he ripped the hatchet back and swung it downward once more. It cleaved through Palmer's forehead and into his brain, exposing bloody gray matter when Randy pulled it back. It was disgusting, and it was relieving to know this man would no longer be in his way to reach his boys. He was about to swing it again when he noticed the Lewis sisters galloping toward him.

Their arms stretched with wild claws, and their legs dug into the ground the way Randy imagined a cheetah would as it hunted. Frieda's broad, hollow chest snapped with fangs ready to take him, and Randy knew the small hatchet would not be enough to bring her down.

He spun again and scrambled toward the shotgun. The sisters growled like a pair of predators as they closed in. Randy spun back, pulling the long gun to his shoulder and pulling the trigger.

Simultaneously, a boom shook the entire space, a blinding flash filled Randy's eyes, and Cherry's head exploded.

The beast tripped and rolled as half of its legs curled in and ceased moving. Frieda screamed, and two clawed feet and two clawed hands dragged the flopping monstrosity toward Randy.

It was almost on him. He could feel the heat from it and smell the rank breath from its gaping chest. He aimed the shotgun and pulled the trigger.

Click.

"Shit!" He was so scared he had forgotten to chamber a new shell.

A gurgling, rattling sound came from the Frieda thing. It spit blood on the floor as he racked a round and aimed.

"This is for Bobby," he said as he pulled the trigger.

Another boom shook the building. Buckshot tore through the middle of Frieda's chest, and the thing that had been Cherry and Frieda Lewis flopped backward, only strands of skin holding Frieda's upper half to the rest of her body.

With that explosion, the red strands began to fade. The fire started to shrink, and light from the hole in the floor dimmed.

The door was closing.

Randy hurried to his feet, grabbed the hatchet, and sprinted to the hole. He didn't look down. He just jumped in.

Chapter Fifty-Three

THE TENDRILS WENT LIMP AROUND Drew's arms and legs. He groaned as he tried scooting away from the dead creature and pulling its twisted thorns from under his skin.

"Mom!" Dean yelled from the other side. He crawled to the wall, tentacles hanging from his body. "Mom!"

Mom wasn't moving. She was crushed and bloody, and the back of her head was cracked open against the wall.

"No." Drew crawled to them. Lance and Eric sat up and began plucking the thorns from their arms and legs.

Dean looked into her blank eyes. They were still. They followed nothing.

"Dean?" Drew put his hand on Mom's arm. "She can't be..."

"She's dead," he confirmed.

"No." Drew shook his head. Had she followed them there? Were they responsible for her death? He leaned over her and hugged her.

Dean leaned over them both.

Pain rippled through Drew's arms and legs from the hundreds of wounds. "What do we do?"

During their entire time in this weird place, Drew had been scared. He had wondered if they would ever get back home, but there was always a little shred of hope. This was unimaginable. This was an end that he could never have fathomed. It was hopelessness in physical form, his dead mother in his hands. She was the one who always told him things would be okay. She was the only one he could go to when he was sad and worried about the world. She taught him to smile and laugh and walk. She was what held their family together. And now she was gone. He couldn't help but think smiling and laughing and living were gone with her.

Nothing would ever be the same again.

"We have to go home," Dean said. "She would want us to."

"Leave her?"

"She wouldn't want us to be trapped here forever, Drew."

But if they left her, she would be here forever.

"She'd want us to get out of here. Bobby said there was a way home in this canyon, and we need to find it. Besides," Dean glanced down at his bloody belly, "I'm shot, man. If I don't get home to a doctor..."

Those words gave Drew chills. He couldn't help but finish Dean's thought. If Dean didn't get to a doctor, he would die too, and he would be stuck there forever.

Drew looked at Mom's face one more time and prayed. *Let her get up. Please.* The wound on her head must have been too much. She was dead, and she was staying that way.

He couldn't lose Dean too.

Drew stood up and started working the rest of the barbs from his skin. Lance finished first and helped Eric get his loose. Then, they both helped Drew and Dean.

When the last dead tentacle flopped to the ground, they stood there for a minute, taking each other in. They had been through hell. They were all wounded, and Eric had died. They had been scared and battered and stabbed with spines. They all deserved to go home.

"We gotta go," Drew said. He didn't say how much he was worried about Dean. He didn't say how sad he was about Mom or for Eric. He wondered if that was what it was like for grownups, always knowing things were worse than you let on and forcing yourself through life regardless.

"Yeah," Lance agreed

"That way." Dean pointed toward the direction Mom had come from.

They were about to leave Mom and the squid thing and that weird man on the glowing rocks when a scream came from above. Drew looked up into the floating fire, and out of nowhere, a man dropped from the flames. He landed on his rear on top of the dead guy that had come with Mom, and all four kids jumped back. A second later, the man was looking around and locked eyes with Drew.

They shouted at each other at the same time, "Dad!" and "Drew!"

Drew, Dean, and Dad hugged and cried for Mom, but they did it as they walked through the passage toward the main canyon once Dad saw that Dean was shot.

"You saw Bobby?" Dad asked. He walked with Dean's arm braced around his neck for support. Dean carried Dad's hatchet in his other hand.

Lance and Eric shushed him. There was no guarantee that those flying things wouldn't return and swoop down to grab them again.

"We did. He told us there was a way home if we get to the end of the canyon." Drew couldn't believe his dad was there. They had almost reached the exit home, and there he was. They might not have found the end yet, but he felt like they had been rescued. Dad would know what to do, and soon, they would be back in their house, and—as much as he was excited, he knew that without Mom everything would not be okay. But he couldn't think about that right now.

"Where is he now?" Dad asked.

"We got separated," Dean explained. "These giant bird things took us in different directions."

They stopped behind a group of boulders and peeked up the canyon path. Dad watched each direction closely. He scanned above for the flying things. He gripped his shotgun tightly and gestured ahead.

"I guess you can tell me all about it when we get home." Dad looked each of them in the eyes. "Right now, we focus and get out of here."

Each of them gave Dad a nod. It was time to end this trip. Drew followed closely behind Dad and Dean, and Lance and Eric trailed them. They all felt the end coming. It was an instinctual understanding. But Drew was unsure exactly what that end would mean.

Yes, they had Dad. Mom was gone. He hurt everywhere from stings and gashes from that tentacled thing. There was an abundance of hope and pain and sadness all mixed together over the past few minutes. There was supposed to be an exit, and he could sense it coming; he could also sense something else, and after all they had been through, he couldn't assume it was good. The feeling that they were being watched from above was still there, even if they saw nothing. The stench of death was still inside every breath. This place would only be satisfied once they were dead, so there was no safety until they reached home.

The main canyon was as ominous as it was when Bobby had led them. They moved along the wall and gauged each shadow for potential dangers, whether they were undead pixies, giants, or flying beasts. Cold winds sailed past them, making Drew's chills worse. He rubbed his hands together to keep warm. They were gritty from the dried blood and grime. They told the story of their pain and fear.

There was whispering from somewhere up ahead. It traveled on the air with the light sound of flapping. Drew jerked his gaze upward. There were none of those bird beasts, but there were rippling waves of light in the sky. They were bluish indigo, reminding him of the water's shimmer the day they moved in and he stared out onto the lake. It was magic, the same magic this place leaked out into his world, and it was coming from up ahead.

Drew tapped Dean and pointed. Dad looked, as did the others.

They were getting close.

The rocky ground and walls were wetter. The canyon narrowed. The whispers grew louder, and a creeping feeling walked up Drew's spine.

"That's gotta be it." Dad pointed. Ahead, the walls closed in to a mere three-foot gap. They shone within the passageway in the same wavering light, and the whispers echoed over each other, layering their voices, chanting, calling on something Drew knew was not of his world.

Dad motioned to Drew to come closer, and when he did, he draped Dean's arm over him. Dad raised the shotgun to his shoulder and chambered a shell. He went first into the narrow passage.

Randy hated the smell of this place. With the wind in his face, it was like the stench was being shoved down his throat. The shotgun at his shoulder helped a little with traces of gun smoke, but it wasn't enough to shroud the rot that saturated the air. He wondered how the kids had dealt with it the entire time. And Emma...

Emma was another mystery. Randy thought he understood how the kids got there—it was like his brother, promised by Mom and then allowed in by The Shadow Man (like he had doomed his future grandchild, but he couldn't think about that at that moment). Emma would have been refused entry like he had been. So how was she there?

His heart ached at the sight of her lying in that mess of tentacles near that man's corpse and whatever that monster was. Yes, they had been going through troubles, but she was his love. No matter the arguments, even the years of distance between them, she was what he thought of at the uttering of the word love. He knew they would get through their troubles. Maybe it would have been once the kids were out of the house, when they had the time to focus more on each other, maybe once their finances had improved and things weren't so hard anymore. Now, that would never happen. They had ended things how their relationship was now, and he hated that. He wished he could have lifted her body, removed those things that were wrapped around her, and carried her home. There was just no time to free her; he had to get Dean to a doctor, and he couldn't carry both Dean and her. It was his final failure in their relationship, and he would live with that forever.

But he would save these boys, whatever the cost.

Randy stared down the shotgun's sights and led them through the narrow passage. The chanting was the same as the bonfire by the lake, the same as the Lewis sisters' place, the same as Palmer's house. They were getting close to whatever this was, and even in the cold wind, he could feel himself sweating. He could hear his heart pounding in his ears. He gritted his teeth and hoped the deal he made with The Shadow Man had worked, even if he did slam a hatchet in the thing's face—*blood for blood* indeed.

The grim gloom of the canyon gave way to a brighter area ahead. Through the end of the passage, Randy could see swirling strands of gold and red. The distant walls sparkled like the shimmering lake. This was it; he knew it. They were almost there.

The path ended, opening into a large, black-walled room. They were walls like the stone structure that started this whole thing. As the blue-indigo shimmer passed from surface to surface, rounding the room and rising in waves toward the sky, pictographs and writing glowed. When the shimmer reached the top of the walls, probably a hundred feet up, they lit the sky above.

In the center of the room was a ten-foot-wide pool of golden fire. Red and golden strands of energy twisted and rose from the flickering flames. They lifted to the sky like smoke and continued onward. It was a sight that could have been beautiful if it wasn't for the endless chanting that whispered in his mind like a call to insanity. It translated into thoughts as he moved closer, showing him what to do, images of him holding the shotgun under his chin and pulling the trigger. Images of each of his four wards walking back through the canyon into that cursed world, dead. He saw Emma, skin dripping from her face but welcoming him with open arms. He wanted to accept her. He wanted to fire the gun, have this all be over, and hug her once again.

They neared the fire, and he felt the stock of the gun lower. The barrel was pivoting from forward to up and leaning back toward him. He was letting it. He felt his finger drift down within the trigger guard and stretch for the trigger.

He wanted to pull it. He wanted to save his kids, but the whispers. They were right, weren't they? Wouldn't this all be better if it was just over for good?

The cold steel of the trigger pressed against his finger, and before he knew it, a wave of stinging pain flashed across his face. The shotgun lifted from his hands, and staring into his eyes was his baby brother.

"Bobby?"

Chapter Fifty-Four

I T WAS BOBBY, BUT IT wasn't. Randy wanted to laugh and he wanted to cry. His baby brother was dead, and he was standing there with a tentative grin on his face. He was missing an arm and an eye, and his chest seemed to be eaten away by something. His insides were barely within him, and his face was as determined and kind as ever.

"Don't let him get inside your mind," Bobby said. He addressed them all as he pointed the shotgun at the flaming pool. "That's the way home."

He had barely spoken the words when a clawed hand rose from the fire—and then another.

Bobby shoved the shotgun flat against Randy's chest. "Are you okay?"

Randy took the gun and nodded. He wanted to grab his brother and pull him close despite the state of him. There had been a hole in his heart since he lost Bobby, and that hole ached right now, seeing what his brother had become. He knew it wasn't yet the time to understand all this; he just had to hope that time would come.

He slid a hand onto the pump, another on the grip, the stock against his shoulder, and a finger on the trigger. He aimed into the flames as another clawed hand gripped the ground. He recognized those hands. He knew what was coming.

They were the shape of the hands Randy had seen by the lake and at Palmer's, though they were somehow more real. They were solid, gnarly flesh. They bled from the gaps of skin between their knuckles, and their matted fur was soaked in vile pus. Even before Randy saw the beast's face, he knew this thing was not going to crawl into a bonfire for the sake of a ritual this time. It was coming from the fire as its real self, and it was coming after them.

The barrel of the shotgun trembled with the shake of Randy's aim. He prayed the gun was powerful enough to do the job as he saw the top of the creature's skull emerge from the fire. The golden flames danced over its head as it rose, and golden strands reflected in its eyes as they locked onto Randy.

He held back. He wanted to fire at that second, but he didn't dare to until he was sure. This type of shotgun typically had a five-shell magazine, and he knew he had already fired it twice at Palmer's place. That meant he only had three shots—and that was assuming the ex-sheriff had fully loaded it.

The disgusting head fully surfaced. It had five eyes, all of them a dense, milky white leaking deep-brown liquid. Its mangy hair was spiked and matted. Its tongues whipped through the air like snakes, and inside its mouth hung a thousand worms from holes inside its cheeks and jaw. All of it made Randy want to retch, and all of it made him tremble even more.

"Now!" Bobby shouted.

His brother was right. He firmed himself, centering the shot-gun's sights on the demon-dog's head, and as he pulled the trigger, he saw the thing he was dreading: another pair of claws emerged on the other side of the pool.

The monster's head exploded into a ball of gore that rained

backward into the fiery pool. Its claws and arms went limp, and its body sank back into the flames. The other pair of claws, however, was joined by the top of another head, and on the right side of the pool, another pair of claws. And on the left, another.

Three more monsters were coming, and Randy had at most two more shells.

Drew stood in frozen terror as his fears were confirmed. It wasn't going to be a simple trip back home. In front of him, yet another horrific thing was crawling into his path, and it was like a feeling of impending doom becoming reality.

Dad aimed his gun, and the thing's head disintegrated into a cloud of pulpy blood and mist. The sound shook the ground and vibrated through Drew's bones, making his insides drop. The creature's death should have made Drew feel better, but he knew this was only the start. Three more of them were climbing up from the pool of fire. *Three more!*

"Back!" Dad stepped between the creatures and Drew.

Drew was glad Dad was there to protect them and terrified for his father at the same time. He had wished for help all this time, but now that it was here, he was terrified that Dad would end up like Bobby or Eric or Mom.

"Stay back, guys!" Dad aimed his shotgun at the closest rising beast, and he pulled the trigger. Like the first, its head was vaporized, and the body dropped back into the pool. But a new set of claws immediately rose to fill its spot. "Shit!"

Dad glanced at his gun. He flipped it around in his hands and ran to the left side of the pool, where he smashed the butt of the thing down into a rising demon's face. It howled as its skull split, and it fell backward into the pool. Dad ran to the next beast and repeated the action.

Dean rose from Drew's shoulder and let go of his brother. He leaned forward and back, fighting for balance, and he walked toward the pool.

"Dean, stop!" Drew called, but Dean wobbled forward. He gripped the hatchet tight and raised it as he moved in on a rising beast. He swung the blade down, and Drew had to look away. He wasn't concerned for the monster; it was Dean that he couldn't stand to watch get hurt again. He had already been shot. He had taken control of the group and helped them get this far, and he didn't deserve to get hurt again. Those claws were huge, and it made Drew sick thinking about what could happen.

"Ahh!" Dean brought the hatchet down in the center of the demon's forehead. Its skull split like a rotten melon, gushing, with half of its head falling to each side.

"Dean, get back!" Dad shouted as he bashed another one on the opposite side. It dropped, but a clawed hand seized his leg, ripping clothes and flesh. He screamed, and Dean ran around the pool. Dad was raising his shotgun like a club, and Dean slammed the hatchet down on the monster's wrist, severing the limb.

"Dammit!" Dad backed away from the pool, dragging the hand with him. Two heads were rising from the fire. Both with busted-up faces from the butt of Dad's shotgun.

Dean circled the pool. He was trying to run, but it was obvious he was out of energy. He hefted the hatchet up as the closest monster's head and chest cleared the edge of the fire. He brought the blade down, and the monster dodged.

Dean stumbled, and the beast squatted, ready to pounce.

"Dean!" Drew had turned to watch—he couldn't help it. But he wished he hadn't. Dean didn't have the strength left in him to do this. He needed to get away from there!

"Hit him!" Lance shouted.

"Get him, Dean!" Eric hollered.

Drew couldn't understand these cheers. Didn't they see how weak Dean had become? He was shot and dying. He couldn't do this.

"Run, Dean!" Dad ripped the clawed hand from his bleeding leg and climbed to his feet.

The beast leaped, and Dean swung. Its arms were long, and the power behind its massive legs propelled it into a blur. Dean's face was a mask of pain over hope and fear. His lip curled. His teeth clenched.

He brought the small ax down against the demon's head, cutting through cheek and snout and into eye and brain. But that wasn't enough to stop the monster's advance.

It fell dead, but it fell on Dean. Its enormous arms and torso slammed into him and smashed him into the ground.

"Dean!" Drew ran to him. The only thought in his mind was helping his brother out from under that thing.

Bobby joined Drew, and they reached Dean together. They grabbed the beast's corpse and heaved, pushing it slowly off.

The other monster charged them. It jumped, claws wide and teeth spreading. Drew looked up and saw it coming down. The anger in its eyes, the pure viciousness—it froze him. Those fangs. The sparkling drool within its rotting jaws. It was like a two-ton blender descending toward him.

A boom vibrated through everyone and everything.

The last demon's head shot sideways from its severed neck and rolled. Its body thudded on the floor next to Bobby. Dad stood on his good leg with the shotgun smoking and out of ammo.

Drew watched the fiery pool, sure another beast was coming. After a moment without one, he turned back to his brother. Dean's eyes were closed.

"Dad?" Drew felt his eyes burn as tears welled.

Dad kneeled there with them. He felt Dean's chest. "He's still breathing. We need to get him help."

Bobby pointed at the pool of fire. "That's the way home. Go, now."

Dad stared at Bobby as he took a breath. It trembled when he exhaled. There was pain from so many directions. Everyone could feel it. He looked over his long-lost brother, and it radiated like a furnace. "What about you?"

Bobby held out a shaky hand and rested it on Dad's shoulder. "I can't go. But I got to see you again. And I got to meet my nephews. It was worth the wait."

"What about him?" Lance asked. He pointed at Eric.

Bobby shook his head. "If he goes through, he'll be dead when he reaches the other side."

They all looked at Eric. His face was wrinkled but stern. "I'm going." He clenched his fist as if someone was going to fight him over this response.

"Didn't you hear him?" Lance snapped. "You have to stay here or—"

"I'm already dead." There was no emotion in Eric's voice. It was a statement as plain as declaring the weather.

The space was silent other than the popping of golden flames.

Eric gestured at Bobby. "I can't live like that. I'm glad you could, but I won't make it. I have to get out of here."

"We can come back for you..." Lance said.

"Lance..." Drew reached out, but Lance pulled away.

"It's not fair."

"Goodbye." Eric widened his arms, and Drew stepped over and hugged him.

"Goodbye," Drew said. He remembered a thousand moments from time spent with Eric, and more than anything, he remembered the kindness that always flowed from his friend. It was warm, and it hurt as they embraced. He leaned back and they slapped hands, that secret handshake that started as a meaningless thing but meant so much right now.

They let go, and Drew joined his dad, who was lifting Dean up over his shoulders.

"Lance?" Eric held open his arms.

"Fuck." Lance pulled away, then returned, delivering a hard embrace to his friend. "Surely, I'm going to miss you."

"I'll miss you, man. And don't call me Shirley."

They chuckled to each other. It was lame, and they loved it. They hated it. They started to weep and turned away.

Bobby took a step back. The others stepped toward the fire.

"Here we go," Dad said. He flexed at the knees, preparing to jump, and a skinless head rose from the fire in front of him. A large gash went down the side of its face. Dad whispered, "The Shadow Man."

But there were no shadows. The demon emerged from the pool with a body of skinless flesh, not of fog. Its muscles bulged across its arms and legs and a pair of tentacles that spread from each side of its ribs. Its body gleamed as raw redness glistened both from tissue and from an aura of red magic that pulsed across its being in sheets.

It hovered closer, and they all stepped back. It raised its arms and spread its clawed fingers. Its tendrils whipped and stood high, ready to stab and wrap at a moment's notice. Its voice boomed inside them with rage.

"*Blood for blood. These are mine.*"

"They're my blood!" Dad screamed back.

"My blood is mine!" Bobby howled. He was in the air. He was moving toward the demon with the hatchet up high. The blade sank into the demon's chest, rending a line through muscle and shattered bone, and The Shadow Man twisted and flung Bobby off like he was nothing but a mild inconvenience.

The demon turned to Dad. "*We had a deal.*"

"The deal's off," Dad shouted. "I'm taking my kids home."

There was a clink as metal hit the floor. Drew turned to Bobby. Bobby released the hatchet and pulled a slice of his own rotting flesh from his gut, a slice he had made that sizzled with the rot from the river. He held it in his one good hand and charged at The Shadow Man once more.

"*Blood for blood,*" the demon repeated. "*All mine.*" He didn't see Bobby until Bobby's hand was shoving the slice of diseased flesh into the open wound in his chest. A moment of anger flashed across the demon's face, and he flung Bobby harder this time. The undead boy crashed into the wall, his head cracking open. He hit the floor, unmoving except for a smirk on his face as he watched what happened next.

The demon twitched. He snarled. He gazed down at his chest to see the wound festering and bubbling. The flesh was eating itself. It was eating him.

The Shadow Man grabbed at its chest in a panic, tearing away chunks of meat, trying to remove the infection before it took him, but it didn't work. The hunks of red meat slapped the stone floor and sizzled, but the wound only grew. Then its hands sizzled as well, spreading the curse as it tried to remove it.

"Go," Bobby whimpered. His voice was weak and wet, but it was filled with relief.

Dad grabbed Drew by the hand and pulled. Drew grabbed Lance. Lance grabbed Eric. They darted to the side of the flailing monster and jumped into the flames.

Drew caught one last glimpse of the room as he sank into the fire. He saw the rage on The Shadow Man's face as bubbling rot ate into it. And he saw his uncle, finally resting.

Epilogue

FROM THE LAPPING TENDRILS OF FIRE, Drew was delivered into the cold wetness of Lone Wolf Lake. From the darkness a dozen feet under, he forced himself up. Up.

His lungs burned as he held his breath and climbed. He saw red and purple through the rippling surface above. He moved his feet and his hands as fast as he could, fearing that even after seeing The Shadow Man fall he could still be coming. He could be right below.

His head breached the surface, and water splashed in every direction. Air burst out over his lips, and he sucked in a gulp of the atmosphere he had been missing for—he didn't know how long. It was fresh and delicious, with no hint of rot or any other stench. It was the glorious air of home at sunset, and a shimmer of blue indigo was fading from the water.

"Drew!" Dad was by the shore, waving Drew over. Dean was there. His eyes were closed. Lance was there, crying. Eric's body floated between them. "Come on!" Dad yelled.

Drew came. He pulled Eric with him. They had to leave his friend by the shore as they rushed to the house and then called an ambulance. The ten minutes they waited for it to arrive were scarier than anything that had happened since the fair.

Maggie was in the house. She was safe but crying. She wouldn't say a word until they were out of the house. Janet was gone, but there was nothing they could do about that other than ignore the blood. Dad said it would only slow them down trying to get Dean to the hospital, and they couldn't help her. So no one said anything about the mess upstairs to the EMTs.

Dad called the cops about Eric, Janet, and Emma being missing after Dean was out of surgery. Lance's mom picked him up from the hospital, screaming at Dad and the hospital staff. She smelled like marijuana, and no one argued with her. They just let her yell and leave.

When cops showed up, Dad told them a story about coming home and finding the kids the way they were. He told Drew to tell the truth, which he did, and of course no one believed him. When the police interviewed Maggie and then Lance, they didn't know what to think. They called Eric's death a drowning even though the medical examiner disagreed; he couldn't figure out the real cause, so they kept it simple. They opened a missing-persons case for Janet and even threatened to charge Maggie with something because of all the blood, but since Maggie didn't have a drop of blood on her and there was no body, that stalled out.

Until they found Mom's car.

It was a few days before the cell phone company released Mom's last known GPS location to the cops. When they discovered her car and James's woodland torture shack, everything got even more complicated. There was blood evidence from at least fifteen different missing girls on the blades in that shack. They didn't know if Mom was a victim or an accomplice since none of the blood was hers. They assumed she was either dead or on the run with James, and James had to be the one responsible for Janet's blood and missing body.

Dad didn't mention a word about Mom for quite a while, but

Drew could hear him crying through the walls at night.

It took three weeks before Dean was well enough to come home from the hospital, and when he did, it was with three feet less of his small intestine. They were grateful that was the extent of the damage. When he was able to start school, he mustered up the courage to walk right up to Nancy Hanning at her locker and ask her out. He told her they could go anywhere in town she wanted as long as it wasn't too spicy—doctor's orders. She said yes. That Friday, they had a picnic and then went to a movie, and he didn't come down from the clouds all weekend.

Lance didn't show up on the first day of school, and his mother immediately put him into therapy. Drew called and Lance wouldn't talk. They didn't see each other until the following weekend at Eric's funeral, and they didn't say a word there other than *Hi*.

While the immediate weeks after Drew's return were surrounded by something of a haze, he found that it grew clearer each day, and as it did, the entire town of Lone Wolf seemed to brighten with it. The feeling of being watched everywhere in town lifted. The smell he had known since childhood sweetened, replaced by a piney aroma that filled him with hope. The townspeople smiled more, or at least it seemed that way to him, and though there was a shared sense of loss throughout the school for Eric and those that were taken in the accident at the fair, a sense of hope slowly emerged for the future among them all.

The house on the lake was a mess for Dad to deal with. None of the family wanted to stay there after the hell they had been through, and since Dad couldn't sell it, nor could he afford the property taxes, he decided he would rent it out after a heavy cleaning, and they moved back into their old house.

It wasn't ideal. With the loss of Mom and her income, things were hard on Dad for a few months until the rental income from the lake house started to come in, though that wasn't nearly as much as they would have liked—being known as a house where kids were murdered or went missing has an effect on rental pricing. Still, though, they got by, and in the spring, the new year brought the miracle of the lumber mill reopening, and not only was Dad called back to work, but he was offered a foreman job.

It took a while before Drew and Lance were able to enjoy time together like they used to. The first few times they tried it felt like a ghost was there. Eventually, they realized that ghost wanted them there, that Eric, wherever he was, would want his friends together and enjoying their lives, even he couldn't do it with them. They even watched *Airplane!* and *The Pink Panther* in his memory. When they heard both "don't call me Shirley" and "a bomb" in Peter Sellers's hard fake-French accent, they each felt chills. They each went silent. They decided those movies would return every year on Eric's birthday, even if they didn't understand half the jokes.

By the following summer, Lance had asked out and broken up with two girls, then found another girlfriend. Drew had pined over a girl of his own for most of the year, and after spring break, he asked her out, and they lasted through the summer. All four of them went to the fair together when it returned to Lone Wolf Fairgrounds. They shared cotton candy and funnel cakes and rode the rides. They went into the fun house, and though Drew would have rather not, he smiled and followed through, his eyes open for Zeetee and his gaze watching the empty shadows.

In the end, the fair went fine. No zombie pixies, no one watching them from the shadows, no malfunctioning rides. He did feel Eric, though. He could tell his cheerful friend was wishing them well, wishing them fun through a life he could no longer join them in.

When the night was over and the girls had been picked up by their parents, when Drew and Lance were back at Drew's house, staring at the living room ceiling from within their sleeping bags, they finally said what each had been thinking but hadn't quite wanted to say out loud.

"It's too bad Eric wasn't there tonight," Drew said.

It was quiet for a long few seconds before Lance agreed. "Yeah. I miss him."

"Me too."

It was another long pause. The compressor on the fridge clicked and there was a creak from someone walking around upstairs—Dad or Maggie. She coughed and the toilet flushed.

"You think his soul made it home?" Lance wondered. "I mean… did they both come through? Or was it just his body?"

Drew was sure. "All of him came home."

"I think so too. I just—I wonder sometimes about that place. My shrink says it wasn't real. He said we made the whole thing up in our minds after the shock of seeing Eric drown. I—I wish he was right. I want him to be right sometimes. Wouldn't that be easier?"

Drew pondered this. Would it be better if Eric had just drowned? If Mom had run off with a psycho and Janet had been taken by them? If Bobby was really just a runaway? In some ways, he figured it would better if that was the case. If he didn't still see movement in the shadows from time to time and could just ignore it like everyone else did.

Because as confident as he was that The Shadow Man was gone and the portals to that other place had been closed in Lone Wolf, he wasn't sure that they had been closed everywhere. That was a big world, just like Earth, and what if another town somewhere had portals like Lone Wolf had? If there was another demon demanding people make good on their deals of *Blood for blood*.

"I guess I'd like that," Drew finally said. "But it'd be a fantasy. And in the end, when he got to choose, Eric chose to let go. And I feel like we should honor that." And regardless of what Mom did to get there, Drew knew she died trying to save him. She didn't run away from their family. He would remember that forever.

"I guess so," Lance said. He rolled onto his side, away from Drew.

"Sup, weirdos?" Maggie walked through the living room toward the kitchen.

Drew watched her pass. There was something different about her over the last few days, though he wasn't sure what it was. Something made her seem just a little bit happier despite her saying she had a stomach bug.

Her shadow followed her into the kitchen, and Drew felt a strange sensation, a series of prickles across his shoulders. That shadow wasn't flat on the ground as she moved. There was a small swirl inside it, a dark fog that hovered above each surface it touched as the absence of light chased her. It was something that pulled Drew up so he was sitting in his sleeping bag and watching her open the pantry door.

"What?" She saw him looking and squinted at him. Her shadow fell flat.

He was probably just seeing things, a mild PTSD flashback as Lance's shrink would have said. It didn't mean anything.

"Nothing." Drew lay back down. He looked at the plaster popcorn hanging down from above, and soon Lance was snoring gently, and Maggie was headed upstairs with whatever snack she had found in the pantry.

He thought about Lance's question and about how everyone was doing right now. The fair had been good. Dean was out with his girl-friend and friends, happy. Maggie, despite her bug, seemed happier than before. Dad still had moments of sadness—he tried to hide them, but Drew could tell—but overall, he was doing well. The town seemed happier.

He decided that it didn't matter what Lance's therapist or anyone else wanted to think. Despite their losses, life was moving on and, for the most part, moving on for the better. He could stop looking at the shadows if he wanted to. He decided he would.

Shadows were just shadows now.

Acknowledgements

The Shadow Over Lone Wolf Lake was a lot of work, through long nights and weekends. It would not exist without the effort and kindness of many people. I thank you all and regret those I may have missed. This is just a token.

Christina Hitz — Thank you for sacrificing time together, encouraging me, and picking up all the pieces I missed through my absent-mindedness. Thank you for encouraging me and being there when I needed you.

My Kids — You inspire me more than you know. Thank you for your patience, understanding, and support.

Melinda Parrish — Your endless support always helps to keep me going. I appreciate you more than you know.

My Editor: **Heather Ann Larson**, your keen eyes and attention to detail really helped to pull this book together. Thank you.

My Cover Artists: **Matt Seff Barnes**, your beautiful cover was an inspiration. Like all your work, it is amazing. Thank you. **Don Noble**, you always know what I'm asking and knock it out with that demented beauty. Thank you.

My Patreon members: Thank you for your support along this journey. Special thanks to **Jay Bower** and **Jordan Triplett**.

About the Author

D.W. Hitz loves the outdoors and enjoys making it a background character in his work. He devours stories in all mediums. He enjoys writing in the genres of Horror, Supernatural/Paranormal Thriller, and Science Fiction/Fantasy. He aspires to tell stories that thrill the heart and stimulate the imagination.

When not writing, D.W. enjoys spending time with his family, hiking, camping, and playing with the dogs.

Stay up to date with D.W. by becoming a member at patreon.com/dwhitz

THE SHADOW OVER
LONE WOLF LAKE
D.W. HITZ

After nightmares begin in the small town of Custer Falls, Montana, in 1992, it'll be thirty years before they end.

After Wes Henson and his friends' field trip to Bloodtooth Caverns, everything changes. All they did was stray off the path. They didn't expect to break their bones and discover an ancient relic. But once it's in Wes's hands, he's the one that has to put it back. Because when this evil is awake, no one's dreams are safe.

Something is stirring in the woods outside Custer Falls. A haunted place that's been waiting a very long time. Wanda heads out on a hike with friends. Stevie and Honey flee into the woods from the cops. They all think the woods will be their salvation until they find the terrors at Garrets Lodge.

In this 1990s schlocky horror throwback, a group of Floridian teens get summer jobs at the mall to pay for their trip to a music festival. Unfortunately, working at this mall's food court comes with a price, and they will be lucky if they escape with both their lives and their souls.

Nikka was normal until she saw something horrific. Now, after years of unrelenting nightmares, she learns of a mystic who could save her from the terrors driving her toward ruin. For the promise of a cure, Nikka makes a deal: one month's work to end her nightmares. But can she do the witch's tasks? Or are her dreams destined to destroy her?

Fedowar Press presents: Always Darker Inside, a cursed objects anthology. Nine diabolical tales of Cursed Object Terror from Master Storytellers: Jay Bower, Eric Butler, Micah Castle, M Ennenbach, Robert Essig, Patrick C. Harrison III, D.W. Hitz, Megan Stockton, & Will Suffer

Winner of the 2023 Spatterpunk Award for Best Anthology.
A tribute to the glorious slasher movies of the 1980s.
Featuring stories from: John Adam Gosham, Gerri R. Gray,
Patrick C. Harrison III, Carlton Herzog, D.W. Hitz, Derek
Austin Johnson, J.D. Kellner, Brian McNatt, Nicholas Stella,
& Vincent Wolfram

A tribute to the glorious slasher movies of the 1980s, Volume 2. Featuring stories from: Jay Bower, Justin Cawthorne, Kay Hanifen, D.W. Hitz, Brett Mitchell Kent, Aaron E. Lee, Kevin McHugh, Carl R. Moore, Daniel R. Robichaud, Darren Todd, & Mark Wheaton.

A tribute to the glorious slasher movies of the 1980s, Volume 3. Featuring stories from: Jonathan Maberry, Will Suffer, MJ Mars, Brian G. Berry, Megan Stockton, Jay Bower, Eric Butler, M Ennenbach, RJ Roles, Angel Van Atta, and D.W. Hitz.

THANK YOU FOR READING!

A tribute to the glorious slasher movies of the 1980s, Volume 3. Featuring stories from: Jonathan Maberry, Will Suffer, MJ Mars, Brian G. Berry, Megan Stockton, Jay Bower, Eric Butler, M Ennenbach, RJ Roles, Angel Van Atta, and D.W. Hitz.

THANK YOU FOR READING!